Murder Most

Romantic

Murder Most Most

Romantic

Passionate Tales of Life and Death

Edited by

MARTIN H. GREENBERG AND DENISE LITTLE

Cumberland House
Nashville, Tennessee

Published by Cumberland House Publishing, Inc., 431 Harding Industrial Drive, Nashville, TN 37211

Cover design: Gore Studio, Inc.
Text design: Lisa Taylor

Library of Congress Cataloging-in-Publication Data

Murder most romantic : passionate tales of life and death / edited by Martin H. Greenberg and Denise Little.
    p. cm.
  ISBN 1-58182-156-5 (alk. paper)
   1. Detective and mystery stories, American. 2. Love stories, American. I. Greenberg, Martin Harry. II. Little, Denise.

PS648.D4 M8757 2001
813'.0872083543--dc21

                                                 00-065561

Printed in the United States of America
1 2 3 4 5 6 7—05 04 03 02 01 00

Contents

Introduction

Denise Little

Murder and romance are an unlikely combination...or are they? If given a choice in the matter, most of us would prefer them to remain entirely separate. Yet, there's no denying that an edge of danger can heighten tension and intensify feelings, particularly romantic feelings. Love, after all, is often at its most intense when it is threatened. And when that threat is mortal, well...it gives a whole new meaning to the phrase *a love to die for....*

That's exactly what this collection of stories is about—romance experienced in the teeth of mortal danger, when every decision is life-or-death and the smallest mistake could kill you. Many award-winning writers have joined together in this volume to bring you the best in romantic suspense. From Laura Resnick's heart-stopping story of a honeymoon gone very wrong, to Diane Stuckart's look at the scary side of cyber, to D. R. Meredith's tale of love and death in small-town Texas, and beyond, every story adds a new twist to *Murder Most Romantic*. It's a collection guaranteed to make your heart beat faster...in more ways than one. So sit back, put your feet up, and take a ride along the knife-edge where love and murder meet.

Enjoy!

Homicidal  Honeymoon

Laura Resnick

A s soon as she woke up next to the corpse, she knew it was going
to be a bad day.

Her first words were, "Blagh! Argh! Murrrrgh!"

She followed this with a more articulate arsenal of curses: "Jesus
H. Christ! Holy shit! What the hell! Ohmigod, ohmigod, ohmigod!"

She only realized she had leaped out of the sagging double bed
and staggered backward across the room when she stepped on something that made her yelp in surprise. Cold and hard, it slid out from
under her foot, causing her to fly up in the air, flail briefly, and then
land heavily on the hard tile floor. She lay there winded and dazed,
her head throbbing, her heart pounding.

"Ohmigod," she murmured weakly when she could speak again.
"Ohmigod, ohmigod, ohmigod..."

Stop panicking! Think this through.

She was utterly bewildered. Rational thoughts were hard to seize,
never mind formulate and examine.

Maybe he's not really dead. Maybe he just looks dead.

After all, all that blood would make *anyone* look dead.

"Ohmigod, ohmigod, ohmigod..."

She opened her eyes and stared at the ceiling. High overhead, a tropical fan whirled lazily. She rolled her head sideways, looking for the object she had slipped on. The big white tiles she was lying on were old and worn, but relatively clean.

Where the hell am I?

She saw the object she'd stepped on. It lay a few feet away, its smooth, cold surface gleaming a dull metallic gray.

A gun.

He'd been shot. The dead man in the bed had been shot.

All right. Get up and look. Then call the cops. And...

"Oh, my God!"

And get dressed!

She was naked. And alone in a strange room with a corpse and a gun.

I was naked in bed with a dead man.

Jesus, Mary, and Joseph, I beg you, don't let my mother ever find out about this.

The thought came as a reflexive response to the scene...but once she examined it, she realized she couldn't form an image of her mother. Some unconscious instinct suggested this was probably a blessing, but it nonetheless worried her. Particularly when she realized, a moment later, she couldn't even remember her mother's name. Or...her own name.

"Oh, my God."

She sat bolt upright, stark naked in the humid warmth of the shabby room as the realization hit her with full force.

My name? What's my name?

Nothing came to her.

What's my goddamn name? Who am I?

She stood up, looked around, and shivered despite the heat.

Where was she? What was she doing here? Who was the guy— *oh, Jesus, the dead naked guy*—in the bed?

The room possessed few amenities. No TV, no phone, no refrigerator with overpriced beverages and fattening snacks. Just the sagging double bed (complete with bloody male corpse), a nightstand, a smashed lamp lying on the floor next to the dead man's crumpled clothes, an armoire that had seen better days, a sink, a mirror, and a few towels.

She walked over to the mirror and looked into it. She was brown-haired, brown-eyed, slim, perhaps thirty. Not a knockout, but attractive enough that, were there not a corpse in her bed, she wouldn't even consider flinging herself off the balcony in hopeless despair now.

Balcony...

She looked around for her clothes. Not seeing them—*good grief, did I come here naked?*—she reached for the sheet on the bed and gave it a tug. The sight of its red-stained folds slithering down the dead man's body brought her to her senses.

"Not a good idea."

She turned in the direction of the sink again. The sudden movement made her head ache painfully. The room swam in and out of focus. That wasn't just from waking up in a panic or falling on the floor, she realized suddenly. She reached up to gingerly examine her scalp and discovered a big lump beneath her hair.

She developed a theory.

Someone hit me over the head and killed him....

But who? And why? And what should she do now?

Trying to ignore her aching head, she wrapped a threadbare towel around herself, turned, and went out onto the balcony. Her room, she discovered, was on the second floor of a grubby pale building in a rundown semi-urban street.

She looked around, starting to feel like she might throw up. There were a few street signs, mostly garish and hand-painted. She couldn't read them.

Am I illiterate?

Two young men were walking down the opposite side of the street, partially hidden in the shadows. The sun was low in the sky, and she didn't know if it was dawn or sunset.

"Excuse me," she called. "Hello? Excuse me. Could I ask you a few questions? Hello! Excuse me!"

They finally paused, looked up, and saw her. After a moment of immobile surprise, they both grinned broadly and started across the street toward her building. It suddenly occurred to her that a woman wearing only a towel who summoned two strange men to her bedroom balcony could conceivably create entirely the wrong impression.

She took immediate steps to correct any misapprehension on their part. "I've just got one or two questions about—"

"*No hablo inglés.*"

"Huh?"

The young man who had spoken repeated himself and, it seemed, added an apology. The other simply shook his head and kept grinning at her.

"Um...is that Spanish?" she ventured.

"*Sí, señorita. Español.*"

"Now that's just lovely," she muttered. She was pretty sure she didn't speak Spanish, whoever she was. Was everyone here Hispanic, or just these two guys? Unfortunately, there didn't seem to be anyone else on the street whom she could ask.

The young man who had spoken now said something else. She didn't understand the words, but the suggestive tone was unmistakable. The silently grinning one looked like he was trying to find a way to climb up to her balcony.

"No!" she said, backing up a step. "No, thanks. I mean, sorry. I mean...Everything's fine up here, thanks." She gestured vaguely behind her. "I've just got a...There's a man who...No!" she uttered when she realized they seemed to regard her gesturing at the bedroom as an invitation. "No!" she repeated forcefully, holding her hands out as if to ward them off. Fortunately, *no* was a word they seemed to understand. Looking disgruntled and perplexed, they started muttering comments that she was certain weren't complimentary. However, the moment her gaze was caught by a glimmering reflection on her outstretched left hand, she stopped listening.

A wedding ring?

Good grief, a wedding ring? She was *married*? She had forgotten an entire husband?

"Oh, no!" She forgot about her two young swains as she raced back into the room and, forbidding herself to be sick, examined the dead man's left hand. Yes, there it was: a wedding ring. One that matched her own.

"Oh, my God..."

We're married?

Her head was pounding. Her stomach churned. Panic raced through her veins.

Or we were married? I guess I'm a widow now.

She forced herself to study the dead man.

Evidently she wasn't shallow, since she certainly hadn't chosen this man for his dashing good looks. He had been ten or fifteen years older than her, a little jowly, with a small mouth and a bland face. His thin, mousy hair was long enough in front that she guessed he usually tried to comb it over that big bald patch now so carelessly exposed. He clearly didn't work out or get much sun, and it looked like he enjoyed fatty foods.

He was also wearing a diamond-studded pinkie ring on his right hand—a particularly cheesy-looking one, even by the standards of pinkie rings.

"Good God," she muttered. This was her husband?

She wondered if she had loved him very much. It seemed that if she had, surely there ought to be at least some quiver of recognition in her heart when she gazed at him, but she felt nothing. Well, nothing except panic, revulsion, fear, and bewilderment—which was really quite enough, for now, anyhow.

She wondered what she should do now. One thing she was certain she shouldn't do was pick up the gun. Her memory might be gone, but she was nonetheless pretty sure she had seen any number of movies wherein the heroine, suffering from shock and a lack of common sense, picked up the murder weapon in confusion, only to be immediately pounced upon by some cop who jumped to the inaccurate (but, frankly, understandable) conclusion that she was the murderer.

She went to the sink and splashed cold water over her face. Her head throbbed. Her stomach contracted threateningly.

Try to remember. There must be at least one thing you can remember.

She closed her eyes and concentrated on breathing in a slow, soothing rhythm.

Relax, relax... Think...

The image of a man penetrated her thoughts. He was tall, dark, and handsome.

Don't fantasize—think!

His image grew stronger, though. Clearer. Coming fully into focus. He had dark piercing eyes, lush brown hair, a sexy smile, broad shoulders....

Was I cheating on my husband?

She was an adulteress married to a balding, jowly man who wore a pinkie ring. An adulteress without any clothing, it seemed.

Perhaps losing her memory had been an unconscious choice, an escape from reality, rather than a result of this bump on her head.

"Ohhhhh..." Trying not to weep in frustration and despair, she buried her face in her hands and wondered who had murdered her husband. Wondered who the handsome man in her memory was.

She suddenly gasped as she realized that the most likely person for her to remember, at this particular moment, was...her husband's murderer!

"Oh, no!"

She needed to get the cops. Whoever she was, wherever she was, she needed to report her husband's death. She also needed to seek police protection until the murderer was caught. What if she had seen the killer? What if the killer knew she had seen him?

She didn't even think, just reacted. She gave in to her panic and ran for the door. She had to get out of this room! She had to find a phone, a police station, a safe place! Preferably a place at some distance from the corpse of her forgotten husband—at least until she could compose herself. She reached for the doorknob, and then—

And then leaped backward in startled fear when it rattled slightly. She stared stupidly at it, watching it turn slowly. The door latch gave a soft click. Her heart pounded with blind terror. She stood frozen on the spot, incapable of motion, as the door swung open.

The tall, dark, handsome man whom she remembered now stood in the doorway, his familiar eyes blazing with some powerful emotion.

The killer!

Her mouth worked silently in mindless, breathless terror.

He stepped into the room and swiftly closed the door behind him. "You're here," he said with almost violent intensity.

He reached for her. Unable to scream, she finally gave in and fainted.

Someone was dousing her with bitterly cold water. It was inhumane! It was *outrageous*.

She sat up shivering, sputtering, and waving her arms around.

"Come on," he said. "Get it together. We have to talk."

She opened her eyes, saw him, and—feeling much better now—screamed her head off

"Stop that," he snapped. "You want to bring everyone in the whole hotel crashing through that door?"

"Yes!"

He put his hand over her mouth. In that same instant, she realized she was stark naked again. Her towel lay beneath her in a lumpy heap. Renewed terror gave her strength to act. She bit him. Really hard. He gasped and snatched his hand away, giving her a wounded look. She screamed again, more forcefully this time.

"What's the *matter* with you?" he demanded.

"Arrrrgh!" She snatched the towel up, jumped to her feet, covered herself, and staggered away from him.

Still cradling his hand, he stared at her as if she had gone mad. "What is it?" he demanded.

"Stay away from me!" she ordered.

His increasingly bewildered gaze raked her from head to toe.

"Don't look at me!" she shrieked.

"O...kay...," he said slowly. "Want to tell me why not?"

"Because I'm not dressed, you idiot!" she raged, momentarily forgetting that modesty should really be the least of her concerns at this particular moment.

He frowned. "Huh?"

"Clothes! Clothes!" she cried. "I don't have any clothes on!"

"Yes, I noticed that." He sounded testy again. "And, believe me, I was planning to ask about that."

"Turn around!" she shrieked, beside herself now. Bad enough that he should murder her, but ogling her, too, was really beyond the limit.

"Will you stop?" he snapped, going over to the bed to examine the corpse. "It's not as if I've never seen you naked before."

That stopped her. "It's not?"

"Christ," he muttered, studying the body, "what happened here?"

"You...you've seen me naked before?"

"Did *you* kill him?"

"Are you sure?"

He glanced back up at her. "Sure about what?"

"That you've seen me naked before?"

He squinted at her. "What are you talking about?"

"I don't..." She spread her hands helplessly for a moment, then scrabbled at the towel as it started to slip. "I don't know who you are."

"*What?*"

"I don't know who he is." She shook her head, then winced as it throbbed again. "I don't know who *I* am."

"What are you talking about?" he repeated.

"And I don't remember what happened here."

His jaw dropped. "You're kidding."

"Oh, good grief, do you think I would kid about a thing like that?" she snapped.

"At least you're starting to sound more like yourself." He eyed her uncertainly. "So all this screaming and this, um, modesty....It's because you..." He tried out the phrase with obvious difficulty: "You don't recognize me?"

"No. I thought you might be...you know."

"No, I don't know."

"The killer."

"Jesus." He looked down at the corpse again. "We're in even more trouble than I thought."

She ventured, "Who exactly *are* you?"

Something about the corpse made him suddenly exclaim, "Hey!" He seized the dead man's left hand and stared at it with an expression of outrage. "I'm the guy who normally wears this ring."

She staggered toward the bed and stared at it, too. "It, um, matches mine." She held up her own left hand, careful not to touch the corpse.

"I know," he snapped.

"What?"

Still staring at the dead man, he murmured, "We got married six days ago."

"Huh?"

He looked up at her, then suddenly dropped the dead man's hand

and said, "You and me, I mean."

"You're my husband?"

"You don't really think you'd have married a guy who wears a pinkie ring, do you?"

She sat down on the edge of the bed. "Oh, this is a big relief."

"I think I'm flattered," he said dryly.

"Really, you have no idea." She sighed and felt some of her panic dissolving. "I'm not married to him. I'm not a widow. And I'm not an adulteress."

"Well, it's only been six days." When she gave him an irritated look, he said, "Kidding, kidding."

"And I haven't killed my husband." She paused and added, "Of course, it's only been six days."

He ignored that. "You're sure you didn't kill him?"

"I'm not sure of anything," she admitted.

There was a sudden pounding on the door accompanied by what sounded like a trio of confused Spanish voices. She looked at him in mingled fear and confusion.

"I *asked* you not to scream like that," he muttered. "Get rid of them."

"I'm not dressed," she argued.

"They're more likely to go away if *you* tell them to than if *I* tell them to," he pointed out. "You're the one who screamed for help."

She experienced another moment of doubt as she looked at him. He was tall and well-built, and she wouldn't have a chance against him, she suspected, if he was lying to her.

He caught her dubious expression and said, with the exasperation only a spouse could muster, "Will you *stop*?"

She nodded. "I'll get rid of them."

She went to the door, opened it slightly, and found two men and a very fat woman in the hallway. The two men looked concerned. The woman looked annoyed. It took some effort, but she bridged the language barrier with enough tenacity to assure them there wasn't a problem, after all. She might have been more convincing, she thought, if she were wearing more than a towel.

After closing the door, she turned to find him searching the room. "What are you looking for?"

"Where are your clothes?" he demanded.

"I don't know." She studied him and said slowly, "If you're my husband, then you should remember what I was wearing when I disappeared."

"You were wearing..." His dark eyes went wide and he said, "Oh."

"What?" she pounced.

"You were naked the last time I saw you."

"What?"

"In our room," he added. "We were, uh, consummating the marriage. Yet again."

"Oh."

"Then we had some wine....And that's all I remember until I woke up alone." He plucked the dead man's shirt and trousers off the floor. "You're going to have to wear his things."

"Yuck! No!"

"Don't worry, he wasn't wearing them when he was shot." He glanced at the naked corpse and added, "Obviously." He sniffed the clothing briefly and made a face. "But I'm afraid they reek of aftershave."

"Figures," she muttered. She took the clothes from him, started to lower the towel, then paused and made a gesture asking him to turn his back.

He looked insulted. "But I look at you naked all the time! You *like* me to look at you naked."

"Even so—"

"You like me to do a lot more than look."

"Nonetheless—"

"Just before you disappeared, you tore off all my clothes and we—"

"I don't want to hear this right now!" She took a steadying breath and said more calmly, "Right now, I don't really know who you are, and I'd appreciate it if you'd turn your back. Surely I wouldn't have married a man who would refuse me that much?"

He sighed. "Fine. Whatever." He turned his back and, while she got dressed, spoke over his shoulder. "Tell me what you *do* remember."

"Nothing. Well, no," she amended, "I remember you."

"But you just said—"

"I mean, I remembered your face."

"Yeah?" He sounded pleased.

"Yeah, but nothing else. I woke up a few minutes ago. Here. No memory. No clothes. With a dead man."

He was silent for a long moment before asking, "Woke up where?"

"Here," she repeated, pulling the dead man's trousers up over her hips. "Gosh, he was chubby. Give me your belt."

"Here, *where*?" he demanded, unbuckling his belt.

"In bed. With him," she admitted reluctantly.

He went still for a moment. His voice was strained as he said, "His name was O'Mallory."

"Oh."

"You didn't like him."

"What a surprise. Did you?"

"No."

He finished taking off his belt and held it out to her, still keeping his face averted. Instinct told her that he probably was indeed her husband, because she didn't need to see his face to know exactly what expression was on it right now.

While she put on his belt, he lowered his head and studied the floor with intense concentration. Still standing behind him, she realized she recognized that posture, too.

After a moment, he said, "Did he, uh...Do you remember if...I mean, if he...Oh, Jesus."

She looked at the dead man. "If anything happened, then I sincerely, truly, profoundly hope that I never ever remember it as long as I live."

"Do you...feel okay?" he asked.

"Somebody hit me on the head," she complained.

"Hit you?" He turned his handsome face and looked at her, his brown eyes soft and concerned.

Now this is more like it.

She had evidently married well, after all.

"I think that's why I can't remember anything," she opined.

"Let me see," he murmured.

She stood still while he came to her and examined the bump on her head, a dark frown on his face. His fingers were gentle, and his touch stirred a memory.

"You like sailing," she murmured.

His frown lifted. "Yeah."

"And you cook."

"That's right," he encouraged.

"I like to watch your hands...." She took one of his hands between hers and tried to remember more. "And you're so good at unbuttoning things that the first time...." A wave of heat washed through her. "Oh."

"Hmmm?"

"I think I remember the first time," she whispered.

"That's good," he murmured. "I worked hard, after all. I'd hate to think—"

"We're...on our honeymoon," she ventured.

He nodded. "We flew here the day after we got married."

"Wait." It was coming back to her. "The honeymoon suite at the Hilton?"

He nodded again. "The night we got married." He grinned and added, "Some complaints about the noise."

"We knocked over furniture," she said suddenly.

"Ahhhhh, you're remembering."

"And then we came here...wherever this is."

"Costa Rica. Because you like wildlife. Especially—"

"Birds," she interrupted, pleased she was recalling more details now.

"Birds," he repeated with a notable lack of enthusiasm. "I really wanted to go to the Virgin Islands, but *nooo*. You said if there was one place you'd alw—"

"Do you have to bring that up now?" she snapped. Her eyes flew wide as she realized, "Wow, I really am married to you, aren't I?"

"Is that a problem?"

"No, no, I'm sure I'll get used to it—"

"Thanks."

"But how did I wind up here? And who the hell is O'Mallory? And how did you find us?"

"O'Mallory is a creep who turned up at the hotel—"

"Please tell me this isn't our hotel."

"No, no," he assured her. "We're staying at a nice place on the coast."

"That's a relief."

"Yesterday morning, I came to. It was late, I felt really hung over—"

"You were drunk?"

He shook his head. "The bottle of wine in our suite must have been drugged. I woke up face-down on the floor, naked and alone. You were gone." He glanced at the bed and added between his teeth, "So was my wedding ring."

"But why?"

"O'Mallory called and said if I ever wanted to see you alive again, I had to get one million in U.S. dollars, in cash, and have it ready."

"Ready for what?"

"His next call."

Her eyes widened. "You've got a million dollars on you?"

"No." He shook his head. "I couldn't get my hands on that much money in one day, especially not in Costa Rica."

"But if we were at home—"

"If we were at home and I had a week or two, then I could do it."

"Wow, I really married well, didn't I?"

"Mind you," he added, "then we'd have to live in a tent and clip lots of coupons for a while."

"But I'm worth it?" she prodded.

"Usually," he agreed with a smile. "Anyhow, when O'Mallory called again last night, he told me to meet him in the lobby of this hotel. After I got here, I waited downstairs for thirty minutes. When he didn't show up, I thought he might have you hidden in one of the rooms, and so I started searching for you."

"That's it?"

He shrugged. "He sounded really scared during that second call. He didn't even seem to care that I didn't have the money yet, just wanted me to come anyhow."

"You didn't call the cops?"

"He said you would die for sure if I did." He shook his head. "All I could think of was getting to you. So I got a car and drove all night to get here."

She looked out the window. The sky was brighter. "So it's morning."

"You didn't know that?"

"I don't know anything," she reminded him.

"Not even how he wound up dead?"

"No. Or whose gun that is."

His gaze followed hers to the weapon lying on the floor. "Or what he was scared of, I guess?"

"Well, I think we can safely deduce he was scared of winding up like this."

He nodded. "Good point."

"What do we do now?" she wondered.

"Go to the cops." He went back to the bed and grabbed O'Mallory's left hand.

"What are you doing?" she demanded.

"I want my wedding ring back."

"Oh, yuck! No! Eeeuuuw! Leave it."

"But it's my wedding ring!"

"You can afford another," she said with forced patience.

"But this is the one you put on my hand when we got married. This one has sentimental value. It's—"

"It's on a dead man's hand!" she snapped. "Leave it there!"

"But—"

"If you put it back on now," she informed him through gritted teeth, "you will never again touch me with your left hand."

He dropped the corpse's hand. "I see amnesia hasn't affected your stubborn streak at all."

"Why did he even take your wedding ring, for goodness' sake?"

"To pass himself off as your husband, of course."

She shuddered. "But why?"

"He had to haul your naked unconscious body from our suite to his car, and later from his car into this hotel." He shrugged. "With matching rings, all he had to say was that you were his wife and you'd had too much to drink."

"If I were his wife," she said with feeling, "I would indeed drink too much."

He glanced down at the big tangle of blood-soaked bedsheets and said, "I suppose he stole one of these from our room and wrapped you up in it."

"So there's no doubt that he saw me—even touched me—naked."
She felt faint again. "Oh, God."

Someone pounded at the door again. There was more shouting in
Spanish. Deep male voices this time, and what sounded like a stern
warning.

Her husband sighed. "Get rid of them."

She nodded and turned to do so. Before she reached the door,
however, it suddenly flew open with a loud crack of splintering wood
and snapping metal. Four uniformed policemen stampeded into the
room, all of them armed and clearly ready to shoot.

She raised her hands. They stared at her. She stared back. When
she could finally make a sound, it came out as, "G...ga...gahhh..."

A short, stout, smirking man walked in slowly behind the four
cops. He seemed to be their superior officer.

She gasped. "Oh, my God! Wait minute!" She stared. "Yes! I
remember you! You ambushed us! O'Mallory was afraid of you! *You're*
the one who hit me on the head, you jerk!" Her eyes flew wide as she
realized, "You killed him!"

"Ah, Mrs. Smith," he said. "A pleasure to see you again."

She glanced at the bed. "Smith? He checked us in under the name
Smith? Of all the unoriginal, clichéd, hack—"

"Uh, honey," her husband interjected, "that's *our* name."

She squinted at him. His hands were raised, too. "I'm really Mrs.
Smith?" she asked.

He nodded.

She shrugged. "Oh, well. At least it's easy to spell."

The stout man cleared his throat. When he had their full attention,
he introduced himself. "I am Captain Lopez."

"I'm not at all happy to see you," she replied.

Her husband said to the other cops, "Listen to me. My wife has
been kidnapped and—"

"Your wife, *señor*," Lopez interrupted, "is a murderess."

She gasped. Her husband argued. The cops, in response to a command from Lopez, handcuffed both of them, then went around the
room gathering evidence. When they collected the gun, her husband
swore.

"Her fingerprints are on it," he guessed, "aren't they?"

"A very astute prediction," Lopez replied.

"I didn't shoot him!" she snapped at her loving spouse.

"I know," her husband said, his gaze still fixed on Lopez, "but he means to prove otherwise."

"He can hardly prove otherwise," she argued, "since I never touched the gun...." She choked and whirled to stare at Lopez. "You planted my prints on it while I was unconscious!"

"I'm afraid it was necessary."

"No wonder O'Mallory said I would die for sure if...if what's-his-name here went to the cops!"

"Scott," her husband supplied. "It's Scott."

"The cops are in on it!" she continued.

"No, no," Lopez said. "Just me."

She looked at the four cops busily tearing apart the room in search of damning evidence against her. "What about them?"

"They don't speak a word of English," Lopez advised her. "They just follow orders."

"So O'Mallory prowled the resorts in search of wealthy victims," Scott guessed, "and you gave him police protection in exchange for a cut of the take."

"Sadly," Lopez said, "he was inept at his duties, so there hasn't been much 'take' so far. I've been obliged to find a replacement."

"O'Mallory found out," Scott surmised. "He realized you'd try to get rid of him."

"Of course!" she said, understanding now. "You couldn't just fire him and count on him to go away quietly."

"So you're framing his final kidnap victim for his murder," Scott concluded.

"Especially since," Lopez said with a noticeable quiver of outrage, "his final victim is not the surgically enhanced young trophy wife of Alan Scott Smith, the fifty-six-year-old heir to a mining fortune worth four hundred million dollars. Noooo!" Warming to his theme, Lopez went on, "Instead, that incompetent moron O'Mallory zeroes in on Scott Alan Smith, a newlywed from Seattle with a wife who—may I be excused for saying?—has the temper of an angry cobra and a head as hard as granite!"

"You may be excused," Scott said.

"Hey!" she said.

"Love isn't blind," Scott told her, "it's just incredibly tolerant."

"If we could return to the subject of my upcoming murder trial," she prodded.

"I'm open to bribery," Lopez said with the air of a man trying to demonstrate goodwill and a desire to cooperate, "but I fear that you can't meet my price."

"Which is?" she prodded.

"One million, U.S., cash."

Scott sighed. "Well, as you've remarked, I'm not the mining fortune heir with the trophy wife, so I'd need time to get that much money together."

"We're not giving a penny to this slimy worm!" she snapped.

Scott glared at her. "There goes my whole 'give me time' ploy."

"It wouldn't have worked anyhow," Lopez assured him.

"You can't convict me of a murder I didn't commit!" she insisted.

"Of course I can," Lopez said. "I am an expert at manufacturing evidence."

"Oh." She thought she was going to throw up.

"Yes, I'm afraid things do look really bad for you," Lopez said with a touch of sympathy. "And on your honeymoon, too. Such a shame, but it can't be helped."

"Look, why don't you arrest *me* for his murder?" Scott suggested desperately. "Say I found them here together, and in a jealous rage I—"

"Sorry," Lopez said. "Your gallantry is admirable, but the gun is covered with her fingerprints, not yours.... However, we'll be happy to arrest you, too."

"On what charge?"

"I'm sure I'll think of something."

"You won't get away with this!"

"What that warning lacks in originality it makes up for in sincerity," Lopez replied. "However, sincerity is unlikely to prevent your conviction or—"

There was a sudden shout behind her, so loud it made her jump. More men came pouring through the door, and there was a great deal of yelling, confusion, and shuffling around. When a gun went off,

Scott knocked her to the floor and landed on top of her. She gasped for air and struggled to see what was going on. She saw scuffling feet coming toward her. She tried to roll away, but Scott's weight pinned her down. One of the feet kicked her in the head.

"Ow!"

"What? What's wrong?" Scott demanded.

"Someone kicked me! Get off of me!"

"Stay down!" he ordered.

"What's going on?"

When Scott finally let her up, Lopez was face-down on the floor with his hands cuffed behind him. The four cops who had come here with him were spread-eagled against a wall and submitting to a search, all the while protesting (it seemed) their innocence. And a dozen heavily armed men in combat fatigues were in charge of the scene.

"What's going on?" she said again as someone helped her and her husband to their feet.

"O'Mallory must have betrayed Lopez," Scott said.

She looked around. "You mean...he realized you might not get here in time to save him—"

"To save you," he corrected.

"—and so he blew the whistle on Lopez!"

"Does anyone here speak English?" Scott asked.

"*No, señor.*" An earnest-faced uniformed man apologized for this, then spoke at great length in Spanish.

They tried to understand, but their efforts at communication were frustrating.

"Oh, mother of God!" Lopez exclaimed from his undignified position on the floor. "He's saying you have to accompany him to the station and give your statements to an interpreter! Really, if you people can't even learn a few words of Spanish, why not honeymoon in a place like the Virgin Islands?"

"You see?" Scott said to her.

"Oh, will you drop it?" she replied.

"Didn't I tell you—"

"Saying 'I told you so,'" she warned him, "would be a bad way to start off our marriage."

He seemed ready to argue for a moment, but then all the fight went out of him. He leaned down and kissed her. "I'm just glad you're safe now," he whispered.

She tried to put her arms around him, then winced when the handcuffs bit into her wrists. "Hey, Lopez, we need the key to these cuffs."

Lopez grumbled, then gave some instructions to one of his captors. A few moments later, someone removed the handcuffs, and she sank into her husband's arms—an embrace that now felt wonderfully familiar.

"You stink of O'Mallory's after-shave," he murmured.

"Nothing happened," she muttered in relief.

"You remember now?"

"It's coming back to me."

He tightened his arms around her for a moment, then said, "I don't think we should tell your mother about any of this."

She froze for a moment, and then groaned, "My mother."

"What's wrong?"

"Oh...I had just mercifully forgotten her for a little while there."

She felt him shake with laughter, and then he kissed her hair. He ran a hand down her back and over her bottom, snuggling her hips against his. A bunch of other memories started returning, and she felt her skin flush.

"Come on," she whispered. "Let's go give our statements and get this over with. We have a honeymoon to get back to."

"Okay, Harry."

She flinched and pulled away. "Harry?"

He nodded. When she continued to stare blankly, he said, "Harriet. Harriet Bryniarski Smith. You didn't know?"

"Harriet Bryniarski." She put a shaky hand to her brow. "No wonder I forgot."

"Honey..."

"What else have I forgotten?" she demanded.

"I don't know."

"You're not a bigamist?"

"No!"

"Or a serial killer? Or the leader of some kind of perverted cult? Or—"

"No! Will you *stop*?"

"Just give me the bad news now. I can take it."

He sighed. "There is no bad news."

She studied him hard. "We'll see."

"The bad news," Lopez insisted, as his captors hauled him off the floor and out of the room, "is that he is not the heir to a mining fortune worth four hundred million dollars!"

"On the other hand," Scott pointed out to Harriet, "*that* Smith is a notorious bisexual philanderer. Whereas I'm straight and entirely monogamous."

"Well, it's only been six days," she pointed out.

He kissed her hand, a courtly gesture that she now remembered was typical of him. "In sixty years," he promised, "I'll still be able to say it to you."

She smiled. "I think today has sort of spoiled Costa Rica for me. So if you still really want to go to the Virgin Islands..."

"That's a good idea." He looked around and grinned. "But I swear to you, I don't normally go this far to win our fights."

The Scottish Ploy

P. N. Elrod

Cassie Sullivan slammed her clipboard onto the props table, causing the sword collection that lay there to jump. One fell to the floor with a solid clank. The abrupt noise startled everyone, giving her the undivided attention of the whole cast and crew. "If just one more thing goes wrong, I'm calling in an exorcist!"

Nell Russell left off wiring together tree branches that were to be part of Burnam Wood. "What's happened now?"

"Trevor Hopkins backed out."

"What?" Similar expressions of dismay flowed from the others who stopped work on the set to come closer, faces tense.

"Hopkins got a starring role in a straight-to-video horror movie and grabbed it."

Nell's mouth twisted. "He chose that over the lead in *Macbeth*? Why?"

"Money. They can pay him more. The option's in his contract."

Everyone nodded, understanding perfectly. The Sullivan Theater Company, for all its members' sincere enthusiasm, was small change to an actor like Trevor Hopkins. Apparently his commitment to keeping theater alive wasn't deep enough to survive the lure of Hollywood dollars. Cassie herself could side with Hopkins to a degree, but there was such a thing as fair warning.

Opening night was only a week away.

"What'll we do for a new Macbeth?" asked Willis Wright, the stage manager.

"Hopkins' agency is sending over Quentin Douglas as a replacement."

"Who?"

Cassie shrugged. "He's done some commercials."

A general groan. Nell joined in. "What kind of commercials?"

"Who knows? Foot powder, shaving cream, talking sandwiches— I don't care so long as he can project the lines. They said he played Macbeth in college—"

Another groan.

"—so he knows the part. If Isabel likes him, he's in."

"Great. Did he save his old costume?"

Cassie glowered. "Don't get me started. At this point I may do a nude production."

"That would sell more tickets. Think of all the sword jokes."

"Argh!" Cassie looked around for something else to slam or throw, but nothing non-breakable presented itself. The company watched her, somewhat wall-eyed. Her tempers were infrequent and short-lived, but infamous for their intensity. Everyone knew to get out of the line of fire for the brief duration, but this time no one seemed to know which way to jump.

She put her hands palm-out in a peace gesture. "It's okay, boys and girls. I just hate surprises. Chalk this up to the production poltergeist and get back to work. Let's keep it to one life-and-death crisis every ten minutes instead of every five. Okay?"

A rumble of agreement. They resumed their tasks. Nell hung close, though. "When's the foot-powder wonder boy due?"

"Sometime today. I just got the call from—"

"Miss Sullivan?" Baritone voice. Rich. Chocolate-smooth delivery. Built-in projection. No need for a body microphone.

Cassie turned to take in the owner of the voice. *Oh, my gawd.* Hair like jet, soap opera hero's face, body of personal trainer, thin line of beard edging his jaw—perfectly in keeping with a Shakespearean character—straight white teeth in a friendly, open smile.

"I'm Quentin Douglas—the Gilbert Agency sent me?" Hand outstretched. Expecting her to respond.

"Yes, they certainly did," she murmured, still goggling. She put her own hand out and connected with his firm grip.

The vision spoke again. "I hope I can work out for you."

His "hope" momentarily sparked a variety of emotions in Cassie, which she quickly snuffed out. *You're off actors, Cassie-girl, you are immune no matter how gorgeous they are. Anyone that good-looking is going to be attached or gay.* "I'm sure you will, Mr. Douglas." She was still holding his hand. Belatedly, she released it.

"Please, call me Quentin."

Before she could call him Quentin, she felt an urgent tugging on her shirttail; Nell obviously wanted to be included in the first-names fan club.

"Quentin, this is Nell Russell, she's playing Lady MacDuff, Hecate, and Young Siward."

"I'm very versatile," Nell purred, oozing forward to shake his hand, too. She had no misgivings about fraternizing with actors, usually bestowing one broken—or at least slightly bruised heart—per production.

Quentin tendered another easy smile, his royal blue eyes twinkling.

"Glad to meet you. Is there much doubling up for roles in this one?"

"A few," Cassie answered, since Nell seemed to have forgotten her next line, basking as she was in his presence. "None of the principals, of course. Go through there to my office, the red door. I'll be right along."

Quentin Douglas departed, walking smooth as a panther on ball bearings. Nell made a low moan of appreciation deep in her throat, ogling at the snug fit of his jeans on his perfect backside—not to mention the muscular set of those sculpted shoulders....The view wasn't lost on Cassie, but she made herself look elsewhere, gritting her teeth.

"Oh, I didn't think they made them like that anymore," Nell sighed.

"Down, girl, I don't want you breaking him before we even start."

"But he's the one."

"What? Your own true love? You've said that on every—"

"No, I mean I know who he is! He's the sports drink shower guy." Cassie blanked. "O—kay."

"You know, that commercial where the guy takes the shower and they pour sports drink all over his sweaty body. Relief from the heat in sloooow-mooootion."

"I'm surprised you even noticed his face." Not much of a TV watcher, Cassie had no recollection of the ad. She quelled a sudden feeling of deprivation.

"I've seen him in *As the Planet Revolves*, too. He can act."

"On TV. I've gotta find out if he's any good for stage work."

"Cassie, he looks like he'd be good for all kinds of things!"

"We'll see." Cassie hurried to her office before she caught Nell's terminal case of carbonated hormones. Yes, Quentin Douglas was a prime physical specimen; yes, he could probably act, but having once fallen far too hard for that type, Cassie had sworn them off forever. Of course, that was difficult to remember when face-to-face with Quentin across her cluttered desk. He had an energy that beat against her like a sunbeam. She refused to be burned by it, but quietly rejoiced; that sort of dynamism was highly valuable. He just might be able to make a whole theater feel it.

"Here's my résumé," he said, handing over a sheet of paper stapled to a head shot.

She compared the photo to the reality. Usually publicity pictures were an idealized improvement of the subject. Not with this guy, though. Would his looks detract from the production? On the other hand, it couldn't hurt to have a drop-dead handsome, extremely virile Macbeth leaping around the stage waving his sword. "Know how to play with your weapon?" she asked. "I mean—do you know stage combat?"

"It's a passion of mine." He flashed those perfect teeth. "I don't get much call for it in commercials."

"This job doesn't pay as well as TV work."

"It's experience. I'm always looking to hone my skills." He kept up with the eye contact.

Is he flirting with me? she wondered, conscious she was only in her second-best work shirt, her third-best jeans, with her blazing mane of red hair piled every which way from its hasty morning pinning. But Quentin had live theater in his background; he'd know how grungy things could get. No matter. *I'm immune to his type now. Stick to business.* She found a copy of *Macbeth* and handed it over. "Let's have a reading, then."

"Sure. What would you like to hear?" Quentin was remarkably self-possessed. Most of the actors she'd dealt with had panic attacks at the prospect of a cold reading. Not this wavy-haired cool cucumber.

"How about Act Three, Scene Four? Macbeth's talking with the First Murderer at the banquet." There, a highly charged scene to work with; would he know the right level to hit?

Quentin found the spot in the book right away, indication that he knew the play well. She fed him the lines of the First Murderer. After a glance at the pages, he delivered flawlessly and in such a manner as to make the arcane language easily understandable to a modern audience. He also got the emotions across without snacking on the scenery.

Cassie tried not to look too enthusiastic. "Okay. I'm happy, but the decision rests with the show's angel, Miss Isabel Graham. I'm directing, but she's the producer and star and has final say." She expected some sort of response from the name. Millions of people knew of her. Even Cassie had seen an episode or three of Isabel's hit comedy series, *I Love Isabel.*

"Shouldn't be a problem," said Quentin, not batting an eye. "I've worked with Bel before."

"Really?" Cassie did not miss the affectionate diminutive of Isabel's name. Only a very select few had the privilege of calling her that.

"She and I were in college together," he explained. "In fact, we were in *Macbeth* one semester. The same roles."

"How...convenient." Cassie spotted the confirmation of this on the résumé.

"Bel's career took off faster than mine. I did a stint in the navy to pay for college, which delayed things for a couple of years. I'm catching up."

"That's great." *I think.* "So Isabel already knows you're here?"

"She's the one who recommended me to the casting agency. But I wanted to get the part on my own, not just because she told you to put me in."

"That's very considerate of you. What if I'd turned you down?"

"Then I'd go back to New York and nag my agent for other jobs. No point being in a show if the director doesn't think I'm right for the part."

Her respect for him went up a few notches. "Just as well it all worked out, then. Let's introduce you to the others. Rehearsal starts in an hour. We'll go over the blocking for Act One."

"All right. How's the curse going for this production?"

At this out-of-nowhere shot, Cassie paused in mid-boost from her desk, and sat down again. Rather abruptly. "Curse? Who told you?" she blurted before thinking.

"This is the bad-luck play," he said, his eyes twinkling again. "So what troubles have you had?"

"I don't believe in the curse," she answered dismissively.

"The Weird Sisters' spells are supposed to be real, and it's always been bad luck to quote from the Scottish play while backstage."

"Only because in the old days it meant the current production was about to close. Companies could quickly throw *Macbeth* together to fill up the schedule gap. If an actor heard anyone rehearsing lines from it backstage, it meant his show's run was doomed."

"I've not heard that one." He fixed her with a rather intense look. "But you've not really answered my question, Miss Sullivan."

"Cassie," she said automatically, and let it hang there between them for a very long moment. Or did time just telescope when he looked at her like that? *Oh, but he does have riveting eyes.* She broke out of their spell and came up with a reluctant response. "We've had a few glitches that we blame on the production poltergeist, but there's been no more now than for any other show."

"Forgive me, but that's not what I've heard."

She could fix people with a formidable look herself and did so now with Quentin, her green eyes stiletto-sharp. "And just what have you heard?"

Unlike others she'd ever used it on, he didn't seem to recognize the danger signal and leaned forward, quite unintimidated. "When I found out I was going to be sent to replace Trevor Hopkins, I phoned Bel to thank her for the boost. She gave me an earful. I know about the missing costumes, props breaking, sets falling down, electrical shorts, flooded bathrooms—the works."

"We found the costumes in the trash and put that down to cleaning staff error, the rest is just accident and coincidence. It's an old building. It would be odd if things didn't go wrong with...things."

"What about the rash Bel got from her makeup?"

"Allergic reaction to a new brand. We changed it."

"And Trevor Hopkins finding that dead rat in his codpiece?"

"It crawled in there to die. We made him a new one and set out traps."

"And the needle that turned up in Bel's corset? She got a bad scratch from that."

Good grief, he knew everything. Cassie fought down her anger. "The costume crew was careless. They apologized. The rest is coincidence. What are you getting at with all this, Mr. Douglas? Do you think someone is after Isabel?"

"I think Isabel thinks someone is out to kill the production."

"That's ridiculous. I've been with the people here for years, there's no way—"

"Bel worked herself into a good upset once she started talking. She's willing to lay the blame on the play's traditional curse, but she's also willing to consider non-supernatural alternatives. You may know and trust everyone here, but she's an outsider."

"Mr. Douglas, I can tell you right now that all the people in this company are two hundred percent behind this production. We're working to make it a success because we need her money. Isabel's agent approached me with her offer to foot the bill for the whole thing so long as she gets to play Lady Macbeth, and I gratefully accepted. The publicity this playhouse will get from her name will give us the financial help we've always needed. There is no way anyone here is going to jeopardize that."

"But maybe talk about a curse might embarrass her in some way? The tabloids love this kind of thing."

Ouch. He knew how to hit low. "Miss Graham wants to prove

to the world she can play high drama as well as middle-America comedy, and a little bad publicity is not going to stop her. She's a total professional and knows that the show must go on."

Quentin, his gaze still steady, nodded slowly, as though he'd found something he'd been looking for and liked it. "You seem to be aware of just how important this is to her."

"If she blows it the critics will be merciless. She's put a lot of trust in me, an unknown backwater director—"

"Whose parents were the darlings of Broadway once upon a time."

It was no secret, but she was surprised he knew that. "Yes, they were, and they taught me everything they knew when they invested in this theater. I want to do proud by their memory, and I will give Isabel my best effort."

"Then we're all in accord." He suddenly relaxed and smiled.

She couldn't help but smile back. "Yes, I suppose we are, but—"

Someone banged urgently on her red door. "Cassie! Emergency!" It was Willis Wright, stage-managing in overdrive from the sound of him.

Heart thumping, she shot from her chair, on full alert. In any given production there were a hundred emergencies, but his tone of voice made this one serious. She tore the door open and nearly collided with him. "What is it?"

"We've found a body up on the gridwalk."

"*What?*" She pushed past, tearing toward the stage. There she saw the whole company staring upward to the dark heights of the grid, the steel construction that held the lights and backdrops. She stared herself, trying to pierce the shadows. "Flashlight!"

Willis slapped one into her hand. Its beam was pale from use and didn't reach far, but she saw a man-sized shape dangling ominously over stage center.

"Oh, my God. Is that for real? Someone get up there and find out."

Willis himself saw to it, scrambling up the metal ladder affixed to the backstage wall. He reached the grid and gingerly stepped onto it. The hanging figure swung heavily. Several of the people around her gasped.

"Everyone back out of the way!" she snapped.

Still staring up, they reluctantly moved clear.

And only just in time. Willis yelled, "Look out!"

The thing high above suddenly plummeted. The body smacked into the stage with a resounding thud, inspiring screams. Cassie jumped in reaction, but held her place. She became aware of someone looming close behind her. Quentin. Generating a lot of heat. He stared over her shoulder at the body.

It was only a dummy—for which Cassie heaved a great sigh of relief—but its appearance sent a chill right up her spine. Female, with a hangman's noose around the neck, it was dressed in her own private working uniform of jeans, cowboy boots, and her best blue work shirt, which had gone missing yesterday. Topping all was a red wig, the color matching her own wild mane. Most disturbing was a huge prop butcher knife, smeared with dark red paint, sticking out of the thing's chest.

She felt Quentin's warm hand on her shoulder, gripping tight. "Good God...that's supposed to be you."

She recoiled at the suggestion. "I hope not."

"That's sick!" Nell all but shrieked. "Absolutely sick! Which one of you did this?"

No one stepped forward; no one looked the least bit guilty or smug, but then, most of them were actors.

No. I'm not going to go there, Cassie thought. *These are my friends, they're family!* An unfamiliar hollowness invaded her guts. Fear. Real fear. That fake knife had been buried right to the hilt in her effigy's chest. She steeled herself, went over, and pulled it out. All eyes were on her as she held it up like a trophy.

She fully milked the moment, making a slow turn to take them all in, keeping her voice rock-steady. "All right. Listen up. I am not amused. Somebody could have been killed if this thing had fallen at the wrong time. There's no harm done, but no more tricks. I'm talking zero tolerance, folks. I find anyone, absolutely anyone, screwing around like this, and I will personally bury them. Is that clear?"

Nods of comprehension all around. She tried to read their faces for any clue as to who might be the guilty party, but it was impossible, so she concentrated on not trembling from the adrenaline rush. Rule One for any good dramatic scene: never let them see you sweat.

"Cassie? What's going on here?"

She turned to face Isabel Graham, the show's patron, producer, and leading lady. Though known as a brilliant comedic star by means of her hit TV series, at the moment Isabel truly resembled Lady Macbeth. Her blue eyes were wide with shock, her mouth set in a grim downward turn. She looked at the bloody knife, then at the dummy.

"Just a sick joke, Isabel," Cassie wearily explained, wishing she could lose the knife.

"Another one?" This came from Isabel's manager, James Keating, also her most recent fiancé. Like Nell, Isabel fell in love a lot, but had been careful not to follow through to marriage just yet. According to the tabloids, though, Keating just might be the one to break the rule. He was movie-star handsome, had a shark's attitude when it came to business, and was totally devoted to Isabel. He stared at the dummy sprawled all over center stage.

"Cassie, this isn't a joke."

"That's supposed to be you?" asked Isabel, horrified.

"It's a rotten likeness. I have a much better figure."

Isabel puffed out a short, mirthless laugh. "Not funny."

"Absolutely not," agreed James. "This is a deliberate and cold-blooded—"

"Quentin!" Isabel squealed, suddenly noticing her new co-star standing behind Cassie. Cassie dodged clear just as Isabel launched herself at him. He obligingly grabbed her up in a full body hug and spun her slender form around.

Short attention span, thought Cassie. Isabel had loads of talent, but when she wasn't performing she was as easily distracted as a kitten was by a new piece of string.

"You've grown!" crowed Isabel when Quentin set her down.

"Nope, you just got shorter."

"Did not! You get those big muscles in the navy?"

"They're rented, but if they work out, I might buy them."

James Keating watched the exchange between the two old friends with thin-lipped tolerance. Cassie knew how he felt. Her last—completely last—actor-boyfriend had thrown her over for someone else. He'd been just as public about it, too. Was James worried about a rival?

Willis came up then, or rather down, having just quit the metal ladder. He also inspected the "body," especially the noose rope. His focus served to draw Isabel back to the immediate problem.

"What is it, Will?" Cassie asked.

He shook his head. "This was set like a booby trap. I found fishing line leading from the dummy's noose to the ladder and down the rungs on the inside. The noose was just barely snagged on a hook up there with a fancy knot; one good pull on the line and it's off and dropping. I accidentally tripped the gag when I got to the top. Whoever set it wanted to pull it down from a distance. It would have worked, but the setup was clumsy. If there'd been a good draft it might have come tumbling down beforetime and killed someone."

She felt cold. All over.

"Cassie, you should call the cops on this. James is right, this isn't a joke anymore. Maybe the rest of the stuff you can fob off on the poltergeist, but somebody put work into this thing—and it had to be somebody with free access to the building. This came from the basement props and costume storage."

"Not the clothes," she said.

"Those are your own clothes, aren't they?" asked Isabel.

"Don't hold it against me. I'll buy something nice for opening night."

"Stop with the joking already," said Nell. "This a deliberate act of terrorism!"

"I agree," said Quentin. "You need to report it."

"And have the tabloids eat us for lunch? I don't think so." She'd already had to deal with several overly friendly reporters looking for the inside scoop on a perfectly ordinary—well, almost ordinary— production of *Macbeth*. They'd been interested in any sort of dirt on Isabel, of course.

Isabel shook her head. "Never mind the so-called press. I can take a little heat so long as they spell my name right. This could be a life-threatening situation. You have to call the police!"

Cassie raised her hands in a placating gesture. Unfortunately, the prop knife was still in one clenched fist, causing everyone to back away a step. "Okay! I'll phone them, but I am not terrorized, I'm mad as hell. Everyone here should get mad, too."

Nell visibly thought that one over. "What? Like an acting exercise?"

"No! I mean if you put all the poltergeist stuff together, most of it doesn't mean squat, but this is different. I think that someone wants to kill this show, for reason or reasons unknown."

"Over my dead body," said Isabel, her eyes flashing blue fire. "I'll call in a security firm and lock this place up like Fort Knox before I let that happen."

"Right," said Cassie. "That's what I'm looking for—I want you and everyone else mad and on red alert. If we all play watchdog, look out for each other, anticipate problems before they happen, then they can't happen. Am I brilliant, or what?"

"Or what," Nell deadpanned. "You want us up here twenty-four/seven to revoke Murphy's Law? Lemme tell you, girl, when it comes to theater, Murphy was an optimist."

For the rest of the rehearsals Cassie concentrated on directing, which almost made her forget about the poltergeist. For whole minutes at a time.

It helped to have really good actors to work with, though. Quentin Douglas's romantic, hot-blooded—if slightly psychotic—Macbeth quite overwhelmed the brooding, anger-driven version Trevor Hopkins had attempted. Even without the drawing power of Isabel Graham's star name, this production was shaping into something special. Cassie was thrilled. She wanted the audience to see the characters, not the actors playing them.

Complications still arose. Mostly in the form of Quentin finding all kinds of ways to stick close to her when he wasn't busy killing people on stage. She pretended not to notice his attentions and focused on rehearsal business, which drove Nell up the wall.

"He likes you, Cassie! Are you nuts? Total studs like him are thin on the ground."

"He's an actor. Actors are off my menu."

"Unbend a little, girl. At least have coffee with him sometime so he doesn't think you hate him."

"I don't hate him! I'm being professional. Go for him yourself."

"I tried—but all he did was get me to talk about you. The least you can do is date him so I can have a vicarious thrill when you tell me all about it."

"I've no time. The play opens soon, and in four weeks it closes; he'll be history. End of problem."

"You wish."

Despite everyone looking out for each other, Murphy's Law continued with a vengeance. Opening-night jitters became the norm days too early, with more missing or damaged costumes, broken props, and damaged scenery flats. Frustration rose, tempers shortened, and arguments were frequent. Isabel's presence helped; she could stop a fight with her star-powered smile alone. At her own expense she had all the locks changed and hired off-duty policemen to keep an eye on things. To no avail, with so many crew and actors milling hurriedly about trying to bring the production together it was impossible for the security types to watch everything. The incidents continued.

After the effigy business, Cassie started sleeping over in the theater. She'd often done so when work had gone too late to drive home. With spare clothing, a comfy couch in her office, and showers in the dressing rooms, it was no hardship.

She didn't tell anyone, having gotten over her fit of denial to face the ugly fact that someone in the group was out to kill the show. Cassie absolutely hated the idea, but she found herself looking at familiar faces with new eyes. She began to come up with motives for each and had to bite her tongue to keep from blurting out an accusatory question that could destroy a lifetime of friendship.

So she kept quiet about her after-hours guardian duty, hoping that if she did discover the culprit they could settle things privately.

As for the possibility that an anti-Shakespearean ghost had taken up residence in the theater...well, Cassie had yet to meet a poltergeist who was any match for a furious redhead armed with a baseball bat.

The first two nights were uneventful, giving her much time to think back on all the various pranks—especially the deadliest. The guilty party behind the effigy had to have access, time, and privacy to set it up. The knot made her think of sailors, but ex-navy man Quentin Douglas, so newly come to the show, had no motive. Besides, most of the company knew how to do special knots; it was part of their normal stagecraft training.

That clue shoved to the side, she thought seriously about motivation. Why would anyone want to kill the production? Not one of her people would benefit if it died—quite the contrary.

What about Isabel? She believed in this show, but was that just cover? Her plan to prove herself to be a powerful dramatic actress as well as a comedy star was backfiring in the tabloids. Derisive articles were surfacing without any of the writers having seen her work. Unfair, but bad news sold. If Isabel stopped the production in the face of the mishaps, then maybe the critical feeding frenzy would never happen. Of course, she lost the chance to disprove all that derision with a solid performance, as well.

Perhaps James Keating? He'd more than once voiced the thought that they should quit and close down the show before anyone got hurt, but he always deferred to Isabel's wishes. Could he be tired of playing second banana?

By the third night at watch, Cassie was exhausted. At eleven she locked out the last of the crew and made a round of the dark and silent theater. While others might find its cavernous quiet and deep shadows ominous, she was in her home element, each creak as familiar as her own breath. When no boogeyman obligingly leaped out so she could whack him with her bat and solve her problems, she retired to the dressing room area to get a much-wanted shower.

Having seen enough Hitchcock movies to be sensible about the vulnerability of bathing females, she not only locked the dressing room door, but propped a chair under the knob. Any would-be Norman Bates would have a tough time of sneaking up on her, especially if the toolbox she'd balanced on the chair fell off.

Just as she finished her final rinse and cut the water, a terrific crash nearly made her leap out of her freshly scrubbed skin. Dripping, she struggled frantically into a terry robe and grabbed up her bat. Her heart hammered so loud she could barely hear anything else as she approached the dressing room door, which was being forced open inch-by-inch by a powerful hand.

Swallowing her fear and outrage, she nipped quick as a cat behind the door and raised her weapon high.

The chair abruptly tumbled over, and a black figure cautiously edged inside. She gulped again. He was awfully big for a poltergeist.

No matter. He was a trespasser and she was within her rights. She brought the bat down hard on the back of his head, giving a banshee yell for good measure.

He whirled just in time to whip his arm up, deflecting the blow to the side. He yanked the bat from her grasp and drove bodily toward her. She buried her fist into his belly, using plenty of knuckle. The man doubled over. Cassie ducked, rolled, and grabbed up the bat again, coming to her feet with it ready in hand as he recovered enough to turn on her.

"*You?!*" she screamed, caught between disbelief and rage.

"*Grrg!*" said Quentin Douglas, holding his gut.

"What the hell are you doing here?"

He waved one hand, palm out, backing away from her threat. "Uh-afh-ooo?"

"I'm watching the place," she answered, understanding the question even if articulation was lacking. "Why are you here? You're the poltergeist? I don't understand!"

He violently shook his head, then found a chair and dropped into it. He didn't look like a poltergeist. *But then he's an actor,* she reminded herself.

"I'm here to watch out for trouble," he wheezed out a few moments later. "With the stuff that's going on...it seemed the right thing to do. I was worried about you."

Wow. Her last guy would never have done *that* for her. "I can take care of myself."

"I noticed," he said, rubbing his gut.

"How long have you been here?"

"Since the first night I arrived."

"What? You've been creeping around every night without me knowing?!"

"I happen to be very good at it. That's why Isabel recommended me when Hopkins gave notice. She knew about my navy training.

She thought it might be an asset to theater security."

Cassie relaxed. Marginally. She still held her bat ready. "Are you all right?"

"Just bruised pride. If my service buddies ever found out I was decked by a half-pint like you—"

She growled and tightened her grip on the bat.

"Take it easy! That was a compliment. You've got a great punch. If red hair is mentioned they won't hassle me."

Mollified, she eased off. "Why'd you come in here? Trying to cop a peek?" She tightened the tie on her robe, suddenly aware of drafts.

"That would be great, but I saw someone lurking in the hall outside. I chased him, then lost him. When I returned I found the lock jimmied, so I thought I'd better check to make sure you weren't hanging from a coat rack with a knife in you."

"Oh. Well. Thanks. Shouldn't we go looking for the lurker, then?"

"We—sure, when you've dressed for the part, but don't go to any trouble on my account. In the meantime, I'll start looking around."

Growling, she retreated to the shower area and threw on clothes, then went to find Quentin.

Apparently recovered from the blow to his gut, he reported that all was quiet. "He's probably gone by now. I didn't get a good look at him. It was too dark. It might even have been a woman."

"Let's turn on all the lights and see what we find." She headed for the master switches backstage.

"Wait a second...do you smell gas?"

She sniffed. He was right.

"Basement," she said decisively, pivoting and running for the stairs. "We have butane tanks there to fuel stage-fire effects, but they're locked up in a cage. I don't see how—"

Quentin followed her, using the flashlight he carried to light the way down the stairs for them both. "Who has the keys to the cage?"

"There is no key, just a trick padlock, it's a joke around here—" She stopped cold. On the bottom step was a single candle burning in a holder. She scrambled the rest of the way down the stairs and slapped the flame out. The gas smell was worse here; she felt a headache coming on from it.

Quentin surged past her. Some of the cage wire had been cut

through. He thrust his hand into the hole and shut off the valves on the hissing tanks.

"Out!" he ordered, and she did not argue with him.

An hour before the final rehearsal Cassie called a meeting. She was mad as hell, but not showing it. In fact, she looked quite pleasant and rested. That was enough to alert her people that something was up.

"We're going to have the best show we've ever put on," she said as an opening.

Nell, who knew her very well, showed alarm.

"We can also relax, our troubles are over. The poltergeist blew it. I know who's been trying to kill this production."

"Who?" demanded James Keating, holding tight to Isabel's hand.

Cassie grinned. "Someone who didn't know all the ins and outs of this old place. One of the jokes here is the fact that there is a huge dummy padlock on the butane cage." She quickly explained about what she and Quentin had discovered the night before. "This place was supposed to blow up, or at least be so damaged as to make the show impossible. The culprit, not knowing that a trick catch on the padlock would open it, didn't have time to cut through the hasp, and smashing it would have been too noisy, so he cut the cage wires instead—and that was his giveaway."

"How so?" asked Isabel.

"A woman or a small man could have got a hand through the cage wires without too much trouble, and wouldn't have needed to cut the wires to turn the tank valves on. Anyone inside the Sullivan company would have known to just pop the trick padlock. Only an outsider, a man unable to get his big hand through, would have thought it necessary to cut the wire to get to the tanks. So why the hell were you trying to kill this production—Mr. Keating?"

Keating, no actor, went a sickly gray. "That—that's slander!" he finally stammered out. "My lawyers will strip you to the bone!"

Isabel shot to her feet. "You bastard!"

"B-but, sweetie-pie—it was getting too expensive, even as a tax write-off. And the critics were eating you alive even before opening night. Besides, you're a *star*, not an *actress*...."

Cassie calmly fitted her baseball bat into Isabel's hand. "Here, honey, have a party."

The Graham-Keating engagement, along with James Keating's right arm, which he'd raised to ward off the blow, was officially broken. Despite his threat of legal reprisal for slander, assault, and battery, no one in the company would admit a thing, so the police investigation into his broken arm stalled, while the show went on. Isabel Graham, drawing from that afternoon's inspiration, gave a riveting performance as one of the most vicious, bloody-minded Lady Macbeths the critics had ever had the pleasure to cower from; they also enthused about newcomer Quentin Douglas, sparking talk of a Broadway revival of the play.

"Four weeks and he's history," chided Nell to Cassie at opening night's celebration party. "Yeah, sure. You change your mind about dating actors yet?"

"Maybe," Cassie admitted, returning Quentin's look from across the stage. He started toward her, eyes twinkling again. "He didn't seem to mind too much when I clobbered him, so there's some hope...."

"Then you go, girl!" Nell pushed her forward. "And give him one for me!"

www.gonnahavekelly.com

Diane A. S. Stuckart

He had been there for the past half-hour, perched atop an empty bicycle rack in front of the West End art gallery where Kelly Winslow worked part-time. *Waiting for someone*, she tried to tell herself, noting his scrutiny of the pedestrian traffic in this, one of Dallas's most popular historic districts. Indeed, he looked little different from the typical West End hanger-on with his black T-shirt, black jeans, and fashionably cropped black hair. Just some thirty-ish Goth-wannabe... maybe a neophyte hit man who hadn't yet learned the art of blending with a crowd.

Then he turned his black sunglasses in her direction, and Kelly shivered.

"Get a grip, girl," she muttered, deliberately focusing her attention on the inventory list she was compiling. Chances were, the man couldn't even see past the reflection of sun against glass to make out who might be standing behind the gallery window.

No reason to assume he was staring at her, in particular. No reason to suspect he was the same person who, unbeknownst to her until a few days before, had been following her for weeks now. No reason to fear that he was the Internet stalker who had a website dedicated completely to her, a frightening little corner of cyberspace he called www.gonnahavekelly.com!

Come visit my website, Kelly. I think you'll find it very interesting, the message appearing in her e-mail box a few days earlier had read. She had almost deleted it, certain it was one of those invitations to a porn site halfheartedly disguised as an e-mail from a friend. But some impulse had made her click on the link, anyhow.

Its unsettling domain name notwithstanding, the website appeared to be nothing more sinister than an unauthorized tribute dedicated, as it claimed, "to the beauty and power of Kelly Winslow's extraordinary paintings." Three page links each suggested that she click. Feeling rather smug, Kelly had.

The first link, entitled See Who Kelly Is, consisted of the same photo she used in her gallery publicity. A box of statistics followed: age, 28; eyes and hair, brown; height, 5′5″; and so on. At the bottom of the page was a list of various galleries that had shown her work, information that, while hardly secret, must have taken some effort to compile.

Next was See What Kelly Has Painted, featuring perhaps a dozen photos of the various oils she'd displayed over the past year. Under each, the unknown webmaster had added comments of his own...all complimentary, some surprisingly insightful. She had clicked from there onto the final if oddly titled page See What Else Kelly Does, and her initial satisfaction had swiftly deteriorated into dismay.

The images that had followed would, under other circumstances, be dismissed as innocent, even boring: shopping at the health food store; drinking coffee at a table outside Starbucks; dancing with friends at a Greenville Avenue bar. Nothing special about them, at all...save for the fact they had been taken without her knowledge or consent!

"Kelly, darling, be a lamb and ring up Mrs. Criswell," an affected voice abruptly broke in on her thoughts.

The speaker was a tall, thin man with shoulder-length blond hair...Billy Criswell, the gallery's flamboyant owner and, in a manner of speaking, Kelly's employer. He displayed her works in his gallery in return for her few unpaid hours a week helping him run the place. It was a setup that benefited them both.

So what would he say if she told him about the website? she wondered as she wrapped the aforementioned Mrs. Criswell's new watercolor. Probably, not much. *Free publicity, darling*, he'd likely declare, dismissing her fears as casually as the police had.

There's not much we can do, ma'am, the polite voice that had identified itself as Detective Ted Ralston, of the Computer Crimes Division, had told her. *Unfortunately, it's not illegal to post pictures of someone without their consent. I can record your complaint but, unless this person ever actually threatens you, I suggest you don't worry.*

That, basically, had been the good detective's advice in one neat package. It had been easy enough for him to say...and a hell of a lot harder for her to do. In the past week, she'd been certain at least half a dozen times that some man or another was following her, only to realize after a few nerve-wracking minutes that she simply had let her imagination run wild. So, maybe the detective had been right. Chances were that he'd be too shy ever to approach her, anyhow. Fantasizing about her in cyberspace was likely as far as this wacko would ever go.

But he *had* wanted her to know about this fantasy, she reminded herself.

Which brought her back to the man in black. Was he her stalker, or just another victim of her paranoia? *If he's not there when you look out the window again, then that means he's not the one.* The mental bargain with herself made, she began counting to ten—very slowly—then dared another glance back out at the street.

The man was gone.

She breathed a thankful sigh that was loud enough to draw the attention of Billy, who had just hustled another, non-buying customer to the door. "Really, darling," he drawled, shaking back his bleached mane, "if you're that bored, why don't you go home early. Heaven knows they're not rushing in to buy *your* work."

His snide reference was to her pair of as-yet-unsold abstracts that had been on display for the past week. *Love Is a Pain*, she had wryly named the second of the two, with its tortuous angles in shades of charcoal and red that captured the essence of a bleeding heart...hers, to be exact. The other, painted well before the romantic breakup that had spawned its bleaker companion, was a study in brilliant primaries and more optimistically titled, *Love Is Bliss*.

"If you won't mind closing up alone, then I will go. If I hurry, I can catch the early bus."

A few minutes later, she was out on the sidewalk. Though freshly released from her air-conditioned haven, she still felt sweat begin trickling from her temples before she'd gone a block. For once, however, the oppressive heat might be considered a friend. *No stalker in his right mind would be following someone around on a day like this*, she told herself in satisfaction. Not with the June sun as hot as a ripe jalapeño, and no breeze in evidence to help cool the fire.

If she had a choice, she wouldn't be walking, either. She'd be tooling around town in her car like any other good Dallasite, with the windows rolled up tight and the a/c cranked down to polar. Unfortunately, said vehicle required $600 worth of repairs to be drivable, according to the local shop. Kelly grimaced. Since she didn't have the spare cash this month, she had reconciled herself to getting around on foot and on public transportation, for the time being.

She paused at a sliver of shade provided by the awning of a trendy clothing store window, and sighed. She damn well couldn't afford this place's three- and four-figure price tags, either; still, it didn't cost anything to look. But barely had she begun to lust after a bright red leather halter-top—on sale at $295—when a movement in the window reflection caught her eye. Her could-be stalker was behind her now, standing perhaps twenty feet away!

Kelly took off toward the next corner at a pace somewhere between race-walking and jogging. All she had to do was reach the bus stop unscathed, and she'd be home in half an hour. Just one more block, she reassured herself and stepped into the crosswalk.

Barely had she registered the blat of a car horn before a strong hand clamped around her upper arm and jerked her back onto the curb. A heartbeat later, a beat-up yellow mustang made a swift right turn in front of her, tires squealing and exhaust belching. When the smoke cleared, she found herself staring in dismay at the fresh tread marks now laid over the very spot where she'd been standing on the crosswalk.

Wincing a little at the pressure of his fingers, she slowly turned to face her rescuer. Had he not pulled her back, those tire marks would have been decorating her body, instead. But now he had her where he probably wanted her...firmly in his grip. They were close enough so that she could see the faint beading of sweat on his brow from the heat, could breathe in the faintest hint of the expensive-smelling after-shave he wore. And he was even more attractive than she'd realized, Kelly thought in dismay.

At least, I'm not being stalked by some butt-ugly loser wearing a pocket protector.

Just as quickly as the irrelevant thought flitted through her mind, she mentally tromped it down. *Damn it, Kelly, focus.* To her advantage, half a dozen cars now were stopped at the light alongside them, their occupants all potential witnesses to any altercation. The man could hardly carry her off without being noticed, so she didn't have to panic...at least, not yet. But she damned sure wasn't going to stand there playing helpless victim, either.

"All right, asshole," she declared in a voice that squeaked only slightly. "You've got exactly two seconds to let go of me, or else I'm going to start screaming."

"No need to scream, Ms. Winslow. I was just keeping you from being roadkill...nothing more sinister than that." A faint smile tugged at his lips. "It's okay, I'm one of the good guys."

Releasing her, he slipped a finger beneath the gold neck chain he was wearing and pulled it up to reveal a badge that glinted in the sunlight. Then he reached into his jeans pocket and extracted a business card stamped with the Dallas Police Department logo. "Detective Ted Ralston, Computer Crimes Division," he said and handed it to her. "We talked on the phone last week."

"I—I remember."

She glanced from the card to him, and then back to the card again. *This* was the cop she'd talked to? Maybe she should call the police on a more regular basis. Perhaps his voice was a bit different—deeper, sexier—from what she remembered but, then, their conversation had lasted maybe all of two minutes. But if he was a cop, then what in the hell was he doing...

"...Following me," she finished aloud. "Damn it, you were following me, weren't you?"

"My apologies if I alarmed you, ma'am."

He pulled off his sunglasses to reveal a pair of the sexiest blue eyes she had ever seen on a man. They were rimmed with thick black lashes that would make any model in a mascara ad weep with envy, while a fine spray of squint lines radiated from each corner, as if those eyes were habitually crinkled from grinning. Unfortunately, his expression now as he stared down at her was anything but amused.

"Actually, I wasn't so much following you, as hoping to spot your cyber admirer," he went on, that blue gaze making a quick sweep of the street around them before locking on her again. "You see, I did another check on that website you reported to us. Turns out there have been a few significant...well, changes...since the last time I looked at it."

"Changes? What kind of changes?"

He hesitated, and then nodded in the direction of the Starbucks across the street. "Why don't you let me buy you a cup of coffee, and I'll tell you about it."

⚲ ⚲ ⚲

"He's been inside my house!"

The few sips of iced latte that Kelly had managed to swallow threatened to come back up in a fear-laced spray of milk and coffee. With an effort, she managed to hold back that unseemly tide, even though Detective Ralston would have been the only witness. At his urging, they had eschewed the air-conditioned comfort of the coffee-house for the hot if relatively private sidewalk patio, with its row of empty, umbrella-shaded tables. Even so, she leaned across the table and dropped her voice to a whisper.

"He's been inside my house," she softly repeated. "How do you know that?"

"He added a few new pictures to the website this morning. Pictures of your studio, your kitchen, your living room...your bedroom."

Her bedroom. Dear God, surely he hadn't come prowling in the night, snapping pictures of her while she was sleeping! She briefly shut her eyes as she steeled herself to ask the next question. "What about...I mean, did he—"

Ralston shook his head. "He didn't take any pictures of you, if that's what you're asking. They're just shots of empty rooms. I don't suppose you've noticed any signs of a forced entry in the past few days?"

"No, nothing...but then, it's not like the place is a fortress," she faintly answered, picturing the tiny, tree-draped bungalow off Greenville Avenue that she called home.

The single-story house was just large enough for one person to spread about comfortably, with its combined living/dining room, two bedrooms—one of which she had converted into her studio—a bath, and a kitchen. Furnished with garage sale oddities and vintage store leftovers, the place dated from the thirties. Its door locks were original hardware; flimsy things that she'd always meant to replace with deadbolts, but never had gotten around to doing so. And the wood-sash windows with their little thumb locks weren't much better, considering that a couple of them didn't even close completely to start with. Breaking in would be an easy feat for anyone with a couple of spare minutes and a nail file.

"...think we've discovered his identity," Ralston was saying, and Kelly snapped her attention back to the detective. "He covered his tracks pretty well, but I was able to trace the website back to a guy by the name of Jason Todman. He's twenty-nine, single, makes pretty good bucks. By all accounts, he's smart, successful, not bad-looking—"

"So why in the hell does he need to stalk me? Can't he get a date?"

The detective had slipped his sunglasses back on, so that the cool black barrier was between them again. "It's not a matter of not being able to get a date," he replied, and a matching coldness crept into his tone. "I don't think even he could completely explain his reasons, except that it's a power trip. Controlling women that way makes him feel, well, sexy."

"I see. So how do you know all that, Detective Ralston? Did my friend Jason send you an e-mail or something?"

"Nope, just guessing. Must be those psych classes I took at the academy, kicking in after all this time."

Another grin tugged at his lips, dispelling the momentary chill between them...if, indeed, it had even existed. Kelly allowed herself a wan smile in return, even as she persisted, "But I don't understand. If you know who the guy is, why don't you just go arrest him? After all, he broke into my house. Surely that's still against the law, even if his webpage isn't."

"But unless we have a witness, or some physical evidence he was there—fingerprints, hair samples —we can't charge him with anything. For all we know, he took those pictures while he was in the house on legitimate business. Or maybe he got them from you."

Right. Like she was in the business of handing out photos of her living quarters to every guy who rang her doorbell. She didn't say that aloud, however, but merely swirled a straw in her latte—already thawed into a lukewarm brown concoction—as she strove for a reasonable reply.

"All right, Detective, let me make sure I understand what's happening here," she finally said. "Some crazy computer nerd has the hots for me; he takes pictures inside my house when I'm not there and posts them on a website; the police know who he is...and they can't arrest him for a damn thing. Does that about cover it?"

"That about covers it."

She shoved aside her half-full drink and stood. "Fine. Thanks for the coffee. Now, if you'll excuse me, I think I'll go home and wait to be murdered in my sleep."

To her dismay, those last few words verged dangerously on a wail. Blinking back tears of frustration, she started at a swift walk toward her bus stop. Just wait until the next time the issue of police pay raises came up on a city bond issue, she silently fumed. She'd check off a big fat "no" faster than Detective Ralston could blink those sexy blue eyes of his!

"Wait, Ms. Winslow..."

She heard the soft scrap of athletic shoes against pavement, and then Ralston was beside her again. "Just because we can't arrest the man, doesn't mean there's nothing we can do. At the very least, I can check out your place, make sure your friend isn't hiding in the closet."

She halted in mid-step and shot him an outraged look. "Excuse me?"

"Sorry, bad joke," he quickly amended. "What I really mean is that I can look things over for you, see if I can figure out how he got in, and fix it so he can't do it again. Besides, I'm parked down the block from your place, so I have to ride back with you, anyhow."

Yeah, or you could wait and take the next bus.

Still, the detective had a point. The thought of returning home alone, knowing that some stranger had been prowling within its walls, was more than unsettling. It made sense to let a professional make the rounds with her; maybe recommend a few security tips. And if her cyber stalker did happen to be lying in wait with his camera, it wouldn't hurt for him to see a man around the place...particularly a hunk like Detective Ralston.

The heat that abruptly warmed her cheeks wasn't entirely from the afternoon sun. *Don't get ahead of yourself, Kelly.* Probably, cops had rules about getting involved with crime victims. Of course, since they weren't going to arrest this Jason Todman unless he killed her, or did something equally vile, then maybe she didn't yet count as a victim.

She ventured a sidelong glance in Ralston's direction. He flashed her another smile, and she wondered if maybe he was thinking the same thing. Or maybe he was just feeling guilty about his earlier flip comment, and wanted to make amends. For now, either was fine by her, so long as it meant she didn't have to walk into her house alone.

She nodded. "All right, you win. Might as well get my taxpayer's money's worth."

"Might as well," he agreed, and his smile broadened into a grin that, to her consternation, did quite interesting things to her insides. "If nothing else, I'll pull a few strings and get you the city discount on new locks."

Detective Ralston...or Ted, as she had called him for these past two weeks...had been as good as his word. The day after their first meeting, he had returned to her place with two shiny new deadbolts, which he proceeded to install on both front and back doors. He'd also fixed the sticking windows, so that she could close them all the way. And since he'd done all this work on his off-hours, Kelly had offered to reciprocate by picking up the tab for Tex-Mex at one of Greenville Avenue's hot spots that night.

Not a date, she had hurried to clarify, when he had begun to mumble something about departmental policy. *Just a little thank-you for your help.* But a shared pitcher of margaritas, combined with the sight of him in snug jeans and an equally tight black T-shirt, had proved a devastating combination. Halfway through a platter of fajitas, she'd gathered the courage to point out that, technically, she wasn't yet a crime victim...so maybe it was okay if they counted this as a date, after all? And matters had proceeded quite satisfactorily from that point on.

He had left her place early the next morning, but not before retrieving the business card he'd given her at their first meeting.

"Don't bother trying to get hold of me at the precinct," he told her, scratching through the printed phone number with a felt-tip pen, and scrawling in another number above it. "You call there, you get someone who transfers you to someone else, who transfers you to another someone else, who'll probably end up having to take a message for me. Anytime you need me—day or night—call my cell phone."

But she'd had little need to dial that number, for he usually called her first...sometimes, while she filled in at the gallery; other times, just before she settled in for the night. Unfortunately, he'd been able to break away from work for a full evening only twice more in that time, but both those occasions had ended quite satisfactorily in her bed. In the meantime, though, and to her very great relief, her cyber stalker finally seemed to have tired of his game.

Two days after her first date with Ted, she had checked the Kelly website again, only to find a lone THIS SITE UNDER CONSTRUC-TION banner. When she'd gleefully told Ted what she had learned, he merely flashed her that sexy grin and mentioned something about having sent an official, unofficial "cease and desist" e-mail to the site. Thus, by the end of the second week, her cyber stalker had become all but a distant memory.

That was, until she came home from the gallery that afternoon to find her latest painting askew on its easel.

It was the oil she'd begun work on just a few days earlier, rounding out her series of abstracts with love as their theme. Rather than using the brilliant shades of *Bliss*, or the stark, contrasting tones of *Pain*, she had opted for a more thoughtful feel with this as-yet-unnamed work, indulging in muted primaries and softer lines. While the painting was but half-finished, she had been so pleased with the results that, yesterday, she had done something she rarely did...allowed someone other than herself to view a work in progress.

"Don't take this wrong, but I'm beginning to see your friend Jason's fascination with you," Ted had told her as he studied the canvas from all angles. "You have a wonderful gift, this ability to turn your own emotion into something we all can recognize." Then he'd unleashed his sexy grin on her, adding, "Actually, it's a bit scary, just how well you can do it...but, then, I'm the kind of guy who likes being scared."

Half an hour later—and after an impromptu session on the floor of her studio that was anything but frightening—Ted had returned to work, and she had covered up the wet canvas until she could return to it the next morning. Unfortunately, she'd ended up putting in an entire day at the gallery, so that it had been late afternoon before she went back again into her studio and made the unsettling discovery.

Perhaps Ted had taken a final look at the canvas before leaving yesterday, she tried to tell herself as she stared now at the painting, its protective cloth hanging slightly askew, like a curtain that had been twitched aside. But she remembered walking him to the door immediately after their impromptu lovemaking. Certainly, he couldn't have stopped by while she was at the gallery, since he had warned her yesterday that he was going to be working a double-shift today.

Cautiously, she lifted the cloth, half-fearing to find the canvas beneath damaged. The painting, however, was just as she had left it. No one had been prowling about her studio in her absence; no one had been splashing about with her oils. She shook her head at her paranoia, straightened the picture...and only then noticed a smudge of robin's-egg blue along one edge.

It was a small defect, as if someone's thumb might have slipped as he held the canvas, and smeared the still-wet oil. The damage was easily repairable, something she could have caused herself. Reflexively, she glanced at both hands but saw no telltale blue paint. Somebody else, then. But, who?

The stalker, that's who.

Impulsively, she grabbed for the phone and began dialing Ted's cell number. Maybe she was being paranoid, but she'd feel a lot better if he were the one to tell her so. When the call finally rang through, however, instead of Ted's familiar voice, or even his crisp message—*You've got me. Leave a message*—coming on the line, a prerecorded voice explained that all circuits were busy, and asked that she please try her call again later.

Kelly slammed down the receiver. Of all times for the system to be overloaded, why did it have to be now? She could call the local precinct, but would they have any better luck than she in getting through to him? Swiftly, she reached into her desk drawer for Ted's business card. She could still make out the original number, despite the heavy black line he'd drawn through it. She'd try him there, and she would leave as many messages as it took for them to find him.

A moment later, an efficient female voice answered, "Dallas Police" and, at her request, promptly transferred her. She heard a click; then her call rang through but a single time before a voice answered, "Computer Crimes Division, Detective Ralston speaking."

"Ted, it's me, Kelly. I think he's been in the house again," she began in a rush, only to hesitate as she registered what she had just heard. The voice on the other end of the line was oddly familiar...but it wasn't his.

"Kelly?" the voice questioned with an air of professional reserve. Then, abruptly, the polite tone took on an urgent edge. "Is this Kelly Winslow?"

"Y—Yes...but who—"

"I've been calling you for the past three days, Ms. Winslow," the voice went on. "Didn't you get any of my messages?"

She glanced over at the answering machine beside her phone, frowning. No flashing red light signaled any unplayed messages. Come to think of it, there hadn't been a single message on her machine for almost a week now. And surely she'd misheard the name this person had given when he'd answered the phone. "I—I'm sorry, who is this again?"

"This is Detective Ralston," the voice replied. "I'm the one you talked to a couple of weeks ago about your cyber stalker, remember?"

Kelly sank back in her chair and tried to corral her rapidly racing thoughts. Large as the Dallas Police Department was, surely there weren't two detectives by that same name in the same precinct. So who in the hell was the man on the other end of the phone? Deciding it was best to play along with him, at least for the time, she hesitantly replied, "Y-Yes, I remember. So, why were you trying to get in touch with me?"

"I've tracked the Kelly website back to its owner, and I think we need to talk about this guy." He paused, and then went on, "Look, Ms. Winslow, maybe I shouldn't be dumping all this on you over the phone. My shift's about up, anyhow, so why don't I just drive over there and tell you the rest? Besides, I've got a picture of him that I think you should check out, just in case."

"Sure...good idea...that'll be fine," she heard herself agree. "You have the address?"

"In your file. With traffic, I should be there in, say, thirty minutes."

It wasn't until she heard the buzzing of the dial tone over the sound of blood pounding in her ears that Kelly realized he had hung up some moments earlier. With shaking hands, she slowly returned her own receiver to its cradle. What had just happened here...and who in the hell had she been talking to?

The phone rang again, the unexpected sound practically sending her leaping from her chair. She snatched up the receiver and put it to her ear, then ventured, "Hello?"

"Kelly?"

It was Ted. Or, she abruptly wondered, was it merely the man she thought was Ted? She pressed the heel of her palm to her forehead and tried to think. Was it a good sign that a wave of relief had swept through her at the sound of his voice...or was it merely an indication that she'd been thoroughly taken in by a suave stranger who was pretending to be someone he was not?

"I'm between shifts," he was saying, in the meantime, "and since I'm just a few blocks from your place, I thought I'd stop by, if that's okay with you."

She choked back a laugh that was perilously close to a sob. Hadn't they just had this conversation, she and one of the two men who called himself Ted Ralston? "Sure, why not?"

"Kelly, is everything all right?" he replied, and she heard the frown in his voice. "You sound kind of strange."

"Well, that must be because strange things are going on. By any chance, did you accidentally erase my phone messages for the past couple of days?"

"Erase your phone messages?" he echoed. "No, not unless I did it in my sleep."

"And I don't suppose you remember smudging my painting when you looked at it yesterday, do you?"

"No, I never touched it. And what the hell kind of questions are these, anyway?"

Kelly took a deep breath, aware that she must sound like a stereotypical hysterical female. "Sorry, Ted. It's just that I found a thumbprint on my painting that I'm sure wasn't there yesterday. And if I didn't put it there, and you didn't, then someone was in my studio today."

"That's it? A thumbprint?" he asked, the tension in his voice easing. "I'll take an official look at it but unless you've been handing out door keys, I'd almost guarantee you it's yours. But why didn't you call me, instead of worrying yourself into a frenzy?"

"I tried, but all the cellular lines were all busy. I had to call you at the precinct, instead."

"You did?" Something momentarily sharpened his tone—surprise...anger?—before he went on in the same unconcerned tone. "Let me guess. They transferred you from department to department, and then cut you off before you could leave a message, right?"

"Not exactly. I got transferred to the Computer Crimes Division right away. Someone answered the phone who said he was you, and told me that he's been trying to get hold of me for days. He's on his way over here right now to talk about the cyber stalker."

"I see."

"You see?" she echoed in disbelief. "Well, that's great, because I don't. What am I supposed to do now? He says *he's* Ted Ralston...you say *you're* Ted Ralston. So who am I supposed to believe, him or you?"

Me, she waited for—prayed for—him to say. Rather than answering her, however, he said in a very deliberate voice, "Kelly, I want you to think back very carefully to that phone call. When the dispatcher transferred you over, did you hear anything on the lines...any tones, any clicks...before you were connected with this guy?"

"It did click once," she recalled in a puzzled tone, "but what does that mean?"

"It means our cyber stalker friend is a hell of a lot more clever than I gave him credit for being. Damn it, Kelly, he must have tapped into your phone line, maybe through your modem. That's why, when you dialed the precinct, he could intercept the call and pretend to be me."

She hesitated, wanting desperately to believe he spoke the truth. After all, if computer hackers could shut down multimillion-dollar corporations with simple e-mail viruses, surely they could play equal havoc with phone lines.

"I know it all sounds crazy," he went on, "but you've got to trust me on this one. The guy you just talked to is your stalker, not me... and he damn sure has crossed over the line if he's ready to meet with you in person."

Crossed over the line. She'd read the papers enough to know what happened when a stalker did just that. Usually, the headlines blared words like *shot* and *dead.* But even as she shut her eyes against those disturbing images, she heard his voice take on a more urgent note as he went on, "Listen, Kelly. This is very important. When you talked to this guy, did you give him any reason to imagine that you already knew me?"

She opened her eyes again and shook her head; then, remembering that he couldn't see her through the phone lines, she replied, "I don't think so. I was too shocked to do anything but listen to him talk, and then tell him it was okay when he asked to come over. I—I didn't know what else to say."

"Don't worry, you handled it just right." She relaxed a little as she heard a note of warmth replace the earlier sternness in his voice, only to gasp in disbelief as he added, "That means he won't suspect a thing when you let him inside the house."

"You really want me to let him inside the house?" she repeated a few minutes later, after Ted—wearing very uncop-like jeans and a torn white T-shirt—had slipped in through the back door and joined her in her tiny living room.

He nodded and twitched back the front window curtain just enough to give them a glimpse of the street beyond. A few battered sedans were parked along the curb, but Ted's sleek black BMW was nowhere to be seen, as he'd taken care to leave it on the next street over.

"We already went over this on the phone," he answered, his attention fixed on the encroaching dusk. "Sure, I could arrest him the minute he knocks on the door, but hosting a website—or even pretending to be me on the phone—isn't enough to justify charging him with a crime. The judge would kick him free, and you'd be right back at his mercy. The only way I can make anything stick is if we can prove some sort of threat against you."

"And what if he *does* threaten me, and you try to arrest him, and he resists?" she wanted to know, still not convinced this idea was anything but insane.

He glanced over and flashed her his sexy grin. "I'm pretty sure I can handle him...but just in case I can't, I've got backup waiting." Then he returned his attention to the window, and his grin abruptly faded. "All right, it's showtime," he murmured, indicating the dark green pickup that was pulling into her driveway.

He let the curtain drop, and turned to her. "Remember, I'll be in the hallway, just out of sight, but where I can hear everything. Now, chances are he's going to throw you a few curves, show you some reports or pictures that make him look like he's the genuine article. But don't let him rattle you with smoke and mirrors...just keep him talking until he says something to incriminate himself, okay?"

Keep him talking. She silently repeated those words as she opened her front door, letting out a blast of air conditioning into the muggy dusk. The man who stood on her porch was maybe a year or two older than she, of medium height and build, and with features that were pleasant if rather ordinary: straight nose, sandy hair, mild brown eyes behind wire-rim glasses. His clothes were equally run of the mill, blue slacks and a white shirt, topped by a tan jacket that was slightly too heavy for the day's remaining heat.

The single, irreverent corner of her mind that wasn't currently frightened shitless by the entire situation chortled. He might be believable as the guy delivering UPS packages, or as the person who sold printers and peripherals in the local computer superstore, but as a cop...never. The question for the moment was, however, was he also her cyber stalker?

"Ms. Winslow?" he politely inquired. At her nod, he flipped open a leather wallet to reveal a badge remarkably similar to Ted's, then reached into his jacket and pulled out a business card. It was identical to the one on her desk, save that it lacked the handwritten phone number.

"I'm Detective Ralston. May I come in for a moment?"

Nodding again, she opened the door wider. He stepped into her living room, his gaze taking in each detail as he casually paced it, a thick manila folder clutched in one hand. He paused at the darkened hallway, and for a heart-stopping moment she feared he would keep going. To her relief, however, he turned and asked, "You're here alone, ma'am?"

"Yes...I live here by myself." She gestured toward the balding horsehair sofa, which was well away from the hall, and suggested rather breathlessly, "Maybe you'd like to sit down now?"

He took the seat she'd indicated and set his folder on the old steamer trunk she used as a coffee table. Kelly perched on a straight-backed chair a cautious distance from him; then, conscious of the man in the hallway listening to every word, she went on in as casual tone as she could muster, "I believe you said you had some information?"

The man who called himself Detective Ralston nodded. "The first time we spoke, I told you there wasn't much I could do about the situation," he began. "I checked out the website, anyway, and got the name of the domain owner...one Jason Todman. When I ran a check on him, nothing came up, but since he's only been in Dallas a few months, I decided to dig deeper."

He flipped open his folder and pulled out what appeared to be an official-looking form, its numerous blanks filled in with blue-inked writing. "His last known addresses were Chicago and L.A., and it turns out that both departments had pretty thick files on the guy. You see, you're not the first woman he's stalked."

"So you mean he's put up websites like the Kelly one before?"

"Not exactly. The common denominator is that our friend Jason has a thing for women in the arts...dancers, musicians, painters. He finds a woman who catches his fancy, and picks a role to play with her, something that would fulfill an immediate need for the victim.

"Usually, he chooses an actual person to impersonate," the man continued, "someone whose name people might have heard before, but who doesn't have an immediately recognizable face, someone he can re-create with a handful of stolen business cards and an answering service. Then he arranges to meet his victim, and he usually ends up dating the woman for a while...under his assumed identity, of course.

It's a real cozy arrangement, until she decides to call it quits."

"Th—Then what happens?"

He pulled out a photograph from the file and slid it toward her. *Smoke and mirrors*, Kelly reminded herself, steeling herself to see a gruesome crime scene photo. To her relief, however, the picture was instead a black-and-white publicity still. Its subject was a dramatic-looking woman about her own age, her bleached hair chopped and spiked in last year's style.

"Her name was Millie Donovan," he said, and she shivered a little at his use of the past tense. "She was the lead singer with one of the local club bands in Chicago. She died in a house fire a month after she broke up with Todman, though he was using the name Kurt McAfee at the time. The arson guys ruled it an accident, said a lit cigarette caught the bed on fire. Odd thing was, her friends all insisted she didn't smoke."

He pulled another picture from the file and flipped it toward her. This woman was a brunette wearing a leotard and long, gauzy skirt, posed gracefully on pointe. "Tammy Jacobs, partner in a struggling dance company based in Los Angeles. Two days after she broke up with a guy named Ben Tresome—who turned out to be Todman— paramedics pulled her out of a one-car wreck. The skid marks and some paint damage indicated that her car was run off the road, though she wasn't able to tell us much about what happened." He glanced up at Kelly's unspoken question and added, "Oh, she survived the acci- dent...but she doesn't dance anymore."

"My God," she breathed, letting the photographs drop back to the table as she strove for calm. If this man truly was Detective Ted Ralston, and he simply was trying to convince her she was in danger, he was doing a damn good job of it. And if he actually was Jason Todman trying to scare the hell out of her, just for sick thrills, he was succeeding with that, as well.

"But I don't understand. If this Jason Todman has done what you say he has, why isn't he already in jail?"

"The local cops picked him up, but he had alibis in both cases, and there was absolutely no physical evidence to tie him to either crime scene. Even the fact that he'd used a false name to get close to those women wasn't sufficient cause to hold him." Ralston quirked a wry brow. "Like it or not, it's not a crime to use a fake name just to get laid."

Kelly would have blushed at that last, save that she was struggling against the sudden sick feeling that had enveloped her. "You said he assumed roles with these women," she managed in a voice that shook only slightly. "What exactly did you mean by that?"

"With the Donovan woman, he claimed to be the owner of a record label looking to sign new talent. Turns out that Kurt McAfee really is a record executive, but he happened to be out of the country during the time that Todman was using his name. He told Tammy Jacobs that he'd just sold out his dot-com company to a big conglomerate and was looking for places to invest his profits. With a couple of others, he played a surgeon, and the son of a well-known televangelist. He makes a point of choosing positions of power...of trust."

Positions of power...of trust. She briefly shut her eyes, then softly asked, "Like, maybe pretending to be a cop?"

"That's possible. Listen, I know the website is upsetting, but I don't think you're in any immediate danger. Those other women had been involved with Todman awhile, and it wasn't until they dumped him that all hell broke loose. So, as long as you don't start seeing the guy—"

He broke off abruptly, frowning, and then casually pulled another photograph from his file. "I guess that, between your painting and your work at the art gallery, you meet all sorts of interesting people," he resumed in a conversational tone as he slid the sheet toward her. "Are you currently seeing anyone...involved in any relationships?"

While he was speaking, she'd had time for a clear look at the page before her. Unlike the others, this one was a police booking photo, complete with dual views and the requisite identifying numbers across the bottom. The suspect had worn what appeared to be jail issue, and looked as if he hadn't slept in a couple of days; still, he had stared into the camera with the hint of a grin, as if confident this was the closest he'd come to paying for his crime.

Kelly slowly looked up from the photo of the man she'd been sleeping with these past couple of weeks, to the man before her. Steeling herself, she gave Ralston the barest of nods, even as she said, "I have been going out with someone, but it's nothing you'd really call serious."

"You're hurting my feelings, Kelly," a cool voice spoke up from the direction of the hallway. "And here I thought we had something real...something special."

Jason Todman—or was he Ted Ralston?—was leaning against the doorjamb, the blue steel finish of the revolver he held glinting dully in the room's low light. Kelly gasped and scrambled from her chair. The man beside her rose more slowly, still clutching the incriminating folder as he eased away from the sofa.

"I can't believe you're listening to this loser," he addressed Kelly in the same chill tone. "Everything he's shown you, he could have pulled off a website, or created himself. Real cops carry guns...and I'm the one with the gun. And you saw the badge, and the business cards with my name on them. They all looked pretty damn real to me."

"You can buy replica badges a dime a dozen on the Internet," Detective Ralston—or was he Jason Todman?—countered calmly. "Guns are just as easy to get. As for the business cards, whenever I give a seminar at the local community center, mine are always there for the taking."

"Yeah, but you're forgetting one thing. Who looks more like a guy who has problems getting women...me or him?" the other man demanded, and jerked a thumb at his rival.

Kelly didn't reply, her attention held by a hint of color...a tiny smear of robin's-egg blue paint on his extended hand. He followed her gaze, and then allowed himself a wry smile.

"Stuff's a bitch to get off without turpentine," he casually observed, shaking his head in mock dismay as he let his hand drop again. "I didn't even notice I'd gotten any on me until after I left. By then, you were already on your way home from the gallery, so I couldn't come back."

"Convinced now, Ms. Winslow?" the detective softly asked. At her frightened nod, he returned his attention to Todman. "All right, Jason, it's over with. Now, why don't you hand the gun to me, and we can talk about what to do next."

"I've got a better idea. Why don't we quit talking?" Todman countered and pulled the revolver's trigger twice in swift succession, catching him squarely in the chest with both shots.

By the time the sound of gunshots and Kelly's answering scream had faded, Ralston lay slumped against the far wall. A folder's worth of scattered pages had settled over him in a bureaucratic drift, mercifully obscuring any blood or gaping flesh. She probably should check to see if he was still alive, she faintly told herself, but surely there wasn't a need.

"Well, that's settled," Todman observed with a final look at Ralston, and then turned to her, pistol raised. "Unfortunately, it also means that things are over between us, too, Kelly."

"This isn't necessary," she protested in a voice that sounded weak to her own ears, even as she tried to summon a smile. "You know I don't want to see you go to jail...not after what we've had together. Maybe we could—"

"Cut the bullshit, Kelly," he interrupted in a conversational tone that was far more frightening than any overt threat. "I've just killed a cop, and I'm not about to leave you around to testify against me. Now, why don't we go into your studio and get this over with."

He gestured with the pistol in the direction of the hallway, and she took a deep breath. She had little hope of a police rescue; gunfire was common enough in this part of town not to draw undue interest from the neighbors. If she tried to flee, he would shoot her down long before she made it to the door; once in the studio, however, she'd be effectively trapped. Still, the latter choice left her with a few more precious moments in which to come up with a plan.

"I'm thinking murder-suicide," Todman went on in the same casual tone as she walked on shaky legs into the studio. "That seems to be a pretty popular cause of death with couples in this town. Oh, yes, people will think you're a couple," he confirmed as she shot him a confused look. "You see, I borrowed one of his credit cards and set up the cell phone account in his name. When they check, they'll find plenty of activity between that number and yours. And, of course, there'll be a few personal possessions of his scattered about your house."

So saying, he reached over to the wall switch and flipped on the light, illuminating the half-finished oil that sat upon the easel. "You know, I really do like that painting," he mused, gripping her by the arm as he walked her over to it. "Such beauty, such power. Too bad you didn't get to finish it. But those are the breaks."

His gaze lingered on the abstract a moment longer before he let her go and took a step back. His tone was businesslike once more as he said, "Since your friend Detective Ralston was shot from a distance, we're going to have to make you the suicide instead of the murder victim. Powder burns, angle of bullet entry, and all that. But we have to make it look right."

"Please," she whispered, "don't do this. Leave, and I'll never mention your name to the police. I swear it!"

"I've read that women commit suicide differently from men," he went on, as if she'd never spoken. "They never put the gun to their temple, or in their mouth...guess they don't like the idea of blasting their pretty faces all over the place. So, how do you think they do it?

"They go for the heart," he answered his own question, and she gasped as she felt the sudden, painful pressure of the muzzle directly over that wildly beating organ. "It's quick, it's clean, and they can still have an open casket at the funeral. So tell me, Kelly, does that work for you? Because I'm equally comfortable with the head, if you were planning on being cremated—"

"Lower your weapon, and step away from her!"

The words lashed whiplike through the room, momentarily jerking Kelly from her terror. Todman stiffened, and she heard his swift intake of breath before he slowly turned to look over his shoulder. Cautiously, she raised her own gaze to look in the direction of the voice.

Detective Ralston—minus his jacket and glasses—stood in the doorway of her studio, looking remarkably alive and unbloodied for a man who had just taken two bullets in the chest. Except that Kelly barely recognized him as the mild-mannered guy she had dismissed as harmless only minutes before. Maybe it was just the automatic pistol he gripped with businesslike efficiency in both hands. Or maybe it was simply the way his ordinary features had hardened into the cold, implacable expression of a man prepared to finish an unpleasant job.

"You were right, Jason," he said in the same chilled tone. "Real cops carry guns. They also wear body armor when they know they're going up against scumbags like you." And, indeed, Kelly could see where the bullets had torn two holes through the fabric of his shirt. As she stared at him in something akin to awe, she heard him repeat,

"Now lower your weapon and step back."

Before Kelly realized what was happening, Todman had slipped behind her so that he now faced Ralston. "I'll kill her," he threatened, his pistol pressed into the back of her ribs as he used her for a shield. "You put down *your* gun, and let the two of us walk out of here, and maybe I'll let her go once we're out of the county."

"Not a chance. It ends here, now."

Ralston moved one step closer, then two. Abruptly, Kelly felt her captor's free hand grip her shoulder, pulling her closer to him as he raised his revolver and leveled it at the detective.

"You'll have to shoot her to get at me," he shouted. "You don't want to be responsible for the bitch dying, do you? Now, put down the gun and get the hell out of my way before I—"

He broke off abruptly as Kelly reflexively slammed an elbow into his gut, and then dived for the floor. She had barely landed in an ungainly heap when she heard the crack of gunfire for the second time that day. She lay where she was, waiting for the sound of a second bullet, the one that would rip through her body. Instead, all she heard was the thunk of something small but heavy landing on the wooden floor beside her.

Cautiously, she lifted her head just enough to see that the object was a familiar blue steel revolver. Next to it was a rapidly widening puddle of crimson. Biting back a gasp, she raised her head still higher to see Jason Todman swaying as he clutched his gut, blood dripping from between his fingers and splashing at his feet. He moaned once, and then sagged to his knees.

As she scrambled a safe distance from him, his dull gaze met hers. He managed a brief, sickly shadow of his familiar grin. "I had you, Kelly. I had you," he whispered and collapsed against the easel, tumbling the painting on top of him.

In the silence that followed, Ralston reached down and picked up the fallen revolver. Wincing slightly as he clutched at his bruised ribs, he straightened again and stuck the gun in the waistband of his trousers, then walked over to where she still huddled on the floor.

"Are you all right, Ms. Winslow?" he asked as she tentatively took his proffered hand and scrambled to her feet.

She nodded. "I—I'm fine," she managed in a halting voice, adding as she looked over at the body in the middle of her studio floor, "but I guess he's not, is he?"

Even as Ralston shook his head, Kelly heard a faint wail of sirens and raised her brow in surprise. Apparently, there was a limit, after all, to the amount of gunplay that her neighbors would tolerate before calling the cops. "Backup will be here in a minute," Ralston told her unnecessarily as he reached for her fallen oil painting, and then settled it back on the easel.

Careful not to look down at the dead man again, Kelly moved closer to the painting, gasping a little at what she saw. A large smear of drying blood now bisected the canvas, almost obliterating the abstract heart that, moments before, had glowed so brightly. At her sound of dismay Ralston—who had shrugged off his torn shirt and now was unbuckling his bulletproof vest—glanced over at her. "Sorry about the painting. It looks like it was something special. What did you call it?"

"*Love Takes a Chance*," she softly replied, belatedly dubbing it with the title that had come to her just this very afternoon, as she worked at the gallery. "It was the last of three, but I guess I'll never finish it now."

"Are you sure? I rather like the title, myself."

Kelly glanced back over at him. By now, he had shed the vest and the T-shirt beneath it, and was gingerly examining the pair of purplish bruises on his chest. *Not a bad body, especially for a computer geek*, her inner voice irreverently decreed. *I wonder if he likes Mexican food.*

As if feeling her gaze on him, he looked up and flashed her a faint grin. While not as devastatingly sexy as Jason Todman's had been, Ralston's grin hinted at definite possibilities. Feeling far more cheerful than she should have, considering that she'd almost been murdered a few moments before, and a dead man was lying practically at her feet, Kelly smiled back.

"Actually, I was considering expanding the series to four paintings," she said over the blare of sirens that was now right outside her window. "So tell me, Ted, what do you think of this for a new title... *Love Tries Again?*"

The Perfect Man

Kristine Kathryn Rusch

Paige Racette stared at herself in the full-length mirror, hands on hips. Golden cap of blond hair expertly curled, narrow chin, high cheekbones, china blue eyes, and a little too much of a figure—thanks to the fact she spent most of her day on her butt and sometimes (usually!) forgetting to exercise. The black cocktail dress with its swirling party skirt hid most of the excess, and the glittering beads around the collar brought attention to her face, always and forever her best asset.

Even with the extra pounds, she was not blind-date material. Never had been. Until she quit her day job at the television station, she'd had to turn men away. Ironic that once she became a best-selling romance writer, she couldn't get a date to save her life. Part of the problem was that after she quit, she moved to San Francisco where she'd always wanted to live. She bought a Queen Anne in an old, exclusive neighborhood, set up her office in the bay windows of the second floor, and decided she was in heaven.

Little did she realize that working at home would isolate her, and being in a new city would isolate her more. It had taken her a year to make friends—mostly women, whom she met at the gym not too far from her home.

She saw interesting men, but didn't speak to them. She was still a small-town girl at heart, one who was afraid of the kind of men who lurked in the big city, who believed that the only way to meet the right man was by getting to know him through mutual interests—or mutual friends.

In fact, she wouldn't have agreed to this blind date if a friend hadn't convinced her. Sally Myer was her racquetball partner and general confidante who seemed to know everyone in this city. She'd finally tired of Paige's complaining and set her up.

Paige slid on her high heels. Who'd ever thought she'd get this desperate? And then she sighed. She wasn't desperate. She was lonely.

And surely, there was no shame in that.

Sally had picked the time and location, and had told Paige to dress up. Sally wasn't going to introduce them. She felt that would be tacky and make the first meeting uncomfortable. She asked Paige for a photograph to give to the blind date—one Josiah Wells—and then told Paige that he would find her.

The location was an upscale restaurant near the Opera House. It was The Place to Go at the moment—famous chef, famous food, and one of those bars that looked like it had come out of a movie set—large and open where Anyone Who Was Someone could see and be seen.

Paige arrived five minutes early, habitually prompt even when she didn't want to be. She adjusted the white Pashmina shawl she'd wrapped around her bare shoulders and scanned the bar before she went in.

It was all black and chrome, with black tinted mirrors and huge black vases filled with calla lilies separating the booths. The bar itself was black marble and behind it, bottles of liquor pressed against an untinted mirror, making the place look even bigger than it was.

She had only been here once before, with her Hollywood agent and a movie producer who was interested in her second novel. He didn't buy it—the rights went to another studio for high six figures—but he had bought her some of her most memorable meals in the City by the Bay.

She sat at the bar and ordered a Chardonnay that she didn't plan

on touching—she wanted to keep her wits about her this night. Even
with Sally's recommendation, Paige didn't trust a man she had never
met before. She'd heard too many bad stories.

Of course, all the ones she'd written were about people who saw
each other across a crowded room and knew at once that they were
soul mates. She had never experienced love at first sight (and sometimes she joked to her editor that it was lust at first sight) but she was
still hopeful enough to believe in it.

She took the cool glass of Chardonnay that the bartender handed
her and swiveled slightly in her chair so that she would be in profile,
not looking anxious, but visible enough to be recognizable. And as
she did, she saw a man enter the bar.

He was tall and broad-shouldered, wearing a perfectly tailored
black suit that shimmered like silk. He wore a white scarf around his
neck—which on him looked like the perfect fashion accent—and a
red rose in his lapel. His dark hair was expertly styled away from his
chiseled features, and she felt her breath catch.

Lust at first sight. It was all she could do to keep from grinning at
herself.

He appeared to be looking for someone. Finally, his gaze settled
on her, and he smiled.

Something about that smile didn't quite fit his face. It was too personal. And then she shook the feeling away. She didn't want to be on
a blind date—that was all. She had been fantasizing, the way she did
when she was thinking of her books, and she was simply caught off-
guard. No man was as perfect as her heroes. No man could be, not
and still be human.

Although this man looked perfect. His rugged features were
exactly like ones she had described in her novels.

He crossed the room, the smile remaining, hand extended. "Paige
Racette? I'm Josiah Wells."

His voice was high and a bit nasal. She took his hand, and found
the palm warm and moist.

"Nice to meet you," she said, removing her hand as quickly as possible.

He wore tinted blue contacts, and the swirling lenses made his
eyes seem shiny, a little too intense. In fact, everything about him was

a little too intense. He leaned too close, and he seemed too eager. Perhaps he was just as nervous as she was.

"I have reservations here if you don't mind," he said.

"No, that's fine."

He extended his arm—the perfect gentleman—and she put her
arm through his, trying to remember the last time a man had done
that for her. Her father maybe, when they went to the father-daughter
dinner at her church back when she was in high school. And not one
man since.

Although all the men in her books did it. When she wrote about
it, the gesture seemed to have an old-fashioned elegance. In real life, it
made her feel awkward.

He led her through the bar, placing one hand possessively over
hers. This exact scene had happened in her first novel, *Beneath a Lover's Moon*. Fabian Garret and Skye Michaels had met, exchanged a few
words, and were suddenly walking together like lovers. And Skye had
thrilled to Fabian's touch.

Paige wished Josiah Wells's fingers weren't so clammy.

He led them to the maitre d', gave his name, and let the maitre d'
lead them to a table near the back. See and Be Seen. Apparently they
weren't important enough.

"I asked for a little privacy," he said, as if reading her thoughts. "I
hope you don't mind."

She didn't. She had never liked the display aspect of this restaurant anyway.

The table was in a secluded corner. Two candles burned on silver
candlesticks and the table was strewn with miniature carnations. A
magnum of champagne cooled in a silver bucket, and she didn't have
to look at the label to know that it was Dom Perignon.

The hair on the back of her neck rose. This was just like another
scene in *Beneath a Lover's Moon*.

Josiah smiled down at her and she made herself smile at him.
Maybe he thought her books were a blueprint to romancing her. She
would have said so not five minutes before.

He pulled out her chair, and she sat, letting her shawl drape
around her. As Josiah sat across from her, the maitre d' handed her the
leather-bound menu and she was startled to realize it had no prices on

it. A lady's menu. She hadn't seen one of those in years. The last time she had eaten here had been lunch, not dinner, and she had remembered the prices on the menu from that meal. They had nearly made her choke on her water.

A waiter poured the champagne and left discretely, just like the maitre d' had. Josiah was watching her, his gaze intense.

She knew she had to say something. She was going to say how nice this was but she couldn't get the lie through her lips. Instead she said as warmly as she could, "You've read my books."

If anything, his gaze brightened. "I adore your books."

She made herself smile. She had been hoping he would say no, that Sally had been helping him all along. Instead, the look in his eyes made her want to push her chair even farther from the table. She had seen that look a hundred times at book signings: the too-eager fan who would easily monopolize all of her time at the expense of everyone else in line; the person who believed that his connection with the author—someone he hadn't met—was so personal that she felt the connection, too.

"I didn't realize that Sally told you I wrote."

"She didn't have to. When I found out that she knew you, I asked her for an introduction."

An introduction at a party would have done nicely, where Paige could smile at him, listen for a polite moment, and then ease away. But Sally hadn't known Paige that long, and didn't understand the difficulties a writer sometimes faced. Writers rarely got recognized in person—it wasn't their faces that were famous after all but their names—but when it happened, it could become as unpleasant as it was for athletes or movie stars.

"She didn't tell me you were familiar with my work," Paige said, ducking her head behind the menu.

"I asked her not to. I wanted this to be a surprise." He was leaning forward, his manicured hand outstretched.

She looked at his fingers, curled against the linen tablecloth, carefully avoiding the miniature carnations, and wondered if his skin was still clammy.

"Since you know what I do," she continued in that too-polite voice she couldn't seem to shake, "why don't you tell me about yourself?"

"Oh," he said, "there isn't much to tell."

And then he proceeded to describe his work with a software company. She only half listened, staring at the menu, wondering if there was an easy—and polite—way to leave this meal, knowing there was not. She would make the best of it, and call Sally the next morning, warning her not to do this ever again.

"Your books," he was saying, "made me realize that women look at men the way that men look at women. I started to exercise and dress appropriately and I..."

She looked over the menu at him, noting the suit again. It must have been silk, and he wore it the way her heroes wore theirs. Right down to the scarf, and the rose in the lapel. The red rose, a symbol of true love from her third novel, *Without Your Love*.

That shiver ran through her again.

This time he noticed. "Are you all right?"

"Fine," she lied. "I'm just fine."

Somehow she made it through the meal, feeling her skin crawl as he used phrases from her books, imitated the gestures of her heroes, and presumed an intimacy with her that he didn't have. She tried to keep the conversation light and impersonal, but it was a battle that she really didn't win.

Just before the dessert course, she excused herself and went to the ladies' room. After she came out, she asked the maitre d' to call her a cab, and then to signal her when it arrived. He smiled knowingly. Apparently he had seen dates end like this all too often.

She took her leave from Josiah just after they finished their coffees, thanking him profusely for a memorable evening. And then she escaped into the night, thankful that she had been careful when making plans. He didn't have her phone number and address. As she slipped into the cracked backseat of the cab, she promised herself that on the next blind date—if there was another blind date—she would make it drinks only. Not dinner. Never again.

The next day, she and Sally met for lattes at an overpriced touristy café on the Wharf. It was their usual spot—a place where they could watch crowds and not be overheard when they decided to gossip.

"How did you meet him?" Paige asked as she adjusted her wrought-iron café chair.

"Fundraisers, mostly," Sally said. She was a petite redhead with freckles that she didn't try to hide. From a distance, they made her look as if she were still in her twenties. "He was pretty active in local politics for a while."

"Was?"

She shrugged. "I guess he got too busy. I ran into him in Tower Records a few weeks ago, and we got to talking. That's what made me think of you."

"What did?"

Sally smiled. "He was holding one of your books, and I thought, he's wealthy. You're wealthy. He was complaining about how isolating his work was and so were you."

"Isolating? He works for a software company."

"Worked," Sally said. "He's a consultant now, and only when he needs to be. I think he just manages his investments, mostly."

Paige frowned. Had she heard him wrong then? She wasn't paying much attention, not after she had seen the carnations and champagne.

Sally was watching her closely. "I take it things didn't go well."

"He's just not my type."

"Rich? Good-looking? Good God, girl, what is your type?"

Paige smiled. "He's a fan."

"So? Wouldn't that be more appealing?"

Maybe it should have been. Maybe she had overreacted. She had psyched herself out a number of times about the strange men in the big city. Maybe her overactive imagination—the one that created all the stories that had made her wealthy—had finally betrayed her.

"No," Paige said. "Actually, it's less appealing. I sort of feel like he has photos of me naked and has studied them up close."

"I didn't think books were that personal. I mean, you write romance. That's fantasy, right? Make-believe?"

Paige's smile was thin. It was make-believe. But make-believe on any level had a bit of truth to it, even when little children were creating scenarios with Barbie dolls.

"I just don't think we're compatible," Paige said. "Sorry."

Sally shrugged again. "No skin off my nose. You're the one who doesn't get out much. Have you ever thought of going to those singles dinners? They're supposed to be a pretty good place to meet people...."

Paige let the advice slip off her, knowing that she probably wouldn't discuss her love life—or lack of it—with Sally again. Paige had been right in the first place: she simply didn't have the right attitude to be a good blind date. There was probably nothing wrong with Josiah Wells. He had certainly gone to a lot of trouble to make sure she had a good time, and she had snuck off as soon as she could.

And if she couldn't be satisfied with a good-looking wealthy man who was trying to please her then she wouldn't be satisfied with any other blind date, either. She had to go back to what she knew worked. She had to go about her life normally, and hope that someday, an interesting guy would cross her path.

"...even go to AA to find dates. I mean, that's a little crass, don't you think?"

Paige looked at Sally, and realized she hadn't heard most of Sally's monologue. "You know what? Let's forget about men. It's a brand-new century and I have a great life. Why do we both seem to think that a man will somehow improve that?"

Sally studied her for a moment. "You know what I think? I think you've spent so much time making up the perfect man that no flesh-and-blood guy will measure up."

And then she changed the subject, just as Paige had asked.

As Paige drove home, she found herself wondering if Sally was right. After all, Paige hadn't dated anyone since she quit her job. And that was when she really spent most of her time immersed in imaginary romance. Her conscious brain knew that the men she made up were too perfect to be real. But did her subconscious? Was that what was preventing her from talking to men she'd seen at the opera or the theater? Was all this big-city fear she'd been thinking about simply a way of preventing herself from remembering that men were as human—and as imperfect—as she was?

She almost had herself convinced as she parked her new VW Bug on the hill in front of her house. She set the emergency brake and then got out, grabbing her purse as she did.

She had a lot of work to do, and she had wasted most of the day obsessing about her unsatisfying blind date. It was time to return to work—a romantic suspense novel set on a cruise ship. She had done a mountain of research for the book—including two cruises—one to Hawaii in the winter, and another to Alaska in the summer. The Alaska trip was the one she had decided to use, and she had spent part of the spring in Juneau.

By the time she had reached the front porch, she was already thinking of the next scene she had to write. It was a description of Juneau, a city that was perfect for her purposes because there were only two ways out of it: by air or by sea. The roads ended just outside of town. The mountains hemmed everything in, trapping people, good and bad, hero and villain, within their steep walls.

She was so lost in her imagination that she nearly tripped over the basket sitting on her porch.

She bent down to look at it. Wrapped in colored cellophane, it was nearly as large as she was, and was filled with flowers, chocolates, wine, and two crystal wine goblets. In the very center was a photo in a heart-shaped gold frame. She peered at it through the wrapping and then recoiled.

It was a picture of her and Josiah at dinner the night before, looking, from the outside, like a very happy couple.

Obviously he had hired someone to take the picture. Someone who had watched them the entire evening, and waited for the right moment to snap the shot. That was unsettling. And so was the fact that Josiah had found her house. She was unlisted in the phonebook, and on public records, she used her first name—Giacinta—with no middle initial. And although her last name was unusual, there were at least five other Racettes listed. Had Josiah sent a basket to every one of them, hoping that he'd find the right one and she'd call him?

Or had he had her followed?

The thought made her look over her shoulder. Maybe there was someone on the street now, watching her, wondering how she would react to this gift.

She didn't want to bring it inside, but she felt like she had no choice. She suddenly felt quite exposed on the porch.

She picked up the basket by its beribboned handle and unlocked her door. Then she stepped inside, closed the door as her security firm had instructed her, and punched in her code. Her hands were shaking.

On impulse, she reset the perimeter alarm. She hadn't done that since she moved in, had thought it a silly precaution.

It didn't seem that silly anymore.

She set the basket on the deacon's bench she had near the front door. Then she fumbled through the ribbon to find the card she knew had to be there.

Her name was on the envelope in calligraphic script, but the message inside was typed on the delivery service's card.

Two hearts, perfectly meshed.
Two lives, perfectly twined.
Is it luck that we have found each other?
Or does Fate divine a way for perfect matches to meet?

Those were her words. The stilted words of Quinn Ralston, the hero of her sixth novel, a man who finally learned to free the poetry locked in his soul.

"God," she whispered, so creeped out that her hands felt dirty just from touching the card. She picked up the basket and carried it to the back of the house, setting it in the entryway where she kept her bundled newspapers.

She supposed most women would keep the chocolates, flowers, and wine even if they didn't like the man who sent them. But she wasn't most women. And the photograph bothered her more than she could say.

She locked the interior door, then went to the kitchen and scrubbed her hands until they were raw.

Somehow she managed to escape to the Juneau of her imagination, working furiously in her upstairs office, getting nearly fifteen pages done before dinner. Uncharacteristically, she closed the drapes, hiding the city view she had paid so much for. She didn't want anyone looking in.

She was making herself a taco salad with Bite-sized Tostitos and bagged shredded lettuce when the phone rang, startling her. She went to answer it, and then some instinct convinced her not to. Instead, she went to her answering machine and turned up the sound.

"Paige? If you're there, please pick up. It's Josiah." He paused and she held her breath. She hadn't given him this number. And Sally had said that morning that she hadn't given Paige's unlisted number to anyone. "Well, um, you're probably working and can't hear this."

A shiver ran through her. He knew she was home, then? Or was he guessing?

"I just wanted to find out if you got my present. I have tickets to tomorrow night's presentation of *La Bohème*. I know how much you love opera and this one in particular. They're box seats. Hard to get. And perfect, just like you. Call me back." He rattled off his phone number and then hung up.

She stared at the machine, with its blinking red light. She hadn't discussed the opera with him. She hadn't discussed the opera with Sally, either, after she found out that Sally hated "all that screeching." Sally wouldn't know *La Bohème* from Don Giovanni, and she certainly wouldn't remember either well enough to mention to someone else.

Well, maybe Paige's problem was that she had been polite to him the night before. Maybe she should have left. She'd had this problem in the past—mostly in college. She'd always tried to be polite to men who were interested in her, even if she wasn't interested in return. But sometimes, politeness merely encouraged them. Sometimes she had to be harsh just to send them away.

Harsh or polite, she really didn't want to talk to Josiah ever again. She would ignore the call, and hope that he would forget her. Most men understood a lack of response. They knew it for the brushoff it was.

If he managed to run into her, she would just apologize and give him the You're-Very-Nice-I'm-Sure-You'll-Meet-Someone-Special-Someday speech. That one worked every time.

Somehow, having a plan calmed her. She finished cooking the beef for her taco salad and took it to the butcher-block table in the center of the kitchen. There she opened the latest copy of *Publisher's Weekly* and read while she ate.

During the next week, she got fifteen bouquets of flowers, each one an arrangement described in her books. Her plan wasn't working. She hadn't run into Josiah, but she didn't answer his phone calls. He didn't seem to understand the brush-off. He would call two or three times a day to leave messages on her machine, and once an hour, he would call and hang up. Sometimes she found herself standing over the Caller ID box, fists clenched.

All of this made work impossible. When the phone rang, she listened for his voice. When it wasn't him, she scrambled to pick up, her concentration broken.

In addition to the bouquets, he had taken to sending her cards and writing her long e-mails, sometimes mimicking the language of the men in her novels.

Finally, she called Sally and explained what was going on.

"I'm sorry," Sally said. "I had no idea he was like this."

Paige sighed heavily. She was beginning to feel trapped in the house. "You started this. What do you recommend?"

"I don't know," Sally said. "I'd offer to call him, but I don't think he'll listen to me. This sounds sick."

"Yeah," Paige said. "That's what I'm thinking."

"Maybe you should go to the police."

Paige felt cold. The police. If she went to them, it would be an acknowledgment that this had become serious.

"Maybe," she said, but she hoped she wouldn't have to.

Looking back on it, she realized she might have continued enduring if it weren't for the incident at the grocery store. She had been leaving the house, always wondering if someone was watching her, and then deciding that she was being just a bit too paranoid. But the fact that Josiah showed up in the grocery store a few moments after she arrived, pushing no grocery cart and dressed exactly like Maximilian D. Lake from *Love at 37,000 Feet* was no coincidence.

He wore a new brown leather bomber jacket, aviation sunglasses, khakis, and a white scarf. When he saw her in the produce aisle, he whipped the sunglasses off with an affected air.

"Paige, darling! I've been worried about you." His eyes were even more intense than she remembered, and this time they were green, just like Maximilian Lake's.

"Josiah," she said, amazed at how calm she sounded. Her heart was pounding and her stomach was churning. He had her trapped— her cart was between the tomato and asparagus aisles. Behind her, the water jets, set to mist the produce every five minutes, kicked on.

"You have no idea how concerned I've been," he said, taking a step closer. She backed toward the onions. "When a person lives alone, works alone, and doesn't answer her phone, well, anything could be wrong."

Was that a threat? She couldn't tell. She made herself smile at him. "There's no need to worry about me. There are people checking on me all the time."

"Really?" He raised a single eyebrow, something she'd often described in her novels, but never actually seen in person. He probably knew that no one came to her house without an invitation. He seemed to know everything else.

She gripped the handle on her shopping cart firmly. "I'm glad I ran into you. I've been wanting to tell you something."

His face lit up, a look that would have been attractive if it weren't so needy. "You have?"

She nodded. Now was the time, her best and only chance. She pushed the cart forward just a little, so that he had to move aside. He seemed to think she was doing it to get closer to him. She was doing it so that she'd be able to get away.

"I really appreciate all the trouble you went to for dinner," she said. "It was one of the most memorable—"

"Our entire life could be like that," he said quickly. "An adventure every day, just like your books."

She had to concentrate to keep that smile on her face. "Writers write about adventure, Josiah, because we really don't want to go out and experience it ourselves."

He laughed. It sounded forced. "I'm sure Papa Hemingway is spinning in his grave. You are such a kidder, Paige."

"I'm not kidding," she said. "You're a very nice man, Josiah, but—"

"A nice man?" He took a step toward her, his face suddenly red. "A nice man? The only men who get described that way in your books are the losers, the ones the heroine wants to let down easy."

She let the words hang between them for a moment. And then she said, "I'm sorry."

He stared at her as if she had hit him. She pushed the cart past him, resisting the impulse to run. She was rounding the corner into the meat aisle when she heard him say, "You bitch!"

Her hands started trembling then, and she couldn't read her list. But she had to. He wouldn't run her out of here. Then he'd realize just how scared she was.

He was coming up behind her. "You can't do this, Paige. You know how good we are together. You know."

She turned around, leaned against her cart and prayed silently for strength. "Josiah, we had one date, and it wasn't very good. Now please, leave me alone."

A store employee was watching from the corner of the aisle. The butcher had looked up through the window in the back.

Josiah grabbed her wrist so hard that she could feel his fingers digging into her skin. "I'll make you remember. I'll make you—"

"Are you all right, miss?" The store employee had stepped to her side.

"No," she said. "He's hurting me."

"This is none of your business," Josiah said. "She's my girlfriend."

"I don't know him," Paige said.

The employee had taken Josiah's arm. Other employees were coming from various parts of the store. He must have given them a signal. Some of the customers were gathering, too.

"Sir, we're going to have to ask you to leave," the employee said.

"You have no right."

"We have every right, sir," the employee said. "Now let the lady go."

Josiah stared at him for a moment, then at the other customers. Store security had joined them.

"Paige," Josiah said, "tell them how much you love me. Tell them that we were meant to be together."

"I don't know you," she said, and this time her words seemed to get through. He let go of her arm and allowed the employee to pull him away.

She collapsed against her cart in relief, and the store manager, a middle-aged man with a nice face, asked her if she needed to sit down. She nodded. He led her to the back of the store, past the cans that were being recycled and the gray refrigeration units to a tiny office filled with red signs about customer service.

"I'm sorry," she said. "I'm so sorry."

"Why?" The manager pulled over a metal folding chair and helped her into it. Then he sat behind the desk. "It seemed like he was harassing you. Who is he?"

"I don't really know." She was still shaking. "A friend set us up on a blind date, and he hasn't left me alone since."

"Some friend," the manager said. His phone beeped, and he answered it. He spoke for a moment, his words soft. She didn't listen. She was staring at her wrist. Josiah's fingers had left marks.

Then the manager hung up. "He's gone. Our man took his license number and he's been forbidden to come into the store again. That's all we can do."

"Thank you," she said.

The manager frowned. He was looking at her bruised wrist as well. "You know guys like him don't back down."

"I'm beginning to realize that," she said.

And that was how she found herself parking her grocery-stuffed car in front of the local precinct. It was a gray cinderblock building built in the late 1960s with reinforced windows and a steel door. Somehow it did not inspire confidence.

She went inside anyway. The front hallway was narrow, and obviously redesigned. A steel door stood to her right and to her left was a window made of bulletproof glass. Behind it sat a man in a police uniform.

She stepped up to the window. He finished typing something into a computer before speaking to her. "What?"

"I'd like to file a complaint."

"I'll buzz you in. Take the second door to your right. Someone there'll help you."

"Thanks," she said, but her voice was lost in the electronic buzz that filled the narrow hallway. She opened the door and found herself in the original corridor, filled with blond wood and doors with windows. Very sixties, very unsafe. She shook her head slightly, opened the second door, and stepped inside.

She entered a large room filled with desks. It smelled of burned coffee and mold. Most of the desks were empty, although on most of them the desk lamps were on, revealing piles of papers and files. Black phones as old as the building sat on each desk, and she was startled to see that typewriters outnumbered computers.

There were only a handful of people in the room, most of them bent over their files, looking frustrated. A man with salt-and-pepper hair was carrying a cup of coffee back to his desk. He didn't look like any sort of police detective she'd imagined. He was squarely built and seemed rather ordinary.

When he saw her, he said, "Help you?"

"I want to file a complaint."

"Come with me." His deep voice was cracked and hoarse, as if he had been shouting all day.

He led her to a small desk in the center of the room. Most of the desks were pushed together facing each other, but this one stood alone. And it had a computer with a SFPD logo screen saver.

"I'm Detective Conover. How can I help you, Miss…?"

"Paige Racette." Her voice sounded small in the large room.

He kicked a scarred wooden chair toward her. "What's your complaint?"

She sat down slowly, her heart pounding. "I'm being harassed."

"Harassed?"

"Stalked."

He looked at her straight on then, and she thought she saw a world-weariness in his brown eyes. His entire face was rumpled, like a coat that had been balled up and left in the bottom of a closet. It wasn't a handsome face by any definition, but it had a comfortable quality, a trustworthy quality that was built into the lines.

"Tell me about it," he said.

So she did. She started with the blind date, talked about how strange Josiah was, and how he wouldn't leave her alone.

"And he was taking things out of my novels like I would appreciate it. It really upset me."

"Novels?" It was the first time Conover had interrupted her.

She nodded. "I write romances."

"And are you published?"

The question startled her. Usually when she mentioned her name people recognized it. They always recognized it after she said she wrote romances.

"Yes," she said.

"So you were hoisted on your own petard, weren't you?"

"Excuse me?"

"You write about your sexual fantasies for a living, and then complain when someone is trying to take you up on it." He said that so deadpan, so seriously, that for a moment, she couldn't breathe.

"It's not like that," she said.

"Oh? It's advertising, lady."

She was shaking again. She had known this was a bad idea. Why would she expect sympathy from the police? "So since Donald Westlake writes about thieves, he shouldn't complain if he gets robbed? Or Stephen King shouldn't be upset if someone breaks his ankle with a sledgehammer?"

"Touchy," the detective said, but she noticed a twinkle in his eye that hadn't been there before.

She actually counted to ten, silently, before responding. She hadn't done that since she was a little girl. Then she said, as calmly as she could, "You baited me on purpose."

He grinned—and it smoothed out the care lines in his face, enhancing the twinkle in his eye and, for a moment, making him breathlessly attractive.

"There are a lot of celebrities in this town, Ms. Racette. It's hard for the lesser ones to get noticed. Sometimes they'll stage some sort of crime for publicity's sake. And really, what would be better than a romance writer being romanced by a fan who was using the structure of her books to do it?"

She wasn't sure what she objected to the most, being called a minor celebrity, being branded as a publicity hound, or finding this outrageous man attractive, even for a moment.

"I don't like attention," she said slowly. "If I liked attention, I would have chosen a different career. I hate book signings and television interviews, and I certainly don't want a word of this mess breathed to the press."

"So far so good," he said. She couldn't tell if he believed her, still. But she was amusing him. And that really pissed her off.

She held up her wrist. "He did this."

The smile left Conover's face. He took her hand gently in his own and extended it, examining the bruises as if they were clues. "When?"

"About an hour ago. At San Francisco Produce." She flushed saying the name of the grocery store. It was upscale and trendy, precisely the place a "celebrity" would shop.

But Conover didn't seem to notice. "You didn't tell me about the attack."

"I was getting to it when you interrupted me," she said. "I've been getting calls from him—a dozen or more a day. Flowers, presents, letters and e-mails. I'm unlisted and I never gave him my phone number or my address. I have a private e-mail address, not the one my publisher hands out, and that's the one he's using. And then he followed me to the grocery store and got angry when the store security asked him to leave."

Conover eased her hand onto his desk, then leaned back in his chair. His touch had been gentle, and she missed it.

"You had a *date* with him—"

"A blind date. We met at the restaurant, and a friend handled the details. And no, she didn't give him the information, either."

"—so," Conover said, as if she hadn't spoken, "I assume you know his name."

"Josiah Wells."

Conover wrote it down. Then he sighed. It looked like he was gathering himself. "You have a stalker, Ms. Racette."

"I know."

"And while stalking is illegal under California law, the law is damned inadequate. I'll get the video camera tape from the store, and if it backs you up, I'll arrest Wells. You'll be willing to press charges?"

"Yes," she said.

"That's a start." Conover's world-weary eyes met hers. "But I have to be honest. Usually these guys get out on bail. You'll need a lawyer to get an injunction against him, and your guy will probably ignore it. Even if he gets sent up for a few years, he'll come back and haunt you. They always do."

Her shaking started again. "So what can I do?"

"Your job isn't tied to the community. You can move."

Move? She felt cold. "I have a house." A life. This was her dream city. "I don't want to move."

"No one does, but it's usually the only thing that works."

"I don't want to run away," she said. "If I do that, then he'll be controlling my life. I'd be giving in. I'd be a victim."

Conover stared at her for a long moment. "Tell you what. I'll build the strongest case I can. That might give you a few years. By then, you might be willing to go somewhere new."

She nodded, stood. "I'll bring everything in tomorrow."

"I'd like to pick it up, if you don't mind. See where he left it, whether he's got a hidey-hole near the house. How about I come to you in a couple of hours?"

"Okay," she said.

"You got a peephole?"

"Yeah."

"Use it. I'll knock."

She nodded. Then felt her shoulders relax slightly, more than they had for two weeks. Finally, she had an ally. It meant more to her than she had realized it would. "Thanks."

"Don't thank me yet," he said. "Let's wait until this is all over."

All over. She tried to concentrate on the words and not the tone. Because Detective Conover really didn't sound all that optimistic.

The biggest bouquet yet waited for her on the front porch. She could see it from the street, and any hope that the meeting with Conover aroused disappeared. She knew without getting out of the car what the bouquet would be: calla lilies, tiger lilies, and Easter lilies, mixed with greens and lilies of the valley. It was a bouquet Marybeth Campbell was designing the day she met Robert Newman in *All My Kisses*, a bouquet he said was both romantic and sad. (Not to mention expensive: the flowers weren't in season at the same time.)

She left the bouquet on the porch without reading the card. Conover would be there soon and he could take the whole mess away. She certainly didn't want to look at it.

After all this, she wasn't sure she ever wanted to see flowers again.

When she got inside, she found twenty-three messages on her machine, all from Josiah, all apologies, although they got angrier and angrier as she didn't answer. He must have thought she had come straight home. What a surprise he would have when he realized that she had gone to the police.

She rubbed her wrist, noting the soreness and cursing him under her breath. In addition to the bruises, her wrist was slightly swollen and she wondered if he hadn't managed to sprain it. Just her luck. He *would* damage her arm, which she needed to write. She got an ice pack out of the freezer and applied it, sitting at the kitchen table and staring at nothing.

Move. Give up, give in, all because she was feeling lonely and wanted to go on a date. All because she wanted a little flattery, a nice evening, to meet someone safe who could be—if nothing else—a friend.

How big a mistake had that been?

Big enough, she was beginning to realize, to cost her everything she held dear.

That night, after dinner, she baked herself a chocolate cake and covered it with marshmallow frosting. It was her grandmother's recipe—
comfort food that Paige normally never allowed herself. This time,
though, she would eat the whole thing and not worry about calories
or how bad it looked. Who would know?

She made some coffee and was sitting down to a large piece, when
someone knocked on her door.

She got up and walked to the door, feeling oddly vulnerable. If
it was Josiah, he would only be a piece of wood away from her. That
was too close. It was all too close now.

She peered through the peephole, just as she had promised
Conover she would, and she let out a small sigh of relief. He was shift-
ing from foot to foot, looking down at the bouquet she had forgotten
she had left there.

She deactivated the security system, then unlocked the three deadbolts and the chain lock she had installed since this nightmare began.
Conover shoved the bouquet forward with his foot.

"Looks like your friend left another calling card."

"He's not my friend," she said softly, peering over Conover's shoulder. "And he left more than that."

Conover's glance was worried. What did he imagine?

"Phone calls," she said. "Almost two dozen. I haven't checked my
e-mail."

"This guy's farther along than I thought." Conover pushed the
bouquet all the way inside with his foot, then closed the door, and
locked it. As he did, she reset the perimeter alarm.

Conover slipped on a pair of gloves and picked up the bouquet.

"You could have done that outside," she said.

"Didn't want to give him the satisfaction," Conover said. "He has
to know we don't respect what he's doing. Where can I look at this?"

"Kitchen," she said, pointing the way.

He started toward it, then stopped, sniffing. "What smells so
good?"

"Chocolate cake. You want some?"

"I thought you wrote."

"Doesn't stop me from baking on occasion."

He glanced at her, his dark eyes quizzical. "This hardly seems the time to be baking."

She shrugged. "I could drink instead."

To her surprise, he laughed. "Yes, I guess you could."

He carried the bouquet into the kitchen and set it on a chair. Then he dug through the flowers to find the card.

It was a different picture of their date. The photograph looked professional, almost artistic, done in black and white, using the light from the candles to illuminate her face. At first glance, she seemed entranced with Josiah. But when she looked closely, she could see the discomfort on her face.

"You didn't like him much," Conover said.

"He was creepy from the start, but in subtle hard-to-explain ways."

"Why didn't you leave?"

"I was raised to be polite. I had no idea he was crazy."

Conover grunted at that. He opened the card. The handwriting inside was the same as all the others.

My future and your future are the same. You are my heart and soul. Without you, I am nothing.

Josiah

She closed her eyes, felt that fluttery fear rise in her again. "There'll be a ring somewhere in that bouquet."

"How do you know?" Conover asked.

She opened her eyes. "Go look at the last page of *All My Kisses*. Robert sends a forgive-me bouquet and in it, he puts a diamond engagement ring."

"This bouquet?"

"No. Josiah already used that one. I guess he thought this one would be more spectacular."

Conover dug and then whistled. There, among the stems, was a black velvet ring box. He opened it. A large diamond glittered against a circle of sapphires in a white gold setting.

"Jesus," he said. "I could retire on this thing."

"I always thought that was a gaudy ring," Paige said, her voice shaking. "But it fit the characters."

"Not to your taste?"

"No." She sighed and sank back into her chair. "Just because I write about it doesn't mean I want it to happen to me."

"I think you made that clear in the precinct today." He put the ring box back where he found it, returned the card to its envelope and set the flowers on the floor. "Mind if I have some of that cake?"

"Oh, I'm sorry." She got up and cut him a piece of cake, then poured some coffee.

When she turned around, he was grinning.

"What did I do?" she asked.

"You weren't kidding about polite," he said. "I didn't come here for a tea party, and you could have said no."

She froze in place. "Was this another of your tests? To see if I was really that polite?"

"I wish I were that smart." He took the plate from her hand. "I was getting knocked out by the smell. My mother used to make this cake. It always was my favorite."

"With marshmallow frosting?"

"And that spritz of melted chocolate on top, just like you have here." He set the plate down and took the coffee from her hand. "Although in those days, I would have preferred a large glass of milk."

"I have some—"

"Sit." If anything, his grin had gotten bigger. "Forgive me for being so blunt, but what the hell did you need with a blind date?"

There was admiration in his eyes—real admiration, not the sick kind she'd seen from Josiah. She used her fork to cut a bite of cake. "I was lonely. I don't get out much, and I thought, what could it hurt?"

He shook his head. That weary look had returned to his face. She liked its rumpled quality, the way that he seemed to be able to take the weight of the world onto himself and still stand up. "What a way to get disillusioned."

"Because I'm a romance writer?"

"Because you're a person."

They ate the cake in silence after that, then he gripped his coffee mug and leaned back in the chair.

"Thanks," he said. "I'd forgotten that little taste of childhood."

"There's more."

"Maybe later." There was no smile on his face anymore, no enjoyment. "I have to tell you a few things."

She pushed her own plate away.

"I looked up Josiah Wells. He's got a sheet."

She grabbed her own coffee cup. It was warm and comforting. "Let me guess. The political conferences he stopped going to."

Conover frowned at her. "What conferences?"

"Here in San Francisco. He was active in local politics. That's how my friend Sally met him."

"And he stopped?"

"Rather suddenly. I thought, after all this started, that maybe—"

"I'll check into it," Conover said with a determination she hadn't heard from him before. "His sheet's from San Diego."

"I thought he was from here."

Conover shook his head. "He's not a dot-com millionaire. He made his money on a software system back in the early nineties, before everyone was into this business. Sold his interest for thirty million dollars and some stock, which has since risen in value. About ten times what it was."

Her mouth had gone dry. Josiah Wells had lied to both her and Sally. "Somehow I suspect this is important."

"Yeah." Conover took a sip of coffee. "He stalked a woman in San Diego."

"Oh, God." The news gave her a little too much relief. She had been feeling alone. But she didn't want anyone else to be experiencing the same thing she was.

"He killed her."

"What?" Paige froze.

"When she resisted him, he shot her and killed her." Conover's soft gaze was on her now, measuring. All her relief had vanished. She was suddenly more terrified than she had ever been.

"You know it was him?"

"I read the file. They faxed it to me this afternoon. All of it. They had him one hundred percent. DNA matches, semen matches—"

She winced, knowing what that meant.

"—the fibers from his home on her clothing, and a list of stalking complaints and injunctions that went on for pages."

The cake sat like a lump in her stomach. "Then why isn't he in prison?"

"Money," Conover said. "His attorneys so out-classed the DA's office that by the end of the trial, they could have convinced the jury that the judge had done it."

"Oh, my God," Paige said.

"The same things that happened to you happened to her," Conover said. "Only with her those things took about two years. With you it's taking two weeks."

"Because he feels like he knows me from my books?"

Conover shook his head. "She was a TV business reporter who had done an interview with him. He would have felt like he knew her, too."

"What then?" Somehow having the answer to all of that would make her feel better—or maybe she was just lying to herself.

"These guys are like alcoholics. If you take a guy through AA, and keep him sober for a year, then give him a drink, he won't rebuild his drinking career from scratch. He'll start at precisely the point he left off."

She had to swallow hard to keep the cake down. "You think she wasn't the only one."

"Yeah. I suspect if we look hard enough, we'll find a trail of women, each representing a point in the escalation of his sickness."

"You can arrest him, right?"

"Yes." Conover spoke softly. "But only on what he's done. Not on what he might do. And I don't think we'll be any more successful at holding him than the San Diego DA."

Paige ran her hand over the butcher-block table. "I have to leave, don't I?"

"Yeah." Conover's voice got even softer. He put a hand on hers. She looked at him. It wasn't world-weariness in his eyes. It was sadness. Sadness from all the things he'd seen, all the things he couldn't change.

"I'm from a small town," she said. "I don't want to bring him there."

"Is there anywhere else you can go? Somewhere he wouldn't think of?"

"New York," she said. "I have friends I can stay with for a few weeks."

"This'll take longer than a few weeks. You might not be able to come back."

"I know. But that'll give me time to find a place to live." Her voice broke on that last. This had been her dream city, her dream home. How quickly that vanished.

"I'm sorry," he said.

"Yeah," she said quietly. "Me, too."

He decided to stay without her asking him. He said he wanted to sift through the evidence, listen to the phone messages, and read the e-mail. She printed off all of it while she bought plane tickets online. Then she e-mailed her agent and told her that she was coming to the City.

Already she was talking like the New Yorker she was going to be.

Her flight left at 8:00 A.M. She spent half the night packing and unpacking, uncertain about what she would need, what she should leave behind. The only thing she was certain about was that she would need her laptop, and she spent an hour loading her files onto it. She was writing down the names of some moving and packing services when Conover stopped her.

"We leave everything as is," he said. "We don't want him to get too suspicious too soon."

"Why don't you arrest him now?" she asked. "Don't you have enough?"

Something flashed across his face, so quickly she almost didn't catch it.

"What?" she asked. "What is it?"

He closed his eyes. If anything, that made his face look even more rumpled. "I issued a warrant for his arrest before I came here. We haven't found him yet."

"Oh, God." Paige slipped into her favorite chair. One of many things she would have to leave behind, one of many things she might never see again because of Josiah Wells.

"We have people watching his house, watching yours, and a few other places he's known to hang out," Conover said. "We'll get him soon enough."

She nodded, trying to look reassured, even though she wasn't.

About 3:00 A.M., Conover looked at her suitcases sitting in the middle of the dining room floor. "I'll have to ship those to you. No sense tipping him off if he's watching this place."

"I thought you said—"

"I did. But we need to be careful. One duffel. The rest can wait."

"My laptop," she said. "I need that, too."

He sighed. "All right. The laptop and the biggest purse you have. Nothing more."

A few hours earlier, she might have argued with him. But a few hours earlier, she hadn't yet gone numb.

"I need some sleep," she said.

"I'll wake you," he said, "when it's time to go."

He drove her to the airport in his car. It was an old bathtub Porsche—with the early seventies bucket seats that were nearly impossible to get into.

"She's not pretty anymore," he said as he tucked Paige's laptop behind the seat, "but she can move."

They left at five, not so much as to miss traffic, but hoping that Wells wouldn't be paying attention at that hour. Conover also kept checking his rearview mirror, and a few times he executed some odd maneuvers.

"We being followed?" she asked finally.

"I don't think so," he said. "But I'm being cautious."

His words hung between them. She watched the scenery go by, houses after houses after houses filled with people who went about their ordinary lives, not worrying about stalkers or death or losing everything.

"This isn't normal for you, is it?" she asked after a moment.

"Being cautious?" he said. "Of course it is."

"No." Paige spoke softly. "Taking care of someone like this."

He seemed even more intent on the road than he had been. "All cases are different."

"Really?"

He turned to her, opened his mouth, and then closed it again, sighing. "Josiah Wells is a predator."

"I know," she said.

"We have to do what we can to catch him." His tone was odd. She frowned. Was that an apology for something she didn't understand? Or an explanation for his attentiveness?

Maybe it was both.

He turned onto the road leading to San Francisco International Airport. The traffic seemed even thicker here, through all the construction and the dust. It seemed like they were constantly remodeling the place. Somehow he made it through the confusing signs to Short Term Parking. He found a space, parked, and then grabbed her laptop from the back.

"You're coming in?" she asked.

"I want to see you get on that plane." He seemed oddly determined.

"Don't you trust me?"

"Of course I do," he said and got out of the car.

San Francisco International Airport was an old airport, built right on the bay. The airport had been trying to modernize for years. The new parts were grafted on like artificial limbs.

Paige took a deep breath, grabbed her stuffed oversized purse, and let Conover lead her inside. She supposed they looked like any couple as they went through the automatic doors, stopping to examine the signs above them pointing to the proper airline. Conover was watching the other passengers. Paige was checking out the lines.

She had bought herself a first-class ticket—spending more money than she had spent for her very first car. But she was leaving everything behind. The last thing she wanted was to be crammed into coach next to a howling baby and an underpaid, stressed businessman.

She hurried to the first-class line, relieved that it was short. Conover stayed beside her, frowning as he watched the people flow past. He seemed both disappointed and alert. He was expecting something. But what?

Paige stepped up to the ticket counter, gave her name, showed her identification, answered the silly security questions, and got her e-ticket with the gate number written on the front.

"You've got an hour and a half," Conover said as she left the ticket counter. "Let's get breakfast."

His hand rested possessively on her elbow, and he pulled her close as he spoke. She glanced at him, but he still wasn't watching her.

"I have to make a stop first," she said.

He nodded.

They walked past the arrival and departure monitors, past the newspaper vending machines and toward the nearest restrooms. This part of the San Francisco airport still had a seventies security design. Instead of a bank of x-ray machines and metal detectors blocking entry into the main part of the terminal, there was nothing. The security measures were in front of each gate: you couldn't enter without going past a security checkpoint. So different from New York, where you couldn't even walk into some areas without a ticket. Conover would have no trouble remaining beside her until it was time for her to take off.

She went into the ladies' room, leaving Conover near the departure monitors outside. The line was long—several flights had just arrived—but Paige didn't mind. This was the first time she'd had a moment to herself since Conover had arrived the night before.

It seemed like weeks ago.

She was going to be sorry to say goodbye to him at the gate. In that short period of time, she had come to rely on him more than she wanted to admit. He made her feel safe for the first time since she had met Josiah Wells.

As she exited the ladies' room, a hand grabbed her arm and pulled her sideways. She felt something poke against her back.

"Think you could leave me?"

Wells. She shook her arm, trying to get away, but he clamped harder.

"Scream," he said, "and I will hurt you."

"You can't hurt me," she said. "You can't have weapons in an airport."

"You can bring a gun into an airport," he said softly, right in her ear. "You just can't take it through security."

She felt cold then. He was as crazy as Conover said. And as dangerous.

"Josiah." She spoke loudly, hoping that Conover could hear her. She didn't see him anywhere. "I'm going to New York on business. When I come back, we can start planning the wedding."

Wells was silent for a moment. He didn't move at all. She couldn't see his face, but she could feel his body go rigid. "You're playing with me."

"No," she said, letting her voice work for her, hoping it sounded convincing. She kept scanning the crowd, but Conover was gone. "I got your ring last night. I decided I needed to settle a few things in New York before I told you I'd say yes."

Wells put his chin on her shoulder. His breath blew against her hair. "You're not wearing the ring."

"It didn't fit," she said. "But I have it with me. I was going to have it sized in New York."

"Let me see it," he said.

"You'll have to let me dig into my purse."

She wasn't sure he'd believe her. Then, after a moment, he let her go. She brought up her purse, pretended to rummage through it, and took a step toward the ladies' room door, praying her plan would work.

He was frowning. He looked like any other businessman in the airport, his suit neat and well tailored, his trenchcoat long and expensive, marred only by the way he held his hand in the pocket.

She waited just a split second, until there were a lot of people around from another arriving plane, and then she screamed, "He's got a gun!" and ran toward the ladies' room.

Only she didn't make it. She was tackled from behind, and went sprawling across the faded carpet. A gunshot echoed around her, and people started screaming, running. The body on top of hers prevented her from moving, and for a moment, she thought whoever had hit her had been shot.

Then she felt arms around her, dragging her toward the departure monitors.

"You little fool," Conover said in her ear. "I had this under control."

He pushed her against the base of the monitor, then turned around. Half the people around Wells had remained, and two of them had him in their grasp, while another was handcuffing him. Plainclothes airport police officers. More airport police were hurrying to the spot from the front door.

Passengers were still screaming and running out of the airport. Airline personnel were crouched behind their desks. Paige looked to see whether anyone was shot, but she didn't see anyone lying injured anywhere.

Her breathing was shallow, and she suddenly realized how terrified she had been. "What do you mean, under control? This doesn't look under control to me."

Security had Wells against the wall and were searching him for more weapons. One of the uniformed airport police had pulled Wells's head back and was yelling at him. Some of the passengers, realizing the threat was over, were drifting back toward the action.

Conover kept one hand on her, holding her in place. With the other, he pulled out his cell phone. He hit the speed-dial and put the small phone against his ear.

"Wait a minute!" Paige said.

He turned away slightly, as if he didn't want to speak to her. Then he said into the phone, "Frank, do me a favor. Call the news media— everyone you can think of. Tell them something just happened at the airport....No. I'm not going through official channels. That's why I called you. Keep my name out of it and get them here."

He hung up and glanced at Paige. She had never felt so many emotions in her life. Anger, adrenaline, confusion. Then she saw security lead Wells away.

Conover took her arm and helped her up. "What's going on?" she asked again.

"Outside," he said, and pushed her through the crowd. After a moment, she remembered to check for her laptop. He had it, and somehow she had retained her purse. They reached the front sidewalk only to find it a confusion of milling people—some still terrified from the shots, others just arriving and trying to drop off their luggage. Cabs honked and nearly missed each other. Buses were backing up as the crowd spilled into the street.

"Oh, this is so much better," she said.

He moved her down the sidewalk toward another terminal. The crowd thinned here.

"What the hell was that?" she asked. "Where were you? How did he get past you?"

"He didn't get past me," Conover said softly.

She felt the blood leave her face. "You set me up? I was bait?"

"It wasn't supposed to happen like this."

"Oh, really? He was supposed to drag me onto the nearest flight? Or shoot me?"

"I didn't know he had a gun," Conover said. "He was ballsier than I expected. And he wouldn't have taken you from San Francisco."

"You know this how? Because you're psychic?"

"No, he wanted to control you. He couldn't control you on a plane. I had security waiting outside. A few plainclothes cops have been around us since we arrived. He was supposed to grab you, but you weren't supposed to try to get away."

"Nice if you would have told me that."

He shook his head slightly. "Most people wouldn't have fought him. Most people would have cooperated."

"Most people would have appreciated an explanation!" Her voice rose and a few stray passengers looked in her direction. She made herself take a deep breath before she went on. "You knew he was going to be here. You knew it and didn't tell me."

"I guessed," he said.

"What did you do, tip him off?"

"No," Conover said softly. "You did."

"I did? I didn't talk to him."

"You booked your e-ticket online." His face was close to hers, his voice as soft as possible in all the noise. "He'd hacked into your system weeks ago. That's how he found your address and your phone number. Your public e-mail comes into the same computer as all your other e-mail. He's been following your every move ever since."

"Software genius," she muttered, shaking her head. She should have seen that.

Conover nodded. Across the way, reporters started converging on the building, cameras hefted on shoulders, running toward the doors.

Conover shielded her, but she knew they would want to talk to her.

"Why didn't you warn me?" she asked again.

"I thought you'd be too obvious then, and he wouldn't try for you. I didn't expect you to be so cool under pressure. Telling him about the ring, pretending you were interested, that was smart."

One of the reporters was working the crowd. People were turning toward the camera.

"Where were you?" she asked. "I looked for you."

"I was behind you all the time."

"So if he took me outside...?"

"I would have followed."

"I don't understand. Why didn't you tell me not to get the ticket online?"

"The ticket was a gift," Conover said. "I didn't realize you were going to do it that way. You told me when you finished. His file from the previous case mentioned how he had used the Internet to spy on his first victim. He was obviously doing that with you."

"But the airport, how did they know?"

"I called ahead, said that I was coming in, expecting a difficult passenger. I faxed his photo from your place while you were asleep. I asked them to wait until I got him outside, unless he did something threatening."

She frowned. More reporters were approaching. These looked like print media. No cameras, but lots of determination. "You could have waited and caught him at home."

"I could have," Conover said. "But this is better."

She turned to him, remembering the feel of the gun against her back, the screaming passengers, the explosive sound when the gun went off. "Someone could have been killed."

"I didn't expect a gun," Conover said. "And I didn't think he'd be rash enough to use it in an airport."

"But he did," she said.

"And it's going to help us." Conover watched another set of reporters run into the building. "First, his assault on you in an airport makes it a federal case. The gun adds to the case, and all the witnesses make it even better. Then there is the fact that airports are filled with security cameras. There's bound to be tape on this."

She frowned, trying to take herself out of this, trying to listen like a writer instead of a potential victim.

"And then," Conover said, "he attacked you. You're nationally known. It'll be big news. Our DA might have lost a stalking case against Wells, but the feds aren't going to let a guy who went nuts in an airport walk, no matter how much money he has."

"You set him up," she said. "If this had failed—"

"At the very least, I would have been fired," Conover said. "But it wouldn't have failed. I wouldn't have let anything happen to you. I didn't let anything happen to you."

"But you took such a risk." She raised her head toward his. "Why?"

He put a finger under her chin, and for a moment, she thought he was going to kiss her.

"Because you didn't want to leave San Francisco," he said softly.

"I get to stay home?" she asked.

He smiled, and let his finger drop. "Yeah."

He stared at her uncertainly, as if he were afraid she was going to yell at him again. But she felt a relief so powerful that it completely overwhelmed her.

She threw her arms around him. For a moment, he didn't move. Then, slowly, his arms wrapped around her and pulled her close.

"I don't even know your first name," she whispered.

"Pete," he said, burying his face in her hair.

"Pete." She tested it. "It suits you."

"I'd ask if I could call you," he said, "but I'm not real good on dates."

That pulled a reluctant laugh from her. "Obviously I'm not, either. But I make a mean chocolate cake."

"That's right," he said. "Let's go finish it."

"Don't we have to talk to the press?"

"For a moment." He pulled back just enough to smile at her. "And then I get to take you home."

"Where I get to stay." She couldn't convey how much this meant to her. "Thank you."

He nodded. "My pleasure."

She leaned her head against his shoulder, feeling his strength, feeling the comfort. It didn't matter how he looked or whether he knew

La Bohème from Don Giovanni. All that mattered was how he made her feel.

Safe. Appreciated. And maybe even loved.

Celtic  Cross

Yvonne Jocks

"Someone's going to die," whispered Didi, staring at the tarot card.

Her new employer, Annie Tregaron, glanced down from where she stood by the cash register. "The death card doesn't always mean death," she prompted gently. *Too gently*, Didi thought, considering the garish picture of a skeleton that she'd just drawn from the store's sample deck.

"I asked the cards what I should know about taking this job, and then I drew *this*!"

"It usually means beginnings and endings." Annie plucked the card neatly from Didi's hand, tucked it back into the deck, and shuffled all seventy-eight with practiced hands. With her gauzy skirts and all those rings and bracelets and all that brown hair, Annie Tregaron looked like some kind of high priestess. She sounded so sure, and yet...

Someone's going to die, thought Didi again. And she had the sick feeling it might be her.

Was taking this job a mistake?

Annie handed back the cards with quiet confidence. That confidence had drawn Didi back to her store, Avalon, again and again, even before the clerking job became available. Didi liked other things about the store, too—the incense and candles, the Celtic and Native American music, the crystals and jewelry. It felt like maybe magic really worked, in here, like a place where the harshness of the world could never intrude....

Didi O'Sullivan longed to believe such a place existed. But...the card!

"Try again," advised Annie, since Didi had already learned her tasks for the day and now was just killing time. "A whole spread, not a one-card pull. It'll tell you more."

Didi didn't understand tarot all that well yet, despite the books she'd bought—books her husband had pitched a fit about. As she laid cards out on the glass-topped counter, she murmured a chant beneath her breath to remember the basic spread: "Cover me, cross me; over me, under me; behind me, before me."

But instead of admiring the knot-work design that backed the face-down cards, she found herself noticing her gold wedding band. *Had she made a mistake?* Annie seemed so safe, so capable of taking up anybody's problems in those many-ringed hands!

Inhaling scented air, Didi turned the first card, called the significator, which represented the center of the matter. The breath whimpered out of her. She stared down at the same picture of a horseback skeleton.

Death.

Someone...

"Well," said Annie steadily. "That *is* what you were asking about, right? Let's see what the cross card tells us." While Didi sat on the stool behind the counter, near to paralyzed, Annie turned the next card. It lay across the first, indicating obstacles. "Ah..."

It was a face card, the Knight of Swords.

Even without books, Didi knew what—or who—that card represented. Apparently, so did Annie.

"Your husband?"

Didi's gaze again dropped to the wedding ring, with a mixture of misery and hope.

Conn...

🎷🎷🎷

"I've never loved anyone like I love my wife, Mr. Delaney," said the man sitting across the desk from Sawyer, earlier that day. "Maybe nobody has. I'd die if anything happened to us."

Die? That seemed extreme, but Sawyer was no expert on true love. All he said was, "And you're hiring me to...?"

Connor O'Sullivan shifted restlessly. He had shaggy black hair, a long and shadowed jaw, stubborn blue eyes. He wore jeans and a WWF T-shirt. "This isn't real comfortable for me, you know. Coming to another guy for help."

Sawyer could've guessed that from the shirt. "So don't think of me as a guy, Mr. O'Sullivan," he advised, leaning farther back in his chair. He opted against propping his booted feet up on his desk. *Too gumshoe.* "Just think of me as a private investigator."

O'Sullivan scowled at him a long moment more.

"Is it your wife you want investigated?"

"*Yes.* I mean—" O'Sullivan closed his eyes, shook his head. Either he really was upset, or he was an excellent actor. "It's not that I think she's cheating on me or anything. Didi would never in a million years do something like that."

Sawyer had heard *that* before. It was usually a lie.

"*Never!* She knows it would kill me."

Again with the dying. "So..."

O'Sullivan opened his fists, spread his fingers. "My wife's gotten sucked into some kind of cult."

Suddenly, this wasn't just another is-my-wife-cheating case after all. "A cult," Sawyer repeated, propping his elbows on his wood-veneer desk.

"People are always taking advantage of Didi. That's why she needs *me*. About a month ago, she starts bringing home weird books and crystals and shit, you know? From this hocus-pocus bookstore she's found down on 7th Street. Next thing I know, she's following her horoscope and talking about the freaking moonphase and just going *spacey* on me."

Sawyer considered that. "New Age spacey is one thing, Mr. O'Sullivan. But a cult has to have a leader. A figurehead. Like David Koresh, or that Jim Jones bastard. Remove the figurehead, you end the cult."

"Yes!" agreed O'Sullivan. "There's this woman at the bookstore, Annie something-or-other. She gives classes in fortunetelling and shit,

and women get together there after hours in some kind of *coven*, and...
and they've got my Didi."

"Kidnapping is a job for the police." Only as he heard himself all
but turning down money did Sawyer admit the truth. As much as this
case intrigued him, he had a bad feeling about it. A *real* bad feeling. No
crystal ball required.

And yet...

"I mean, they have her brainwashed or something," insisted
O'Sullivan. "But the way they're turning her against me, she might as
well be kidnapped. She even got a job at the place—can you believe it?
Like I haven't been providing for her just fine! Like she has any business hanging around those lesbo crazies doing their voodoo shit."

Lesbo crazies? How sad—yet Sawyer was intrigued. "What exactly is
it you want *me* to do, Mr. O'Sullivan?"

"You probably wouldn't go for killing them all, huh?" asked his
client, with a sudden, awkward laugh.

Sawyer just stared, unamused. *You couldn't afford me.*

"Never mind," said O'Sullivan quickly. Dropping his gaze, he
scraped his open hands down his blue-jeaned thighs. "Bad joke. What
I need is information on this Tregaron woman and what kind of a woo-
woo cult she's running. I need to show Didi what a batch of loonies
she's getting into, before it's too late. I don't...I don't think she'll listen
anymore, if it comes from me. They've got her that turned around. But
cold, hard proof..."

"From a professional like myself," clarified Sawyer, not smiling.

"Yeah," said O'Sullivan. "Look, I'm desperate. If this doesn't work,
I don't know what else I can do. Get me something to make my wife
see sense, okay? Before I wake up one morning and find her dead and
mutilated, some kind of satanic sacrifice. We...this isn't the kind of
love that you just let go of, you know? This is the kind of love a man's
got to fight for—or die trying."

There it was again, the bad feeling. But...Sawyer *did* need the business.

"I'll give it a day and see what I can find out," he said. By quoting
his price, he mentally accepted responsibility for whatever came of it.

He just hoped whatever-came-of-it didn't end up being his fault.
Again.

"*Calm down,*" repeated Annie. "You won't hear anything the cards are advising if you overreact."

"*Overreact?*" squeaked Didi.

Annie had found herself drawn to the redhead's vulnerability early on, drawn to the potential of it. She would be interested to see what Didi could become—with the right influences, of course.

But the woman wasn't particularly well grounded.

"Remember what I said about the Death card." If she spoke steadily, she could help slow a listener's brainwave cycles toward the alpha end of the spectrum. It was like a mild form of hypnosis. "You said you were asking about the job, so that makes sense. You're leaving remnants of the old Didi behind. That's not such a bad thing, is it?"

Didi shook her head, but reluctantly. She still looked pale.

"Standing in your way, though—the cross card—is a man, possibly dark-haired. He makes up for his insecurities by pretending to know everything, no matter whom he hurts in the process. You think that's your husband?"

Annie thought she saw a nod hidden in Didi's shrug. She'd figured as much, ever since the day Didi brought a moon pendant back to the store, claiming that her husband wouldn't let her wear it. Wouldn't *let* her! It bristled Annie's every female instinct.

"Your hope for the situation, its highest good, is…" Annie's bracelets jingled as she turned the card that made the top of the cross shape. "Justice. Well…maybe it has to do with you paying your own way, like you said you wanted to."

That didn't feel quite right, but Didi nodded again, so Annie continued.

"And the foundation of the situation is…" *Huh. Eight of Swords.* She never had liked the drawing of a woman, bound and blindfolded, blades on all sides. "Isolation," she murmured. "Confusion. Self-doubt…"

How could *that* have led to Didi's life change, registering for classes at Avalon, getting involved with the woman's circle, *taking this job*?

That *was* what this spread was about, wasn't it? Didi taking this job? *Something didn't feel quite right, at that…*

Annie turned over the card that symbolized the immediate past—the Devil, humanity's tendency to chain itself with negativity or obsession.

But whose? Didi's, or her husband's? Or someone else's?

Faster now, Annie turned the next card to reveal the immediate future—and stared.

It showed a tower, lightning blasting the roof off, innocents tumbling from its windows toward their death. A portent of devastation, the Tower was arguably the worst card in the entire deck.

Oh, crap, she thought, taking in the main body of the tarot spread. *Maybe someone IS going to die.*

Great. Absolutely peachy.

"What is it?" asked Didi. "What's wrong?"

"I...I'm not sure," Annie admitted. She'd already made Didi more susceptible to suggestion by easing her brainwaves down toward alpha state. She could too easily plant prophecies for the girl to self-fulfill. "The future is fluid, after all."

"It's bad news," guessed Didi.

"It—" Annie took a deep breath. "It shows that there could be some kind of blowup in your near future, because of these cards." She indicated the Devil, the Eight of Swords. "They indicate self-denial, unwillingness to take responsibility, a tendency to dwell in negativity." Annie considered her new part-time clerk. "What the heck's been going on in your life lately, anyway?"

Didi drew herself up straight. "That's my own business."

Now she grows a spine.

To complicate matters, the bells over the doorway chimed and an auburn-haired man walked in.

He didn't look like Annie's type—or Avalon's. She sold to black-lipsticked Goths, RenFaire types, hold-over hippies. She also helped housewives, dentists, college professors, computer programmers.

And yet, despite the jeans and scuffed bomber jacket, this man *still* didn't look like her usual customer.

"We'll talk in a minute," she instructed Didi. "In the meantime, go choose a nice black crystal—jet, or obsidian—for extra protection. On the house. And *don't worry.*"

Nodding, Didi headed for the back of the shop.

Annie turned to the not-a-customer, a tallish man with sideburns and gray eyes and an air of purpose about him that she didn't fully trust. "May I help you?"

"I hope so," he said. He looked her up and down—but like a regular guy would. *That* part didn't set off any warnings. Then he offered his hand. "Sawyer Delaney. Can I ask you a few questions?"

What Connor O'Sullivan couldn't stand was the not knowing. He tried to just go on to his job like nothing had happened, like he could just sit behind the office building's security desk with his video feeds and his badge and his headset and not care. He tried to distract himself by laying out his umpteenth game of solitaire, using a worn pack of casino cards. But how was a man supposed to stay calm when crazies were threatening his *wife*?

It wasn't like he could take off his worry the same way he changed out of his T-shirt and into the stupid white monkey-shirt management forced him to wear. Uniform or not, he could barely think past his upset.

Didi...

From the moment he saw her, he'd known they were meant to be together. Within weeks of their first date they were living together; within months, they'd married. Something like that didn't happen any old day, right? But he and Didi, they were special.

What kind of unfeeling bitch would turn a man's wife, his soul mate, against him like this?

Connor split his attention between the playing cards and the video feeds, a voyeurism he normally enjoyed. Did the people he watched know what he was going through? Were any of them involved with that Tregaron woman's cult?

He wrenched his attention away from the vid-screens and, since he couldn't concentrate anyway, scooped the playing cards off the counter and into the trash.

The ace of spades fluttered to the floor, a stray. He wondered what the Tregaron woman would make of that?

Anyone who put a stop to her kind of craziness was a real man, in his book.

Most of the con-artists Sawyer had run into didn't stay anywhere long enough to get caught—or prosecuted, anyhow. They tended to decorate in such a way that they could pull up and move on.

In contrast, a computer check from his office told Sawyer that the store called Avalon had been in business at the same location for over three years. It had its own website, announcing new merchandise and listing classes and retreats for the next six months. The store itself had stained glass worked into its display windows and murals on the upper walls.

The proprietor clearly had no intention of moving anytime soon. Either she was legit, or...

Or she had her own, less legal reasons for confidence.

Two women occupied the store. One, a pale young redhead, fit Didi O'Sullivan's description. The other had long, wild brown hair, and a wide mouth, and clear green eyes so direct that he could think of no other word than "wise."

So this was the Jim Jones of the New Age set?

He'd have thought she'd be taller.

"Sawyer Delaney," he said in a neutral voice. "Can I ask you a few questions?"

"Annie Tregaron," she said back. "You can *ask*."

No promises about answers, though...

"I'm a private investigator, Ms. Tregaron, looking into some concerns about the, um, *occult* stores in town."

She kept her expression remarkably neutral, but her eyes cooled. *Something to hide, Dark Lady?*

"'Metaphysical,'" she said. "The word *occult* means 'hidden,' and as you can see, we aren't hiding anything."

"Well, that should make my job easy." Fun though the hard-boiled private-eye routine was on TV, he generally caught more information with honey than with vinegar. "Do you have a few minutes? We could talk here, or go across the street for a cup of coffee—my treat."

She glanced over her shoulder toward the redhead, who was sorting through a bin of colored rocks. "I have a new clerk today."

At least that meant she'd talk to him. Then again, after her "occult means hidden," speech, she'd look damned suspicious otherwise.

More damned suspicious.

"Here's fine," he said.

"Do you have an ID?" she asked.

He dug it out for her.

As he was showing her his credentials, he noticed the tarot cards laid across the glass counter. "Have I interrupted something?"

"Nothing to worry about."

But the skeleton card drew his interest. "Death, huh?"

"The Death card," said Ms. Tregaron, "doesn't always mean death. It usually means endings and beginnings."

Sounded like a line to him.

"But sometimes it means death, right?"

She met and held his gaze for what felt like a very long moment. She was a helluva lot prettier than Jim Jones.

Sawyer looked away first. Because he didn't want to alienate her, he told himself.

"Sometimes," she admitted.

"So," he asked, his voice coming out deeper than usual. "Who's going to die?"

"So," she countered. "What is it that has *'people'* so concerned?"

"You don't know?"

"Folks usually complain that we're Satanists, sacrificing babies and having orgies in the back room."

"I hadn't heard the orgies part," he admitted—and she smiled. Annie Tregaron had a hell of a smile. *Oh, hell,* Sawyer thought. He was in trouble.

"You needn't sound so intrigued, Mr. Delaney," she chided, her own voice deepening.

He was in deep, deep trouble.

※ ※ ※

Annie answered the private investigator's questions with her usual speech—the we're-not-witches, we're-not-Satanists, we-don't-target-minors speech. She never knew if a person would actually buy it, of course, but she found herself hoping the investigator would. He could be trouble, otherwise.

And, okay, he *was* attractive in a lanky sort of way.

"Could I see the back room where you hold your classes?" he asked, and she led him back through the curtains, only briefly glancing toward Didi O'Sullivan.

Annie was proud of her "classroom" in back. A storage area opened off of it, but she knew Mr. Delaney's peek would show him nothing more damning than a lot of boxes and empty shelving. The main room had dark blue linoleum, a large table and a dozen chairs, and a refrigerator, which Mr. Delaney checked.

"No dead bodies," she said, and he spun around, as if surprised by her voice. "But there's a Dumpster out back, if you want to be sure."

"I'll keep that in mind," he said, looking down at her. She could feel his nearness against her, like an expectation.

"Will there be anything else?"

"*Would* you like to get a cup of coffee?" he asked. "Maybe after you've closed up for the day?"

"I don't drink caffeine."

"Herbal tea, then."

"Wouldn't that be a conflict of interest? What about whoever hired you to dig up proof about our brainwashing, child-sacrificing, demonic orgies?"

He narrowed his eyes, cocked his head suspiciously. "I hadn't mentioned brainwashing."

"Goodbye, Mr. Delaney," she said. She headed for the front door, confident that he would follow her. He did.

"Can I call you if I have more questions?" he asked.

"You can *call*," she demurred.

He stopped in the doorway, folded his arms, looked her up and down like a man who knew what he was doing.

Annie waited for it.

"Are you a good witch," he asked, "or a bad witch?"

"I told you, I'm not a witch."

He glanced toward the tarot spread on the counter.

"Witches," she said, "have too many rules about ethics."

Then she smiled her best, most evil smile, and turned away from him. She didn't need him distracting her any further.

She had Didi to take care of.

The more frightened Didi felt, the more dangerous her magic book-store seemed. She tried not to be scared, but...a private investigator? He'd asked Annie some scary questions.

Had she made a mistake, taking this job?

It didn't help when Annie glanced at her with those all-knowing eyes and predicted, "You're having second thoughts?"

"I..."

"How long have you been married?"

Then Didi understood. "Second thoughts about *Connor*?"

"You said your husband wasn't happy with you taking this job," said Annie. "He made you return that amulet."

Both of which were true, but...

"Well, we'd agreed that he'd work, and I'd stay home and take care of the house." Or the one-bedroom apartment, as the case may be. "Conn's family thinks it's an insult to the husband if his wife works. That's not *his* fault."

Annie looked unconvinced.

"And he *didn't* tell me to return the moon amulet." True, he'd yelled at her about it. Worse, he'd thrown her new crystal ball across the living room, right through the window. It had shattered on the concrete out-side, so of course she couldn't return *that*. He'd gone off to the bar to cool off. Afterward he'd apologized for losing his temper, held her tight, told her she was the most important thing in the world to him.

Didi loved it when Conn told her things like that.

Since she had to somehow pay the apartment complex for a new window, she'd decided on her own to get the money back on the moon pendant. Did Annie resent the return? Was that it?

"I suppose," said Annie slowly, "that I misunderstood."

But she sounded suspicious, and that made Didi mad.

"Conn and I have our problems, but he loves me," she insisted. "He loves me more than anything in the world. He says so."

Annie, she remembered, had never married. Didi had admired her quiet confidence...but maybe it was a ruse.

She didn't want to be like Annie, if it meant alienating Connor. She didn't want to be empowered, if it meant being alone.

"I should probably go," Didi said. She wasn't sure she would come back, either. But she would rather tell Annie that over the telephone. "It's after four."

"What about the tarot reading? Don't you want to finish it?"

"No." For all she knew, Annie had arranged the cards to lay out that way on purpose. "It's probably nothing. Like you said, endings and beginnings."

Didi retrieved her purse from behind the counter.

"See you tomorrow," said Annie.

And Didi, hurrying out the front door with a jingle of bells, called back, "Bye."

When she remembered the onyx in her pocket, she decided to worry about it later.

She wasn't likely going back.

The cards said scary things in that place.

❧ ❧ ❧

"You cheat!"

One of the suits crossing the marble foyer glanced nervously toward Connor O'Sullivan. Well, the hell with him. *He* wasn't the one on the phone with a no-good PI.

"I checked Tregaron out thoroughly," said the cheat. "Court records. Credit report. Better Business Bureau. She's clean."

"You didn't look hard enough," protested Conn. "Didn't ask enough questions."

"I've worked all day on this! I spent a half-hour at the store myself, and Ms. Tregaron was…"

Delaney hesitated, which made Connor immediately suspicious. "What already?"

"Impressive. And I, uh, found no bodies in the Dumpster."

Connor felt suddenly cold. "She got you, too."

"What?"

"You son of a bitch!"

Another passing businessman cleared his throat.

"Mind your own damn business," Connor snarled at him.

"Look," said Delaney into the phone, "I know this isn't what you were looking for—"

"And don't expect to get paid for it, either!" Connor slammed down the phone, dug for his car keys with a shaking hand. He needed a beer. It wasn't quite time for him to go off shift, but he didn't give a rat's ass about the time.

If you wanted something done right, you did it yourself.

"Nevertheless, I'll include an invoice with my written report," muttered Sawyer to dead air as he hung up the phone. "You paranoid *jerk.*"

But he had a bad feeling about this.

Maybe he was just bummed about Annie Tregaron. It was dicey, pursuing a woman when he'd seen everything from her credit report to her spotless driving record.

Too spotless, maybe?

But, no, that wasn't the same kind of bad feeling.

On a hunch, he leaned over his computer and ran another check. But this time, he typed in a different name entirely.

Within minutes of seeing the results, Sawyer was on the phone to Avalon. When he just got the answering machine, he headed out the door.

At a run.

Annie used Didi's job application to find her clerk's apartment complex—one of the rundown types from the sixties building boom, with smaller windows and communal balconies. Once she'd spotted the apartment, she parked her car, but she didn't get out right away. Instead, she used her cell phone to try Didi's number one last time.

Not even an answering machine.

After turning over the last four cards of Didi's Celtic-Cross spread, Annie knew she had to find her new clerk. As Mr. Sawyer Delaney had so simply pointed out, sometimes the Death card really *did* mean death.

And sometimes you did what you had to do.

Annie got out of her car, locked it, and headed toward the apartments. She heard a car screech to a stop in the parking lot behind her; heard a door slam shut. "Annie!"

Speak of the devil—Sawyer Delaney!

"What are you doing here?" But she couldn't help glancing over her shoulder, toward Didi's apartment, as she asked.

"I followed a hunch." Delaney took her by an arm, tried to guide her off the cement walkway, tried to stop her. She pulled away—and he let her.

That's when she decided he really was a good guy.

Bad guys didn't let go.

"Look, I've got to check on Didi. Her car's here, but she's not answering the phone."

"Let me do it," insisted Delaney.

"She doesn't even *know* you."

"Yeah, well, her husband knows *you*. By reputation, anyway. And he's not real happy with you today."

Then Annie understood who had hired Sawyer Delaney. She understood her certainty that something was wrong with Didi's marriage.

She hesitated, glanced toward the stairs.

"Look, he's got a record," insisted Delaney. "Bar fights. Threats. Battery."

Annie nodded. "Fine. You check. But get her out of there."

He searched her eyes, then nodded, turned. He took the stairs two at a time, like someone who could get the job done.

But he couldn't reach the landing before the gunshot.

The gun just went off—and now there was a body on the floor. They'd been fighting about the job again. Didi said she would quit, but Connor lost his temper worse than ever, and...

Yes, that was it. They'd been fighting about the job.

Somehow they ended up in the kitchen, with its sink full of dirty dishes and its overflowing trash can. He'd started yelling. She'd yelled back—Annie Tregaron's influence, maybe?

He'd screamed his frustration and grabbed a knife.

Even that didn't seem real, even as he slashed at her, even as she cowered behind bloody arms, because after all he loved her. He loved her more than anything—kept trying to tell her that. They would be together forever. But there was the knife, and there was the pain, and his gun hung off the chair where he always put the holster after work....

With a loud, crisp *bang!* the body crumpled, too neat, too sudden. Then someone was at the front door, banging on it and yelling something about calling 911. The bloody, shaking hands couldn't hold the gun steady.

It was now starting to feel horribly real after all.

But...he'd loved her!

The gun clattered onto the table—so much heavier than you'd think, guns—and the banging at the door got louder until shaking feet found their way across the living room, until blood-slick hands fumbled the lock, until the door swung open.

Then Didi O'Sullivan looked into the panicked eyes of the man who'd been in Annie's shop this afternoon, and she didn't know why he was there at her apartment. But she guessed she knew what had happened, after all.

"I killed him," she whispered. "He's on the floor. The cards said someone was going to die, and it was Connor."

Then she began to weep.

*   *   *

"She said he loved her," whispered Annie Tregaron, staring down into her cup of herbal tea.

Sawyer glanced around the all-night diner. "This is not what I meant about taking you out for coffee."

But she'd been so shaken in the aftermath of the shooting—after the ambulance had taken Didi to the hospital, after the police cars, after the reports—that he'd had to do *something*. Attraction aside, he owed her that. As angry as he'd been, Connor O'Sullivan could have gone after Annie almost as easily as he'd gone after his wife.

His wife was just the safer target.

"He said he loved her, too," Sawyer offered. "For what it's worth."

"So why'd he try to kill her?"

"Why did she stay with him?" He shrugged. "Love's not all hearts and flowers, you know? Women are more likely to be killed by a husband or boyfriend than a stranger. When people's emotions and self-image get involved..."

She was staring at him, but she didn't look empowered or wise. She looked scared.

Sawyer said, "That's probably the worst possible lead-in to asking a woman out that I could ever come up with, huh?"

She said, "Yes."

He nodded, and looked down into his mug of coffee. *Oh well.*

Then she said, "But *any* date would have to top this, right?"

He nodded, looked up, grinned.

Annie's face twisted into a kind of wince. She wasn't ready to smile quite yet. She'd held Didi until the paramedics showed up, putting pressure on the towels they'd wrapped around her lacerated arms, wiping tear-streaked spatters of blood off the girl's face. Only when Didi's parents had arrived at the hospital, had Annie agreed to leave her.

Finding someone like that really *was* a kind of magic. Sawyer had no intention of letting her slip away, after all that.

Unless, of course, she told him to.

"So...," he prompted. "What do the tea leaves say, anyway?"

"I don't read tea leaves." But she inhaled deeply, then straightened her shoulders, sat up a bit. "Give me your hand."

Sawyer did.

Annie Tregaron studied his palm, stroked a single finger across the lines of it. He enjoyed her touch, firm and purposeful but not clinging.

She nodded and looked up, still holding his hand. "Yes. I'll go out with you."

So he had to ask. "Just what did you see?"

"Nothing," she admitted, with the barest of smiles. "I don't read palms, either. Just cards."

Their fingers interlaced.

It was a beginning. A good one.

Hostage  to Love

Mary Watson

"Promise we won't stay long."

Brand-new Assistant Prosecuting Attorney Jo Haynes heard the hint of desperation in her voice, but there was nothing she could do about it. Anticipation of the ordeal ahead made her restless and fidgety. She jabbed a button on her armrest to lower the power window and sucked humid eighty-degree air into her lungs.

Sharon Hancock, Jo's part-time secretary and full-time friend, used the driver's control panel to close the window. "Want me to park at the curb and leave the engine running?"

Jo reminded herself that Sharon was barely twenty-five, and that most of the time her flippancy was one of her more appealing traits. Still, if she hadn't been driving, the crack probably would have earned her a punch on the arm.

"No one appreciates your impudent wit more than I," she said dryly. "But I don't think *you* appreciate how much I hate these places. They give me the creeps."

"Then you shouldn't have agreed to come with me," Sharon

replied. "We have to stay for a decent amount of time. The whole purpose of visiting a funeral home is to pay your respects."

"Well, yes, sure," Jo muttered. "I know *that*. But—"

"It would sort of defeat the purpose to dash in, blurt 'So sorry for your loss,' then race for the nearest exit."

Jo grimaced, conceding the point. "I would never blurt out 'So sorry for your loss.' Ugh. Sounds like a chintzy generic sympathy card."

"Well…yeah. But what should you say? What would be appropriately sympathetic, compassionate, but not schmucky?"

"You're asking the wrong person. Not knowing what to say is one of the reasons I avoid funeral homes. That, and besides—"

"They give you the creeps."

"Big time. Think about it—you stand around with a bunch of other people who don't want to be there, all of you uncomfortable as hell, trying to think of nice things to say about a dead person most of you barely knew and maybe didn't even like that much…."

"Like how good she looks."

"As if! How can dead look *good*?"

Sharon grinned. "But that's what a lot of people comment about. The makeup, the hair, how natural the corpse looks, what an attractive dress she's wearing…that kind of thing."

"Creepy," Jo declared, feeling vindicated. "At least we won't have to listen to that sort of asinine drivel."

"Probably not. I doubt Flo's casket will be open. You never know, though. Last year, when Ralph Forstner fell headfirst into that corn auger? His mother insisted on an open casket, said his friends should have one last chance to see him before they put him in the ground."

"Oh, Lord," Jo murmured, wiping suddenly damp palms on her skirt. "Surely they won't—" Her right hand levitated in an involuntary gesture of dismay. "—*show* her."

She thought Sharon's mouth tried to twitch into another grin before she got it under control. "I wouldn't think so. If it was *my* family, I know they'd want a closed casket. But cosmetologists can work miracles nowadays, so maybe."

Jo closed her eyes and offered up a heartfelt prayer that she wouldn't have to think of something appropriate to say while gazing down at Flo Johanssen's dead, painted face. The biggest reason funeral homes gave her the creeps was because they were always occupied by dead people. Who were usually wearing too much rouge. By the time Sharon found an empty space in the Bates Mortuary parking lot, Jo's stomach felt like a giant clenched fist.

"Looks like half the town is here," Sharon said as they headed up the sidewalk toward the entrance. She sounded a little too enthusiastic in Jo's opinion, as if they were about to enter the Elks Lodge on singles night.

Sharon was right, though. The joint wasn't exactly jumping, but a sizable crowd spilled out of the "parlor" that held Flo's mortal remains and into the large foyer. While waiting in line to sign in as a visitor, Jo spotted the mayor, the bank president, the owners of several local businesses, three ministers, approximately half the high school faculty, and about a jillion teenagers. The number of teachers and students wasn't surprising. The recently departed Flo and her husband, Bob, both taught at the high school. Most of the kids looked as miserably uncomfortable as Jo felt. Of course it was possible that their misery was actually caused by grief.

"Quite a turnout, huh?"

Recognizing the deep, sonorous baritone, Jo turned to face Sheriff Angus McCormick. Damn. Of all the people she'd have wished *not* to run into....

"Hello, Sheriff. Yes, evidently Flo had a lot of friends."

One side of his full mouth lifted in a mocking half smile. "C'mon, Madam Prosecutor. We both know most of these people are here just to get a look at her, see if the rumors are true."

Jo ducked her head and studied the glossy gray marble floor, caught between the impulse to agree with him and a more politically correct conditioned response. Of course he was right, but damn! The man was either the most scrupulously honest person she'd ever met, or the most tactless, insensitive clod. Unfortunately, she didn't know him well enough to make the call. This was only the third time they'd met, and he'd managed, with no apparent effort, to completely discombobulate her the first two times. He was on a roll, three for three, batting a thousand.

Deciding that any response would be better than stupefied silence, she murmured, "That's a pretty harsh judgment."

"I wasn't passing judgment."

Jo tilted her head to give him a skeptical look.

"Curiosity isn't a crime, or even a sin, so far as I know." He lowered his voice and leaned a few inches closer. "And considering some of the rumors...." He trailed off with a shake of his head that could have signified either disgust or amused disbelief.

"I know," Jo muttered. Although at the moment she wasn't really focused on the rumors about the circumstances surrounding Flo Johanssen's death. She was wondering whether the sheriff was wearing musk cologne, or if that was just his own natural essence. Whichever, the effect was potent, which only intensified her uneasiness. Belatedly realizing that all the people between her and the visitors' book had moved on, she seized the excuse to step away from him. McCormick and the pheromone cloud surrounding him followed her.

"Is the, uh...the casket, is it open?" Jo stammered as she scribbled her name.

"I don't know. I came in right behind you and Sharon. Funeral homes make you uncomfortable?"

"Gee, how'd you guess?" she said dryly. "Was it the sweat on my forehead? The desperate glint in my eyes?"

His grin was startling, wide and spontaneous, until he remembered where they were and replaced it with an appropriately solemn expression.

"No, it was the way you almost choked on the word *casket*," he said as he added his signature beneath hers. "Speaking of which..."

Casually planting a hand on the small of her back, he steered her toward one of four wide doorways leading off the foyer. A discreet sign on an easel beside the door identified this particular parlor as the temporary resting place of Floradora Johanssen.

"Floradora?" he murmured in surprise.

"She was named for a rose," Jo explained.

"No wonder she preferred Flo. What kind of person would name a baby Floradora?"

"An avid rosarian."

She knew what he was doing. The small talk served as a distraction while that hand on her back gently but firmly urged her forward, through the thinning crowd and across the room. She was pleasantly surprised that he made the effort. Maybe he wasn't such a hard case after all.

"You've done this a lot, haven't you?"

"Looked at dead people? Too many times."

She didn't doubt it; he'd served two tours in Vietnam and spent twenty years with the DEA before "retiring" to his hometown in southern Indiana and ending up as the county sheriff.

"I meant escorted people to places they'd really rather not go."

"That, too," he acknowledged. "So, what have you heard?"

Jo stopped so abruptly that his left shoulder collided with her back. "About Flo?" she said under her breath, at the same time thinking, *Surely not, he couldn't be asking what rumors she'd heard.*

"Yeah. I heard she had a delayed reaction to something the plastic surgeon gave her, and her face swelled so much the stitches ripped loose."

"Good God," Jo muttered.

She was appalled. What was he thinking, for heaven's sake— gossiping about Flo's death right there in the room where her casket was on display? Only a couple dozen feet from her grieving family! She pivoted to poke a discreet elbow into his solar plexus and gave him an exasperated look.

"Shush! Someone will hear you."

The admonition was a bit late. Mitch Pierce, who owned the town's hardware store, sidled up on McCormick's right to confide in what he probably thought was a whisper, "But that wasn't what killed her. I heard it was the liposuction she had last month. The thingamajig they used to suck out the fat was contaminated, gave her a blood infection."

"No, no, that's wrong!"

This from Mitch's wife, Elaine, who suddenly materialized to join the discussion. "I just heard from Erma Hudgins that it wasn't the infection that killed her." Elaine paused a beat for dramatic effect, then declared, "It was a heart attack."

"That's what I heard, too," chimed in Pete Rautenberg, who had been headed for the door when Elaine's news flash snagged his attention.

Jo glanced around anxiously. Lord, how far were their voices carrying?

"Who'd you hear it from?" Mitch demanded. Evidently he didn't consider Erma Hudgins a reliable source.

"Trish Eberhardt, who got it straight from Heidi West. Heidi works for Doc Dennison, and he's Lloyd Bates's vet."

"Well, then," Elaine said with a "see, I told you so" nod at her doubting husband. Lloyd Bates was the county coroner, so naturally information that had originated with an employee of the veterinarian who gave Lloyd's dogs their rabies shots had to be considered irrefutable.

Pete suddenly grinned and reached out to tap Jo's upper arm with his fist. "Hey, Jo, great to see you." Evidently he'd just noticed her standing there.

Startled out of her dumbfounded spectator status, Jo stared at him blankly for a second.

"Hi, Pete. Good to see you, too."

The pressure of the sheriff's hand, which had never budged from her lower back, increased for a moment. A gesture of support? A heads-up caution? (Pete did reek of gin, but he hadn't tapped her that hard.) A signal for her to move?

"Sheriff, I'd think if anybody would know the cause of Flo's death, it'd be you," Elaine remarked coyly.

McCormick smiled and shook his head. "Sorry, Elaine. The death occurred in Vanderburgh County. All I know is what her obituary said—that she died 'from complications following surgery.'"

This time there was no question about the message his hand was conveying; it pushed so hard that Jo had to take a hasty step or land face-down on the carpet.

"Excuse us," McCormick said as he moved forward with her. "They'll be closing soon and we haven't paid our respects."

When they were several feet from Pete and the Pierces, he murmured, "God, I love this town." Jo looked over her shoulder at him and saw laughter dancing in his eyes. "Never a dull moment," he elaborated. "And the people are so…"

"Eccentric?" she suggested. "Nosy? Downright rude?"

"Honest. Plainspoken and often nosy, yeah, I won't argue that. But most of them are honest to the bone. I didn't realize how much I'd missed that—the knowledge that what people say to me is almost always going to be the unvarnished truth, as opposed to what they think I want to hear."

"Even the criminals and miscreants?" Jo asked.

"Especially them. My interview technique is very persuasive."

That was an understatement if she'd ever heard one. Even out of uniform, in khakis and sans tie, he radiated authority and physical strength. And of course there was that voice, which had a power all its own. A couple of weeks ago she'd seen him use it to quietly "persuade" an insolent, tattooed, two-hundred-pound jerk to make an abject apology to his wife for the verbal abuse he'd been dishing out, and then make an appointment to arrange for anger management counseling.

Just as Jo was reflecting on the restraint and diplomacy he'd demonstrated on that occasion, McCormick shoved her between two enormous floral arrangements. She opened her mouth to complain, then closed it when she realized he'd saved her from being trampled by the high school football team, who'd apparently decided to leave en masse and in a hurry.

"Sorry about that," McCormick said. "You okay?"

"Everything but my dignity seems to be intact," she replied from the depths of a miniature rain forest. All she could see of him was the hand that appeared between leaves the size of dinner plates. "Is it safe to come out?"

"Yeah, the stampede's over. So many people left that I can see Floradora's casket. You'll be relieved to know it's closed."

Jo was so gratified by the news that she grabbed his hand and started gingerly making her way out of the jungle…only to be roughly pushed back.

"Hey! What the—"

"Quiet! Stay there," the sheriff ordered. His voice was barely audible, but commanding enough to make her clamp her lips together midsentence.

A second later she heard a shriek—a startled, frightened cry that raised the hair on her arms. Then someone else shouted something unintelligible. Jo squeezed McCormick's hand, though she couldn't have said whether it was a reflex action or a wordless plea for explanation.

But apparently the sheriff was preoccupied with the disturbance, whatever it was. His only response was to yank his hand from her grip. Although Jo couldn't hear anything over the incomprehensible babble of alarmed voices, she thought he was moving away. Determined to find out what was going on, she parted the foliage in front of her face and peered out.

She was just in time to see Zane Wilkes point a gun at the ceiling and fire a round into one of the air-conditioning vents.

Jo ducked back behind the greenery, her heart pounding so hard that for a while the whooshing thud of her own pulse was the only sound she was aware of. She sagged against the wall at her back and breathed deeply through her mouth. Holy shit. Why in God's name had the president of the high school chess club brought a *gun* to the funeral home?

When her initial shock started to recede, two things became clear. First, a smart, levelheaded kid like Zane Wilkes wouldn't do something like this unless he'd completely flipped out. Second, and even more alarming, in addition to the handgun he'd fired into the ceiling, Jo was sure she'd seen another weapon—a hunting rifle, she thought—slung over his shoulder, alongside a large backpack. Which meant that whatever he was doing, it probably hadn't been a spur-of-the-moment decision.

She had no idea what *she* could or should do, but she was the assistant prosecutor, an officer of the court. She couldn't just stand there hiding behind a bunch of plants, despite McCormick's instruction to do exactly that. And where the hell was he, anyway? He was the county sheriff; he should be dealing with this situation. Jo scrunched into a half squat to peek through a gap in the foliage, hoping to see that he'd taken charge and "persuaded" Zane to hand over his weapons. Her view was severely restricted, but McCormick's khakis were nowhere in sight. The only person talking now was Zane. He pointed the handgun at David Nesbitt, who, if she wasn't mistaken, was the Johanssens' family physician.

"Over here, next to Mr. Johanssen. You, too, Reverend. Take a seat next to the doctor, but don't get too comfortable."

Not much chance of that, Jo thought. All three men looked terrified. Zane, on the other hand, seemed focused and in control. She had no idea whether that was a good sign or a bad one. McCormick would probably know. Where *was* he?

Zane was facing the opposite side of the room, gesturing with the gun for a fourth person Jo couldn't see to come forward. She might be able to slip out if she moved now. She backed up slowly, one hand behind her to locate the wall. Fortunately a lot of individuals and local businesses had sent potted plants and floral arrangements. Some sat on the floor, others on tables or pedestals of varying heights, so that they provided fairly dense cover almost all the way to the door. Almost, but not quite. She'd have to cross about six feet of open space, and hope that no one saw her and called attention to her.

She impulsively crouched to remove her shoes and set them behind a large vase filled with irises and oriental lilies. A tingly itch in her nose caused a moment of panic. Oh no, what a time for her pollen allergy to kick in. She hunched over and pressed a finger under her nose, exhaling through both nostrils to check the incipient sneeze. When she lifted her head, she was startled to find herself looking at a narrow door. It was covered with the same wallpaper that had been used on the walls, so well camouflaged that she might not have noticed it from five feet away even if it hadn't been hidden by the flowers. Holding her breath, she grasped the dainty porcelain doorknob, turned it, and gently pushed...just enough to create an opening she could fit through. Despite her fears, the hinges didn't screech and give her away. Still, she waited to exhale until she was on the other side of the wall and the door was closed behind her. She sank to her knees and rested her forehead against the smooth, cool wood framing this side of the door.

"Please, Lord, don't let this be the embalming room," she whispered.

A large hand covered her mouth an instant before a godlike voice murmured in her ear, "It's just an office."

Jo knew she would have died, right there on the spot, if the spot had been anywhere else—the county courthouse, a church, the Dairy Queen, a public restroom—but no way was she going to check out in a funeral home.

She pulled McCormick's hand from her mouth. "Give me a heart attack, why don't you!"

He grasped her upper arms and lifted her to her feet. "Sorry. Scaring you out of your wits wasn't my intention. I just didn't want you to scream."

"Well, I probably would have," Jo admitted as she hitched the strap of her shoulder bag back into place and turned to face him. "I guess we know what caused the stampede. How'd you get here?"

"I slipped out with a couple of other people during the initial confusion, right after the kid marched in waving his nine."

"His what?"

"He's got a nine-millimeter semiautomatic, plus God knows what else in the backpack." Taking her arm again, he pulled her toward a door on the far side of the office. "C'mon, we can't stay here.

"He was watching a group of people at the front of the room, near the casket," he continued as they hurried across the office and a small interior hallway. "Either he didn't notice us leaving, or he did notice but didn't care. I'm inclined to think it was the latter."

"His name is Zane Wilkes," Jo said as he ushered her into another, larger office across the hall from the one they'd just left. Kevin Bates, Lloyd's son and partner in the mortuary, was there, standing at one of three desks while he spoke to someone on the telephone. Also present were Erma Hudgins and Flo Johanssen's teenage nephew, Billy Merckle. All three were obviously distraught, but Billy looked like he might start weeping at any second.

"I know who he is," the sheriff said in reply. "Billy here identified Zane for me and was about to enlighten me about why he's using the ductwork for target practice, when I heard you open the door."

Jo stared at him in amazement. He'd *heard* the door open? A second later the rest of what he'd said sank in. She whirled on Billy.

"You knew Zane was going to do this?"

He flinched as if she'd struck him. "No! I thought it was just talk, you know, that he was blowing off steam."

His voice was thin and high-pitched, bordering on hysteria. Jo cast a worried look at the door to the hall, which McCormick had left standing open.

"Shouldn't we—"

"No, it's okay." He put a hand on Billy's bony shoulder and guided him to a chair, then moved another chair and took a seat facing the boy, so close that their knees were almost touching. "Would you please get Billy a glass of water."

He spoke to Jo, but Billy had a hundred percent of his attention. He was working to calm the boy's fear, his movements slow and nonthreatening, his voice soft, patient. Jo placed her shoulder bag on one of the desks and looked around for a water cooler, a fountain, a restroom...

"I've got it." Erma bustled forward carrying a pitcher of water in one hand and a glass in the other.

Jo perched on the desk to the sheriff's left and restrained the urge to start bombarding Billy with questions. He wasn't in the witness box, though he might well end up there. McCormick gave the boy a brief respite, a few seconds to collect himself, while he took the phone from Kevin.

"Okay, Ed, I'm back," he said tersely. "Nothing, Ed, don't do anything, just stay on the line....No, dammit, don't notify anybody until I tell you to. Send one car—that's one car, Ed—to block the entrance to the property. No lights, no siren. Nobody gets closer than that. And Ed? I mean nobody....I don't care what the hell you tell people. Tell 'em we're having an orgy, or the place is under emergency quarantine. But understand this—if I look out the window and see any state police cruisers or television vans, it's your ass. Got it?"

Evidently Chief Deputy Ed Steinmetz replied in the affirmative, because McCormick handed the phone back to Kevin and once again focused his attention on Billy. The kid looked stunned. Not stunned as in intimidated or scared, but awestruck. Jo empathized. She was remembering why she had been less than thrilled to encounter Sheriff McCormick a half-hour or so ago...and reflecting that she was damn glad he was there now.

"Okay, Billy," he said as if the conversation with his chief deputy hadn't taken place. "What's Zane doing here? What provoked this?"

Billy drew a shuddering breath. "He's mad. Really pissed."

"Yeah, I sensed that," McCormick drawled. "Who's he mad at, and why?"

Billy hung his head. "Everybody who hurt Aunt Flo, or didn't do anything to help her. By rights, that should include me, I guess."

McCormick shot Jo a questioning look. She shook her head in response.

"Hurt her how, Billy?" she asked.

He shrugged. "Lots of ways. Uncle Bob was always criticizing, telling her she was getting fat and starting to show her age...said she was a lousy cook and she spent too much money on stupid things. Then Mr. Yellig gave her two bad evaluations in a row, so it was like he was on her case, too."

"Teacher performance evaluations, you mean?" Jo asked. Virgil Yellig was the high school principal.

Billy nodded glumly. "She was afraid she'd lose her job. Uncle Bob is...what do you call it?"

"Tenured," McCormick said.

"Yeah, right. He's been a teacher forever, but Aunt Flo just got her certificate a couple years ago and she was still on probation. She knew if she lost her job, Bob would blow his stack. 'Cause he was already gripin' about all the money she spent on clothes and makeup and stuff, I mean."

"Which she thought she needed because he'd convinced her she was a fat, ugly hag," Erma chimed in, sounding outraged.

The sheriff ignored the outburst, signaling his impatience and a sense of urgency with a quick glance at his watch. "Tragic as all this may be, Billy, it doesn't explain why Zane Wilkes is holding several people at gunpoint right now. Don't tell me he always reacts this way to emotional abuse."

"No," Billy mumbled. He lowered his gaze to stare at the water glass, which he was clutching with both hands. "Zane and Aunt Flo..." He squirmed in discomfort, his neck and face turning bright red. "They were...uh..."

"Lovers," Jo finished for him when it seemed he might choke

trying to get the word out.

Billy's muffled "Yeah" was drowned out by Erma's strangled gasp and Kevin's shocked, "Lovers!"

The sheriff silenced them both with a freezing look. "I need you to think, Billy," he murmured, laying a hand on the boy's arm. "Besides Bob Johanssen and Virgil Yellig, who else does Zane blame for Flo's death?"

Billy shook his head in abject misery. "Lots of people. He didn't tell me who all of 'em are, just said a lot of people were to blame."

Jo abandoned her perch on the desk to stand beside McCormick. "Doctor Nesbitt? Reverend Tyler?" she asked. When Billy nodded, she explained, "Zane singled them out, made them sit with Bob Johanssen."

"Who else?" McCormick pressed.

But the boy had reached his breaking point. "I don't *know!*" he wailed. "Oh, Jesus, is he gonna kill them? He won't really kill all those people, will he?"

McCormick squeezed the boy's arm, at the same time pressing him back into the chair. "No." His voice was quiet but rock solid, his gaze locked with Billy's. "That's not going to happen. I'm going to go talk to him, and we'll straighten out this mess so everybody can go home."

His reassurance had begun to visibly calm the boy, but that last sentence made Billy bolt upright, eyes wide with panic.

"He won't talk to you! He won't *listen* to you! If you go in there, it'll just make him more pissed!"

The brusque shake of McCormick's head told Jo that he'd automatically dismissed the boy's opinion. Billy obviously thought so, too. He turned to her in desperation.

"You gotta believe me, Miss Haynes. A couple months ago Zane talked to one of the city cops. Don't ask me which one, 'cause I won't tell. Zane told him how Bob was treating Aunt Flo and said somebody should have a talk with him, tell him to either treat her right or leave."

Jo was fairly sure the city officer Zane had spoken to was George Kelly, Bob Johanssen's best friend since high school.

"The cop told Zane to mind his own business," Billy said bitterly.

"Said it wasn't his job to make husbands and wives get along with each other, and if Aunt Flo wasn't happy, *she* could leave, or maybe talk to a marriage counselor."

"So Zane feels let down or betrayed by the policeman he went to for help," Jo murmured. Then, addressing the sheriff, "Billy's probably right. You may not be the best person to approach him."

"I bet he'd talk to *you*, though," Billy said before McCormick could reply.

The sheriff vaulted out of his chair and barked, "Absolutely not!" at virtually the same instant Jo stammered, "Who...me?"

"He knows you," Billy pointed out. "He likes you, too. He says you're the smartest woman he's ever met."

Jo gaped at the boy. "Zane said that?"

"Don't even think about it," McCormick growled. "Get the idea right out of your head."

"He does know me," she argued, and wondered if she'd lost her mind. "I'm one of the chess club sponsors."

"Good for you," McCormick shot back. "Zane Wilkes didn't come here to take part in a chess tournament."

"Uh, excuse me, Sheriff," Kevin interrupted in his most soothing undertaker's voice. "Ed wants me to tell you that the patrol car is here, blocking the drive."

"Thanks," McCormick snapped without breaking eye contact with Jo.

"I could appeal to him with reason and logic," Jo suggested. "Zane is extremely intelligent. He has a real talent for strategic analysis."

"Which means he's probably anticipated that we'll send somebody in—"

"But he won't have anticipated that it'll be me."

"And it won't be. You aren't qualified—"

"I beg your pardon!" She interrupted him for the second time, indignation prevailing over courtesy. "For your information, I've questioned and cross-examined hardened criminals."

McCormick's left eyebrow rose a sardonic centimeter. "How many of them were pointing a loaded gun at you at the time?"

Jo couldn't immediately produce a retort to that, but Erma

chose that moment to weigh in with her opinion.

"I agree with the two of them—Jo should go in there and try to talk some sense into him," she said confidently.

If looks could kill, the one McCormick shot her would have put Erma in intensive care. She didn't flinch.

"For heaven's sake, Sheriff, disconnect your stupid male ego for a minute and think. This boy is full of anger at the *men* he holds responsible for Flo's death. Now, who's he more likely to be willing to listen to—a male authority figure, or a woman he already trusts and respects?"

Jo managed not to smile, but she couldn't resist the impulse to remark, "I believe that would qualify as some of the plainspoken honesty you value so highly."

For a second she thought McCormick was going to let her have it, really rip into her. But then his mouth twisted in an ironic smile and she felt her tensed muscles relax.

"Tell Ed we're going in," he said to Kevin. "If we're not back in thirty minutes, he should call Captain Richmond at the state police post."

"Good luck," Erma called softly as they left.

They took the long way around, approaching the parlor via the front foyer so Zane wouldn't think someone was trying to sneak in and take him by surprise.

"Scared?" McCormick asked as they approached the end of the hallway.

"Oh, yeah," Jo murmured.

"Good. You should be. The nine-millimeter holds eleven rounds—enough for the two of us and nine other people."

"If this is your idea of a pep talk, I have to tell you, it sucks," she replied. "Anyway, he fired one round into the ceiling, so now he has ten, not eleven. Of course that's not taking the rifle into account. Please don't tell me how many bullets a rifle holds, I'd really rather not know."

McCormick grabbed her arm and yanked her to a halt halfway across the foyer. "He has a rifle?"

Panic flared in her chest. "Christ, I thought you knew that." She thought she might faint. "You didn't know about the rifle?"

He inhaled a long, deep breath, then released it in a rush. His lips compressed to form a taut seam. Jo could almost *feel* him suppressing the urge to shake her. "Damn it, I should've trusted my own judgment. You're going back to wait with the others."

He'd pulled her a couple of yards before she collected her wits and started resisting. Unfortunately, the feet of her pantyhose provided no friction whatsoever on the polished marble floor.

"No, stop!" she hissed. "I'm all right, really. I just got a little—"

"Hysterical." His harsh whisper made it an indictment, but at least he stopped dragging her across the foyer.

"Anxious," she corrected stubbornly. "Oh, all right, petrified, but only for a second. I'm okay now. Anyway, you *said* it was good that I'm scared!"

She saw a faint glint of surprise, and just maybe admiration, in his eyes. She quickly pressed on, not giving him a chance to argue.

"I can do this. I can. Back to the rifle—I could be mistaken; it might be a shotgun. I saw a long black barrel, hanging on his backpack. Come to think of it, it looked too fat to be a rifle barrel."

McCormick shook his head decisively and started walking again, but back in the direction they'd originally been headed, pulling her with him. As relief washed through Jo, she reflected giddily that his left hand had spent so much time pushing or pulling or grabbing or yanking her around tonight that it might as well be surgically grafted to her body.

"I saw it, too. But whatever it is, it isn't a gun," he whispered as they reached the parlor entrance.

They stopped simultaneously, frozen in surprise and confusion as they took in the scene before them. McCormick was right. The long black tube they'd both seen wasn't a gun. It was one leg of a tripod.

A video camera, which Zane had presumably carried in the backpack, sat on top of the tripod, beside Flo's casket. Sharon had been drafted to serve as vidcam operator. She sat on a chair behind the tripod, evidently using the camera to document individual statements. As Jo and McCormick watched, Zane instructed Reverend Tyler to take the seat Dr. Nesbitt occupied directly in front of the camera. The doctor got up without a word and moved to the last folding chair in the row, distancing himself from both the reverend and Bob Johanssen. He didn't appear to be in fear for his life, but rather completely demoralized.

Jo turned to the sheriff with a perplexed frown—were they witnessing what she thought they were witnessing? He nodded pensively, then inclined his head to indicate that they should enter the parlor. Despite a careful scrutiny of his eyes and his facial expression, she couldn't detect the slightest hint of uncertainty. Personally, Jo thought it might be better to wait until Zane finished taping what appeared to be a series of forced confessions, let him finish what he'd started. He probably wouldn't appreciate being interrupted. But on second thought, what if his plan was to force the men to confess and then kill them?

She might have stood there the rest of the night, seesawing between equally ruinous possibilities, if McCormick hadn't planted his hand in the middle of her back and given her an impatient push.

She drew a steadying breath and stepped forward as if she knew precisely what she was going to say and what the result would be.

"Zane?"

Her voice emerged so soft and embarrassingly timid that she wondered if he'd heard her. He looked up, blinked in surprise, then saw McCormick and scowled.

"Hi, Miss Haynes. You can come in, but he has to wait outside."

As Zane spoke he raised his right arm, which had been hanging relaxed at his side, and pointed the gun at McCormick. Jo was close enough to see that his hand trembled slightly. She wished she knew whether it was because he was on the brink of a total emotional meltdown, or because pointing a gun at the county sheriff scared the bejesus out of him.

"No, Zane, you need him here," she said with a lot more confidence than she felt. "If you're doing what I think you're doing, who better to serve as an official witness?" She continued into the parlor as she made the point, managing to put herself between the gun and McCormick. She could imagine how Mr. Macho Lawman was reacting to that, but he'd get over it. In her considered opinion, Zane was much more likely to shoot the sheriff than her.

Zane blinked again then raised his free hand to rub at his eyes. Jo was now close enough to see that they were red-rimmed and bloodshot, his complexion wan. She also observed that his clothes were wrinkled and his usually neat hair stood in spikes. Poor kid probably hadn't slept since he heard about Flo's death.

"Let him stay." She was careful to make it a request, not a demand.

The boy's head bobbed in agreement. "Sit back there, Sheriff," he directed. A sloppy waggle of the gun indicated a spot in the center of at least four dozen precisely arranged folding chairs. Smart, Jo thought; McCormick would have to clamber over several rows to get to him. She glanced back to check that the sheriff was complying. He was, though he didn't look happy about it.

"You come stand up front, between Sharon and me," Zane instructed. "I wish I'd known you were here. You could've got these bastards to confess a lot faster."

"So that is what you're doing." A quick glance at Sharon eased her anxiety somewhat. Sharon looked nervous, but not terrified. Of course, Jo couldn't imagine what it would take to terrify Sharon Hancock.

"All of these assholes are at least partly to blame for Flo's death," Zane told her, his voice hoarse with emotion. "All three of 'em either mistreated her or betrayed her."

Jo impulsively reached out to lay a hand on the boy's right shoulder. Realizing how close she was to the gun he was waving around as if it were a baton, she glanced at the sheriff. He glared back at her and gave an emphatic shake of his head, which she interpreted to mean: No, for God's sake, you idiot, don't try to take it away from him!

Jo administered a sympathetic pat to Zane's shoulder and withdrew her hand. "Billy gave us a little background information." She saw Bob Johanssen lean forward and start to blurt out something, then look at the gun. His Adam's apple worked as he reconsidered and sank back against the chair.

"Billy didn't know what I was going to do," Zane said. "I didn't tell anybody ahead of time, so nobody but me should take the blame for this."

"Nobody else will." McCormick's deep, imposing voice caused everyone but Sharon to give a nervous little start. "And Billy didn't rat you out. He's your friend and he's worried. He doesn't want anyone else to get hurt, that's all."

Jo caught that "else" and she was sure Zane had, too. McCormick was letting him know that they understood the reasons for his anger, but without endorsing his actions.

"We know why you're so pissed at Bob," he added after a slight pause. "But what about the others? What did the doctor and Reverend Tyler do?"

Zane eagerly seized the opportunity to catalog their sins, as the sheriff had no doubt anticipated. "He"—swinging the gun toward the doctor—"referred her to the butchers who gave her sepsis and caused a fatal heart attack!"

"But Doctor Nesbitt didn't perform any of the procedures, Zane," Jo murmured reasonably.

"He knew she was emotionally unstable!" he shot back. "He should have tried to talk her out of having cosmetic surgery, or at least recommended counseling beforehand. That's what doctors are supposed to do."

"He probably knew that cosmetic surgeons often require potential patients to talk to a therapist," McCormick told him, but Zane wasn't appeased.

"Those guys didn't know her...he did! He knew Bob had destroyed her self-esteem and turned her into an emotional basket case. Doctors are supposed to help people, not just take their insurance money and then pass them off to some other mercenary quack."

His agitation was beginning to alarm Jo. "All right, you've made your case against Doctor Nesbitt," she said briskly. "And you may have legitimate grounds for a malpractice investigation. What about Reverend Tyler? Why is he here?"

The minister, a tall, dignified man in his early sixties, spoke up before Zane could answer. "I failed Flo, too. Several weeks ago she came to me after a friend—" He paused to bestow a sad smile on Zane. "—urged her to seek counseling. Her marriage was deeply troubled. She wanted me to tell her it would be all right to end it."

"But you didn't," Zane accused. "You told her to stay and 'work things out,' be more 'tolerant and forgiving' of her husband's faults."

"Yes," Reverend Tyler admitted. "At the time I truly believed it was the best counsel I could give."

"At the time," Zane repeated bitterly.

"That's right, son." He lifted both hands, palms up. "Would I repeat the same counsel today, considering what's happened since she came to me? Probably not. But I believe strongly in the sanctity of marriage, so neither would I encourage her to file for divorce."

Zane's pale face flushed crimson and the hand holding the gun twitched in angry reaction. McCormick stood up and casually side-stepped to the end of the row of chairs.

"Easy, Zane," he said softly. "Hindsight is always twenty-twenty. We've all done things we regret or wish we could undo."

"Amen to that," Sharon murmured from her place behind the camera.

"But people should have to pay for their mistakes!" Zane cried.

"We do," Jo assured him. "Believe me, we all do pay, every day. Just because you don't *see* someone being punished doesn't mean he isn't suffering a terrible punishment."

"She's right," McCormick said. He'd taken advantage of the boy's distraction to move in front of Reverend Tyler. Zane backed up a step, raising the gun to the level of the sheriff's chest. Jo stopped breathing for a moment, but McCormick completely ignored the weapon.

"Take a look at Doctor Nesbitt," he said. "He's going to have to live with this particular error in judgment the rest of his life. Same for the reverend. He may have strong religious objections to divorce, but something tells me he won't be quite so inclined to dispense trite, simplistic advice from now on."

Zane's lower lip quivered and tears brimmed in his eyes. Jo was sure he was about to hand the gun over, or maybe drop it and col- lapse from sheer exhaustion. Instead, he suddenly spun toward Bob Johanssen, his arm flying up, elbow extended stiffly to aim the gun at Bob's head.

"What about that son of a bitch!" he demanded, his voice shak- ing with rage and grief. "Look at him, the arrogant bastard! He isn't *suffering*, he doesn't even feel guilty for the way he treated her! What's his punishment going to be?"

Everything happened so fast that only later could Jo reconstruct the sequence. Zane took an awkward step forward, lurching toward Bob. There was a startled yelp—presumably from Sharon—and the soft thud of the camera and tripod hitting the floor as Jo impulsively grabbed Zane's left wrist, the only part of him within reach. Reverend Tyler jumped up, frantically attempting to get out of harm's way, stumbled over his chair, and somehow ended up sprawled in the row of chairs behind him.

Fortunately McCormick moved faster and with much better dexterity than anyone, including Zane. His left hand closed over the gun and forced Zane's arm down, so that the barrel pointed harmlessly at the floor. Other than that, he did nothing to restrain the boy.

"No," he said gently. "No, Zane. His punishment will be having to live in this town." He didn't have to add, because everyone present was thinking it: "Where everybody he meets, every single day, will know what a bastard he was to his wife."

Zane made a strangled sound and fell to his knees, wrenching sobs tearing at his chest. Driven purely by instinct, Jo dropped to her knees beside him and wrapped her arms around him as McCormick removed the gun from his hand. Without a word, Sharon righted the tripod, removed the videocassette from the camera, and handed it to the sheriff.

"I...I wouldn't have shot him," Zane managed to say after a while. "I just...I just wanted to scare him, make the bastard *feel* something!"

"I know," McCormick murmured. Holding the gun high so that everyone could see, he explained. "He had the safety set to on."

The next hour passed in a blur for Jo, who felt so emotionally and physically drained that she could barely hold herself upright. McCormick had quickly and efficiently taken care of everything— phoning Zane's parents and arranging for them to be at the county jail when their son arrived, calling a couple of clerks to the funeral home to take the preliminary statements, fielding calls from three area television stations and two newspapers. The man was too damn capable by far, she reflected as she sat on the curb and contemplated the gritty asphalt in front of her. Surely he had a *few* faults or weaknesses.

"You still here?" the object of her thoughts said when he exited the funeral home a few minutes later.

"Believe me, it isn't by choice. I finished dictating my statement and went to collect my shoes. By the time I got outside Sharon had taken off without me. I'm giving her time to get home, then I'm gonna call and lay a humongous guilt trip on her."

"She probably thought you'd caught a ride with someone else."

"Probably." Jo pushed off the curb and his left hand—surprise!— slipped under her arm to pull her the rest of the way up. Suddenly she wasn't quite so exhausted. "But it's too good a chance to pass up," she told him. "Opportunities to make Sharon feel guilty are extremely rare."

He smiled and inclined his head toward his brown and tan county car, parked near the back of the lot. "So save it until you need a big favor. I'll give you a lift. I'll even throw in a hot-fudge sundae from DQ."

"Oh, God, you mean it?" Jo said with shameless eagerness. "I desperately need a sugar fix."

"Me, too," he said as his hand found its spot on her back and they started toward his car. "It's been a hell of a night."

"That it has," Jo agreed. "We deserve to indulge ourselves with some comfort food."

"Absolutely." They reached the car. He unlocked and opened the passenger door, waited till she was inside, then leaned down to add in a conspiratorial whisper, "Besides, don't tell anybody, but funeral homes give me the willies."

Jo smiled and leaned back against the seat. Now that was a weakness, and a man she could relate to.

Dizzy and  the Biker

Susan Sizemore

"Report says the woman said her dog's a cat. That ain't right."

Detective Sergeant Mike Moran looked up over the computer screen. He was happy for the diversion. It was a hot summer afternoon, and the air conditioning wasn't working very well. A lot of work had piled up while he was on vacation. "What you working on, Charlie?" he asked the detective who had spoken.

Charles Boromeo came over with a suspicious eagerness and tossed a folder to him. "You're the animal guy. You tell me. Got a murder in a park. Dead end, so far. Witness got hit on the head. Says she doesn't remember anything. Storm washed away any physical evidence an hour after the crime. There's a kidnapped puppy—dognapped puppy—involved."

"O—kaay." Moran leaned back in his chair and opened the jacket on the folder. A few seconds later he grinned up at Boromeo. "A murder at Franciscan Place. This is great."

Captain Cutler broke through a crowd of uniforms by the water cooler to join them as Moran spoke. "Great?" she asked. "Some poor old guy got whacked for his fancy dog and the only witness was assaulted."

"Well, yeah," Moran agreed. "That's terrible. We have to find the murderer, and the puppy." He ran his index finger up and down the report. "The guy, Alec Penhurst, was in his seventies, with no relatives. This happened a week ago." He couldn't help but sound gleeful. "His place is going to be up for sale—and I'm top of the waiting list!"

"Would that make you a suspect, Sergeant Moran?" Cutler was not happy with his attitude.

Moran was not fazed by her annoyance. "Got witnesses to my whereabouts on—" He checked the date. "June fourth. I've been trying to get into Franciscan Place since Dizzy was a pup. You know how you get a condo at Franciscan Place? Most people inherit them. The whole complex started out as a commune in the seventies. A group of urban animal lovers bought up some abandoned buildings in the warehouse district long before the area was trendy. They renovated the condo building on part of it. Turned the other forty acres into parkland." He gave a cynical laugh. "The last time a one-bedroom place was empty—the old lady died of natural causes—I was all set to move in, when, bam, out of nowhere, a great-niece from down in the bayou decides she wants to come and live in the big city. Association had to give the place to her rather than to me. I'm on a list for two years, then this backcountry Cajun cook moves into my home on a whim. Dizzy was heartbroken. But at least we still get to use the Franciscan Place exercise park. If your application is approved and you pay an annual fee anybody can use the park three times a week."

"That's where the murder took place," Cutler said. "Residents think somebody jumped the fence, grabbed the pooch—"

"A porcelain dog," Boromeo said. He scratched his head. "That makes as much sense as the woman claiming her dog's a cat."

Moran consulted the report again. "A Porcelaine. It's a fancy French breed. Very few in the States. Stupid motive for murder, but it is a rare breed. Are we sure that's the motive for the murder?" Moran wondered. He tapped the report. "No physical evidence."

"Hey," Boromeo asked, "if this was a dog park, how come the dogs didn't notice this old guy being attacked? How come this woman's cat dog didn't come to her defense?"

Moran consulted the witness statement, and quoted, "'You obviously don't know anything about dogs, Officer. They form an instant pack for playing when they're out here. Most of the animals were down by the front pond. And Harley—well, if you want some pigs rounded up from the swamp he's your dog. I don't expect him to be something he isn't—but if he thinks he's getting steak anytime soon after letting me get hit on the head he's sadly mistaken.'" Moran smiled. She understood dogs. He checked the name on the report. Yep, Sugar LaRoux. She was definitely the woman who'd stolen his condo out from under Dizzy's nose.

"Listen," he said to Cutler. "Why don't I take over the investigation? I've got an idea how to handle it...."

୧୧୧

"Be good, Dizzy."

Moran slipped off her leash. She took off down the path, heading straight for the churned-up mud of the pond. Another dog was already splashing around in the reed bed near the stand of young willow trees. It was the middle of the afternoon, and it looked like Moran and the other dog's owner were the only people in this part of the Franciscan animal park. That was fine with Moran. He held back for a moment, studying the woman's profile while she watched her big dog wading in the water.

Frankly, she looked like a Sugar LaRoux. She had lush bosoms peeking above the scooped neck of a mint green T-shirt. She wore tan shorts that emphasized a heart-shaped bottom, and legs that went on for about three weeks. She had dark auburn hair, long and curling, and full lips that were so kissable they looked dipped in honey. He'd always had a soft spot for redheads. Moran would have recognized her as a "Sugar" from miles away.

Of course, the row of stitches and bruises that showed when she turned fully toward him was a strong clue as well. Somebody had hit her very, very hard, and the sight sent an unfamiliar jolt of anger through him. Moran had grown cynical in his job, but not so cynical that he couldn't still feel outrage and anger for a victim. He didn't usually get a sudden urge of protectiveness, though, or an electric jolt of desire when his gaze met that of a witness—who might be a suspect and was certainly...gorgeous.

"Will you get a look at that, Harley?" Sugar asked over the throbbing racket of frog mating ritual. "That is one pretty animal." She was referring to the sleek and happy Irish setter trotting toward them down the path, tongue flapping and a wide, doggie grin on its muzzle. Its dark red coat gleamed like silk in the sunlight. Harley's nose came up out of the mud at the appearance of a new dog. He gave a bark and took off like a shot.

"You be good," Sugar called after her big boy.

Then she looked past the dogs and saw the human following the Setter. She almost whistled. *That* was indeed one gorgeous creature, of the human male variety. Tall, dark, and handsome was the term, right? Well, he filled the bill on all three counts. Nice legs, too, she thought, sweeping her gaze up from his feet to long, strong thighs, narrow waist, broad chest and shoulders and back to the newcomer's face.

He was staring at her, so she didn't feel quite as rude as she might have for staring back. Of course he was staring. She touched her fingers to the bruises on her face, and the ugly aching marks on her left leg. She wasn't exactly an object of desire right now, but her current appearance certainly drew the eye. People usually looked quickly away, though. Not this guy.

The low, throbbing pain had been a part of her existence for several days now, so much so that she'd almost forgotten what it was like without it. What really worried her was that she'd forgotten several other things as well, which left her shaky inside despite her outward show of confidence. For example, this man she'd never seen before might be the one who'd hit her. She didn't *know*. That made her wary, and angry—with herself, and whoever the bastard was who'd smashed her skull and left her worried it would happen again. She was an open, voluble sort of person. Fear did not suit her lifestyle, but she couldn't help but be aware of being nervous at the man's interest in her, even though the slight fear was overlaid by an instant physical attraction.

So she fought down the visceral interest the man evoked, told herself that primal mating urges were on hold at present, and said to him, "Nice dog." If there was one thing that was a safe and neutral subject around here, it was pets—companion animals, babies, darlings—whatever you wanted to call them, love for animals was the one passion everyone indulged in at Franciscan Place. A hit man wouldn't have a pet as flighty as an Irish setter, would he?

She made herself look back at the dogs, and the man on the path did the same. Just as—

"Harley!"

"Dizzy!"

They leaped forward at the same time.

"Get off her!" Moran grabbed the male dog's heavy collar.

"Don't touch him!"

The dog growled. Dizzy snapped. The woman's shoulder banged solidly into Moran's, and the next thing Mike Moran knew he was lying on his back with the lush redhead's body on top of him. Under other circumstances this would have been a most pleasant sensation. Hot breath warmed his cheeks. His gaze went quickly from side to side and saw that the dogs were standing on either side of them. The animals were tense, but at least they weren't fighting, or—

"What kind of dog have you got, lady?" Moran demanded. He put his hands on her trim waist. The intent was to push her off, but his fingers and palms came into contact with warm bare skin, and lingered. "Having sex with a stranger is—"

"That was a dominance game." The woman shifted so that their gazes met. He was very aware of the soft weight of her breasts pressing against his chest. Her eyes were green, flecked with gold. One was swollen nearly shut.

"I know all about dominance games," Moran answered.

"I just bet you do."

His body tightened at the sultry sound of her voice, his body tried to disconnect all higher brain function. He saw that she'd shocked herself. The look on her bruised face told him that she didn't say such provocative things and didn't know where *that* had come from. The round O of surprise that shaped her mouth made kissing her mandatory. He would have, too.

Then Dizzy barked in his ear.

"Jealous bitch," he muttered. He and the woman helped each other up and brushed off the cedar chips and blades of grass that clung to their clothing. He noticed that where she wasn't bruised, she was blushing. That he found it charming bothered him. *Business*, he told himself. *She's an assault victim, murder witness, possible suspect. She's—*

"Cassandra LaRoux," she said.

He grinned. "But everybody calls you Sugar."

"How'd you know that?" She put her hands on her wonderfully curvaceous hips.

Mike tried hard not to look at those hips. "You're a famous celebrity chef."

She shrugged. "I'm a good cook."

Which was something else to find attractive about her. "Hey!" He pushed her dog's huge head away from his crotch. "What the hell kind of dog is that?" he asked Sugar LaRoux, but his attention was drawn away before she could answer as Dizzy took off, with Sugar's dog bounding after her.

"They like each other," Sugar said.

"He likes her all right," Moran said darkly.

"Now there's a protective daddy talking. Better to have them playing than mating, don't you think?"

"Maybe."

"Hey, Harley doesn't take to just any dog. Not usually without whupping 'em in a fight first. He's a rough, tough, stock dog raised in the bayous. Harley don't take nothin' from nobody. But I think we have love at first sniff here. Looks like he and—"

"Dizzy."

"Good name for an Irish setter. Harley's a Catahoula leopard dog. A cat."

"He looks like a biker." He shook his head. "Looks like my little girl's got a crush on a bad boy."

"That happens a lot."

Moran grinned at her as she gave a squeak of surprise and her hand flew to her mouth. "Maybe it's the concussion," he suggested.

Sugar damned her strangely loose tongue and ignored his mention of her injuries. She tried hard to focus on the dogs and not on how sexy his legs looked in his sporty athletic shorts. Harley and Dizzy were currently stalking a pair of ducks who floated serenely in the center of the pond. "There's instant attraction there," Sugar said as the dogs wheeled and chased each other back and forth along the shallow edge of the pond, tongues lolling and fur getting splattered with mud. She tried to keep her attention on the dogs, but was hampered by the same instant attraction Harley was showing toward the silky red-furred beauty who matched him for speed and energy.

"I'm Mike Moran," he finally introduced himself.

She gave him a direct look with her one good eye. "You're not a hit man by any chance, are you?"

He didn't show a bit of surprise. "I'm moving into Mr. Penhurst's place. Sorry to hear about Mr. Penhurst," he added. He whistled at his dog.

After a few moments, Dizzy split away from her new playmate and came running back up the path. Instead of stopping by her owner, she flew past where he and Sugar stood and trotted up the path that led to the rear of the exercise park. Harley followed the Irish setter.

"Walk with me," Mike Moran suggested.

"Look's like Harley's already made up my mind about where we're going today."

"Don't want to go back there where it happened, do you?" Moran questioned. He brushed fingertips lightly across her bruised cheek. "Don't blame you."

Which explained why he wasn't surprised at her silly hit man question. "Read it in the papers, saw it on television, or had a chat with Mrs. Beckett?"

"I haven't met Mrs. Beckett yet."

Which was not an answer. His fingers lingered on her cheek. She did not jump away from his touch. That was the crazy thing—she'd been jumping and ducking being touched by everybody but Harley since it happened. She didn't want to slap Mike Moran's hand away. She wanted to tell him to do it again. She said, "Welcome to the neighborhood. Don't let the murder and assault rate put you off our little community," she added as they climbed the wooded hill away from the pond.

He nodded and came with her. "I won't. Harley on the other hand…"

"Is a sweetheart. Okay, he's a bruiser, but he's mine and I love him. How much do you know about Penhurst?" He shrugged. Since he was moving into Penhurst's place, she figured he had a right to know facts. "He and I were talking while his puppy sniffed at a rabbit hole. I heard a noise behind us—thought it was a dog. I woke up in the hospital. At first I didn't remember being with Penhurst. At first all I recalled was coming out here with Harley, then waking up in the hospital."

She strode up the hill with flagging determination. The dogs ran on ahead, through bushes and intermittent stands of young trees. Mike Moran walked beside her with his hands thrust in his pockets. Swallows darted close overhead. Yellow butterflies fluttered nearer to the ground. The sun was as bright as a lemon in the clear blue sky.

"It's very hard to remember that we're in the heart of a city," Moran said, echoing Sugar's thoughts.

"This fenced forty acres is the most precious real estate in the city. I wouldn't have picked up and moved here without knowing Harley'd have someplace he could run free. With the park, I jumped at the chance to move here and open a branch of *Le Bon Temps*." In a few seconds they would crest the hill and be within sight of where it happened. She did not want to go into the back of the park.

"Come here every day, don't you?" Moran asked.

"No."

"But you try to. I know the feeling."

She stopped a step away from the top of the hill and their gazes met. He had chocolate brown eyes, and thick, dark lashes. Those eyes were very, very shrewd. She didn't see pity in them, or the sort of sick curiosity she was getting used to. The sympathy in his look was tinged with just the right degree of irony. "So, what happened to you?" she asked him.

"Got shot in the line of duty once," he answered. "Made myself go back to where it happened. More than once before I worked through it."

"You're a police officer?"

There was no hint of coldness or suspicion in her question. Moran appreciated Sugar's simple curiosity. What he didn't appreciate was the way Dizzy and Sugar's raw-boned hound started to roughhouse. "Hey!" he shouted as Harley butted his Irish setter in the side. Dizzy went down on her back, feathered legs flailing. "Cut it out!" He turned a glare on Sugar, who laughed at his concern. "That dog of yours is a menace, LaRoux."

"They're just playing."

Dizzy's shining red coat was covered in dust and dried grass when Harley backed off and let her jump to her feet. She and Harley trotted away. "I raised her to be a lady," he complained to Harley's owner.

Sugar smirked, standing in the center of the path with one hand on her hip. "Harley loves the ladies."

"Him and me both," Moran said. She threw back her head and laughed a deep, sexy, infectious laugh.

The sight and sound of her sent a hot flash of desire through him that wiped out every bit of professional detachment he'd brought into this not-at-all-chance meeting. He looked at Sugar, and looking at her was a real treat even with the bandages and bruises, and his highly honed suspicious nature was overridden by lust, protectiveness, and genuine liking. Now, there was a deadly combination if there ever was one. Put those three components together and the chemical reaction could result in something serious indeed. He started to reach for her, to draw her into his arms and kiss her silly, but he stepped back instead. Not going to happen today, he told himself sternly. Fortunately, Dizzy ran up and bumped her head against his leg, which distracted him further from following his libido. He told himself the look of disappointment that briefly flashed across Sugar's face was his imagination. He looked at his dog and rubbed Dizzy's soft head. The two of them did just fine on their own up to this point.

"I never thought I was a dog person until Dizzy came along," he heard himself telling this stranger.

"I don't want to go over that hill today," Sugar said. Stepping around Moran, she called, "Yo, Harley. Let's go, boy!"

Harley came running toward her a few moments later, then spun around at the whirring of wings as a dove shot up out of the grass. He barked and took off toward the back side of the park again. Dizzy went with him.

"Cover me," Moran said, heading over the top of the hill. "I'm going in." He didn't look back, but heard Sugar follow.

Sugar stopped on the crest of the hill and watched Mike Moran explore the open expanse at the rear of the park. The examination he made was careful and professional. He even went over to the spot by the back fence where it was thought the assailant had climbed over and back out again with Penhurst's stolen puppy.

"He knows more than we do about this case," Sugar said to Harley, who'd come up for a bit of attention. She noticed her dog glance after the human male whose lovely Irish setter was now loping beside him, and smiled. "Jealous, huh?"

Moran was certainly a handsome devil, and she felt a definite buzz of attraction for him. She'd have liked him better if he'd said, "I'm a cop and I know about the Penhurst murder" immediately. This omission, plus his less than enthusiastic reaction to Harley playing with his precious Dizzy made her wonder if Mike Moran was someone she wanted to spend time with. She gave his backside one more appreciative look before she put the leash back on Harley and headed for the parkside entrance of Franciscan Place.

"It was something I said, wasn't it?" Moran asked Dizzy as they followed after Sugar and Harley. He knew damn well it was. He'd been friendly instead of professional and Ms. LaRoux caught on. Besides, he didn't like her dog. Well, he'd been nursing resentment because he and Dizzy could have moved in here months ago if celebrity chef Sugar LaRoux hadn't decided to exercise her auntie's option on her condo. Meeting her, he liked her instantly. Maybe he ought to keep some professional distance, but she was a neighbor, and all his protective instincts were kicking in. She was scared, and not just because she'd been traumatized by the attack. He could see it in her eyes, and hear it in some of the things she'd said. People didn't normally ask if strangers were hit men, even people who'd recently been struck on the head. And where had the marks on her leg come from? There was nothing in the hospital report or photos that showed anything but the head injury.

"You know, I didn't like you at first," he said, catching up to her at the door.

Sugar gave him a puzzled look over her shoulder. "At first? Ten minutes ago?"

"No," he said, and explained all about how he'd first heard about her. He didn't mean to do that, but talking to her came far too easily.

"Maybe I should have stayed in Louisiana," she answered, and swiped her keycard through the reader by the door.

When she opened the door, both dogs butted ahead, dragging their humans with them. Moran bumped shoulders and thighs with Sugar on the way through the doorway. He blessed Dizzy and the biker dog for this inadvertent contact, though he did manage a half-hearted, "Bad dog," just to let Dizzy know he expected civilized behavior even if she was running with a bad boy at the moment.

"I should have let you have the condo," Sugar told him as he followed her toward the hall that led to the front of the building and the elevators near the street entrance. "The place has been nothing but trouble."

There was a back stairs at the park entrance, and Sugar looked like the sort of active person who'd normally use them. He didn't think she was trying to dodge his company, but he did notice the glance she gave the stairway. She was nervous about using them. Why?

"Trouble how?" he asked as they reached the front of the building.

"Trouble like them," she said quietly, and tilted her pretty, pointed chin toward a trio of people already standing by the elevators. She looked like she was considering heading back for the staircase, but one of the trio noticed Sugar and waved. Sugar returned the gesture halfheartedly.

The group consisted of two women in their sixties and a man in his late forties. The man was thin and bald, nondescript in every way. He held a plastic bag in one hand. The old ladies reminded Moran of a couple of the fairy godmothers in the Disney version of *Sleeping Beauty*, only dressed in pastel sweatsuits instead of pastel fairy robes and pointed hats. One was thin and tall, the other short and plump. Neither woman looked happy with the thin man.

"Mr. Carlson, really, shopping outside the co-op is frowned upon," the plump one said as Moran, Sugar, and the dogs reached the elevators.

"There's nothing in the bylaws against it, Pansy," the thin woman said to the plump one. The thin woman held a fluffy white Maltese about the size of a longhaired rat in her arms.

"It's traditional, Esther," Pansy answered. Pansy had a definite cat person look to her. "Supporting all aspects of Franciscan Place is implicit in the charter."

"Implicit, yes," Esther replied. "But not required."

Moran looked from the women to the man. There was a stubborn set to Carlson's thin mouth, and deep anger in his pale eyes. Moran noticed that the white plastic bag the man held was imprinted with the logo of a big chain pet supply store. Moran knew there was a pet supply store here on the first floor of the Franciscan Place building. There were also a pet grooming shop, a pet sitting service, a dog training school, an animal psychologist's office, and a vet clinic on site. All these services were open to the public as well as to the residents, but residents manned the counters in the co-op enterprises and received a deep discount for bringing their business to the co-op stores. Looked like poor Mr. Carlson was busted by the tradition police. Moran noticed that while Pansy defended Carlson's rights, she didn't look happy about doing so.

He saw that Sugar looked pained as she pushed the button and waited for the elevator. Her big hound pressed against her leg and bared his teeth at the group, but didn't growl or show any other form of aggression. The Maltese yipped at the sight of Harley, but its owner didn't pay the cat hound any mind. Moran had the feeling that Sugar hoped they wouldn't be noticed and dragged into this conversation by the older folks. No such luck.

"Why, even Ms. LaRoux, here, with her busy schedule and her injuries, puts in time working at the co-op and on the hospitality committee," Pansy said.

"Not to mention taking over the board seat she inherited from her aunt," Esther added.

Sugar gave the women a wan smile. "Thanks."

Carlson glared at Sugar and said, "Once I'm on the board things will change."

"If you're elected to the board," Esther said.

"You won't win any votes if people know you're buying ferret food from an outside source," Pansy said. "It's not the Franciscan way."

Carlson continued to ignore the older women. He shifted his glare from Sugar to Moran, and his angry expression softened, just a little. "Another outsider. Penhurst's replacement, I suppose. Good to have new blood. What's your stand on the proposal?"

Before Moran could ask what Carlson was talking about Dizzy

took it into her pea-brained head to notice the Maltese. He could almost hear her think, *a fluffy mouse!* as she gave a joyful bark—and leaped.

Of course she forgot she was on a leash. Dizzy never remembered when she was attached. She jumped forward—sixty pounds of brainless enthusiasm, and Moran, unprepared, went with her.

"Dizzy!"

Esther and Pansy got out of the way, but Moran slammed into Carlson. The plastic bag flew from the man's hand, busted, and cans of pet food went rolling down the hall.

"Dogs!" Carlson snarled, dropping to his knees to gather up the spilled cans. "I hate dogs."

"Sorry." Mike gathered Dizzy in with the leash and held her close. He would have helped Carlson, but the elevator doors opened, and Sugar pushed him and Dizzy inside. She and Harley followed quickly. Pansy and Esther resumed nagging Carlson as the elevator doors closed.

Sugar pressed the button for the eighth floor, then leaned her head against the back wall as the elevator began a very slow ascent. "Whew. Sit, Harley," she added, tugging on the heavy leather leash. "I mean it."

Moran was surprised when the big dog obeyed. "You, too, Diz." Dizzy sat for a moment, then scuttled over to Harley and started licking his ears. Harley accepted this grooming as his due. Moran concentrated on Sugar. "We both live on eight. That's nice." Penhurst had been her next-door neighbor, he recalled. Was there any relevance to that? "What's with Carlson and the old birds?" he asked. "And what proposal? I'm a cop," he added when she looked at him. "I like to ask questions. It's more of a compulsion."

She gave an understanding nod. "Sort of like my using hot sauce." She touched her swollen cheek. "Time for some pain pills. The old girls are a couple of founding members of the Franciscan commune. Carlson's the first outsider to buy into the place. You must be the fifth or sixth to get a condo that didn't go to an heir. The original residents are getting used to the idea of new residents, but there's still resentment against Carlson."

"For being the first?"

"For being a pain in the ass. Doesn't like dogs or cats or bunnies or snakes or birds or llamas."

"Llamas?"

"There are a pair of llamas living on the second floor. They're housebroken, I'm told."

"Okay. If he doesn't like animals, why does he want to live here?"

"He does like animals. He keeps ferrets. There's a city ordinance against keeping ferrets, Officer Moran. This is the only place in town he can have them."

"Detective Sergeant Moran. Is there? Then why—"

"He can keep them here because Franciscan Place has all sorts of special dispensations from city ordinances. Ferrets are really quite sweet, and clean. People have the mistaken belief that they're wild animals, but they've actually been domesticated for thousands of years."

He was impressed, and grinned to show her. She reacted by blushing a little, and that was impressive, too. He liked her skin all flushed and pink and— "How come you know so much about ferrets?"

"Because I volunteer in the pet supply store. You have to take classes in the history, care, and feeding of all sorts of critters to work in the co-op."

"Good for you," he said. The elevator creaked ominously as it passed the fourth floor. It was an old office building, he reminded himself. Renovated and added onto, but still old. "Tell me about the elections. Am I supposed to run for something?"

"Run from if you're smart. You moved in at a bad time, Moran."

Yeah, he thought, right after someone got murdered. "Afraid the dognapper's going to show up again?" Sugar touched her face, and then her bruised thigh. He wanted to ask her how she'd hurt her leg, but he left it for now. "What's with the election? What proposal was Carlson talking about?"

Sugar's head hurt. She wished Moran would stop asking questions. Then again, she didn't really want to stop talking to him. She liked his deep voice, and his humor, and his lively intelligence. The more time she spent with him, the more she liked him despite her initial skepticism. And she didn't like being alone. Soon they'd reach the eighth floor and go their separate ways. Then she'd be alone with her fears and suspicions, and the sense of helpless dread she hated. She was probably just being paranoid. And bored.

She wished the doctors would let her go back to work. But kitchens were dangerous places. She was still getting dizzy spells and her vision went fuzzy sometimes. Not good conditions around hot stoves and sharp knives. So, she had at least another week of enforced vacation with only Harley—who was no great watchdog—to keep her company. Moran, she thought, might make a very good watchdog. Except that she was a strong, independent woman of the twenty-first century, and not some weak southern belle in need of a big, strong man's protection. And what a pity that was, she thought, giving Moran another once-over with her one good eye. He was not unaware of her scrutiny. Harley nudged her leg with his head, and got her mind back to the present.

"Where was I?" she asked him. "And where are we?"

"Sixth floor. Election. Controversy."

"Mr. Penhurst's death left a space open on the board. That's too bad, because there's an upcoming vote on whether to sell five acres at the back of the park for city development. Penhurst was against the sale. Carlson is running for the open board spot and no one so far is running against him. The election is next week. He's very much in favor of the sale. Those acres are worth millions. Every member of the owners association would receive a share of the proceeds, plus a great deal of the money would be used for needed repairs on the property. On the other hand, it would mean losing five acres of irreplaceable parkland. Some of the original residents argue that giving up a foot of ground goes against the spirit in which Franciscan Place was founded. They've vowed to tie themselves to trees in protest if the sale is approved. Everyone else is divided on the issue. I'm agin' it," she added. "Most of the dog owners are."

"Me, too." He rubbed Dizzy's head, then rubbed his square, masculine jaw thoughtfully.

He looked like he was about to ask another question, and she wanted to know what he was thinking. In fact, a stab of sudden suspicion went through her. But before Sugar could voice anything, an even sharper stab of pain knifed through her head, and then all she wanted was to get to her bathroom to throw up, and then take a pain-

killer and go to bed. Fortunately, the elevator drew to a halt and the
door opened before the pain completely paralyzed her.

"Later," she managed to say to Moran, and she and Harley
squeezed past him and Dizzy and hurried down the hall to her door.

"I brought you a pie."

Moran had made up his mind to pay a call on Sugar when the
doorbell rang. She hadn't looked good when she got off the elevator.
Maybe he should have gone with her to her condo. Instead he'd taken
the chance to be alone. He'd given Dizzy a bath, then paced for hours.
While he thought, Dizzy noisily groomed herself then curled up on
the couch to sleep. When he opened the door Harley came in and
promptly jumped up beside Dizzy. Dizzy didn't mind, and Moran
was too intent on the human visitor to yell at the Catahoula.

Sugar was pale, but beautiful. He looked at the pie she held out to
him. The crust was flaky and golden, and the scent of warm blueberries filled his nostrils. "I love you," he said to Sugar LaRoux. Then he
added, "What kind of food do ferrets eat?"

He pulled her inside before she could answer and shut the door
behind her. "Cat food," she said as he took the pie from her. She followed him into the kitchen. "Why?"

"Why'd you bring me a pie? And thank you. How'd you know I
love pie?"

"You look like a pie kind of guy."

"Oh, I am."

The kitchen, like the rest of the condo, was pretty bare. Penhurst's
furniture had all been donated to Goodwill, his papers and personal
effects were in a police warehouse. Most of Moran's stuff was still at
his old place. He had only the couch, his bed, his clothes, Dizzy's
stuff, the microwave and a few dishes moved into his new home. He'd
arrived to solve a murder first and settle down to enjoy living at Franciscan Place later. He hadn't counted on homemade pie. This was a
real housewarming present. A treasure. He was glad he'd remembered
to bring plates and silverware. He wouldn't have minded eating the
pie with his bare hands straight out of the dish, but that didn't seem

neighborly, somehow. He supposed he'd better offer the lady who'd made it a piece.

"You want some? How are you feeling? And how'd you bruise your leg?"

"Yes, please. Much better. Why do you want to know what ferrets eat?"

Moran busied himself with knives, forks, and plates. When he handed Sugar a slice of warm blueberry pie, he said, "You tell me first."

"Why should I tell you anything?"

"Why'd you make me a pie?"

"I like to cook. And I'm on the hospitality committee."

"Plus, you don't want to be alone." After a moment of strained silence, he added, "And you like me."

"Harley likes Dizzy," she answered. She looked at the dogs on the couch. "They make a cute couple."

"So do we."

His mouth said it before his mind could censor the words. He didn't know where those words came from, but he couldn't bring himself to apologize or back off. "At least, I think we do." She was blushing again. He took a step closer to her, and watched while she concentrated on eating her pie rather than look at him. He liked making her blush, seeing her pale skin take on heat. To get his mind off the thought of seeing more of her skin warmed by his words and his touch, he wolfed down his blueberry pie. The taste only made him wonder about how sweet her mouth would taste with her lips all covered in blueberries. To bludgeon down this thought, he went back into cop mode.

"Why don't you want to be alone? And what do ferrets eat?"

Sugar didn't know which question to answer first, or even if she should answer either of them. Maybe she shouldn't be here. Maybe she should have just dropped off the welcome present and gone back home. She glanced toward the door, but didn't seriously consider leaving. Maybe she'd only met Mike Moran a few hours ago, but there was an undeniable chemistry between them. Maybe the blueberry pie was only the beginning of showing how welcome he was at Franciscan Place. And maybe this was all moving too fast, and she was just reacting to him this way because she was lonely.

The ferret question seemed safer to address. "Cat food," she told him. "The expensive canned kind. There are a couple of kinds of ferret chow, but they're expensive, and vets say they aren't any better than good cat food. Why?"

"Carlson had dog food in his bag."

"Oh." Somehow that seemed ominous. She shrugged. "Maybe there's a dog food that ferrets like. Carlson's an expert on them."

He put down his plate and came forward to put his hands on her shoulders. Lovely, warm, big hands. "You're not exactly the suspicious type, are you?"

"I didn't used to be," she admitted. ""I'm really not a naive and trusting soul," she went on. "I've lived in New Orleans, not Mayberry."

"But you still get mad at yourself for being suspicious of people."

There was no arguing with this. It was like she and Moran had known each other forever. "And you get mad at yourself when you aren't suspicious of people."

"I really did think of you as a murder suspect before I met you," he admitted.

"And you met me on purpose." He nodded. She'd been annoyed about this at first, but her attraction to the man quickly overrode her outrage. "Are you the officer in charge of the investigation, or is moving in here a coincidence?"

"Yes. And yes." He shook his head. "I'm a good investigator, but I keep going off on personal tangents with you. Don't tell my boss, okay?"

She glanced back at the couch. "Would that be Dizzy?"

"She doesn't care right now." The dogs were tangled up in a pile, perfectly content to be with each other. One of them was snoring. "That biker of yours is making me jealous, Sugar."

"And here I thought I was Harley's only love."

"Guess we'll have to settle for each other." He'd done it again! And she was smiling at him with her lovely, kissable mouth. Moran carefully took his hands away from Sugar's shoulders and stepped away. He even put them behind his back to keep from touching her again. "I think it's time for the 'just the facts, ma'am' speech. I've got a murderer to catch."

Sugar had a teasing glint in her one good eye, and he sadly watched it fade. "You don't think Mr. Penhurst was killed by a stranger stealing his dog, do you?"

"You don't either," he answered her. "Why not, Sugar? Why don't you want to be alone?"

She put her hands up in front of her. "I've gotten a little paranoid since I got hit on the head. But—"

"What happened to your leg?"

"I fell down the back stairs. This old building needs some work, and we can't keep caretakers. Our last one left two weeks ago, and since Penhurst was in charge of the hiring committee he hasn't been replaced. The wiring's ancient. Sometimes there're power outages." She shrugged.

"You didn't fall, you were pushed."

"Harley probably knocked me off balance...except I was pretty sure he was a couple of flights ahead of me."

"Why didn't you tell the police?"

"Because I wasn't sure."

"If you weren't sure you wouldn't have even joked about my being a hit man."

"I can't remember what happened when I was attacked. How can I trust my judgment without any concrete proof?" She turned toward the couch. "Could it be that the dognapper is trying to steal Harley? Catahoula leopard dogs aren't too well known outside of Louisiana."

Moran laughed. "Hell, no, I don't think anyone's trying to steal your dog. They'd pay you to take that bruiser back." He ignored her outraged glare. "I think plain old greed's the motive. Why didn't you mention the fight over selling off part of the park to the investigating officers?"

She looked puzzled. "That's Franciscan Place business. You signed the non-disclosure agreement when you moved in, didn't you?"

Yeah, he had. The media was always trying to do cutesy stories on the weirdo hippie animal lovers that lived in the building, and the hippie weirdos were sick of it. Rule was nobody talked about Franciscan Place to outsiders. He considered pointing out to Sugar that non-disclosure agreements didn't count in a murder investigation, but it didn't matter now. Besides, every animal-loving hippie weirdo at Franciscan Place genuinely believed Penhurst had been killed for his dog. Every animal-loving hippie weirdo but one, but he was still an animal lover.

"That dog food is going to put Carlson away. He couldn't get rid of a dog as rare as a Porcelaine without even an animal shelter noticing, and it hasn't occurred to him to kill an animal."

Sugar looked stricken, but not really surprised. "You think Carlson killed Mr. Penhurst? Because of the proposed land sale?" She sighed. "I really didn't want to believe it was one of us."

"He bludgeoned a man to death because he was blocking the land sale Carlson wants. He tried to kill you twice. Don't feel sorry for him."

"And he stole a puppy," She added in outrage. "I don't feel sorry for him. Can I feel sorry for his ferrets?"

"I suppose somebody has to."

"What are you going to do? Search his apartment? Arrest him?"

"A couple of cans of dog food aren't probable cause for arresting the guy. I can start an investigation. Or..." He scratched his jaw. "Yeah."

"Was that a light bulb I saw go off over your head?"

"Uh-huh. Hey, Dizzy, wake up!" He looked at Sugar. "You and Harley want to show me around the building?"

"Isn't he cute? The poor little thing."

Moran listened carefully at the door. "Shhh. I hear someone coming."

"Aren't you sweet?" Sugar whispered behind him. "Poor lonely thing. Been locked up in here all alone when you're just a baby. That's a good Dizzy. You lick his ears like a good mommy."

Despite the approaching footsteps in the hall, Moran took a moment to glance over his shoulder. There were no lights on in the caretaker's empty apartment, but Sugar and a pile of dogs were gathered in a patch of moonlight under a bare window. The place didn't smell so great, but Moran was used to dog mess. There were bowls of water and food on the floor and a stack of empty cans in a corner.

The Porcelaine puppy was in Sugar's lap, with Harley and Dizzy jostling to give the pup attention.

"Shh," he said again.

When Sugar glanced up he motioned to her to get out of the light. She scooted back, the dogs going with her. The steps halted outside the door. Then Harley's head came up, his attention on the door. A low growl started in his throat, but Sugar grabbed the big dog's muzzle to keep him quiet. Dizzy obeyed Moran's hand motion to sit and be quiet. Mostly she was good at obeying...for about fifteen seconds. Then whatever passed for thought in her pretty head would drift off and she'd be ready to play again. Fifteen seconds would do for now.

He stepped to one side and waited as a key turned in the door. A key. More physical evidence. They'd gotten into the basement apartment with the help of a credit card jimmied in the door. Sugar gave him permission to enter as a member of the board. The member of the board who had had a key to the caretaker's apartment was Penhurst. No keys had been found on Penhurst or in his condo. Moran's conclusions about where the puppy was hidden had proved correct. That the puppy was being taken care of by the murderer made sense—if you thought like a typical hippie weirdo resident of Franciscan Place. Which Moran did.

Now he waited to see if the person he expected would come through the door.

Sugar was glad to be in the shadows. She wasn't afraid, exactly. Not with Mike Moran standing there being large and competent. It was just that the idea of facing her attacker was—daunting—even if she'd been talking to him by the elevator only a few hours ago. She watched the door slowly open and hoped it wasn't Carlson. She didn't like the man, but it sickened her that someone she knew had tried to kill her. She held her breath, and a man stepped into the room.

She couldn't stop Harley's growl this time, or his lunge.

Carlson screamed.

Harley pulled so hard his collar came off in Sugar's hands. She shouted. The puppy trotted forward. Her dog drew up his heavy muscles and jumped. Dizzy began barking. Carlson screamed again. Moran slammed the door and put himself between it and Carlson.

Carlson ran into Moran. Harley leaped on Carlson's back. They all went down in a heap. Dizzy kept barking and the puppy yelped in distress. Sugar snatched up the puppy, then circled around the swearing, barking tangle of bodies to switch on the overhead light.

By the time the lights came on Moran was on his feet. Carlson was on his back. Harley straddled him, growling in his face.

"Get him off me! Get him off me!"

Moran looked at her. "I thought you said he wasn't protective?"

"Maybe he's trying to protect the puppy."

"Or impress Dizzy."

"Get him *off!*"

Moran looked at Sugar's bruises, and enjoyed watching Carlson squirm in terror for a few more seconds. Then Sugar frowned at him in that civilized way women have of indicating they disapprove of such manly pursuits as torture and war, and he reminded her, "He's your dog."

"Right. Harley!"

Moran thought Harley backed off more out of boredom than obedience training. Harley turned to Dizzy, whose tongue lolled out in a way that indicated complete hero worship of Harley. "Sucker," Moran muttered. Carlson stared up at him, his face covered in drool. "You're under arrest for the murder of Alec Penhurst." Then he hauled the shaking Carlson to his feet and read him his rights.

When Moran was done Mirandizing his suspect, Sugar stepped forward, the white puppy still in her arms. "Why'd you try to kill me?" she asked.

Carlson would have been smart to wait for a lawyer before he did any talking, but he answered her. "To free up another liberal spot on the board." He sounded like murder was the most reasonable thing in the world. "You stand in the way of progress."

Moran added, "Besides, you thought she might get her memory back. That's why you tried the second time."

Carlson nodded. "That, too."

Carlson was hanging himself. Moran loved it, less work to make the case for him. He took out his cell phone and called in the collar.

A few minutes later a pair of uniformed officers arrived at the front of the building where he'd brought Carlson. He let the uniforms take Carlson away. He'd follow them to the homicide division soon. He went back inside the building.

Sugar and the dogs waited for him in his condo. The first thing he did was the one thing he'd been wanting to do since he first laid eyes on her. He took Sugar LaRoux in his arms and kissed her. It was as wonderful as he'd thought it would be, and went on for a long while.

"My head's spinning," she said when their lips parted. "And I don't think it's from the concussion."

"I have to go," he said. "That was a down payment for later."

She didn't object. "What's going to happen to the puppy?" she asked. "Penhurst didn't have any family."

Harley and Dizzy were on the rug. The Porcelaine was chewing on Harley's ear. Moran shook his head, and put his arm around Sugar's waist. "I think they've already adopted him."

She rested her head on his shoulder. "Looks like it."

"And I guess that means we'll have to stay together. For the sake of the children."

Night  Hawks

Jody Lynn Nye

Footsteps came closer and closer to where Melina Lange hid, terrified, in the recess of the rough brick wall. Somewhere behind her was an assassin who had just killed her boyfriend. If she didn't keep moving, she knew she would be next.

She heard voices coming from the downslope side of Jasmine Garden Park. She left her hiding place and blundered up the hill in the dark. Twigs like fingers reached out of the bushes and pulled out strands of her long, curly hair. They scratched her hands, which were unprotected by her short trench coat. She ignored the pain and kept running.

Allen was dead! Melina's hazel eyes were blurred by tears as she stumbled on the white gravel path. She wished she could have been in love with him—truly, she did. She was ready for a plain, ordinary romance. That didn't mean she wasn't sorry someone had shot him, but at least it hadn't been her. She'd been instantly attracted to him. And what woman wouldn't have been, he was so handsome—muscular and tan with romantic, dark blue eyes and gorgeous sun-streaked hair. But what had really drawn her to him wasn't his looks, it was something else…something she couldn't quite define. He was intriguing, just a little offbeat, just a little dangerous. Though he wasn't more than a couple of inches taller than her five-foot-seven, he walked with a confident swagger, and he always seemed to have plenty of money. When she asked him about his business operations, he was so mysterious. He diverted her questions, or simply ignored them. She'd worried that he was dealing in something exotic and illegal. Now she was sure of it.

She had been titillated when Allen told her to meet him there in the Jasmine Gardens after dark. Twenty acres of fragrant, walled garden looking out over the white-tipped waves of the Pacific Ocean, it was a popular spot for couples seeking a little love fulfillment by moonlight. The Gardens offered plenty of intimate, private areas surrounded by low, mossy stone walls, where they could be alone. But when she arrived, eager and ready, wearing a sexy little dress she knew he'd like under the short raincoat, he'd spoiled the whole thing by telling her he had come there to meet someone—someone important, he'd said.

"And I'm not important?" she had asked, angry and disappointed.

So they'd quarreled, there in the most romantic spot in the city, while the waves tossed and crashed at the foot of the cliff far below the brick walls and night birds called in the trees. Everyone had heard Melina and Allen yelling at one another. Couples passing them to go deeper into the garden gave them pointed looks. If they weren't there to enjoy themselves, couldn't they at least take their noise somewhere else?

In the midst of the argument, Melina had caught sight of a figure, little more than a shadow, coming toward them. She ignored the stranger and continued arguing with Allen until a blue glint caught her eye as the silhouette's hand emerged from the inside of his raincoat.

After that, things had happened so quickly. Allen saw the gun at the same moment she had. With a single movement he'd shoved her into the bushes and dived in the opposite direction. The man—for it was a man—had a narrow, hatchet face and short-clipped hair. As Allen hit the ground and rolled, the gunman stuck

his weapon out at arm's length. The gun's muzzle flashed. It made
so little sound that Melina knew instinctively he'd used a silencer.
Allen quit rolling and sprawled on the ground in a sad, boneless
mass. The man moved up to his victim, kicked him to be sure of
his kill, and turned and walked away. Melina had cowered for a
moment until the assassin was out of sight, then flung herself at
her boyfriend, turning him face upward. Allen's eyes stared sight-
lessly into the night. She could feel no pulse in his neck. Terrified,
she groped for her cell phone. Her fingers fumbled on the keys
several times before she managed to dial Emergency Response.
She'd given her name, Allen's name, and all the details she could
think of, her voice rising toward hysteria until the kindly operator
on the other end of the line stopped her and calmed her down.
He promised to send someone immediately. He asked her to wait
where she was, and instructed her not to touch anything. It was
too late for that, of course.

Melina switched off the cell phone, and sat down on the grass
beside Allen's body, alone with the sounds of the night. Before,
they'd been familiar and friendly. Now they were strange and
frightening.

She heard footsteps approaching. Suddenly, it occurred to her
that perhaps she hadn't waited until the assassin was out of ear-
shot before calling for help. Perhaps he was coming back to elimi-
nate the only witness?

Maybe it was just another lover looking for his beloved in the
park. An enormous shadow passed by her suddenly, cutting off
the light of a distant street lamp. Melina stayed still as long as her
nerves could stand it, then fled into the trees.

The footsteps quickened as the mysterious figure behind her
gave chase. Melina's heart pounded wildly with fear.

She'd missed the winding path, but felt it was smarter not to
take it anyhow. The forest floor was uneven and slippery. Low, leafy
plants whipped her legs, and she felt her stockings tear. The ever-
present creak of tree frogs ceased as she disturbed them in her
headlong dash through the park. She ran with her arms up, elbows
out, to keep branches from striking her in the face. The footsteps
following her got louder, feet crunching on fallen twigs as her pur-

suer plunged into the woods behind her.

She couldn't run forever. What could she use to defend herself? Searching her pocket with her free hand for her keys, she threaded them in between her fingers, points out. But she prayed it wouldn't come to that—mere keys against a gunman.

She ran toward the high stone wall that surrounded the garden. If she followed it, she might be able to get out of the park without being seen. A root caught the sandal strap over her toes. Her shoes weren't intended for sprinting, let alone running for her life. Melina grabbed for the tree to steady herself. Behind her, the following footsteps drew closer. She crouched down and wrenched her sandal free, then she sprang up, ready to run, when an arm wrapped around her from behind.

Her heart leaped in her throat, choking her. Melina almost passed out with terror, but some reflex, ingrained during a long-ago women's self-defense course, caused her to jab backward with her elbow. She caught the assailant in the belly. He, for it was a man, let out an *oof!*, but didn't let go. Frantic, Melina struggled to gouge her keys into his face. Her captor fought back, holding her pinioned with one arm. He pulled her farther into the brush, his other hand clapped over her mouth.

"Shh!" he hissed in her ear. "Don't make a sound."

This man had shot Allen in cold blood. He wouldn't hesitate to do the same to her. Melina had no intention of being dragged off and shot or strangled or knifed. She wriggled her jaw open, and bit the nearest finger of the enclosing hand.

"Crap!" the man growled, letting the hand fall. "No, don't yell," he began as Melina took a deep breath.

"Help!" Melina screamed at the top of her voice. "Help me!"

Her attacker sagged and released her. "I wish you hadn't done that," he said.

"Why shouldn't I have, you bastard?" Melina demanded, turning to face her tormentor.

Ping! A bullet struck the wall over their heads, showering them with stone shards. The stranger seized her hand and started running. She stumbled after him. For it wasn't the same man who'd killed Allen. This man was wearing jeans and a short, zip-up jacket.

"There're two of you?" Melina asked, fighting to free her hand. "Who are you? Why did you kill Allen? No, never mind. Don't tell me. Then you'll have to kill me. And I just want to go home. Please, let me go."

The strange man pulled her around a brick pillar and yanked her down to crouch beside him.

"I'm not going to hurt you. I'm just an innocent bystander here," he whispered. "A witness. My name's Mike Dillon. I'm a nature photographer. I've been working in the conservancy area up near the peak for three weeks. I've been trying to catch nighthawks in action for *Avian* magazine. I was on my way up there when I saw that guy shoot your boyfriend. I ran off to see if I could find a park warden. Old Boscombe is usually driving around at this hour. The park guys all know me, and they're armed and trained to deal with stuff like this. But I couldn't find any of them. I thought I'd better come back and help you."

Melina got a good look at him for the first time. He was thin, just the opposite of Allen, with longish black hair and light eyes. She couldn't tell their color in the meager moonlight that filtered through the bushes, but she found their expression sincere.

He had very pale skin, as though he often stayed up all night and never saw the sun.

"You're not an...assassin?" Melina's voice shook, and she hated herself for being so weak.

"I'm glad you're finally figuring that out," Mike said, a small, ironic quirk lifting the side of his mouth. "No. I'm one of the good guys."

"Oh." Melina swallowed, having to rearrange her thinking. "I'm Melina Lange."

She could see the glint of his white teeth when he smiled. "Pleased to meet you, Melina." He quit talking to listen to the night. The sound of the tree frogs diminished, then stopped again. "I think our bad guy is getting too close. We'd better move. Stay low, and use whatever cover you can find."

Melina had just taken a small step when an ominous *thunk* came from the tree beside them. Leaves flew in all directions. Melina let out a little peep of surprise and threw herself to the ground. Mike flattened himself over her. Another bullet whinged off the wall about twenty feet away from them.

"I think your friend's firing at random." Mike rose to a crouch and grabbed her arm. "Come on. This way!"

"He's not my friend!" Melina whispered furiously, as she ran after him.

"Well, he's sure not mine." He held up a thorny branch and gestured her underneath it into the heavily wooded landscape, then crept along beside her.

Melina bit her tongue as they finally stopped at the edge of a clearing. It was her fault that both of them were now in such danger. If only she had listened to this man and not screamed, giving away their location to the assassin. But what was she to think when he grabbed her? Was she supposed to believe he meant her no harm? For some reason, seeing her boyfriend killed before her very eyes had made her jumpy. Mike raised his head, getting his bearings.

"We're in the gazing pool garden," he whispered. "There's at least two or three ways in. We're not trapped, even if he's in here with us."

"If we can just keep hidden and out of the killer's way, we'll be all right," Melina said. "I called the police. We only have to stay away from him until they get here."

Another bullet ricocheted noisily off the wall, much too close for Melina's comfort.

"Damn," Mike said. "Or we can lay low until this guy runs out of bullets." He shoved her down into a patch of grass deeply shadowed by the surrounding bushes and flopped down beside her. He scattered handfuls of dead leaves over them both and motioned for silence. All too soon the sound of footsteps passed within a few feet of them. Melinda listened, her heart pounding so hard she was sure the killer would hear it. Soon, the sound of steps faded into the distance. Mike shifted.

"I think we're okay. He doesn't know where we are," Mike whispered. "What in hell was your boyfriend into, anyhow?"

Melina was too ashamed to tell him that she didn't really know. She put out a finger and touched his lips, signaling him to be quiet. His lips felt soft. She let her hand drop.

"I'm sorry," he said. "I didn't mean to snap. Are you all right? It's got to have been traumatic to see someone…"

…Die. He hadn't wanted to say the word, but it hung in the air between them. Melina shivered all over. Taking control of herself, she made a face.

"I'll be fine," she assured him. "You know, right now I'm so angry with him. Angry. Resentful. I'm sorry Allen…died, but I'm also totally ticked off that he put me in this situation. He brought me here knowing something was wrong. He as much as told me that before the gunman shot him." She looked up at Mike. His pale eyes picked up the faint light and seemed to glow. "I'm sorry about all this. It's too bad that you got involved, too, but I'm glad you were there. But there's something I don't understand. If you were looking for hawks, how'd you happen to see what happened to Allen? We were nowhere near the wild parts of the park."

The light eyes dropped and were covered by long eyelashes. "I was watching you," he said sheepishly. "I saw you, and I was just wishing I had a someone as beautiful as you in my life when that guy walked right up and pulled the gun out. I didn't hear anything, but I saw a red flash, then…you know." Mike paused and looked at her. "I suppose this is a bad time to ask you if you'd like to have coffee some time?"

In spite of herself, Melina started laughing. The sound of it rang out in the silent park. She knew her life depended on it, but with the adrenaline rush from shock, fear, and relief she couldn't stop. She covered her mouth with both hands. Mike wrapped himself around her to muffle the sound. Suddenly, unexpectedly, inevitably, they found themselves face-to-face, and all Melina could think about was passionately kissing those soft, soft lips.

She pulled away from Mike with a little gasp and started crawling away, into the undergrowth, moving as fast as she could so the gunman wouldn't find them where the laughter had been. Mike followed her into a copse of thick, scratchy arborvitae bushes. He reached for her, but she pulled away, welcoming the sharp prickles against her back as a kind of penance for nearly making love to a stranger when the man she'd been seeing was lying dead no more than a hundred yards from her and a killer was stalking them.

"I'm so sorry," she said, hoping her face was in shadow so he couldn't see how red she knew it was. "I didn't mean to laugh." It was her turn to hang her head. "You know, I came here tonight hoping for a nice romantic encounter. I just thought it would be with...someone else."

Mike's light eyes glinted at her from the darkness. "So, under better circumstances, would I do instead?"

She studied him, liking the way the spare planes of his face threw shadows under his brows and cheekbones. "Yes," she said in a very low voice. "You'll do nicely."

"Do you know who was shooting at your friend?" She could tell he didn't want to say 'boyfriend.' Maybe he was picturing himself in that role. To tell the truth, and she was ashamed of herself for it, given the events of the last hour, she was beginning to picture him in that role, too.

"I never saw that man before," Melina said.

"Neither have I. He's not a regular in the park. But I got a good look at him."

Melina made a face. "Well, *if* we live to describe him to the police, that will be useful."

"My camera bag's at the bottom of the hill. I threw it there when I went after you. I could try to go get it, and take his picture. You know, we ought to do that anyway, in case he leaves before the cops come."

Melina looked at him in astonishment. She wouldn't have been more surprised if he'd said he was going to sprout wings and fly them to the police station.

"Are you out of your mind? That's too dangerous," she said.

"All right," Mike said, his eyes dancing. "I'll draw his fire, you go get the camera."

"This is not an adventure story, Mr. Nature Photographer!" Melina hissed. "This is reality! We could get killed!"

"Fine," he said. "We'll die together, then. We'll both go."

This initiated a short, whispered argument. It ended only when Mike convinced her that staying there was even more likely to get them killed than moving back to the scene of the original crime, where his camera was. After all, he pointed out, the last place the killer would want to be found was right next to the body of his victim. And the killer knew the police were coming.

"I just wish they'd get here faster!" Melina muttered.

They tiptoed out onto the path. It was better that way, Mike had asserted, against Melina's protestations that they should stay under cover. The killer had searched this path, after all. They'd heard him. And they'd make a lot less noise walking on the compacted gravel than crawling around in the bushes. Here in the dark, noise was their enemy, silence their friend.

The camera bag lay exactly where he thought it would be. Mike took out a silver-cased camera, checked its film indicator, and handed it to her. He shouldered the bag, but carried in his hands a giant-sized flash attachment and a coil of wire with a palm-sized box at the end.

"Remote control," he told her as they trotted deeper into the park. His low voice soothed Melina's jangling nerves. "I don't need the flash when I'm using super-high-speed film. I like doing night photography. It's kind of a specialty with me. In the wild the hawks hunt at dusk and dawn, but what with streetlights everywhere in this park, as far as the hawks are concerned it's always dusk, so I have all night to get my pictures. The females are terrific hunters. You ought to see them. We'll stake this guy out, just like I would my birds. Then, we'll nab him."

We shouldn't be doing this, Melina thought, as the entrance disappeared farther behind them. We shouldn't be hunting the hunter. We should be getting out of this park, going somewhere safe, finding the police. But she could never resist that touch of danger. She was also glad to have something to do to help her keep from thinking about the cold reality of Allen's murder, and all those gunshots that had nearly ended her own life. She'd discovered she really didn't like getting shot at—and she wanted to make sure the assassin didn't get away. Until he was caught, she'd never have a moment's peace of mind. She owed it to Allen to find his killer. Surely she owed Allen that much.

At the edge of one of the smallest and darkest walled sections of garden, Mike set Melina in the shelter of a stand of thick bushes with the camera while he headed off into the darkness with the flash unit.

"How can you see where you're going?" she breathed.

"Practice," he said. "I've developed good night vision after stalking hawks."

Melina squinted into the shadows, feeling as though she missed him already. What an odd sensation...but understandable, perhaps. They'd shared something few people did: a life-and-death test of who they were. He'd cared about her during the crisis. He was friendly, funny, self-deprecating, and, as a bonus, good-looking. When this was over, *if* they both lived through it, she did want to go out with him. Maybe she'd join him photographing his hawks. That sounded interesting. She'd always liked birds and had a sympathy for raptors. They, too, had that taste for danger. Speaking of which...

Her heart started pounding again. Mike had been out of sight for a long time. The forest had gone quiet. That probably wasn't good. She stepped out slowly to see where he had gone and if he was all right.

Something crunched right beside the fence. Startled, Melina looked up. Silhouetted in the moonlight, the narrow-faced assassin was looking down at her. He'd come around the bend in the path at just the right time to catch her exposed in the pathway. His feral grin gave away his ill intentions as he drew the gun from inside his coat. Melina was hypnotized by the sight, unable to run away or even move. The barrel lowered toward her until she was looking at the black opening at its end. It looked big as a cannon. She was going to die.

"Hey, killer!" Mike yelled from across the path. The assassin spun around to face the new target.

The night blossomed into blinding light. Melina threw her hands up to protect her eyes. The assassin hesitated only a second, then fired shot after shot at the blazing target. She heard a crash in the dark.

"No!" she screamed, galvanized into action. Not twice in one night! Allen, and now Mike, murdered before she had even gotten to know him. She jumped the assassin, pummeling the back of his head and kicking the backs of his knees with every bit of strength she possessed. The man dropped to the ground, the gun flying out of his hand. Melina jumped on his back, kept pounding him even after he collapsed into unconsciousness until gentle but firm hands pulled her off.

They belonged to Mike. He was alive! A sob of relief burst out of her. She threw her arms around him and held him tightly. Then lights appeared everywhere around them. A couple of uniformed police officers moved in on the shooter, pinioning his hands behind his back with handcuffs.

"You hit him pretty hard, ma'am," the older officer said as they got out the smelling salts. A couple of moments later one of the policemen helped the dazed man to sit up while the other examined the man's wallet with a flashlight. Blood dripped into the gunman's eyes from a cut on his forehead. The cop turned his torch on Melina. "What'd you use on him?"

Melina looked down at her hand, struck dumb with shock. "Use?" She'd forgotten she'd been holding anything. A twisted metal box was clutched in her fingers. Twinkling glass shards peppered her sleeves and front of her coat.

Mike stepped in. "She nailed him with a Nikon F1 camera, Officer. Metal body. He might have a concussion."

The officer was amused. "A pretty expensive weapon, but effective. Couldn't happen to a nicer guy. I know this perp—he's got a blotter sheet you wouldn't believe. Stay here while I put him in the car. I'll need to get detailed statements from both of you in a minute."

Mike returned to Melina, who was staring, mortified, at the wreck in her hands. "I ruined your camera!" she exclaimed. "I'm so sorry. I'll get you a new one, I promise. But I thought he'd shot you."

Mike held up the little box. "Remote control. He got my flash unit. It was in a tree about six feet away from me. Don't worry about it. The equipment can be replaced. And it was worth it," he said with a grin, as he brought his soft mouth close to her ear. "You know, I've been waiting for weeks to catch a female nighthawk in action."

Keeper of  the Well

Deb Stover

Rural Kansas—present day.

Hana Gillespie stared at the key cradled in her open palm as if seeking its permission to enter the rundown old farmhouse. *Face it, Hana—it's really yours.* She looked past the missing shingles and broken windows to sweep the landscape beyond the house, and released a contented sigh. This place was worth every penny it would cost to restore. It was her future.

She looked at the house again and pulled the newspaper article she'd printed from the microfiche at the library. When the woman at the hardware store heard which farm Hana had bought, she'd told her a bizarre tale of murder and ghosts. And, according to this article, at least the murder part was true.

A little girl named Annie had drowned in the well over fifty years ago, murdered by a farmhand. A few days after the man's execution, the girl's mother took her own life. Brokenhearted and alone, the grandmother had simply walked away from the farm.

This farm.

Despite the past tragedies, Hana was determined to make it a happy home for a child, once the adoption agency approved her application. Stuffing the article into her pocket, she faced her front door again.

Each time she entered, she realized what a disaster the place was. The downstairs was clean now, but still decrepit. Today she would explore upstairs.

Glancing across the parlor, she did a double take. In the doorway to the kitchen stood a child. She estimated the girl's age at around five. Bare feet and legs stuck out beneath a faded brown dress that reached just below her knees. Her blond hair hung straggly and unkempt.

Hana's gaze traveled back up to the child's smiling face. Something besides the endearing grin drew Hana's scrutiny. Need. The little girl needed something.

Or someone?

Why would anyone permit a child to roam around the countryside alone? Hana took a tentative step toward her, noting the physical characteristics of Down syndrome in the child's face. The little urchin grinned, crooked a finger in invitation, then simply disappeared.

Vanished.

Hana's blood turned cold and her heart slammed into her chest. She blinked, willing the child to reappear.

No such luck.

Was she imagining things? Was her desire to adopt a child threatening her sanity? Or had the hardware store clerk's tale planted the seeds of this hallucination?

Hana closed her eyes again for as long as she dared, then reopened them and walked into the kitchen. The child couldn't have been real. The way she'd dissolved into nothingness was impossible. But if she was real, Hana would have been aware of her turning to run away, not simply vanishing.

Like a ghost.

Educated, intelligent people like Hana simply didn't believe such nonsense. *It was only my imagination.*

Humming "Lions and Tigers and Bears" as a defense mechanism, Hana peeked around the corner at the back porch, where pails and other discarded items were stored. No little girls—only more evidence of the hard work Hana had ahead of her.

Squaring her shoulders, she walked purposefully outside to her car and opened the trunk. It was time for her to get her act together. Past time.

Ghost or no, Hana Gillespie was moving in.

She removed a box of cleaning supplies and placed it on the ground beside the car and retrieved her flashlight. Determined, she went back inside to open every unbroken window, then started up the stairs.

The old staircase groaned and creaked as she ascended to the second floor. This was an adventure—like Indiana Jones entering the "Temple of Doom." But no snakes, please.

At the top, she looked down a long hall at several closed doors. "There, that wasn't so bad," she said quietly, the sound of her own voice comforting. "What's behind door number one?"

A *real* bathroom. She whooped in delight upon discovering the antique plumbing fixtures. Though covered in fifty-plus years of filth, they were in fair condition. Now all she needed were new pipes, a water heater...and water.

Don't think about the well....

Hana stared for a few moments at the door across the hall. Taking a deep breath, she turned it. No bats. No mice. No snakes. "Whew." She walked around the room, touching the dusty dresser, running her hand along the rusted iron bed frame.

Only one of the three narrow windows had been boarded over. The other two opened rather easily once she released the rusted locks. The temperature lowered a few degrees almost immediately.

She dropped to her knees beside a trunk at the foot of the bed, running her hand along its intricate carving. Relief mingled with foreboding as she discovered it unlocked.

She closed her eyes. "God, please don't let there be anything that moves in here." Wary, she lifted the lid. "Aha." Papers, a Bible, and photo albums. A breeze came through one of the windows, several degrees cooler. Hana peered outside. Thunderheads loomed like harbingers of disaster to the southwest.

Sighing, she reminded herself to hurry through the trunk's contents, then she'd take some of it downstairs to examine more closely.

Curiosity grabbed her by the throat and she removed a photograph album, catching a few loose photos as they fell.

Did these faces belong to the names from the newspaper article? The first was of a little girl standing between two women. Hana squinted as she studied the child's hauntingly familiar face.

"Annie," a small voice supplied from Hana's side.

Forcing herself to remain calm, Hana held her breath and looked at the little girl. Okay, so the ghost was real. She could handle this. Dead or alive, Annie was a child and Hana was a teacher. *No sweat. Yeah, right.*

Hana pointed at the photograph. "Annie?" she repeated, holding her breath.

The child nodded and pointed to the picture of herself. "Me."

"I see." Hana's eyes stung as she considered the little girl's tragic death. "Annie." She moved her finger to the young woman in the photograph. "Who's this?"

Annie giggled as if Hana's question was ridiculous. "Mama."

Hana pointed at the older woman's image. "Grandma?" she asked.

Annie nodded, then reached for the second photograph. "Kayub," she said, looking up at Hana to smile again. "Kayub fun."

Hana stared in silence at Caleb Dawes—the man who'd killed Annie? The skin around Hana's mouth tingled and the acid in her stomach hit a record high.

The photo showed the man smiling and leaning against the hood of an old truck. With his good looks, it was easy to see how Annie's mother, Mildred, might've fallen in love with him. Hana blinked and shook her head. Fictionalizing the missing pieces of this mystery wasn't smart.

Still, it made sense in a sick sort of way.

Caleb's eyes were light, probably blue. It was impossible to tell from the black-and-white print. His full lips were turned up in a grin that belied the morbid tale. This man looked...nice.

Swallowing her fear, she watched Annie take the photo and hold it close to her face. She displayed no fear, no anger toward the man. Surely Annie knew the identity of the person who'd pushed her into the well.

Maybe she just fell. Maybe...

"Kayub," Annie repeated.

"Did—do you like Caleb?" Hana asked.

The child looked up and nodded.

Hana had the overwhelming urge to hold Annie, to rock her, to protect her from a tragedy that had occurred over half a century ago. She closed her eyes.

I'm going crazy—having fantasies about mothering a ghost.

Her biological clock had taken control. Of course, it was beginning to seem more like a sundial at her age. Even so, Hana didn't have to resort to mothering a ghost.

Even an adorable ghost? Enough. When she opened her eyes again, Annie was gone. A protective urge evolved and grew within Hana, more powerful than any she'd ever known.

She had to find Annie. No, she had to save her...

Lightning streaked across the sky and thunder rattled the windows. Every sound sliced right through her, including the small voice crying out for help.

Annie.

Hana ran blindly down the stairs. It didn't matter that Annie Campbell was a ghost—that she was already dead. In Hana's heart, she was a little girl who needed her.

Nothing more, nothing less.

She rushed headlong into the storm. The wind whipped her face and stole her breath—rain penetrated her clothing. Hana leaned over the opening, ducking her head beneath the crumbling cover. She stared into the darkness. "Annie!" Her voice echoed back to her.

"*Annie!*" Tears burned her eyes and fell to join the water pooling at the bottom.

"Mama?"

Squinting, Hana prayed for any sign of the child. It wasn't her imagination. Annie was in the well. Leaning farther, Hana grasped the frayed rope with one hand and called out again. The stones suddenly crumbled beneath her and the rope snapped. A scream tore from her throat as she fell into the well.

She was either going to save Annie from something that had already happened...or become a ghost herself.

Hana struck the cold water and found Annie simultaneously. She grabbed the surprisingly solid child in one arm and held a much-appreciated rope with the other. She remembered the rope snapping and shook her head. Without it, she and Annie would both have—

Don't think. Saving Annie was all that mattered.

She looked up. How far had she fallen? "Help," she shouted toward the top of the well, though her nearest neighbor was a mile away. She had to *try.* "Help!"

Shivering, Annie wrapped her arms around Hana's neck. *Do ghosts feel cold?* It didn't matter—Annie needed her. Hana held her even tighter, fearing the child might disappear again before she could get her out of the well.

"Annie?" A face peered down from the top, and the masculine voice brought with it a surge of hope. "You down there, girl?"

He's calling for Annie?

Hana hugged Annie. "It's all right, honey," she whispered, then turned her attention upward again. "We can't get out."

Their rescuer moved away from the opening, returning within a few seconds. "I'm sendin' down another rope."

The rope landed in the water and she forced herself to concentrate on tying it around Annie's waist. It was no easy task considering how tightly the child clung to her. Hana struggled with the wet rope as her teeth began to chatter along with Annie's.

"We're ready anytime."

A shudder swept through Hana. Was she reliving Annie's death? Was the man at the top of the well another ghost?

Sure. Patrick Swayze to the rescue.

She slammed a mental door on such thoughts. Far more urgent matters demanded her attention now. Like her life...and Annie's.

She gave Annie a reassuring hug. "Did you hear? That man's going to pull us out."

"Kayub," Annie whispered.

Hana must have misunderstood. She kissed the top of the girl's wet head, banishing the crazy notion. She tied a loop in the second rope, large enough for both her feet and soggy tennies. She stood in it and wrapped one arm around both ropes, and the other around Annie.

"Ready," she called, praying their mysterious savior didn't turn out to be more terrifying than a watery grave. Within moments, the ropes grew taut and slowly lifted them up the narrow shaft. Hana held her breath. When they were above the water, she allowed herself a sigh.

Annie wept pitifully until someone reached into the well and pulled her to safety. A second later, those same, very human, arms hauled Hana onto solid ground.

She landed on her rear with an undignified plop, her gaze darting around in search of Annie. Had she vanished again after everything Hana had done to save her?

"Where'd you come from?" The man hovered over her, his legs spread apart as he stared down at her in obvious disbelief.

Hana lifted her gaze from his heavy work boots, traveled upward beyond a pair of overalls and a blue shirt to a familiar face. For a few moments, shock snatched her ability to speak.

"You're Caleb Dawes," she whispered in disbelief.

The man's expression changed to astonishment. "How do you know me?"

Hana struggled to her feet. This couldn't be happening—was it a nightmare? Caleb Dawes was dead. Of course...so was Annie.

"Where's Annie?" Hana demanded. Annie had drowned in 1949. Hadn't she? *God, I'm so confused.* What was happening? "Where's Annie?"

An older woman came out the back door of the farmhouse with Annie wrapped in a blanket. "She's gonna be fine, thanks to you," the woman announced, smiling at Hana.

If other people could see Annie, that meant Hana wasn't crazy. Didn't it? A wave of dizziness enveloped her. Swaying, she reached for the nearest means of support—Caleb's muscular forearm. His other arm circled her waist, preventing her fall.

"Miss Daisy, I think this lady better lie down a spell." He swept Hana into his arms and followed the woman into the house.

Daisy?

Of course. She remembered the name from the article. Daisy Campbell—Annie's grandmother.

Hana was dizzy, but not unconscious, so she couldn't blame this on a dream. She'd never fainted in her life. This was pure nonsense. Insanity.

And this was *her* house.

Wasn't it? Looking around the clean, well-maintained kitchen, Hana had her doubts. Where were the bird droppings? The dust? This couldn't be real. Her throat was dry; her eyes stung.

"P-p-put me down," she said, but the big man simply shook his head. He certainly didn't look or feel like a ghost—or a killer.

"Not 'til Miss Daisy tells me where to put you."

"I reckon we'd best put her in the guest room." The older woman—who also couldn't be real—led them up the stairs. "I swan. How'd that child fall in the well? Caleb, you fix that cover today. I ain't got eyes in the back of my head, and it's a sure thing Mildred ain't gonna watch her."

"Yes'm."

Mildred—Annie's mother?

Had Annie fallen in the well—or been pushed? And what had happened to Hana's old, decrepit farmhouse?

She stifled a gasp when she found herself carried to the first of the bedrooms she'd investigated. It was lovely and bright with a nine-patch quilt on the bed. Lace curtains fluttered in the breeze at the open windows.

Windows that had been broken and boarded over when she'd last seen them....

"Now, you shoo, Caleb," Miss Daisy demanded. "Tell Mildred to try'n get some warm broth into Annie while I tend our guest."

"I'll see to it myself," Caleb said with a frown, taking the child in his strong arms.

Hana blinked at the big man. Could he be trusted with Annie? She took a deep breath to quell her rising panic as Daisy turned to face her.

"What's your name, child?" she asked, assisting Hana in removing her wet clothing.

"Hana." She bit her lower lip when the woman turned to remove a soft cotton nightgown from the trunk Hana'd looked inside of earlier. The empty trunk.

"Hana what?"

The woman politely turned her back while Hana slipped out of her wet undergarments and into the gown. The dry flannel felt wonderful against her clammy skin. "Gillespie."

Daisy patted Hana's shoulder, then turned back the quilt. "How can I thank you for savin' little Annie? You rest and I'll get you something warm if you ain't asleep before I get back."

Hana obeyed the woman's gentle pressure at her back and climbed into the bed.

Daisy pursed her lips and shook her head. "Some folks just don't understand. Just 'cuz Annie ain't perfect don't mean she ain't a blessin' like every other livin' soul."

Living soul?

Hana blinked back her stinging tears, relieved to hear that little Annie was—had been—loved and wanted. *Wait a minute. This is impossible, remember?*

She looked up at the middle-aged woman. It was time to face facts. This woman was Daisy Campbell. *But how?* "What...is the date, please?" Hana asked, holding her breath as she waited.

Daisy moved around the room, looking perplexed when she picked up Hana's soggy Reeboks.

"The date...*please?*"

The woman smiled indulgently. "July 19, 1949. You get some rest now."

$$\text{\textcurrency}\ \text{\textcurrency}\ \text{\textcurrency}$$

Hana slowly opened her eyes. Gazing around the dark room, she wondered where she was—then remembered with a start.

"Oh, my God." She sat upright and clutched the nightgown at her throat. This wasn't a dream. Even in the dark, she realized she was still in the small bedroom at the farmhouse. How could this be?

After crawling from the comfortable bed, Hana rushed over to peer out the window. Moonlight bathed the lawn in silver. She swallowed convulsively at the tranquil scene—so familiar, yet so strange.

Two vintage automobiles occupied the circle drive. A tire swing hung like a dark sentinel from a huge tree she remembered as nothing more than a stump. She rested her forehead against the cool glass.

A figure—a woman—darted across the lawn and climbed into a car parked on the dark road. There was something clandestine about the entire scene. Was it Mildred? But Mildred was dead.

"Am I dead? Are they dead?" She raked her fingers through her hair and shook her head. "Is this all a dream?"

She crossed the room and turned the knob on the wall near the door. The lights illuminated the floral wallpaper she'd last seen hanging in shreds. The soft pinks and blues were bright and pretty, no evidence of time's passage.

Time.

Hana slumped to the floor and covered her face. Tears didn't come, though they'd be welcome relief at this point. She rocked back and forth for several minutes.

"It can't be true," she muttered.

A cool breeze wafted through the window, extricating her from her daze. With a shudder, she drew a deep breath and stood. She had to get out of here. "I need some air."

And a shrink.

Quietly, she tiptoed into the hall and down the stairs to the front door, which opened on well-oiled hinges. The night was perfect—cooler than any since she'd left Kansas City. Taking a deep breath, Hana stepped off the porch and into the damp grass.

Okay. This isn't a dream and I'm not dead. What's left?

Insanity?

She chuckled out loud and continued her stroll toward the old barn she'd planned to have torn down. But here it stood, whole and perfect, silhouetted against the night sky. Mocking her. More proof.

Taking a deep, calming breath, Hana resumed her pace around the edge of the barn toward the fields. Despite the darkness, she needed to feel the wide open spaces surrounding her.

After stepping in something warm and squashy, she realized how foolish it was to traipse across a barnyard with bare feet—in the dark, no less.

"Oh, yuck." Hana backed up, wiping the manure off on the damp grass, then ran smack into something warm and solid.

And laughing.

She turned so quickly she nearly lost her balance, but he reached out to steady her. His grip on her upper arms was warm and strong. She wasn't frightened, even though she knew the impossible identity of the man who had his arms around her in the middle of the night.

In 1949.

She looked up at his face, a face that didn't resemble a murderer's in the least. Moonlight reflected off his blond curls, and his smile was plainly visible. Other than that, his features were a vague blur of light and dark. "Caleb," she whispered.

His smile faded, but his hands didn't move. "Who are you?" he asked softly, his voice melodic and unthreatening. "How do you know my name?"

Hana swallowed, staring at his face. A murderer? *This* man? Impossible. He'd saved Annie...and her.

He tilted his head to the side. "Miss Daisy said your name's Hana."

She nodded, wondering why his touch should feel so...powerful. Men hadn't been a big part of her life. She'd dedicated herself to her career, rarely finding time to even date. Was she so inexperienced that a simple thing like this could spark her libido?

Get a grip, Hana.

She recalled having seen Mildred—or rather a woman she'd assumed was her—leaving the house earlier to climb into an automobile for a midnight rendezvous. Obviously not with this man. Additional testimony of Caleb's innocence? If he wasn't involved with Mildred, then he had no motive to harm Annie. For some reason Hana was relieved that the evidence pointed away from this gentle, handsome man.

Suddenly, she realized something even more important. Annie was *alive*. And that miracle was because of this man's strong arms and her own recklessness. Relief flooded her. She smiled so suddenly it took even her by surprise.

"Annie's alive," she said in awe. "Thank you, thank you, thank you." Overcome with joy and relief, she threw her arms around Caleb's neck and kissed him.

He slid his arms around her and tugged her against him while his mouth returned her impromptu kiss with a raw, primitive hunger that seized her breath.

Hana's shock was quickly followed by a swift surge of yearning. Her legs became rubber bands, and her belly tightened into a coil of blatant need.

She *should* be offended. He was bold. Impudent.

Marvelous.

Hana suddenly became aware of her state of undress, and the way her body molded against his. Intimately. *What am I doing?* Resurrecting her sanity, she pulled herself free and stared down at his tanned hand resting against the stark white nightgown at her waist.

Her face flooded with heat as she continued to stare at his hand. "Stop," she whispered, as much to herself as to him.

He stepped away, his magical hands falling to his sides. They stood staring at one another while the sound of their ragged breathing filled the night.

What had come over her? Hana Gillespie had never done anything so impetuous. She was vulnerable right now. Today's events tumbled over again in her mind. Her nerves were raw. She felt...exposed.

"I think you'd better go wash your foot," he whispered raggedly. "Before I forget my manners again."

"My foot?" Hana looked down, wondering why she should be concerned about her foot when the rest of her body ached for something she must deny it. Then she remembered and raced to the house as fast as she dared, since the moon had set and left her in a dark, lonely world.

A strange world...and an even stranger time.

She paused in the front yard to let her breathing slow as her pulse pounded. She wiped her foot in the damp grass again. The sound of a vehicle stopping out by the road made her dart behind the porch railing.

She heard a masculine chuckle from the vicinity of the road, but no telltale headlights shone in the darkness. Mildred's lover was being very cautious.

Hana remained hidden near the trellis, hoping she wouldn't be seen. The woman she assumed was Mildred stopped to remove her shoes, then quietly entered the house. The car drove away a minute later.

A well-orchestrated rendezvous.

Hana released a ragged breath and turned toward the house. Unless she wanted to explain her own nocturnal behavior, Hana needed to make certain Mildred was upstairs in her room before she went in herself.

But a lone figure caught and commanded her attention as she turned. An imposing figure, he stood in the field between the house and barn, staring toward the road. The fading moonlight distinguished the man's light hair.

Caleb Dawes.

Hana groaned and opened her eyes. Sunlight flooded the bedroom, shimmering through the snowy lace curtains to land in geometric patterns across the polished wood floor.

At least it was morning this time. But it was still 1949.

I'm not crazy. I'm not dreaming. This is real.

Completing her affirmations, Hana rubbed her head and swung her legs over the edge of the bed, struggling into a sitting position. Standing, she stretched and yawned.

The door opened just a crack, then Hana noticed the small hand gripping its edge just before a blond pigtail swung into the opening. After another moment, Annie's face followed, her blue eyes wide and curious.

"Hello, Annie," Hana said warmly, overjoyed to see the little girl alive.

The child came the rest of the way into the room. She wore a blue calico dress with black leather shoes. Her face was clean and shining pink, the blond braids neatly secured with ribbons.

Annie's fingers were in her mouth as she smiled at Hana. "Who you?" she mumbled.

"Don't you remember?" Hana frowned, then realized that the Annie who'd known her had been a ghost. A chill swept through her as she considered how very close the darling little girl had come to never seeing this new day. "I'm Hana."

"Hana," she repeated. "Annie." She pointed at herself, then swung left and right as she continued to stare at Hana with that impish grin.

She's alive, and she's going to stay that way. Hana couldn't begin to explain her fierce need to protect Annie. It was a simple fact—and, she decided, the reason she was here.

She needed facts to help her protect Annie. For one thing, who had Mildred been sneaking out to meet last night?

Jeez. I've fallen into an Agatha Christie novel.

Would the person who pushed Annie try again?

Shocked by her own bizarre thoughts, Hana reached out to touch Annie's shoulder, needing reassurance that the child was, in fact, alive. She mustn't permit her fears to transmit to Annie.

"So, Annie, do you know where your grandma hid my clothes?" Hana asked.

Annie walked over to the trunk and pointed. Hana followed and lifted the lid. Yesterday, in Hana's time, this trunk had held only photo albums and an old Bible. Now there were several old dresses, a pair of overalls, another nightgown, and a few undergarments that more closely resembled items one might expect to find in a torture chamber.

Voices raised in obvious disagreement reached Hana's ears. Two women—Mildred and Daisy, no doubt—were involved in a heated argument. She chewed her lower lip and cocked her head to listen.

Their words weren't discernible, and after a few moments the front door slammed. Remembering Annie, Hana glanced down at the little girl. Her blue eyes were wide and her lower lip trembled.

Hana knelt beside the child and tentatively pulled her into her arms. Annie hesitated for only a moment, then clung to Hana's neck and wept on her shoulder. "Don't cry, punkin'. It's all right."

Hana straightened and carried Annie to the edge of the bed. She sat there for several minutes, waiting for the child's tears to cease. It felt so right to hold this little girl. Fulfillment and contentment threatened to destroy all her efforts at logic. Annie's hair had a clean, little girl scent to it. Her small body was warm and filled a deep void in Hana's heart—a need she planned to fill by adopting.

"Well, I'd better get dressed," Hana said.

A short time later, Annie and Hana went downstairs to the kitchen. Daisy looked up from a letter clutched in her hands. Her eyes were red and puffy when she glanced up at Hana, and she stuffed the letter into her apron pocket.

Hana's gaze swept the tidy room, quite modern by 1949 standards. A Frigidaire hummed away in the corner, and the wood floor gleamed. A monstrous stove took up most of the far wall, and a huge sink sat beneath a square window. Arthur Godfrey's voice boomed to housewives across America from a radio.

The back door opened and Caleb came into the kitchen smiling. "How's my Annie this mornin'?"

The child flew into his arms and he whirled her in a circle. Hana watched them, knowing beyond any doubt that this man would never harm Annie. Yet, in the first history, he'd been executed for her murder.

Hana's journey through time had saved more than one life. She bit her lower lip and released a slow breath. None of this made sense....

Daisy hurried around the kitchen, and a few moments later, a huge breakfast filled the table. "Sit and eat before it gets cold."

Remembering the way she'd responded to Caleb's kiss, Hana avoided his gaze as she sat opposite him with Annie at her side. Daisy filled the coffee cups and poured a glass of milk for Annie, then took a seat.

"Hana, would you be willin' to stay on and help with Annie?"

As if she had anywhere else to go. Hana smiled and said, "I'd like that."

"Good," Daisy said. "Stay as long as you're willing. I'm gonna need the help."

The woman had a distant expression in her eyes. Why had she been crying earlier? Hana didn't want her to be unhappy. Daisy Campbell was a good woman who loved Annie.

As did Hana.

She glanced across the table at Caleb, whose gaze rested on her with warmth and something more that stole her breath. He turned his gaze to Annie and winked. "You gonna help me feed that ornery mule after breakfast?" he asked the girl.

Annie giggled and nodded. She held up some fingers and counted to three.

"Yep, he gets three scoops," Caleb said. "Good, Annie."

Hana's heart warmed as she watched the exchange between the man and Annie. How could anyone have ever believed him guilty of killing a child he so obviously adored?

They're both alive now. Hana sipped her coffee, vowing to keep them that way.

❦ ❦ ❦

Hana bolted upright in bed, drenched in sweat. She scrambled from the bed and paced the room, raking her fingers through her hair. Then she heard it. Annie's voice crying out in her head, just like—

"Oh, God." Hana ran from her room and down the stairs to the back door. "Annie!" she shouted, racing toward the well, reminding herself that Caleb had sealed the well at Daisy's insistence.

Logic be damned—she heard Annie scream again just as the clouds parted and moonlight beamed on that wretched well like a spotlight.

The uncovered well.

"Annie!" Hana grabbed the rope and peered into the well. "Hold onto the rope, Annie."

"Mama!"

Hana had to save her. She shouted toward the house again for help. How had Annie—

Thwap. Something heavy slammed into Hana's shoulder and she fell down the narrow shaft. "Annie!"

The water felt like a million needles against her skin, and her wet nightgown dragged her under. She found Annie's arm and pulled them both to the surface, scrambling for the rope. Shivering, she held the choking but breathing child and clung to the rope.

Hana gulped in a breath to shout, then realized someone was standing over the well. Laughing.

The killer.

Would Annie *and* Hana drown this time? *No.* Tears swelled in Hana's eyes, but she blinked them back. The moonlight vanished as the killer slid the cover in place. Hana screamed and Annie cried.

They were being sealed alive in the well.

God help us.

Caleb heard the screams and raced from his bed and across the field toward the house. *Annie.* His little girl.

A car sped away as he neared the house, the lights vanishing down the dusty road. "Annie!"

He ran to the back door, but a muffled sound stayed him. His blood turned cold as he faced the well. The clouds shifted and the moon illuminated the cover he'd placed over it just yesterday. Nothing seemed amiss. Maybe he'd imagined the sound.

Still, something drew him to the well, and as he approached, he realized the cover wasn't latched, and it sat off-center. The muffled cry came again. Within seconds, he had the cover off and peered into the deep, black pit. "Annie?"

"Help us."

"Hana?" He didn't wait for her answer, but ran to fetch another rope. He shouted into the house for Miss Daisy, who joined him to help pull Hana and Annie to safety again.

Shivering and sobbing, they were both on dry ground again with his arms wrapped around them before he stopped to think. "What happened?" he asked, allowing Miss Daisy to take Annie and wrap her in a warm blanket.

"Talk inside," Miss Daisy said, carrying Annie into the house without waiting for an answer.

"Thank you," Hana said as he led her into the kitchen.

Miss Daisy had hot cocoa in front of Annie before she joined them at the table. "Now tell us what happened," she said to Hana.

"Something woke me." She looked at Annie, who had stopped shivering and crying now and seemed content with slurping her cocoa. "A nightmare."

"You saved Annie again," Caleb said. "I don't know how you knew, but—"

"I know how," Miss Daisy said, pulling two folded pieces of paper from her pocket. "This here's a letter from Mildred. She's gone and ain't comin' back." The woman's voice trembled. "She told me this morning that her lover wanted her to send Annie away. That he wouldn't marry her otherwise. That's when she told me she had to go away, because she wanted to marry him, but she was afraid he'd hurt..." Miss Daisy turned her gaze on Annie.

"Good Lord." Caleb glanced at Annie, who wasn't listening, thank goodness.

"Someone pushed me," Hana said. "Do you...think it was her lover?"

Miss Daisy nodded and bit her lower lip. "Yes."

"I saw a car just before I heard you scream," Caleb said, clenching his fist. "I'm gonna call the sheriff."

Miss Daisy agreed, but said it could wait until morning. Mildred and her lover were gone now, and Annie was safe. Then she looked at Caleb and gave him a sad smile.

"Mildred told me somethin' else," she said.

Caleb studied the older woman's face, realizing she knew the truth. He reached for her hand and squeezed it. "I wanted to tell you, Miss Daisy, but Mildred made me believe she'd send Annie away if I did."

"No child could ask for a better daddy, Caleb," Miss Daisy said, a tear trickling down her wrinkled cheek. "Maybe I lost a daughter today, but I think I got me a son instead. You'll stay?"

He looked at his daughter, who grinned through a cocoa mustache. "There's no place I'd rather be."

He felt and met Hana's gaze. Tears sparkled in her lashes and her dark hair had dried in tiny curls around her face. Right now she and Annie were the most beautiful people he'd ever seen. His heart felt tight in his chest and his throat clogged.

"That's settled then." Miss Daisy turned her attention to Hana. "And you're a guardian angel."

"Guardian angel?" Hana gave a nervous laugh and rubbed Annie's back.

Miss Daisy produced another piece of paper and handed it to Hana, who took it with trembling fingers. "Where did you get this?" Hana asked, her eyes wide.

"What is it?"

"Nothin' for you to worry about, Caleb," Miss Daisy said steadily. "It's between us womenfolk."

"You knew?" Hana asked, passing the piece of paper back to Miss Daisy.

"Like I said, you're Annie's guardian angel, child."

"What are you going to do with that?" Hana asked, a slight tremor in her voice.

Caleb didn't know what was happening, but he knew it was important. He reached across the table and took Hana's hand in his, giving it a firm squeeze. There was something powerful about his feelings for this woman. All he knew for certain was that he couldn't let her leave.

Miss Daisy rose and faced them all. "You both gonna stay here with Annie?" she asked in a no-nonsense tone.

Caleb nodded, knowing he could finally claim his daughter as his own. "Even President Truman couldn't drag me away from here now."

Miss Daisy smiled and said, "Praise be." Then she turned to Hana again, the folded piece of paper held in both her hands. "Hana...?"

Hana looked at Caleb with something burning in her eyes that made his heart do a little flip-flop in his chest, then she glanced down at Annie. When she looked up at Miss Daisy again, she drew a deep breath and said, "I'm here for a reason."

"That you are, child." Miss Daisy was still smiling when she tossed the folded paper into the stove where the glowing embers devoured it.

"Stowy," Annie said, yawning.

Hana gathered Caleb's little girl into her arms and looked up at him, "Tonight," she promised, "and forever."

Dearly  Beloved

D. R. Meredith

Highwater, Texas, population 455, dozed in the shade of its own history. The town began as a division headquarters for the XIT Ranch in the Texas panhandle, considered the largest ranch anywhere ever, but according to the late Jake Palmer, when the XIT started selling off land at the turn of the last century, Highwater couldn't make it as an independent city. Everyone agreed that Jake exaggerated, because at no time in its history did Highwater qualify as a city. Village was more like it. Oh, it still had a post office, a small room on the west side of Highwater Grocery, where Butch Jones, the proprietor, was also the postmaster. There was always some argument down at Buddy's Café during the ten o'clock coffee hour that the postmaster ought to be somebody besides Butch. In a town the size of Highwater, you wanted to spread out the employment as much as possible. Butch already owned Highwater Grocery. It wasn't fair that he earn a salary as postmaster besides. There were whispers that Butch had turned Democrat just so he could get the appointment, but nobody wanted to insult Butch by asking

him. The ranchers and farmers and what businessmen as Highwater had that met every day at Buddy's listened closely to everything
political Butch had to say to see if they could catch him supporting
the administration in Washington. Highwater had voted Republican
ever since Roosevelt declared a bank holiday, and First State Bank
of Highwater closed its doors never to reopen them. The idea that
one of their own would bolt Lincoln's party purely for the money
was nearly more than Highwater could stomach, or at least those
who met at Buddy's, which was everybody who mattered, meaning
everybody who owned a business or land or had managed to stay
out of bankruptcy court. They all knew that another bad drought
like the 1950s, or one bad winter like the one back in 1886–87, and
they were done for. So there was a smidgen of envy mixed in with
principle whenever Highwater thought about Butch Jones being on
the federal payroll as well as being proprietor of Highwater's only
grocery store. Whatever the weather or the commodity markets did,
Butch could always fall back on his government paycheck while the
rest of the folks in Highwater and Bonham County would be hung
out to dry. It stuck in Highwater's craw that it was so.

Butch Jones, his shadowy political affiliations, and his government check was the first topic of conversation whenever Butch
missed the ten o'clock coffee hour—which was around the first
of every month. Everybody figured he drove to Amarillo to get
his check cashed instead of going to the bank in Troutman at
the other end of the county like everyone else did when they
had financial business. It was just one more way of thumbing
his nose at Highwater, according to Buddy, who owned Buddy's
Café where the coffee klatch met, and was therefore listened to
with respect. By doing his banking in Amarillo, Butch put himself
out of the reach of the local grapevine. One way or another, the
ten o'clock coffee hour usually found out what a man had in his
checking account and sometimes his saving account, too, if he
did his banking in Troutman or one of the other towns near Highwater. "Information by osmosis," is what Sheriff Jim Hayworth
called it, since every teller and every bank officer denied disclos-
ing any information about any bank customer whomsoever, yet
details seemed to float like the gossamer down from a cotton-

wood tree to be snatched out of the air by the men sitting at the round table by the front window in Buddy's Café at the south end of Main Street.

One woman sat at the round table—and she by special invitation of Buddy. But Elizabeth Walker had no illusions about why she was the only woman in Highwater history to be accorded the privilege of joining the coffee hour. She was there because she was the first elected official of the female persuasion. She was the Justice of the Peace for the Highwater end of Bonham County, and that made her a woman to be reckoned with. When investigating a death, she and not the sheriff or the commissioners' court or anybody else was in charge of the body and the evidence. Not until she determined the cause of death—natural causes, accident, suicide, homicide—was the case turned over to the sheriff. The fact was, Elizabeth had too much power to be excluded from the coffee circle. No one, including Buddy, was ever quite sure what Elizabeth might do if left to her own devices, so better to invite her into the circle than leave her out. That way they could keep an eye on her. Besides, now that she was an elected official, she had to be taught how the system worked, being that she was a woman and had no experience with public office and local government. They conveniently forgot the civic organizations that Elizabeth had been president of at one time or another, and that had, under her leadership, wrested town improvements out of the commissioners' court, frequently against the will of individual commissioners. Those were ladies' clubs and not on a par with elected officials.

"I don't see Butch Jones here this morning," said D. B. DeBord, a county commissioner forty-five of his eighty years.

"Reckon he's gone into Amarillo to cash his postmaster's check," said Buddy in a loud voice. D. B. had gotten hard of hearing the past year, so everybody had to speak up or get chewed out by D. B. for mumbling.

"I knowed Butch's granddaddy as well as I know my own name," said D. B. "I don't know what he'd think about the way Butch is carrying on."

"Somebody has to be the postmaster, D. B.," said Elizabeth, sipping her coffee and occasionally meeting the eyes of the sheriff.

Lord have mercy, but there was no telling what her own grand-daddy would have said about her own carryings on.

D. B.'s bristly white eyebrows drew together like they did every time somebody disagreed with him. "Don't have to be him. Plenty of people in Highwater could use a cushion like a government check. Ed and Jewel Carruthers sure could."

Everybody sipped their coffee and thought about the Car-rutherses. Ed and Jewell had bought a quarter section—one hundred and sixty acres—after WWI. Everybody shook their heads at such foolishness. There was no way to make a living on a quarter of a section out in the western panhandle, not when the average ranch ran close to a hundred sections, and a farm, what few there were in Bonham County, averaged five sections. With little rain and hardly any surface water, a man had to dig wells and put up windmills just to water his cattle. But Ed Carruthers fooled everybody. He dug a well, put in Bonham County's first irrigation system, and raised veg-etables that he sold to independent grocers. Nobody figured Ed and Jewell were making a killing, but they were sure making a living on that little quarter section.

"Ed and Jewel are close to eighty, D. B., if not already there," said Elizabeth, feeling just put out enough to start a fight. "And they live fifteen miles out in the country. Do you want to drive fifteen miles to pick up your mail? And they're too old to sit all day in that little room Butch has fixed up in the grocery store."

"I beg your pardon, missy, but I'm eighty myself and I ain't ready to put up the plow—and neither is Ed Carruthers," said D. B., his eyebrows now a solid bristly line above his eyes. "I seen him just the other day driving toward his place with a pickup full of lumber, so I guess he's fixing to build something, and if he's fixing to build something, then he's still got starch in his britches."

"That was last month, D. B.," said Buddy. "You seen him driving through town last month with lumber in his pickup. Yesterday you saw him drive through with something wrapped up and tied down in the bed of his pickup. Haven't figured out yet what it was, but it was awful damn heavy. His pickup was riding low to the ground."

D. B. flushed red. His memory had been slipping the last year or so, never about anything important, but he did tend to get his times mixed up—like the Saturday he went to the First Baptist Church thinking it was Sunday. "That's what I meant when I said the other day. That can mean last month same as it can mean yesterday."

"What do you suppose he's building?" asked Elizabeth.

"Well, how would I know?" asked D. B. in a testy voice. "Why don't you go out there and ask him if you're so curious?"

Elizabeth pushed back her chair and stood up. "I think I will. Ed and Jewel haven't been in church for a while, and since they have no family, somebody ought to check on them. Ed doesn't have any business climbing ladders or hammering, nailing, and sawing. And he doesn't have any business being postmaster either. His eyes are so bad, he really shouldn't be driving, much less trying to make out strange handwriting on an envelope. He and Jewel are really self-sufficient with their own water well and generator for electricity, and they have Social Security and Medicare. They don't need another government check."

"Any time you think Social Security pays for more than beans and flour, you're mistaken, Miss Elizabeth," said D. B. "Just ask any of us oldsters."

"I know about living close, D. B.," said Elizabeth. "Don't think I don't."

Embarrassed, D. B. looked down at the red-and-black-checked oilcloth on the round table. "My apologies, Elizabeth. I didn't mean to bring up hurtful subjects."

Elizabeth drew a deep breath to ease the sick feeling in her stomach. Her husband had died without insurance, without money, and without a will. Elizabeth was forced to sell most of her cattle and lease out half her ranch, and still wasn't through paying the inheritance taxes. That's why she had run for justice of the peace. Just like Butch Jones and the Carruthers, she needed a check just to get by.

She patted D. B.'s arm. "Don't worry about it. Everybody knows my situation. I shouldn't be so sensitive about it."

"In Highwater we all know one another's situations," said Buddy, "but we try not to talk about them. That's what good neighbors do. They help but they don't talk about it, and a whole lot they overlook because that's best." That was Buddy's way of apologizing for D. B. DeBord, and reassuring Elizabeth that nobody would allude to her finances again.

Elizabeth knew that she would find a vase of D. B.'s prize roses in front of her office door at the courthouse come tomorrow. That's what men of his generation did when they hurt a lady's feelings. Not that her feelings were hurt, exactly. She always felt sick to her stomach whenever she thought of her finances. But today she was feeling contrary, and couldn't figure out why. Something was out of place in her world and she didn't know what it was.

"Believe I'll go with you, Elizabeth," said Jim Hayworth, grabbing his Stetson off the coat rack and following her out the door.

Jim Hayworth had been sheriff of Bonham County twenty-five of his fifty years, and was nearly as whipcord lean and firm of flesh as the day he got home from Vietnam if you ignored a little slackness about the jaw—and Elizabeth Walker did. Lord knows, at forty-three she had lines around the eyes and her chin wasn't as firm as it once was and the forces of gravity were liable to attack her bosom any day, so who was she to demand that a man have abs like steel? Of course, chances were any man with a washboard belly didn't get it by working in Highwater, and Elizabeth had as much use for a glutton as she did for a man who spent the majority of his time perfecting his manly figure instead of using his brain and muscles to accomplish something that needed done.

Jim Hayworth was neither a glutton nor a fitness freak. He was a man who worked hard at his job as sheriff and as a rancher in his off-hours. Either one of those jobs kept you strong, but didn't necessarily sculpt your body. Elizabeth didn't care. She would take Jim Hayworth as he was, gray in his hair and gray on his chest when he whipped his shirt off those days he came for supper and stayed for breakfast—which was a couple times a week, or less frequently depending on circumstances. She supposed everybody in Highwater knew exactly when Jim stayed and when he didn't, despite the fact that Elizabeth lived ten miles outside of Highwater, five of it dirt road meandering across the prairie until it circled in front of her ranch house. But nobody said anything, and as long as nobody said anything, then she didn't plan on changing her ways.

She was two years a widow, and Jim had lost his wife some years before that, so it wasn't like he was hanging his pants on another man's bedpost. He was her husband's best friend, and now he was hers, and they were best friends who sometimes carried on a little. It wasn't anyone's business but hers and Jim's, but Elizabeth didn't underestimate Highwater's interest in the goings-on of their elected officials. Elizabeth figured it wouldn't be long before somebody mentioned that she and Jim were keeping too close company. Highwater was a town in which the word *seemly* was still in vogue.

She and Jim walked shoulder to shoulder toward the courthouse at the north end of Main Street where their pickups were parked. "I'll follow you to the Carruthers, and then maybe follow you home," said Jim in his slow, deep voice that always sent chills up her spine and set fire to her belly even though she figured she was old enough to be immune to those sorts of feelings. "I can throw a couple of steaks on your grill and help you set the table."

"How much setting does the table need for two people?" she asked with a sidelong look at him. "I figure I can handle it."

He leaned over and whispered in her ear. "Then how about I help you do a little house cleaning, maybe change the bed."

She felt the fire burning hotter in her belly. "I put on fresh sheets this morning."

He grinned at her, like Sam Elliott grinning at Katherine Ross in *Conagher*, and Elizabeth thought she might burn up from instantaneous combustion. "I meant I'd help you do a little housework tomorrow morning."

She wondered if he had any idea how lethal his grin and his voice were. She would hate to think that he did. It would take away from what they shared, and put her in the position of being seduced. She didn't much like that idea.

"What do you really think of me, Jim?"

He lost his grin and looked somber. "You make me hotter than any man my age ought to be, but that ain't the reason I like coming home with you." He grimaced. "That's a lie. I like you setting me on fire, but I like the way you warm me up when how we feel won't send us running to the bedroom. I feel comfortable with you, Elizabeth. You warm me down to the bone until I think I won't ever be cold and lonely again. And when I go home alone, I catch myself talking to you like you were there with me, telling you about my day and how I plan to spend the evening."

He fell silent and walked along with her past the vacant block where the Highwater Hotel stood before it burned down in 1928, and burned most of the town's aspirations with it. "That's as close as I can come to what I feel, Elizabeth. I ain't no Shakespeare. The words don't roll out of my mouth like diamond solitaires to make any talk between us sparkle."

There, in front of Highwater Grocery and Phil's Hardware and Variety Store, she raised up on her toes and kissed the sheriff on the mouth, and she took her time about it, too. If people were going to talk about her, then she would give them something to talk about besides her finances. "You might want to wipe your mouth unless you like strawberry cream lipstick," she said after breaking off the kiss.

Jim licked his lips, then pulled a handkerchief out of his pocket and wiped his mouth. "Always wondered why you tasted so much like strawberries." He tucked his handkerchief back in his pocket and opened the pickup door for her. "You know you gave the gossips enough to talk about for the next year. What do you say to that, Elizabeth?"

She slid into her pickup and rolled down the window so she could talk to him. "To quote my younger son, some folks in Highwater need to get a life, maybe take up watercolor or needlepoint. You'll follow me to the Carruthers place?"

Jim rubbed his jaw and looked off in the distance past the courthouse. "I been thinking about that, Elizabeth. Why don't you let me go out to see about Ed and Jewel. I think Ed would take a visit from me better than from you. Remember, Ed's kind of standoffish around any woman except Jewel. He thinks she hung the moon and the stars." He met her eyes, his a guileless blue. "Why don't you go get that table set while I see about the Carruthers?"

The fire abruptly went out in her belly. His eyes were too guileless, and she suspected he was trying to keep her from going to the Carruthers. Maybe if he had just asked her, she would have let him do it, but not now. "I don't like somebody trying to soften me up to get their own way, Jim. You can follow me to the Carruthers place, then follow me home for dinner, but don't count on anything else. I can change my own bed when it needs it, thank you very much, and it won't need changing for at least a week."

"Walt always said you could dig in your heels worse than a Missouri mule when it suited you," began Jim.

"Nice of you to tell me that my late husband was talking about me behind my back."

Jim looked exasperated. "God Almighty, Elizabeth, Walt told you that to your face. I heard him say it on several occasions. What's gotten into you today? You're snipping at everybody."

Elizabeth couldn't answer him because she didn't know what was wrong except that her intuition was telling her something was, but she could no more tell Jim why she thought so than she could fly. Feminine intuition was like that: reliable but inexplicable. "Why don't you want me going to the Carruthers place?"

"I never said I didn't want you going. I just said I'd run by if you were worried, but the fact is, Elizabeth, I was just out at Ed's place a couple of days ago. Ed's fine, but Jewel is laid up. MS is what the doctors told Ed. She spends a lot of time sleeping, according to Ed, and he said he could take care of her without any help, but I called the home health nurse anyway. She's going to check in twice a week to make sure Ed's managing."

"Why didn't you just tell me that to start with, Jim, instead of leading me down the garden path with talk about how hot I make you?"

"That was the truth, Elizabeth, and it doesn't have anything to do with the Carruthers. Maybe I was pushing a little hard about staying the night, but Lord Almighty, I don't need much of an excuse to do that."

"I'm going to go see the Carruthers for myself, Jim. You can come if you want to," Elizabeth said, rolling up her window and turning the ignition. She deliberately didn't look at Jim because she didn't want to see any expression on his face that might disillusion her further.

He followed her to the Carruthers'—she saw his pickup in the rearview mirror—but she resolutely kept her eyes on the narrow two-lane highway running arrow-straight through the prairie to the New Mexico border, glancing every now and then at the wild-flowers along the road. The yuccas with their dagger-sharp leaves and beautiful long stalks of cream-colored flowers were in bloom. Black-eyed Susans and Indian blankets covered the earth in red, orange, and yellow tapestries. Indian paintbrushes with their brightly colored tips were scattered among them, looking like they had been dipped in red paint. By the time she turned off the high-way and onto the Carruthers place, she felt better; in fact, she felt ashamed of herself for being so contrary with Jim, but too stub-born to turn back.

Elizabeth parked in front of the Carruthers' small, one-story frame farmhouse, and slid out of the truck. She knew for a fact that the house had three bedrooms, two for the children Ed and Jewel had wanted but never had. When Jewel reached menopause, and she and Ed knew for a fact there would be no late pregnancy as they had hoped, Jewel turned one bedroom into an office for Ed. The other she kept as a guest room, although to Elizabeth's knowledge, no guest had ever stayed under the Carruthers' roof. Elizabeth wondered how Jewel could have stood walking by those two empty bedrooms through all her childbearing years, always hoping for a miracle, always wondering who was at fault: her or Ed. More likely they believed children were a gift from God, and not a result of properly functioning reproductive organs, because Elizabeth had never caught a hint of a sour spot in the Carruthers' marriage. In fact, they acted so much like newlyweds that Eliza-beth always expected to hear the echoes of "Dearly Beloved" whenever she was around them.

Jim parked his truck next to hers and joined her at the Car-ruthers' front door. Elizabeth knocked and called out, "Mr. Car-ruthers, it's Elizabeth Walker and Sheriff Hayworth."

The door opened and Ed Carruthers stepped outside on the porch. At past eighty he was a tall, stately looking man with silver-white hair and dark blue eyes, and must have been handsome in his younger days. "Elizabeth, Sheriff, what brings you out this way?"

His eyes were red-rimmed as though he had been crying, logical if his beloved wife had multiple sclerosis, thought Elizabeth. Soon her care would be beyond him even with the help of the home health nurse.

"Elizabeth got a bee in her bonnet because you and Jewel haven't made it to church lately," said Jim. "Nothing would do but for her to come out and check on you folks."

Elizabeth felt foolish, and because she felt foolish she wouldn't give in gracefully. That was part of her makeup and it used to drive Walt crazy, but she couldn't help it. Her stubbornness had solved some crimes in Crawford County that had been overlooked in the past. Not that she thought there was a crime here, she assured herself, but she just wanted to make sure everything was *right*.

"How is Jewel?" Elizabeth asked.

Ed Carruthers turned to Jim with a terrified look. "What does she mean?"

Jim laid his hand on Ed's shoulder. "I told her about Jewel having multiple sclerosis, and that she was spending a lot of time sleeping. I'm sorry but I had to tell her, Ed, or she might have led a platoon of the First Baptist Ladies' Missionary Society out here. Either that or she would have accused you of murder. You know she's done that on occasion, accused other people of murder, that is."

"I'm not accusing Ed of murder," said Elizabeth through gritted teeth. She wished Jim hadn't jumped in with an explanation as to why they had come. She would have liked to hear what Ed had to say without Jim's prompting.

"Of course, you're not," said Jim, seeming not to see her glaring at him.

"May I see Jewel?" asked Elizabeth. "I feel badly that she was so sick and I didn't know a thing about it. I didn't even notice obvious symptoms in her motor skills or speech."

"She is sleeping," said Ed. "Sometimes it's hard to wake her up and she is disturbed when I do."

"Disturbed how?"

"She doesn't make much sense, Elizabeth," said Jim. "Leave her alone, and leave Ed alone, too."

"I don't want you to bother a sick woman on my account," said

Elizabeth. "I'm sorry I bothered you. Give Jewel my best when she wakes up." She turned and walked down the porch steps before turning. "By the way, Ed, what are you building?"

"Beg pardon?" asked Ed, his face blank.

"Everybody at Buddy's was talking about you driving through town with a load of lumber in the bed of your pickup. I just wondered what you were building, and if it wouldn't be best to have someone help you."

"I'm building shelves in the storm cellar," said Ed.

Elizabeth nodded and climbed in her pickup and drove off. She noticed Jim staying and talking to Ed Carruthers and wondered if they were getting their stories straight, because as sure as God made little green apples, Ed's story was full of knotholes. For one thing, MS generally hit women between the ages of twenty and forty, and by eighty they would either be dead or totally bedridden. Jim's wife, Carolyn, had died of multiple sclerosis, so Elizabeth supposed that's where that part of the story came from.

Elizabeth parked in front of her house, a two-story ranch with a wraparound porch and hitching rails still in place. She hurried into the house and consulted the phone book, then dialed a number while keeping her eye on the long dirt road that led up her house. She would see Jim coming long before he arrived by the cloud of dust his pickup stirred up.

She turned her attention to the phone when someone picked up on the other end. "Yes, hello, this is Justice of the Peace Elizabeth Walker. I was just checking to see if the home health nurse could possibly visit Ed and Jewel Carruthers more often than twice a week. They are such an elderly couple and the wife has MS. What did you say? You have no record of home health visiting the Carruthers at all? Sheriff Jim Hayworth was supposed to call, but something must have delayed him. Do I want to order the nurse to visit? No, I think I had better talk it over with the sheriff first."

Elizabeth hung up and began to pace the long living room with its old-fashioned furniture. Jim lied about the home health nurse, and Ed Carruthers lied about the shelves in his storm cellar, too. She and the other ladies of the Missionary Society had been in Ed and Jewel's storm cellar when they were helping Jewel last fall. The cellar already had shelves on all four walls. So that was two lies the men had told, and she would bet her bottom dollar that they had lied about the MS, too. There was no point in asking liars to repeat their lies. She would have to get to the bottom of this case another way, and the first thing she had to do was find Jewel Carruthers and talk to her—if she was still alive, and Elizabeth bet she was because Jim Hayworth would never cover up a murder. But knowing that, why was she so dead set on knowing what was going on? Because her best friend lied to her and she wanted to know why, or she would never trust him again or let him in her bed, either. And she didn't think she could stand dismissing him from her life.

After a tense meal, Jim dialed his answering machine at the courthouse to see if all was well in Bonham County. Elizabeth could have told him it wasn't, but she didn't intend to tell him anything until she ferreted out the truth. Then she would confront him, him and Ed Carruthers both.

Jim hung up the phone and picked up his hat. "I gotta run, Elizabeth. One of the messages was from the XIT Bar. Eddie Gomez and John Turley are liquored up and talking big. I figure I can get there before the fighting gets started good and throw a loop around the two of them and lock 'em up until they sober up. Then I guess I'll go home. I don't figure there's any need in coming back here."

"You know when to take a hint," said Elizabeth, handing him his hat.

As soon as she could no longer see his taillights, she got into her pickup and drove to the Carruthers place, parking halfway down the long dirt road leading to the house. Grabbing a flashlight, she climbed out of the pickup and began walking toward the house, thankful that she hadn't noticed any dogs that afternoon. No lights shone in the house, and Ed's old Ford pickup was parked close to the barn. Elizabeth hesitated and wondered if she was being foolish. Maybe Jewel did have MS and Ed really was building shelves in the storm cellar. And maybe Jim just told her about the home health nurse to keep her calm. But why would he do that?

And why did Ed need more shelves in the storm cellar when Jewel was unable to do any home canning? For that matter, why would Ed lie about the lumber to begin with?

Elizabeth stood irresolute in the shadow of a cottonwood tree in the front yard. She needed to talk to Jewel—if Jewel was around to be talked to. And *how* was she to find out? She couldn't very well go around looking in windows like some sort of Peeping Tom. Or was it Tomasina? On the other hand, she could peek into the barn and outbuildings and the infamous storm cellar to see if she saw the lumber. Mind made up, she did exactly that. There was nothing in the barn but a pickup covered by a piece of canvas. The outbuildings were similarly innocent of anything suspicious. At last, she lifted one of the double doors of the storm cellar and carefully walked down the steps. She shone her flashlight on an object sitting on two sawhorses in the middle of the cellar.

"Oh, God!" she cried, and turned to run up the stairs when two bright lights shone in her eyes. She turned her head and covered her eyes with her arm. "Ed Carruthers, is that you?"

"Yes, Elizabeth, I reckon it is."

"Who's that with you?"

"It's me, Elizabeth," said Jim Hayworth. "I'm surprised you didn't guess."

"I was hoping that it was Jewel!" retorted Elizabeth. "I was hoping that she wasn't in that pine casket on the sawhorses."

"She ain't in there," said Ed. "That pine box is mine."

"What! You built your own casket?"

"Jewel and I were from the Appalachian Mountains, and it was the custom there for the family to build a casket for the loved one who passed away. That's what I did for Jewel, but I built my own because I don't have no family left to do it for me. Me and Jewel never had anybody but each other. When she died, I built her a casket, the finest one I could. I stained it mahogany and lined it with pillows covered in velvet. But I wanted a tombstone for her—for both of us—so everybody would know we were buried together and nobody would dig us up someday and separate us."

"My God, you can't do that, Ed. You can't just bury somebody in a pine box anymore. By law the body has to be embalmed and the casket has to be set inside a vault. Tell him, Jim."

Jim walked down the steps and put his arms around Elizabeth, pulling her tight against him despite her pushing and shoving. "Hush, Elizabeth. Don't you believe in love stories? Don't you believe in two people planning their final resting place together?"

"This is not a love story!" shouted Elizabeth. "This is a violation of the law."

"Elizabeth, do you remember what Buddy said this morning? That we all know each other's situations, but sometimes we overlook things because that's best. I've been sheriff of Highwater and Bonham County for twenty-five years, and in that time I've learned to overlook some things. Ed's burying his wife by himself may not be the American way of death, but it's the right thing for him and Jewel. And when he goes, I'm to see to it that he's buried next to Jewel in that very pine box you see. And I'll do it. I'm not arresting Ed for burying his wife. He had his reasons, some of which he's already explained. There's one more reason: Social Security. Jewel and Ed were too feeble to farm anymore, and they never made enough to save very much. In other words, they needed two Social Security checks to live."

"Ed's been cashing Jewel's checks even though she's dead," said Elizabeth. "That's welfare fraud."

"I prefer to think of it as Jewel's money," said Jim. "We're not talking about a couple of no-goods taking money they didn't earn from the government. We're talking about an elderly couple who've worked hard all their lives and made barely enough to survive."

"Jewel and me talked about it, and we agreed on what the survivor would do," said Ed.

"Take my hand, Elizabeth, and walk with me up the knoll in back of the house to that grove of cottonwood trees," said Jim. "I protected you from the truth as long as I could, but when I called for my phone messages this afternoon, there was one from home health asking about the Carruthers. I knew you had called, and I could pretty well guess you wouldn't let this lie, so I drove over here and hid my pickup in Ed's barn and pulled a tarp over it. Then Ed and I waited for you."

Jim released her and held out his hand. Elizabeth stared at him for a while, then finally placed her much smaller hand in his. Again, she couldn't fathom why, but her intuition told her it was right. She felt Ed take her other hand, and they climbed up the cellar steps and walked up the knoll.

Ed shone his flashlight on a pink granite tombstone. One side had Jewel's name and the date of her birth and death on it. The other side was blank except for Ed's name and his birth date. At the top of the stone were the words *Dearly Beloved*.

Jim stepped behind Elizabeth and put his arms around her. "Dearly Beloved, we are gathered here today to join this man and this woman in holy matrimony." He clasped her tighter and rested his chin on the top of her head. His voice seemed to echo inside her head. "Change holy matrimony to eternity, and I figure the words fit, don't you?"

Elizabeth swiped at the tears flowing down her checks. "How many laws do you figure we've broken?"

"This is Highwater, and the law works a little different here."

The Show  Must Go On

Neesa Hart

Scene 1:

For an opening day, things were going fairly well.

As usual, I'd arrived at the church auditorium three hours before the cast and crew were scheduled to arrive. I had checked and double-checked the props table. I'd posted a new sign-in sheet on the call board. I'd inspected the deck for possible tripping hazards and the occasional loose staple that could imbed itself into the sandalless foot of a shepherd or wise man. And I'd ensured that the ushers had everything they needed to seat the two thousand or so patrons who would soon arrive for the twelfth annual Majesty of Christmas Pageant and Holiday Spectacular at Cornova Baptist Church.

No last-minute crises—which seem to be the hallmark of opening days. The children's choir director knew where her angel costumes were, and, more important, wasn't bugging me about them. We'd managed to scavenge a relatively realistic-looking myrrh bottle. Our original prop got smashed at the previous evening's dress rehearsal when a member of Gaspar's entourage took exception to a comment from the Balthazar camp. One thing led to another, and the next thing we knew, we were minus one perfume bottle. Fortunately, the pastor's wife works part-time at a department store, and, at three this morning, I learned that fingernail polish remover will dissolve the ink on a display bottle of Calvin Klein's Obsession. Better yet, popcorn oil, it turns out, looks just like myrrh—not that any of us know what myrrh looks like, but the yellowish-orange tinge of the popcorn oil looks a thousand times more convincing than regular olive oil.

With that problem behind us, I felt fairly confident that we were in good shape for the opening. All the principal cast members had arrived early or on time for makeup and costuming, and I had just given the forty-five-minute call.

And then we found the body in the baptistery.

Forty-two minutes to curtain and there she was, floating face-down in the baptismal waters.

My assistant stage manager, Colleen Dufree, found her. The call light on my headset starting furiously blinking. I knew we had trouble when Colleen asked me to switch to a private channel. Usually, the entire technical staff remains on one channel. I have the control box and can ask someone to switch to a second channel if I think it's necessary. A little wary, I told Colleen to take channel five. I then switched my headset.

"Oh my stars," she was blubbering. "You aren't going to believe this."

"Calm down, Colleen. Where are you?"

"In the baptistery closet. I wanted to inspect the fog machine again to make sure the water was heating."

"Is there a problem with it?"

"NO!" She was starting to sound panicked. It is never a good sign when the assistant stage manager panics less than an hour before curtain. She's supposed to be well past the panic stage by then, and far into the automatic response mode. I heard Colleen draw a shaky breath. "The problem is," she choked out, "that Lisa Eggerston is floating face-down in the baptistery. Geez, Kel, I think she's dead."

Through some miracle of self-control, honed to a razor-sharp edge by years of doing this job, I managed not to visibly react. I did, however, immediately switch off my headset just in time to avoid swearing in Colleen's ear.

Well, great. We've got less than an hour to go and our director, in a final fit of melodramatics, decides to prove she really is in charge. If I didn't know better, I'd swear Lisa had done this just to get even with me. I switched my set back on. "I'll be right there, Colleen. Don't panic."

I wended my way through the milling actors, careful to keep my expression neutral. I answered questions, provided the occasional safety pin or strip of gaffer's tape. I assured Joseph that I'd repaired the loose board on the stable floor that morning, and then I ducked into the narrow hallway that led to the baptistery. I found Colleen, staring numbly at Lisa's body. "What happened?" I asked.

"I don't know," she wailed. "It's like I told you, I came back here to check the fogger—and there she was. The baptistery's not supposed to be full." She was wringing her hands, I noted. I was fairly certain I'd never actually seen anyone wring their hands.

"Are you sure she's dead?"

Colleen looked at me, wide-eyed. "I checked. Oh, Lord, Kel, this is horrible."

"Horrible," I concurred, and looked closely at Lisa's body. Now, I will confess to you that I was not overwhelmed with grief at this moment. And, as long as I'm being honest, I'll even confess that I was more than a little relieved.

Lisa Eggerston was the kind of director every production manager hates to work with—temperamental, demanding, and more than a little flaky. If I hadn't agreed to take on this show as a favor to the producer, a longtime friend of mine, I'd have quit weeks ago. Actually, I'd have quit the first time I met Lisa Eggerston. Like most church drama programs, this one had its institutions—and she was one of them.

"Control freak" didn't begin to summarize this woman's problems. Over the course of the past few months, she'd systematically angered or offended the costume designer, the set designer, the lighting designer, the props coordinator, most of the cast and crew, and generally everyone else she came into contact with. One night, a design meeting nearly ended in a fistfight when Lisa insisted on making the set designer justify his color choice for the stable interior. Last week, I'd spent several hours calming down the props coordinator after Lisa had delivered another six pages of props. Abstraction is lost on the woman.

Generally, the entire last two weeks of rehearsals had proved to be a miserable experience, and I had lived in dread of opening night, knowing full well that if I wanted Lisa to shut up and let me do my job, I'd have to put her in a straitjacket.

So maybe it was that pre-show numbness that sets in, where everything sort of runs on autopilot. More than likely, it was the sure knowledge that we'd get through the next two hours without listening to Lisa screech—the sound of her blistering lecture to the cast after last night's dress rehearsal still rang in my ears. Whatever the cause, I felt nothing but calm relief as I looked at her body.

She was still wearing the clothes she'd had on last night at dress rehearsal—a severe-looking black jumpsuit with silver trim that had made her resemble Cruella De Vil while she'd delivered her blistering lecture on commitment and duty before dismissing the cast three hours late.

Though she was face-down, there was no mistaking her identity. Her platinum hair, straight from a drugstore bottle, fanned around her head like an exotic lily pad.

"What in the world are we going to do?" Colleen insisted.

"Did you call 911?" I asked.

"Not yet."

I nodded and pulled my cell phone from my pocket. While Colleen and I watched Lisa float on the eerily calm pool, I made the call. I hung up and slid the phone back in my jacket. "They'll be here in ten minutes."

"I guess she must have slipped and fallen in last night after rehearsal. I can't imagine who could have filled the pool, or what she was doing back here."

"Isn't this thing computer operated?" I asked.

"I don't know. I guess so. We normally have baptisms on the first and third Sundays of the month. That would be tomorrow, but because of the set, we're not doing them. I guess someone might have forgotten to reset the programming. If that happened, the waters would have started filling during the night."

I touched the water. Cold. "Would she have had any reason at all to come back here?"

"Not that I know of, but you know Lisa." Colleen started to tear up. "Maybe she wanted to check the fogger herself. Oh, I don't know."

"Colleen," I said, my voice deliberately harsh. "You're not going to help anyone if you fall apart right now."

"I know." She visibly struggled for a minute. "I know, but..."

"Get a grip, Colleen," I ordered. "You need to stay in control here."

"It's just that I've never—" She drew a shaky breath. "Kelsey, what if—what if this wasn't an accident?"

"Of course it was an accident," I insisted.

"But what if it wasn't. What if someone killed her?"

"Why would someone do that?" At Colleen's disbelieving look, I coughed. "Well, er, you know what I mean. Sure, plenty of people are mad at the woman, but geez, Colleen, nobody would off her."

She shuddered. "I know. I know. I'm letting my imagination run wild."

"*In control*," I said again.

Colleen closed her eyes. Her black T-shirt made her face look especially pale, but when she looked at me again, her blue eyes were clear and dry. "Do you think we should, you know, pull her out?"

I thought it over. "No. Let's let the rescue squad do it."

"What should we do, then?"

I checked my watch. "I'm going to give the thirty-minute call. I want you to meet the ambulance at the rear entrance. Bring the paramedics in through the stage left door. No one will see them that way."

Colleen's eyes widened. "You aren't going to tell the cast?"

"Not right now," I affirmed.

"But, Kel, I don't think—"

I exhaled a calming breath. "Look, Colleen. There are two thousand people filling up that auditorium. We've got five hundred cast members ready to present a show they've been rehearsing for six months. They don't need Lisa Eggerston right now, and she certainly doesn't need them." I glanced at the body. "If we tell them, it will just cause chaos."

"But don't you think—"

"I think," I said calmly, "that we owe it to all those people to pull it together. Lisa would have wanted that. You know it."

"I know." She looked at Lisa's body. "I just can't believe this."

"I know." I laid a hand on her sleeve. "I can't believe it either. But you and I have a job to do. Go meet the ambulance, and I'll give the call."

"Okay." She grabbed my hand. "Kel—"

"I know," I said again. I gave her fingers a quick squeeze. "It'll be all right, Colleen. We'll get through this."

"I hope so."

"We will," I assured her. "Don't worry."

Colleen hurried down the hall toward the stage left door. I lingered a second longer, looking at the still form of our director. *I should feel something right now*, I thought. *I'm sure I should.* But to be perfectly honest, all I could do was tuck my clipboard under my arm, give the points of my black vest a firm, straightening tug, and think to myself, *The show must go on.*

SCENE 2:

Actually, considering the state of my concentration, not to mention poor Colleen's, I felt pretty good about the way things were going. We were three scenes into the show, and so far, no major bobbles—well, as long as you don't count Colleen's untimely discovery a half-hour before curtain.

I was trying especially hard to make out Colleen's facial expressions during the scene shifts. The near black-out conditions made it particularly difficult, but I strained anyway. I figured the look on Colleen's face was as close to a report as I was going to get on what had happened when the paramedics arrived. I knew Colleen well enough to know she'd followed my instructions to the letter. It's one of the things I love most about my job: I get to rule.

As a production and stage manager, I spend up to six months training the technical and design crews of a show to do exactly as I say. By three days before the show, they've even stopped asking me questions. I control the headset, and everyone on the other end does exactly what I tell them to.

So I knew that if the ambulance had arrived on time, then Lisa Eggerston's body was safely out the door and on the way to the hospital.

Plenty of time to deal with the rest of the consequences later. However, though I'd spent significant time and energy training my people to simply follow my orders, I also knew that the paramedics, and heaven forbid, the police, weren't as likely to simply ignore the matter until after the last curtain call. I mean, a dead body *is* a dead body, and law enforcement and medical personnel have a way of taking that kind of thing very seriously.

Still, with three scenes behind us, I was beginning to relax. There was something comforting in the routine action of calling my cues and watching the drama unfold on stage. I kept one eye on the stage-left action, while I surreptitiously watched Colleen's crew make the difficult shift upstage left. They had to maneuver in the stable, complete with real hay bales, and the castors on the bottom of the flats tended to hang up on the loose hay. They seemed to have the large wagon almost in place, though, when I felt the hand on my shoulder.

This, I knew, was not good news. One of the most important jobs I do during a show is call the cues for the sound, lighting, special effects, and stage crews. *No one* tries to talk to me during a show unless it's an absolute dire emergency. Lisa and I had had several pointed, public arguments over this issue. She really wanted to be in charge of the show—even after we moved past rehearsals and onto stage. But that was my job, and, as I said, I get to rule. It's better for everyone when we all understand that.

So I knew this hand on my shoulder was nothing but trouble. I gathered my calm, made the last set of calls on the page of my prompt script, then slowly turned my head.

I half expected to find one of my shepherds whining about something like a lost prop, or, worse, a lost sheep. In twenty years of church productions, one thing I've learned: shepherds can never find their sheep. You have to put a prop person in charge of that.

What I found, though, left me feeling a little anxious, and greatly annoyed. A pair of intent blue eyes, set nicely apart in a sculpted face, studied mine in the split second before their owner flashed me his badge. Jack Maxwell, it read, homicide detective. He leaned forward. "I need to talk to you."

I glared at him, then called the next few cues on reflex. I switched my headset control to mute. "I, uh, can't right now." I indicated the audience with a nod of my head. "I'm a little busy."

"I don't think this can wait."

"It'll have to."

Detective Maxwell shook his head. "Can't."

"I'm in the middle of a show."

"I'm in the middle of an investigation."

"And it's not going to kill you to wait another hour. She's already dead, Detective."

He tilted his head to one side. The action caused a lock of dark hair to tumble across his forehead. He leaned closer to me. "I'm not a very patient man."

"Too bad," I muttered. My headset crackled, and I heard the sound technician ask me why I'd missed a cue. I flipped off the mute. "Right with you, Charley." Mute again. From the corner of my eye, I could see Mary and Joseph making their way through the streets of Bethlehem looking for a hotel room. Mary, just as she'd done every night in rehearsal, was spending more time playing with her headpiece than looking even remotely distressed that she was about to deliver the pregnancy pillow she wore under her costume. Great. Lisa had warned her a million times that if she didn't keep one hand on that pillow, it would drop like a basketball. Right now, it was hanging down near Mary's thighs. I groaned.

Jack Maxwell—with a name like that, I thought, no wonder he'd become a detective—didn't budge. Blast him. "Ms. Price," he insisted. "I really am going to have to insist."

"I've got a scene shift coming up."

"And there's a dead body in your baptistery."

"Still?" I asked.

An older woman seated near the imposing Mr. Maxwell leaned forward and rapped his shoulder with a set of bony knuckles. "Shhhhh."

He had the good grace to wince. "Sorry."

I looked at the stage again. Mary and Joseph had finally made it to the stable. There was a long song coming up. The choir director, I noted, had moved into place without my prompt. The song would take at least three minutes, and I didn't have any cues to call. I pulled off my headset. "I told my assistant stage manager to call the paramedics. What's the body still doing in the baptistery?"

He gave me a serious look. It would have been more serious if it hadn't made the dimple in his left cheek deepen. And if I hadn't been so annoyed with him, I might have thought he was cute. "I don't want to move it until I'm sure it won't disturb the evidence."

That had my eyebrows rising. "What evidence? She slipped and fell in the baptistery when she went to check the fogger. I'm guessing she hit her head and knocked herself unconscious. The computer must have turned the water on, and when the baptistery filled, she drowned. Case closed."

"You sound really sure about that."

He leaned back in his seat and draped one long arm across the back of two more. Obviously, he wasn't taking my hint that now was not the time for this conversation. I picked up my headset.

"Of course I'm sure," I told him. The song was ending, and I could see the shepherds moving into place. I did a mental count and noted there were two sheep missing. I flagged the page of my script and made a note to talk to Colleen. She had to find someone to handle those sheep before tomorrow night's show.

"Well, I'm not," Detective Maxwell insisted.

I shrugged and pulled my headset on. "Whatever." Flipping the switch to talk, I cued the lighting technician to illuminate the stable. A heavenly kind of glow shone through the wood slats and lit the manger from above. Nice effect. I really liked it.

"Ms. Price," Jack's face was so close to my ear, his breath tickled the back of my neck. "Do you have any idea what we're dealing with here?"

I ignored him and cued the sound operator to turn on Mary's mic for her solo. She sings remarkably well for someone who just gave birth in a pile of straw. Jack tapped on my shoulder. "Did you hear me?"

I nodded, but kept my eyes trained on the stage. The next set of cues was particularly tight, and I didn't want to miss one. I was making the third cue call when Jack seemed to lose his patience. "Ms. Price," he insisted again.

I held up a hand to try to hold him off. He ignored me. "For God's sake. Your director is dead."

My headset crackled to life. *Well, great,* I thought as I watched a lone sheep wander down the center aisle. I turned around to glare at Jack Maxwell. "In case you're interested, you just announced that to my entire crew."

SCENE 3:

Through sheer force of will, I managed to hold Jack, as I now thought of him, at bay until intermission. When he said he wasn't patient, he wasn't kidding. He fidgeted like a six-year-old. To make matters worse, my technical crew was falling apart. Not only were they missing cues, but I sensed the heightened tension through the limited conversation on the headsets. We almost reached a critical point when the rail crew flew one of the angels in too soon. One second earlier, and she would have collided with the flat we were flying out at the time. The increasingly anxious looks I was receiving from the actors told me all I needed to know. News of Lisa's death was spreading backstage with the alacrity of a three-alarm fire.

We persevered, though, and somehow got through two more songs, and the curtain came down on Act I. Feeling simultaneously drained and on edge, I picked up my script and exited the control booth. I walked toward the side door of the auditorium with Jack right on my heels. We stepped outside into a relatively gray December afternoon, but after the semi-darkness of the theater, the light seemed blinding. I had to squint. "All right, Detective, I have fifteen minutes of intermission. What do you want from me?"

He whipped out a notepad. That struck me as a little funny and kind of cute. I think that, right at that moment, I was losing my mind. My show was falling apart, my director was dead as a doornail, and all I could think of was that Jack Maxwell looked like a younger, hunkier version of Joe Friday. I kept waiting for him to mutter, "Just the facts, ma'am." If Jack noted my amusement, he ignored it, and certainly didn't share it. "Who found the body?"

"My stage manager, Colleen."

"What was she doing back in that area at the time?"

"Checking the fog machine to make sure it was heating. It's part of her job."

Jack jotted that down. "What were you doing?"

"Giving orders to the technical crew. That's part of my job."

He gave me a quick look to make sure I was taking him seriously. In the outdoor light, his eyes were an even deeper blue than I'd first thought. "Giving orders?" he prompted.

"Yes." I braced one shoulder against the stone wall of the church. "I was going over the checklist with my audio technician when Colleen asked to speak to me on a private channel of the headset. We switched over, and she told me to come backstage."

He scribbled a few more notes. "Then what?"

"Then, I met her at the baptistery door, she showed me the body, and we agreed to call 911."

"Does anyone else know about this?"

"They do now that you told the entire technical crew over the headset." The door opened and Charley Constantine, my audio technician stuck his head out. "Uh, Kelsey, I hate to bother you, but I think you're needed backstage."

"I'm in the middle of an interview with Detective Maxwell, Charley."

"I know, but, um, everyone knows about Lisa. They're pretty upset. I think you'd better talk to them."

I glanced at Jack. He hesitated, then nodded. I motioned for Charley to lead the way. I followed him with Jack so close on my heels he might have been my shadow.

What I found backstage confirmed my worst fears. I had several cast members in tears, though to be perfectly honest, I'm not sure why. As far as I could tell, no one could stand the woman when she was alive. That's a particularly weird thing about death. People forget how annoying dead people were before they, well, died. As far as I knew, no one had even pretended to like Lisa Eggerston while she roamed the earth spreading theatrical terror.

But now, everyone was standing around in the backstage area doing a pretty good job of portraying hysteria, grief, horror, and shock. No one in the world exhibits these particular emotions quite as well as theatrical people. All the black they wear seems to add to the effect.

"All right," I said. "I need your attention."

"My God," one of the kings groaned. "This is just dreadful."

I ignored that. "You all know about Lisa," I said carefully. "I had wanted to keep the truth from you until after tonight's show. I'll take full responsibility for that."

The innkeeper's wife turned to Mary and threw herself against her shoulder. "Oh, I can't believe this." Mary wrapped a comforting arm around her.

I pulled Jack forward. "This is Detective Jack Maxwell. He's going to ask a few questions."

To my left, the angel Gabriel tried to move forward, but his wings caught on the wagon containing Herod's balcony. So he used what we referred to as his 'announcement voice' to get my attention. "Kelsey?"

I looked at him, almost expecting him to say, "Fear not." "What, Bill?"

"What kinds of questions?"

Jack cleared his throat. "Routine stuff. Just a few things we need to know about who saw her last, what time they saw her, that kind of thing."

Bill frowned. "My God." He looked at Jack. "You think this wasn't an accident, don't you?"

I had to stifle a groan. Just great. I'd suspected as much myself when I realized the water in the baptistery was cold. When the pool fills automatically, it also heats automatically. Since the water was cold, that suggested that someone had filled it deliberately. Under the best of circumstances, it had been a simple oversight by the custodial staff, but I was pretty sure that whoever had filled that pool had done it to drown Lisa Eggerston.

I glanced at Jack. His expression told me that he'd guessed the same thing. Well, good for him. Now his brilliant lack of timing had yielded a theater full of nearly hysterical actors—actors who are more than a little crazy under the best of circumstances. I decided not to help him out of the mess he'd created. I crossed my arms and shot him a knowing look. "*Do* you think it was an accident, Detective?"

He was tugging at the collar of his denim shirt, which he stopped doing long enough to glare at me. "Well, it might be a little too early —"

"You think she was murdered," Joseph insisted. "You think that one of us murdered Lisa Eggerston."

"I didn't say that," Jack said. "It wasn't necessarily someone in this room."

"But it could be?" That came from one of the extras.

Jack nodded. "It could be anyone."

"But you don't know," Balthazar asserted as he took a dramatic step forward, "do you?"

"I don't have any suspects at this time," Jack answered.

Gaspar pulled his crown from his head and began twirling it on his index finger. "Which means that the killer could still be loose in this theater."

A collective gasp filled the humid air.

"There's no need to panic." Jack surveyed the room, then his gaze landed on me. "I can't even say, conclusively, that Ms. Eggerston was murdered. It might have been a simple accident, and that's what I'm here to find out."

As if on cue, Mary clutched her throat and lurched forward. "But my stars. If she *was* murdered, and you don't know who did it, that means that any one of us could be next!"

I believe I mentioned the predisposition of theatrical people to histrionics?

🖈🖈🖈

SCENE 4:
I took my seat in the control booth again, having done the best I could to settle the nerves of my cast and crew. Thirty seconds before the curtain rose on Act II, I glared at Jack, who was still following me like a stray dog. "I hope you're proud of yourself. You've created total chaos back there."

He just shrugged, which, irrationally, riled my temper even more. Shrugging, indeed. The man obviously didn't have a clue what kind of havoc he was wreaking in my well-ordered world. I pulled my headset on and did my best to concentrate on my script, though it was hard with Jack leaning over my shoulder.

We were halfway through the third act when the kings' procession started. I had warned Jack to stay completely out of my way until after this portion of the program. It was by far my most challenging set of cues. With three kings, each with a multi-person entourage, live camels, one elephant, a pair of flying angels, and a two-year-old playing the young Jesus, the potential for disaster was enormous. We had multiple lighting and sound cues to navigate, moving scenery, and an elephant who'd proved to have a little stage fright. By the time the kings had moved into place, I was gripping my pencil so hard my fingers hurt. But, miracle of miracles, we got through the piece. The next song started and the mass of kings began to file off stage.

Belatedly, I noticed that Jack had left the control room.

The rest of the show passed without incident. I authorized two curtain calls, figuring my cast needed the extra encouragement after the night they'd had.

"Colleen?" I paged her on the headset.

"Yeah, Kel?"

I double-checked the control lights on my console to ensure that no one else had an active headset. The other members of my crew had all signed off. "You did a great job tonight. I know it was hard on you."

"Everyone's really upset, Kelsey. I can't believe something like this happened here."

"I know."

"Does Detective Maxwell know what he's going to do yet?"

"I haven't seen him since the kings' procession."

"He's been back here asking questions," Colleen told me.

"I see."

"Do you want to see the cast and crew again for any reason? You know, maybe talk to them about things some more?"

I thought it over. "I don't think so. Why don't you let them go home. They're all pretty stressed out."

"You aren't staying late are you?" she asked me. "I mean, not here? Not with this?"

"I don't think there's a murderer loose in the church, Colleen."

"I know, but it's creepy."

"A little."

"Listen, most of the cast and crew are headed over to Dom's Pizza Kitchen. It's going to be subdued, but I think they need to be together."

"That's probably a good idea."

"Why don't you come with us?"

I drew a deep breath and let my eyes drift shut. "I don't think so, Colleen. What I need is a good night's sleep."

"Are you sure?"

"I'm sure."

"Okay. Uh, Kel?"

"Yeah?"

"Things went well, all things considered."

"Yes, they did."

"I'll see you tomorrow?"

"Yep." I switched off my headset and leaned my head back in the chair. I'm normally energized after a show, but tonight, I felt nothing but bone-deep exhaustion.

I watched from the control booth as people filed out. Colleen was the last to leave. She waved at me just before she flipped off the lights. The glow from my console was the only light in my tiny little space.

Two hands landed on my shoulders. I wasn't startled this time. I'd been expecting him. "Hello, Jack."

"Hi, Kel."

"Learn anything backstage?"

"Some."

"Got any suspects?"

"A cast full." He started rubbing my shoulders. I let him do it because it felt too delicious not to.

"No one liked the woman."

I could see his reflection in the glass window of the room. He met my gaze with a knowing look.

"You warned me two weeks ago that this was going to happen. I should have listened to you."

A smile played across my lips. "I appreciate the fact that you didn't tell the cast I'd suspected this."

"Or that I knew you."

"Or that. If they'd known I'd talked to the police about my suspicions, it would have made things worse. They'd have felt like I was keeping some kind of conspiracy from them."

"Weren't you?"

"Don't frown, Jack," I said, and spun around in my chair to face him. "Part of my job is to keep things running smoothly. Can you imagine what would have happened if people had known what I was thinking?"

Jack dropped into the other chair. He took both my hands in one of his. "Do you think this was deliberate or not?"

"The water in the baptistery was cold."

"I know that. Someone filled it."

"She could have slipped and fallen in without the person who filled it knowing she was in there."

"Why would someone have turned the water on?"

"I don't know." I shrugged. "A prank, maybe. Habit. You don't have any proof it was deliberate."

"No." He shook his head. "I don't. And I'm not sure I can get any."

"Then what are you going to do?" I prompted him.

"Close the show," he responded. "At least until I have time to look around."

I jerked my hands away from him. "Close the show? Close the show? Are you crazy. You can't do that."

"This is a potential murder we're talking about here, Kelsey. I can't just let business go on as usual."

"I know that." I started to pace in the tight confines of the room. "But that doesn't mean you have to close the show."

"I don't see what other choice I have."

"All these people—they've worked so hard. It doesn't seem fair."

"They'll understand."

"You sound awfully sure of that," I accused him.

He shrugged again. It made his shoulders look impossibly broad when he did that. I forced the thought aside and ran my fingers through my hair. "Look, Jack," I prompted. "I'm not sure I can explain to you what a catastrophically bad decision this is."

"Why?"

"Why?" I stopped pacing. "Don't you think we say 'the show must go on' in show business for a reason? It's because a show isn't about one person, or a group of persons; it's the most collaborative of all art forms. It's about team work and sacrifice. It's about pulling together and sticking together, no matter what. It's the only place on earth where every member of the team, from the star to the stagehand, has an equally important role. And if you close the show, you'll take that away from them. This is months in the making, Jack. Months of these people's lives."

He studied me in the green glow of the LED lights. "I'm sorry, Kelsey. I know how much you care about this—and about them."

"But you're going to do it anyway."

"I have a murderer to catch."

"And there's no way I can talk you out of it?"

He leaned back in his chair and crossed his arms over his chest. "I'm afraid not. The only way I can let you raise the curtain tomorrow night is if I know I've got the killer behind bars."

ENCORE:

He looked so smug when he said that. But I also knew he was serious. Jack had believed he'd played his trump card at that moment, that I would finally give in and let him have his way.

But one thing he didn't count on: good production managers don't quit. And I like to think of myself as one of the best. It's my job to make sure the show runs smoothly. It's my job to solve problems and keep the ship moving steadily forward. It's my job to ensure that the cast, the crew, and the designers are cared for. I do it because I love it, and because I'm great at it. I do it because each time the curtain rises on a new production, I get to watch magic happen.

I knew there was no way that Jack was going to back down. If he didn't have the case solved by curtain time the next night, he'd shut down my show. I also knew that there was no way I'd let that happen. My people were very well trained. Colleen knew that show and its cues every bit as well as I did. So I did what any good production manager would at that moment.

I saved the show.

Which is how I ended up here at the Drysdale Women's Correctional Facility. Despite Jack's protests, and despite my lawyers howls of disbelief, I confessed to the murder of Lisa Eggerston. The judge was easy to convince. I repeated several stories of Lisa's antics in the final days of her life. I talked about her fits of temper, her demands, her unbelievable ego. I showed several examples of the memos she'd sent me, and the judge had no problem believing that I'd been driven to take action.

I explained that Lisa and I had fought backstage after dress rehearsal. One thing led to another. She shoved me. I shoved her. She fell in the then-empty baptistery and whacked her head. I didn't know, I said truthfully, how the pool had filled with water, but explained the computerized system that controlled it.

I was very convincing. The judge gave me involuntary manslaughter with extenuating circumstances and sentenced me to two years at Drysdale.

I missed the closing of that show, but I've seen the video. Things went well. Colleen did a super job in my absence. And, I must confess, things haven't been nearly as bad here as I thought. Jack comes to see me fairly regularly. He's still trying to convince me to tell him what really happened that night in the church. I just shrug and ask him how he knows I'm not telling the truth. We usually fight after that. But then he comes to see me again so we can make up.

As of this morning, I've been here exactly thirteen months of my requisite twenty-four. It's been a long time since I sat down and really thought through those final few hours. I suppose it's only natural, though, that the memories would come to me now. After all, I've just given the forty-five-minute call to my cast and crew.

In less than an hour, the curtain—which is made out of several bedsheets stapled together—will rise on the first ever Drysdale Women's Correctional Facility production. The cast and crew consist entirely of my fellow inmates. I expect things to go well. My productions usually do. From the makeshift control booth, I spot Jack. I'm glad he made it. I have a feeling he's going to appreciate my efforts more than most. We're debuting an original play this evening. Written and directed by my cellmate. It's a witty little murder mystery about a production manager who's finally driven to kill her director.

Next season, we're hoping to stage *The Pirates of Penzance.*

Twelve  Days

Laura Hayden

I stared at Stik, trying to see features lost behind the hood of his dark sweatshirt. He had a "one with the shadows" thing going on. I'd stumbled into him twice already because I hadn't seen him. To his credit, Stik didn't curse either time, even when I'd stepped on his foot.

We slipped through the dense foliage, avoiding various detection devices. Our clothing had been impregnated with a chemical that the sci-tech adviser said made us invisible to vid and shielded our heat signatures.

God, I love science.

But technology couldn't protect us from all detection. We still had to avoid guards who patrolled with their own nifty high-tech gear.

Did I mention they had guns?

It wasn't until we'd landed that Stik told me he didn't trust technology so he'd chosen a challenging route into the compound. "Challenging" meant relying less on technology and more on crawling through impenetrable thickets and climbing sheer walls.

Evidently, he'd mistaken me for Spiderwoman.

My problem was—I hated physical activity. My life revolved like my office chair with everything in a 360° arm's-reach circle. But my office and equipment would be useless in twelve days if we didn't stop Doug Post.

Software ka-trillionaire Douglas Post had the world by the virtual gonads and wasn't threatening to squeeze; he'd gone straight to threatening all-out castration. Government brains had accurately anticipated his possible reaction to losing the lawsuit, realizing that—should Post's anger mutate into revenge—he could bring society to its technological knees. The hand that rocks the cradle isn't nearly as influential as the hand that holds the world by its *soft*ware.

When the gavel sounded on December 13, the founder/owner/president/CEO of MultiData was found guilty of creating a monopoly, stealing technology, creating an unfair and unethical marketplace—everything short of RICOH charges. Post dodged the press gauntlet and disappeared into his compound, a.k.a. the "Fortress of Silicon." A few hours later, he issued a warning: if the ruling wasn't reversed, Christmas Day would mark the functional end of every computer on the planet. Thanks to automatic upgrades, he could control every piece of MultiData software by remote. Short of a few antiques, every computer in the free and not-so-free world had at least one Multidata program embedded somewhere in its silicon bowels and one command from him could cause those computers to stop functioning and erase all their data.

A decade ago, we'd lived through the Y2k scare unscathed, but this time there'd be no fixes, no patches, no alternative software solutions. All we could do was surrender to Douglas Post and MultiData and make his Christmas very merry, indeed.

Or then again, we could break in, disable his computers and kill him....

Long story short, they chose me for the "disable his computers" part. Doug Post himself would be terminated by Stik, a man who looked as if he could kill without remorse, concern, or even breaking a sweat.

I shivered. The last thing I wanted to see was an execution—of Post or even a guard. Suddenly, I realized I'd seen no guards, none of the six hundred employees wandering around. Either Stik had picked the perfect route, or the world's richest boss had sent his employees home for a traditional family Christmas.

Yeah. Right.

Stik led us to the main building and it took over two minutes for the reconfigured Omni-Keycard to break the twelve-digit cipher lock. With advanced security like that, maybe Post didn't need guards. The lock clicked, the door opened, and Stik entered.

I counted to ten and followed, immediately tripping over some-thing…someone. Sprawling to my knees, my hand landed in something warm and sticky on the floor. I looked down and stared at the victim, face-to-face. A dead guard. My throat closed until I glanced at my wet hand. Instead of the red stain of innocent blood, a bright yellow-green fluid coated my palm.

I bravely cleaned my hand on the android's sleeve before I scram-bled to my feet. "CyberGuard, 2501 model," I said, wishing my voice didn't shake. "I didn't think they were on the market."

"They're not. These are beta-test units." Stik motioned for me to follow.

He negotiated the maze of corridors with ease, avoiding or disarm-ing the security measures. So far, we'd seen only one inhuman guard. Had Post's megalomania grown so large that he'd replaced his human staff with programmable replicas?

I bumped into Stik when he stopped at a door that looked no differ-ent from the other doors we'd passed.

"He's in there. You ready?"

I gulped, nodded, then reached into my pack for my Silencer and set it up.

MultiData's most popular product was voice recognition soft-ware. Before we might reach him, Post could issue the command that would start a destroy-every-computer cascade effect. But my invention absorbed all sounds, stopping him from issuing any verbal commands such as "Make my coffee black," "Turn on the lights," or "Kill the intrud-ers."

The unit registered a single voice beyond the door. "One," I mouthed. Stik nodded, readied his weapons, then stepped inside.

I waited, counting silently: one MultiData, two MultiData, three…

The Silencer absorbed any sounds of a fight—gunshots, screams of pain, pleas for mercy. At "ten," I entered, praying that Stik had over-powered whatever awaited him.

Sure enough, Stik stood unscathed, staring down at something hidden behind a large desk. I moved closer and saw an overturned chair and a pair of legs ending in Post's signature red Nikes.

I pointed to the shoes. "Post?" I mouthed.

Stik pulled back his own hood, revealing a remarkably average-looking face—certainly not that of a hardened killer. He scanned his victim, registering no emotion, no guilt, and no sense of satisfaction. He placed his large knife in the center of the desk. Instead of blood, a sticky yellow-green substance dripped from the blade.

※ ※ ※

I stared at the screen as my virus program infiltrated the central computer system. Rather than destroy the code, it rewrote it so I could access all levels and circumvent any passwords, inline booby traps or cyber-bombs. I tried not to worry about the body at my feet; it was just a bloodless replica, right?

"Where's the real Post?"

"Here. Somewhere," Stik said quietly. "Pull up a building schematic."

I poked around the computer and found a 3-D wireframe blueprint which I projected into the middle of the room.

Stik circled the hologram, analyzing the structure, then stalked over to a bookcase on the far wall. He wore a fleeting look of irritation; perhaps he was human after all and not a Robo-Stik sent in to do the Dirty Deed.

"Maybe he's in another building," I offered. "Or maybe he's hiding in one of the connecting tunnels between buildings. Or maybe..."

Stik held up his hand, stopping me. "Or maybe..." He pivoted and used that same hand to pull the bookcase from the wall. It teetered for a moment, then fell, scattering books and papers across the floor and landed on the mess with a substantial thud.

"—he's in here."

Behind the bookcase, we could see the outline of a door.

"I thought he was some Boy Genius. A secret room behind the bookcase?" I tried to laugh. "How clichéd."

"Smart men know to hide in plain sight." Stik pointed at the

Silencer. "Set it up."

I hooked up the unit and it registered no audio sounds other than a cyclical click, probably something mechanical in nature. Thermostat? Watch? Time bomb? I shot Stik an "okay."

He pulled out his knife and a small hand laser, then disappeared into the room.

I fought the instinct to close my eyes as I counted. After "ten," I entered the dimly lit room. This time, I stumbled over no bodies, real or synthetic. The room's only occupant was a half-naked body on a med-lab monitor bed.

So where was Stik?

The temptation to retreat was almost overpowering, but our mission's importance superseded my instinct for self-preservation. I searched the shadows for Stik, spotting a single combat boot beneath the bed. I wanted to run—not to abandon him, but to retreat and reassess the situation.

Yeah, right.

I turned and tripped over a cable. Recovering, I scrambled toward freedom, but that same cable snaked around my ankle, tightened, and tugged me backward. I grabbed the door frame as a second cable wrapped around my other leg. The cables pulled hard enough to break my grip and drag me toward the bowels of the machinery.

If this animated jungle of wires and tubes killed Stik, I had no chance in hell of surviving. I couldn't even get satisfaction from screaming thanks to the Silencer.

Inspiration hit. Using the last of my strength, I batted the Silencer from the door, snagged its antenna wire and reeled it in like a fish. I slammed the off switch and suddenly could hear myself bellow in terror and blubber without shame. Between sobs, I screamed, "Computer! Sierra Mike Charlie override."

If my virus had invaded the system's protected core, it had embedded my control signature. If not, I was dead.

The cables grew limp.

"Sierra Mike Charlie override has been activated. Awaiting command." The computer spoke in its creator's voice.

I hyperventilated in relief as I untangled myself from the wires. I scanned the room. Where was Stik? Had the computer killed him, absorbing him into its components?

"Release the other intruder," I rasped.

An empty-looking wall shimmered with movement then spat out Stik's body. Like a cat, he landed on all-fours.

"Thanks," he muttered, sounding as if he seldom had need to thank anyone about anything. He stalked toward the med-lab bed and pulled out a second knife.

"Wait," I commanded.

He paused in mid-step. "Why?"

"Because you owe me a chance to sort this out before you kill him. What if this isn't Post?"

Stik gave me a curt nod. "One chance."

I stumbled toward the bed, trying to digest the medical telemetry. Wires and tubes covered his body, monitoring respiration, heart rate, brain activity—all bodily functions. A mirrored shield blocked his eyes and ears, allowing him to hear and see only what the computer supplied.

"Computer, what is the function of this facility?"

"*To preserve the PostPrime.*"

So it *was* the real Douglas Post.

"Is he dead?"

"*No.*"

"Explain."

"*He is functioning within all parameters but one.*"

"Which one?" I ran through a mental list of physical complications—heart attack, other organ failure, cancer, disease...

"*He is unhappy.*"

Hooboy...didn't see that one coming.

Stik stepped toward the bed.

"Please...not yet." I turned back to the terminal. "Computer, is PostPrime unhappy because he lost the court case?"

"*PostPrime is unaware of outside concerns.*"

Prickles rose on the back of my neck. "Does he know about the court case?"

"*No.*"

"Did PostPrime enter VR to be shielded from outside concerns?"

"*No, we felt it was in his best interest. He was unhappy.*"

So the computer had shanghaied its own creator, maybe issuing the global threats itself without his input, much less permission. Simply put, he didn't deserve to die. Surely, Stik understood that....

"Computer, is PostPrime...happy in the world you have created for him?"

"PostPrime is not as unhappy as before."

I glanced at the monitor, and my heart rate hit warp speed. Post's computer had isolated and invalidated my virus. I couldn't break in. If I told Stik, Post was dead: innocent or not. "Computer, I want to talk to your creator."

"PostPrime is not communicating with the outside world."

I studied the body; he was an ordinary-looking man. Handsome in a sort of studious way. Okay, handsome in a "I'm-richer-than-anybody-on-Earth" sort of way. And he wasn't the hideous, destruction-unleashing Grinch we'd thought he was.

A shiver danced across my shoulders. "Let me enter his VR and talk to him."

Stik shook his head. "You don't know what you're doing."

"Yes I do," I lied. "It'll take time for my virus to give us control." A bigger lie. "I can go in, talk to Post, explain what's going on."

He glared at me as if x-raying my comments for the lie within. Finally, Stik sighed. "Do it."

It's not every day you fool a trained assassin.

"Highest priority status," I ordered. "I want to enter PostPrime's world."

In less than a minute, the computer generated everything I needed for VR.

Stik eyed the preparations with obvious distaste. "How long will this take?" In assassin-speak, it meant *"When can I go ahead and kill him?"*

"Give me eleven days"—I consulted my watch—"eighteen hours and forty-six minutes. If I don't succeed, make sure I'm cleared from VR before you kill him. If I'm there with him when he dies..."

Stik stared back with passionless eyes. "I know."

What I hate most about VR is getting motion sick during initialization, but MultiData's latest generation of VR had no ill side effects. I "landed" in a great hall packed with enough gold and treasure to finance a small monarchy. A decadent jewel-encrusted throne sat at the end of the room.

If Doug Post had conjured this for himself, I was in big trouble.

I heard a noise and hid as a band of women poured into the room, giggling and bouncing around like hyperactive cheerleaders. Their clothing or lack thereof reminded me of Victoria's Secret on parade.

If this was the way Post expected to see his women...

Post shouldered through the throng and plopped down on his throne. To his credit, he didn't ogle or touch them. In fact, he ignored them.

I focused my attention and "thought" myself into an appropriate costume—something with the right flavor but less exposure. Think Barbara Eden in *I Dream of Jeanie*.

I adopted an insipid smile and merged with the vapid audience of admirers. I thought he wouldn't notice me, but I was wrong.

"Oh God. A new one." He gave me a critical once-over. "Don't tell me. You're Jeanie, looking for a new master." He sighed and then grabbed my wrist. "Let's get this over with."

"Not so fast, buster." I pulled out of his grasp.

He looked as if he'd never met opposition before. "Excuse me?" Releasing me, he crossed his arms and frowned. "If this is a new programming variation, I don't like it."

I should've been more careful, but his attitude pissed me off. "What? The Lord and Master never hears the word, *no*?" I scanned the opulent room. "You must get your rocks off playing King of the World." *Yeah, while the rest of the world was sinking like the* Titanic.

A large gong interrupted his response. His harem swarmed in, separating us.

"Gift time!" they chanted, dragging him back to the throne.

One by one, they knelt at his feet in total adoration. A pile of presents grew: rare coins, electronic gadgets, keys to exotic cars—all sorts of expensive gifts, none that apparently pleased him.

After the procession, he glared at me. "What about you? Don't you have a"—he shuddered—"gift?"

I scowled. "It's not Christmas. At least, not yet."

He stiffened. "You know what *day* it is?"

"Gift day!" one nubile lass chortled, stroking his leg. "Let—"

"Quiet." He turned to me. "What day is it?"

"December 13th. Maybe the 14th. It's close to midnight."

He stared into the distance. "I've lost track of time."

I could have mentioned the lawsuit, but somehow I knew it wasn't the right time. *Time...?* I had an idea.

It took some concentration, but finally, a small box appeared in my hand. "Here." I gave it to him. "If this is Gift Day, this is for you."

I thought he was going to dismiss it like the others, but he didn't. He opened it and his dubious look changed to awe.

"A watch? For me?" He examined it carefully. "It works."

I shrugged. "It's no Rolex, but it'll keep time." I pointed at the dial. "And it has one of those calendar thingies so you'll always know what day it is."

He looked up, almost smiling. "Uh...thanks. I appreciate this."

I ducked my head. "You're welcome."

The harem suddenly swarmed the throne, pushing me away. They all sported new presents, coincidentally all watches. The computer learned fast.

"Look, darling. I've brought you a watch."

"No, look at mine. It has diamonds."

"Mine has emeralds..."

I backed away. So much for originality.

As the gaggle overwhelmed him, he looked up and mouthed, "Thank you."

At least he had manners....

VR is funny. Until you get settled, it's more like a dream where a warped logic allows abrupt changes in places, times, and people without question.

So it became tomorrow—December 14. I wandered around lost in a world that looked more like the Playboy Mansion than Alice's Wonderland. Finally I stumbled into the room where King Doug squirmed on his throne.

I tried not to laugh. "You look like my cousin after my uncle caught him smoking in the basement. Talk about a major whupping."

Post looked distracted by his discomfort. "My parents didn't believe in spanking."

Why was I not surprised?

"It's this damn throne," he continued. "I wish it had a cushion or something."

A blond carrying a red velvet pillow trimmed with gold tassels pushed me out of the way. "For you, darling."

And the harem descended, bringing cushions of every size and fabric and jockeying for the top position on the throne. The result? A four-foot-high stack of pillows that left Doug no place to sit.

"C'mere." I grabbed his hand and pulled him toward the door I'd created. His bevy squealed in protest, but he seemed relieved to escape.

When the screen door opened, the hinges made a reassuring creak. The scent of honeysuckle rode the warm fresh air along with the song of a meadowlark.

I led him across the worn plank floor, past terra-cotta pots brimming with red geraniums, and toward what I considered a better throne for His Royal rear end.

"Your choice." I showed him the swing that hung by chains at the end of the porch and beside it, a wooden rocking chair. Each sported one cushion covered in blue-checked gingham.

Doug selected the porch swing, leaving me the rocking chair. It didn't take long for us to start a complementary rhythm.

After a while, he spoke. "This reminds me of something. I'm not sure what, but I like it." Doug hooked his thumb in his waistband and leaned back with a contented sigh.

Ignorance was bliss. I'd always envied kids whose grandparents lived in bucolic countryside settings; mine lived in a midtown high-rise. Lacking suitable personal memories, I'd stolen this setting directly from *The Andy Griffith Show.*

And as long as Opie Post didn't figure this out...

Having witnessed their master's joy in the simplicity of a porch swing, the harem created their own swinging seats for him on the third day. Unfortunately, something had been lost in the translation; they hung a wide assortment of chairs from the ceiling—stools, folding chairs, couches, office chairs....Every time a chair moved, it caused a domino effect, turning the throne room into a swinging hazard zone.

I had no problem coercing Doug into an escape. We headed for the door that led to a rose garden built from my memories of a park where I played as a child.

We strolled down a path between rows of bushes, and he paused to admire the colors. "I forgot flowers could be this pretty."

"You know what they say—take time to stop and smell the roses."

He knelt, selected a blossom and inhaled. "Nice." Suddenly he recoiled from the bush, staring at a drop of blood on his fingertip. "It's a thorn." Perplexed, he examined the bush. "They all have thorns. Why? You could've created roses without them."

"Then they wouldn't have been roses." I inspected his wounded finger. "They would've been...just pretend."

"Pretend," he repeated in a faraway voice, staring at his punctured finger.

"Here, let me." I conjured a Band-Aid and applied it to his forefinger. "There." I placed a maternal kiss on the boo-boo. "All better."

I forgot I had a mission.

I forgot he was a megalomaniacal madman.

I forgot this whole world was indeed pretend.

He turned and, for one moment, I thought he was going to kiss me.

So much for being maternal.

He blushed and smiled. "Thanks."

I know what you're thinking. *Excuse me, Shelley. You're playing nice with a nutcase. Are you crazy?* In my defense, remember that in prolonged VR, it's easy to lose your train of thought, even when the universe's welfare hangs in the balance. But think about it—if my mission was to make PostPrime happy, I was on target.

The next day, the throne room overflowed with huge bouquets of roses, each stem filled with thorns. Not thorns. Spikes, large enough to puncture a tire. Talk about overstating a concept!

"Uh...excuse me?" Doug waved at me from his throne. "Could you give me a hand? I'm stuck."

The spiked roses ringed his seat like a barbed-wire corral. Had he tried to push his way out, the thorn-spikes would have shredded his hands. I imagined a pair of chain metal gloves and some leather boots and they appeared at his feet.

"Perfect." He tugged on the boots and the gloves, and now armed, made an easy path through the roses. When he reached me, he gave me a hug. "Thanks. These were exactly what I needed."

Okay, I'll admit it; I liked the hug. God help me, I liked the man. I grinned like an idiot. "Glad I could help."

He released me, stepped back, and gave me an expectant smile. "Wanna go for another walk?"

"To the garden?"

"Nope." He grinned. "A different type of park..."

As in Fenway Park. Baseball. Hot dogs. All-American entertainment.

Okay, I'll admit I'm no baseball fan, but I had something to cheer about; this was the first time I'd seen Doug actively manipulate VR, creating something for himself.

After the last batter struck out in this perfect shut-out game, the park faded away. We strolled back, hand-in-hand, stopping just short of the throne room.

"Did you enjoy the game?" he asked.

"I liked the hot dogs, the peanuts, the beer, the seventh-inning stretch, and especially the company." I thought I was being highly diplomatic, but he seemed crestfallen.

"But it was a perfect game. I made sure of it."

He swings...he misses. "The fun of baseball—of any sport—is not knowing the game's outcome before it starts. That wasn't a game; it was a predictable rout."

He looked as if he'd never contemplated such a notion. "Unpredictability..."

"Exactly. Constant predictability is boring. Surprises can be good."

Something dark crossed his face. He wandered toward the throne room without me, muttering, "Not always."

So if Doug Post hated surprises, how could I explain the big surprise waiting for him in the real world? Even worse, I'd lost track of the days and could count only by what presents I'd given him—the watch, the porch swing, the rose garden, and the gloves and boots. Four days. Maybe five if we counted the baseball game if that was a different day. Who knew?

It was time to play hardball, time to make Doug come to me. Sure enough, Muhammed came to the mountain. Doug appeared, holding out one red rose.

"For you. With my apologies."

I accepted the rose, noticing the small thorns along the stem. "Apologies for what?"

"For acting like an ass. I didn't even ask if you liked baseball. I'm sorry."

I sniffed the rose. "That's okay."

His look of contrition changed into a shy smile. "Willing to take another chance?"

"Sure. You lead."

We ended up sitting at the edge of the Grand Canyon, watching a brilliant sunset with the canyon changing its array of colors with each passing minute.

"I came here when I was ten," he explained. "I don't think I appreciated it, but I remembered it well enough to reproduce it."

Yahoo! Not only was he manipulating VR, but acknowledging his control. Definitely an improvement.

I tried to control my enthusiasm. "Nice sunset. Reminds me of one I saw on a business trip to Hawaii."

He cocked his head. "You've never told me what you do for a living."

Was it time to take an obvious opening? Maybe. "In the real world, I work with computers."

Shock flooded his features. "The real world..."

"You know...out there. Beyond VR. I work in system security and integrity."

Doug's eyes narrowed and he stood up. "You're a hacker." He stepped back as if putting distance between us would isolate him from danger. "You've broken into our system and are trying to steal data."

I remained seated. "I don't want to steal from you—just stop you."

His face hardened. "From what?"

I'd hoped this would be easier. "From destroying the world. You... or someone representing you, has threatened to release a viral code that will incapacitate every computer in the world loaded with any of Multi-Data software."

His voice remained harsh. "Why would I do something like that?"

"You lost the lawsu—"

Before I could finish, he closed his eyes.

"Computer, stop program."

When he opened his eyes again, he looked shocked to see me still there.

"Computer, I said *stop program*." He glowered at me.

I drew a deep breath. "I'm not part of the program. I'm real."

He raised his hand to shoo me away. "Then leave. I don't want real people here."

Defiant, I moved closer. "Why? Because we disappoint you? We bother you? We hamper your style? We make you unhappy?"

He almost responded, but instead, stormed off. I could've followed him, but didn't. I'd blown a big hole in his world. I could afford to be patient for a couple more days.

On day seven, I found him on his throne as usual. However, his harem were now his security guards, keeping me at bay. Rather than outmaneuver them, I allowed them to isolate me in a distant corner. After a while, Doug approached me, despite the harem's protests.

"I was unhappy," he said in a solemn voice. "Out there."

"I know."

"In here, I feel better."

"I know that, too."

He sat down beside me, and we remained silent until he spoke again. "I haven't been too happy here, either, but..."

I finished his unspoken thoughts. "But it's better than the real world."

"Sure. Look around." He made a sweeping gesture with his hand. "I have everything I could possibly want."

I gave his throne room a once-over, ignoring the harem girls' hostile glares. I noticed the empty chains hanging from the ceiling and the wilted rose petals scattered on the floor.

"Then maybe you ought to want *more* for yourself."

Doug peppered me with questions for the next three days. On the first day, he demanded to know everything about me: my life, my family and my job. Glossing over my job, I spent more time talking about childhood dreams, embarrassing stories about my evil cousin Patrice and anything that highlighted the ups and downs of my real world.

On the second day, he grilled me on current events, including bare details about the lawsuit.

The third day, he talked about himself. I learned he'd been labeled a genius at four and enrolled in college before turning eight, missing an entire childhood along the way. He waxed poetic about his first love, a fellow prodigy with whom he'd shared four magnificent weeks together before her parents stopped the affair. Listening to him, I realize he'd turned out to be much more stable than I'd anticipated. No chemical dependencies or obvious deviancy. No really extravagant lifestyle befitting his fortune.

I had to admit, I liked him. A lot.

But liking him wouldn't save his life. If Doug didn't willingly emerge from VR, Stik would kill him. Pure and simple.

I had to tell him. Time was running out.

Tomorrow...

When tomorrow came, everything changed. When I walked into the throne room, the harem girls were gone. Doug sat behind an old-fashioned desk, his throne replaced by an executive office chair.

He looked up from a stack of papers. "Morning."

"Is it? I've lost all sense of time." A chair magically appeared by the desk and I sat down.

He glanced at his watch. "It's December 23rd. 9:26 A.M." He shot me a brilliant smile. "You know, you couldn't have given me a better present."

Panic rose in my throat. December 23rd? I had less than forty-eight hours to come up with a solution...unless the solution had found me.

"I'm leaving," he stated in a calm voice.

My panic turned into elation. "VR?"

He nodded. "It's time to go back." He pushed the papers away. "I've been hiding from my problems, but they haven't gone away. You've made me realize I have a duty to fix things."

I couldn't believe what I was hearing. "Me? How?"

Doug Post smiled a smile I'd never seen before. "You showed me what it's like to be real, reminded me what I've been missing." A wistful look filled his eyes. "I'd forgotten how much I love life." He touched my hand. "Thank you, Shelley."

I swallowed my disbelief. "You're...you're welcome."

He pushed back from his desk and stood. "It's going to take me longer than you to extract myself since I've been here a while. You go first and tell your superiors I'm going to repair the damage done in my name."

It's exactly what I wanted to hear; not only had he'd recognized his errors and was going to rectify them, but it was all due to little ol' me. What an ego boost.

Something was wrong.

Maybe it was his resolute look, his businesslike demeanor...

This was too damn easy.

There was only one thing I could do. I threw my arms around him and kissed him.

Nothing happened.

All we'd done was talk...about life, liberty, the pursuit of...knowledge. I'd never even thought about kissing him. At least not too often. I had no basis of comparison.

But even if I couldn't predict Doug's reaction, I knew what mine should be. Something. But I felt nothing. Then I realized I'd never told him my first name, yet he'd just used it.

The only way he'd know it was if I'd just kissed a computer.

Maybe not the computer itself, but a simulated Douglas Post, formed for the purpose of stalling me.

What day was it? Maybe I'd lost twelve days and I was living inside the only functional computer on earth. Or maybe the computer figured

Douglas Post was on the cusp of returning to the real world and had to distract me.

I had two choices: confront the computer or let it believe it'd fooled me.

"That's wonderful," I chortled, praying I sounded believable. "Let me get my things." I bolted from the room.

Okay, it was a lousy excuse, but I was desperate. I needed to find the real Douglas Post and I found him...

In the hallway.

Around the corner.

In the next room.

There were Doug Posts, everywhere, all dressed the same, sporting watches on their arms and bandages on their forefingers.

I needed the real Doug Post—now. I started kissing them.

The computer was smart enough to vary their responses to the kiss from tentative to ferocious. But none of them elicited the right response in me.

Until...

When I kissed the real Doug, he blushed, smiled, then kissed me back. A shiver crept across my shoulders. When we broke apart, we gasped for breath.

"Oh boy," we said simultaneously.

We grabbed hands and plowed our way through the Fake Dougs, running toward the door that led to Mayberry. Once outside, we vaulted the porch railing and sped toward the garden. We hid behind a row of rose bushes while a herd of Dougs thundered by.

I turned to whisper something and got a rather intoxicating kiss instead.

"Is this real?" he asked. "What I feel for you?"

"It's got to be."

"But what passes for reality here isn't necessarily real out there." He touched my cheek. "You willing to see if we can make it in the real world?"

"Definitely."

He stood. "Computer, command protocol Delta Delta Papa. Voice recognition verification."

The computer hesitated before answering. *"Voice recognition protocol has been established.*"

"Commence extraction of Delta Delta Papa and..." He turned to me.

"Sierra Mike Charlie," I supplied.

"Insufficient memory for simultaneous extractions."

"Reallocate memory."

"Insufficient memory for simultaneous extractions."

He sighed. "We'll have to do it in shifts." He bowed, slightly. "Ladies first."

"No way. What if the computer releases me, but keeps you? You go first. And tell the guy waiting for you that I'm sorry I stepped on his foot. You fix things there, then you get me out." I kissed him. "In that exact order. Got it?"

He stood. "Computer, commence extraction of Delta Delta Papa."

It wasn't a fancy procedure; he simply faded away. No sparks, no transporter effects like on Star Trek. Even though Mayberry had come from my thoughts, it faded, too. But I was too elated with my relative success to worry about that. After all, I'd saved the world and found love. Not bad for a hard eleven days' work. Or was that twelve?

Or unlucky thirteen?

My heart rate increased. Why? Because of desire? Anticipation? Fear? Whatever emotion spurred my heart also made it hard to breathe. I sat down, hoping to catch my breath.

It didn't work.

"Oxygen readout," I gasped.

Instead of a disembodied voice, a harem girl appeared beside me. "The oxygen levels are at minimum"—she gave me a malevolent smile—"and falling. With PostPrime gone, there is no need to continue life support."

"But...I'm in here."

"Insufficient memory. Fatal error. Would you like to reboot?"

Fatal error indeed. "No."

"Commence diagnostic programming and data compression."

The room began shrinking. The damn computer was going to take revenge one way or the other—suffocating me or squeezing me to death. I wanted to scream, but didn't have enough breath.

I started praying—that I hadn't lost track of time, that the world hadn't been rendered computerless, that Stik hadn't killed Doug the moment he awoke, that Doug could control his own computer and that I'd get out of VR alive.

As I grew weaker and dizzier, I prayed for Doug's survival more than anything else. All I knew was that if Doug hadn't survived, then it didn't matter if I escaped VR.

Didn't matter at all.

The world went black, then turned a brilliant white again.

Doug stood before me.

I drew in lungfuls of blessed air. "Is this heaven?"

He laughed. "Only if you want. You're still in VR."

I didn't have the energy to kiss him. "Are you real?"

"No. But I'm no computer pawn, either. It's a new feature of VR—being able to insert yourself into a running VR program without complete immersion."

"Cool. Wish I'd thought of that. I'd make a million."

"You ready to leave VR?"

"Definitely." I tried to sit up. "But I'm not working well."

"That's because the computer tried to kill you. You're still healing."

"Did we succeed?"

Doug gave me a brilliant smile that seared me to my soul's center. "Yes. Thanks to you." He pointed over his shoulder. "Ready to go?"

I nodded.

He twined his fingers through mine. "Commence extraction, Sierra Mike Charlie."

When I awoke again, I was on the med-lab bed, free of the telemetry equipment. Doug and Stik stood over me. Stik betrayed no emotion, but Doug smiled broadly.

"Welcome back." His kiss was long and deep. He reached behind him and pulled out a single red rose.

With thorns.

"A Christmas present for me?"

His grin flickered briefly. "You were in there longer than you think."

"How long?"

"Be my valentine?"

Authors' Biographies

P. N. "Pat" Elrod is best known for the critically acclaimed Vampire Files, featuring her wisecracking undead private eye, Jack Fleming, in his ongoing battle against the gangster underworld of 1930s Chicago. Beginning with *Bloodlist*, Jack's first head-spinning case is to solve his own murder! *A Chill in the Blood*, her seventh in the series, won the Lord Ruthven Award for best vampire novel of 1999 and her ninth, *Lady Crymsyn*, will be released in the fall of 2000.

She also authored four historical novels with the Jonathan Barrett, Gentleman Vampire series, set during the American Revolution and the best-selling *I, Strahd, Memoirs of a Vampire*, and *I, Strahd, the War with Azalin*, mixing vampirism and magic. All have won rave reviews from *Locus* to *Publisher's Weekly*.

One of her favorite projects has been collaborating with actor Nigel Bennett (LaCroix of TV's *Forever Knight*), on a series of books about the James Bondian vampire, Richard Dun, once known as Lancelot. *Keeper of the King* garnered wildly enthusiastic applause from both fans and critics. "Our premise," said Elrod, "is 'What if Lancelot had been a vampire?' No wonder he was Arthur's greatest knight!' Then we asked,

'What if he has to go after the Holy Grail—again? And this time he'd better find it!'"

Their second novel, *His Father's Son*, will soon be released. "Nigel has spoiled me for collaborations," reports Elrod with a big grin. "He's not only extremely talented, coming up with the best ideas, but has an enviable professional attitude, not to mention a great sense of humor. I am thrilled that our readers enjoy the books as much as we have." Elrod has also co-edited *Time of the Vampires* and the soon-to-be-released *Dracula's London* with Martin H. Greenberg, the latter featuring a short story by Bennett and Elrod.

Elrod has always been a fan of the romance genre and works a strong element of it into all of her novels. "I love a gutsy hero meeting a feisty heroine who not only keeps up with him, but passes him by so he has to work to win her heart. This is a favorite theme for me, especially when the characters take over and start writing their own lines, then I just sit back and relish the ride!

"I was delighted at the chance to contribute to this anthology. The idea of 'The Scottish Ploy' had been banging around in my head for some time and this gave me a means to combine my favorite elements, screwball comedy against a theatrical background. I was a drama major at university and have never lost the kick of working on productions. It has been a great help to my writing as it taught me how to visualize scenes and hear dialogue. I think every writer should take drama courses to enrich their work."

After this, her first foray into the world of romantic suspense, Elrod is planning out additional books in the genre—as soon as she finds the time! At present, she is working on two new Jack Fleming supernatural/mystery novels, two fantasies, and teaming with Nigel Bennett on their third Richard Dun adventure. "But not to worry," she tells her readers, "I'll fit in a romance or three, they're just too much fun!"

Neesa Hart writes contemporary romance under her own name and historical romance as Mandalyn Kaye. Her latest release, *You Made Me Love You*, is a contemporary single-title romance from Avon Books.

Neesa lives in Washington, D.C., where she writes full-time. Sometimes, she lives other places around the country where she manages and produces theatrical presentations for churches large and small. "The Show Must Go On," she swears, is not based on a true story, though some of her former cast and crew do make cameo appearances. Neesa would like to dedicate this story to Ruth and Rose—who make her theatrical endeavors ever so much brighter.

Neesa's work has been honored with multiple awards by readers and her peers. She's a three-time HOLT Medal winner, a Romantic Times Reviewer's Choice winner, and a Gold Congressional Medal winner.

Neesa's books include:

The Promise, historical romance by Mandalyn Kaye. Pinnacle Books, 1995.

Beyond All Measure, historical romance by Mandalyn Kaye. Pinnacle Books, 1996.

A Matter of Honor, historical romance by Mandalyn Kaye. Pinnacle Books, 1996.

Restless, contemporary romance by Neesa Hart. Pinnacle Books, 1996.

Almost to the Altar, contemporary romance by Neesa Hart. Silhouette Special Edition, 1997.

Scandal's Captive, historical romance by Mandalyn Kaye. Zebra Books, 1997.

Seven Reasons Why, contemporary romance by Neesa Hart. Silhouette Special Edition, 1997.

"The Midnight Sky," a historical novella by Mandalyn Kaye in the *Scottish Magic* anthology. Kensington Books, 1997.

Priceless, historical romance by Mandalyn Kaye. Fawcett Books, 1998.

Halfway to Paradise, contemporary paranormal romance by Neesa Hart. Avon Books, 1999.

A Kiss to Dream On, contemporary romance by Neesa Hart, Avon Books, 1999.

Who Gets to Marry Max?, contemporary romance by Neesa Hart, Harlequin American, 2000.

You Made Me Love You, contemporary romance by Neesa Hart. Avon Books, 2000.

Laura Hayden never lacks for a change of pace or venue in her life. The wife of an active-duty air force officer, she has, more than once, started a project while living in one state, sold it while on the road, and finished it while unpacking boxes and setting up a new household halfway across the country. Such versatility in her home life is also reflected in her writing career.

Laura claims 1993 as her banner year. She'd been writing for three years and had completed three manuscripts, two of which were under consideration by publishers. In March 1993, she sold her first project, "The Star of Kashmir," a lighthearted, action-adventure-romance novella written specifically for audio.

In May, she learned she had been selected as a finalist in the Romance Writers of America's prestigious Golden Heart contest for her time-travel manuscript *A Margin in Time*. The air force decided this was a perfect time to uproot her family from Colorado to Kansas for a one-year assignment.

Somewhere on I-70, she learned she'd sold her first novel, a romantic suspense to Harlequin Intrigue. A month later, she won the Golden Heart. Two months after that, her audio book came out to great reviews. A month later, her Golden Heart final-round judge bought *A Margin in Time* on a two-book contract for Pinnacle. Two months later, her first book was released and she sold a second Harlequin Intrigue novel.

After a year in Kansas, she moved to northern Virginia and wrote another romantic suspense for Intrigue and a lighthearted paranormal romance for Pinnacle. The next move was a one-year assignment to North Dakota where she wrote her fourth romantic suspense for Intrigue. When she sold her first short story "Nine Tenths" (featured in the *Dangerous Magic* anthology from Daw), she wrote it while using packing boxes as a desk since her family was moving to Montana. Laura finished the story on the road, somewhere in South Dakota. (She thinks it was at Mount Rushmore.)

It was in Montana that Laura got the idea for "Twelve Days." She reports: "I came up with this story while at the post office. I mailed packages several times a week and struck up a friendship with Doug, the guy behind the counter. We'd discovered some common interests, one of which was computers.

"When the first stories came out about Microsoft's legal troubles, Doug made an innocent observation: 'Boy, I bet Bill Gates isn't happy today!' I nodded, shot the breeze, mailed my package and trudged back through the January snow to my car. By the time I started the engine, I had the basic story—what if the world's biggest computer mogul got pissed and decided to take his toys and go back home? This was January 2000 and the gloom-and-doom warnings about the Y2K death of technology were still fresh in my mind.

"So here's to Doug at the C. M. Russell Post Office in Great Falls, Montana. Thanks!"

After two years in Montana, Laura is moving again, this time packing up three book projects with her household goods. Her next book, *Stolen Hearts*, a time-travel romance, will be available fall of 2001. It's part of the Hope Chest series from Zebra Ballad, a five-book continuity series being written by members of her critique group, the Wyrd Sisters.

She's also embarking on a new writing adventure—working as a ghostwriter on a big mystery series for a major publishing house. And as much as she'd love to tell you all about the project, her lips are sealed!

Laura credits her close ties to the Wyrd Sisters and the wonders of e-mail for keeping her focused on her career, despite all her moves. She enjoys hearing from her fans and welcomes them to e-mail her at: suspense@suspense.net

As she stands by her latest stack of cardboard boxes, she reminds her readers of the wise words of her screen hero Buckaroo Banzai: No matter where you go, there you are.

Yvonne Jocks believes in many magicks, particularly the magic of stories. She has written since she was five years old, and received payment of a transistor radio for her first short story, published by a local paper, at the age of twelve.

Soon after that, she decided writing wasn't lucrative enough to pursue professionally (transistor radios aside). Luckily, this decision did not last like the fun of writing did.

Under the name Evelyn Vaughn (E. Vaughn), Yvonne sold her first romantic suspense novel, *Waiting for the Wolf Moon*, to Silhouette Shadows in 1992. She promptly bought a larger television set. Three more books (*Burning Times*, *Beneath the Surface*, and *Forest of the Night*) completed her "Circle Series," which featured witches and monsters, before the Shadows line closed. The last won Favorite Science Fiction Romance in *Affaire De Coeur* magazine's 1997 reader's poll.

Yvonne's most recent writing project is a series of historical romance novels called "The Rancher's Daughters"—*Behaving Herself* and *Forgetting Herself*—for Leisure Books. She also enjoys writing short stories and novellas in the science fiction/fantasy and mystery genres, and her work has appeared in several books, including *A Dangerous Magic* from DAW books, which combined fantasy and romance.

A resident of Texas for twenty-two years (after living in places as diverse as Window Rock, Arizona, and Pearl River, Louisiana), Yvonne still loves the magic of stories, movies, books, and dreams. Her enjoyment of literature led her to earn a master's degree at the University of Texas in Arlington (her thesis traced the history of the romance novel). An unapologetic TV addict, she lives happily with her cats and her imaginary friends and teaches junior college English to support her writing habit...or vice versa. (All sentence fragments in her story are for effect. Really.)

"Celtic Cross" allowed Yvonne to delve into many of her own interests—she enjoys metaphysical stores such as Avalon and, like any good literature professor, owns a Shakespearean tarot deck. The difference between healthy and unhealthy love and romance has long fascinated her, as well as the emotions that lead to mutual empowerment within healthy relationships.

But mostly, it's the story. And the magic therein...

Feel free to write Yvonne at P.O. Box 6, Euless, TX 76039 or e-mail her at Yvaughn@aol.com.

D. R. Meredith, Doris to family and friends, has a split personality: one persona is that of an ordinary woman with husband, two children, two beagles, and a house in the suburbs; her other persona is a paid killer. After finishing such daily domestic chores as taking out the garbage, Meredith sits down at her computer and commits murder.

Famous for the unique ways in which her victims are "done in," she has created three highly acclaimed mystery series, all set in the Texas panhandle. One series features attorney John Lloyd Branson, another a Texas county sheriff named Charles Matthews, while the third and latest series features an unemployed paleopathologist and female sleuth named Megan Clark. Her first two sherriff mysteries won the "Oppie" for Best Mystery of 1984 and Best Mystery of 1985. Both *The Sheriff and the Branding Iron Murders* and *The Sheriff and the Folsom Man Murders* were selections of the Detective Book Club. Of the John Lloyd Branson series, both *Murder by Impulse* and *Murder by Deception* were finalists for Anthony Awards in 1988 and 1989. "Murder by Reference" was selected to be included in "Murder in the Museum III: A Bibliography," compiled by a panel of museum curators as a study in how the museum is perceived by the public.

A graduate of the University of Oklahoma, Meredith had been a teacher, a librarian, and a bookseller before the publication of her first book in 1984. She was regional director of the Mystery Writers of America, and is the National Liaison Chair for the American Crime Writers League.

She is the book editor for *Roundup Magazine* published by the Western Writers of America, a book reviewer for the *Amarillo Globe News*, has been a contributing editor for *Kirkus Reviews*, and is the current Western Fiction editor for *What Do I Read Next?*, a reference book for libraries and bookstores, published by the Gale Group. She has been a judge for the Spur Awards five times, an Edgar judge twice, and most recently a judge for the Western Heritage Award. She is one of three mystery writers featured in *Texas Monthly*. Meredith is a member of Mystery Writers of America, Western Writers of America, American Crime Writers League, and Sisters in Crime.

When not writing or being a literary critic, she teaches writing seminars at conferences and universities, most recently at the University of Nebraska, or gives programs at libraries and book clubs. *Texas Almanac* names Doris one of the state's best mystery writers, an honor she considers makes her a valuable resource along with natural gas and beef. Both of Meredith's personalities live in Amarillo, Texas.

Jody Lynn Nye has always loved mysteries, from the first Agatha Christie she read to the most recent Tony Hillerman, and confesses that Dorothy L. Sayers's *Gaudy Night* is on her "if I were marooned on a desert island" list of books.

Jody was born in Chicago, and except for brief forays to summer camp and college has always lived in the area. She was graduated from Maine Township High School East and Loyola University of Chicago, where she majored in Communications and English, and was an active member of the theater groups, the student radio stations, and the speech team (original comedy and oratorical declamation).

Jody has worked as a file clerk, bookkeeper at a small publishing house, freelance journalist and photographer, accounting assistant, and costume maker. Before breaking away to write full-time, she spent four years on the technical operations staff of a local Chicago television station, the last year as Technical Operations Manager.

Although she lists her primary career activity as "spoiling cats," since 1985 she has published twenty-two books and over fifty short stories. Among the novels Jody has written are her epic fantasy series, The Dreamland, beginning with *Waking in Dreamland*, four contemporary fantasies, *Mythology 101*, *Mythology Abroad* and *Higher Mythology* (collected as *Applied Mythology*), *The Magic Touch*, and two science-fiction novels, *Taylor's Ark* and *Medicine Show*. Jody also wrote *The Dragonlover's Guide to Pern*, a non-fiction-style guide to the world of internationally best-selling author Anne McCaffrey's popular world. She has collaborated with Anne McCaffrey on four science fiction novels, *The Death of Sleep*, *Crisis on Doona*, *Treaty at Doona* and *The Ship Who Won*. She also wrote a solo sequel to *The Ship Who Won* entitled *The Ship Errant*. Jody co-authored the *Visual Guide to Xanth* with best-selling fantasy author Piers Anthony, and edited an anthology of stories about mothers in science fiction, fantasy, myth and legend, entitled *Don't Forget Your Spacesuit, Dear!* She wrote an episode produced for the animated series *Dinosaucers*, "Tyrannosaurus Store Wars."

Her newest book is *The Grand Tour*, third in the Dreamland series. Due out in 2001 is a contemporary fantasy co-authored with Robert Lynn Asprin, *License Invoked*, and a fourth in the Mythology series, Advanced Mythology.

Jody lives in the northwest suburbs of Chicago, with her husband Bill Fawcett, a writer, game designer, and book packager, and two cats, Lila and Cassandra. Anyone wishing to get in touch with her can write to her at P.O. Box 776, Lake Zurich, IL 60047, USA, or e-mail her at: jodynye@poboxes.com, or visit her website at: http://www.sff.net/people/jodynye.

Jody says:

> "Night Hawks" was inspired mainly by the setting. We have a large backyard, two thirds of which has been allowed to go wild for the sake of the local animal population. Walking in it by moonlight feels mysterious and inviting...even a little dangerous (we have coyotes—and skunks). I'm fascinated by hunting birds. We see red-tailed hawks all summer long, and there are peregrines living on skyscrapers in the city. They aren't alone in their hunting. You have only to read the daily newspaper to know that there are other predators out there besides raptors, and other prey than mice and shrews.

Jody's books include:

The Dragonlover's Guide to Pern. Del Rey, 1989; trade paper, 1992; 2nd ed., 1996.

Visual Guide to Xanth, co-authored with Piers Anthony. Avon Books, 1989.

Mythology 101. Warner Books, 1990.

The Death of Sleep, co-authored with Anne McCaffrey. Baen Books, 1990.

Mythology Abroad. Warner Books, 1991.

Crisis on Doona, co-authored with Anne McCaffre. Ace Books, 1992.

Higher Mythology. Warner Books, 1993.

Taylor's Ark. Ace Books, 1993.

The Ship Who Won, co-authored with Anne McCaffrey. Baen Books, 1994.

Medicine Show (*Taylor's Ark II*). Ace Books, 1994.

Treaty at Doona, co-authored with Anne McCaffrey. Ace Books, 1994.

The Magic Touch. Warner Books, June 1996.

Don't Forget Your Spacesuit, Dear. Editor. Baen Books, 1996.

The Ship Errant (*The Ship Who Won II*). Baen Books, 1996.

Waking in Dreamland (*Dreamland I*). Baen Books, 1998.

School of Light (*Dreamland II*). Baen Books, 1999.

The Grand Tour (*Dreamland III*). Baen Books, 2000.

Applied Mythology (*Omnibus of books 1, 2 ,3*). Meisha Merlin Publishing, 2000.

100 Crafty Little Cat Crimes, "Land Rush." Barnes & Noble, 2000.

Dracula's London, "Everything to Order." Ace Books, 2000.

Warrior Fantastic, "Conscript." DAW Books, 2000.

Forthcoming works:

Oceans of Space, "Pyrats." DAW Books, 2001.

License Invoked, co-authored with Robert L. Asprin. Baen Books, 2001.

Advanced Mythology (*Mythology IV*). Meisha Merlin Publishing, 2001.

The Lady and The Tiger (*Taylor's Ark III*). Ace Books, 2002.

Laura Resnick, a *cum laude* graduate of Georgetown University, where she studied French and Italian, began her career by selling a romance novel to Silhouette Books; it was released in 1989 under the pseudonym Laura Leone. She has won several awards as a romance writer and has sold more than a dozen romance novels to three different publishing houses.

After establishing herself as a romance writer, Laura also began writing science fiction/fantasy short stories under her own name. By 1993, she won the John W. Campbell Award (best new science fiction/fantasy writer) in recognition of her work. Currently under contract to Tor Books, a major publisher of science fiction and fantasy, she now devotes most of her time to writing epic fantasy novels. Her next major release will be *In Fire Forged* (the sequel to her 1998 hardcover, *In Legend Born*, which is currently available in paperback).

In addition, Laura is the author of the award-winning 1997 release *A Blonde In Africa*, the non-fiction account of her seven-month overland journey across Africa. She has also written several short travel pieces, as well as numerous articles about the publishing business; she currently writes a monthly opinion column, "The Comely Curmudgeon," for *Nink*, the newsletter of Novelists, Inc.

You can find her on the Web at www.sff.net./people/laresnick.

Kristine Kathryn Rusch is an award-winning fiction writer. Her novella, *The Gallery of His Dreams*, won the Locus Award for best short fiction. Her body of fiction work won her the John W. Campbell Award, given in 1991 in Europe. She has been nominated for several dozen fiction awards, and her short work has been reprinted in six Year's Best collections.

In 1999, her story "Echea" was nominated for the Locus, Nebula, Hugo, and Sturgeon awards. It won the Homer Award and the Asimov's Reader's Choice Award. In 1999, she also won the Ellery Queen Reader's Choice Award and the Science Fiction Age Reader's Choice Award, making her the first writer to win three different reader's choice awards for three different stories in two different genres in the same year.

She has published twenty novels under her own name. She has sold forty-one total, including pseudonymous books. Her novels have been published in seven languages, and have spent several weeks on the *USA Today* bestseller list and the *Wall Street Journal* bestseller list. She has written a number of Star Trek novels with her husband, Dean Wesley Smith, including a book in this summer's crossover series called New Earth.

Her most recent novel is *Utterly Charming*, a lighthearted romance (with magic) written under the name Kristine Grayson. Her most recent fantasy novel is *The Black King*, the last book in her Black Throne

Series. She has written a science fiction series, The Tenth Planet, with her husband, Dean Wesley Smith. She has also published a mainstream crime novel, *Hitler's Angel*, which was called "a great story, well told," by the *Oregonian* and received a full-page review in the *New York Times*. Her next book will be the second book in her Black Throne series, *The Black King*.

Under the name Kris Nelscott, she has sold two mystery novels set in 1968 to St. Martin's Press.

She is the former editor of the prestigious *Magazine of Fantasy and Science Fiction*. She won a Hugo for her work there. Before that, she and Dean Wesley Smith started and ran Pulphouse Publishing, a science fiction and mystery press in Eugene.

She lives and works on the Oregon coast.

Susan Sizemore lives in the Midwest and spends most of her time writing. Some of her other favorite things are coffee, dogs, travel, movies, hiking, history, farmers markets, art glass, and basketball—you'll find mention of quite a few of these things inside the pages of her stories. She works in many genres, from contemporary romance to epic fantasy and horror. She's the winner of the Romance Writers of America's Golden Heart award, and a nominee for the 2000 Rita Award in historical romance. Her available books include historical romance novels from Avon; a dark fantasy series, The Laws of the Blood, from Ace Science Fiction; science fiction from Speculation Press; and several electronically published books and short stories. One of her electronic books, the epic fantasy *Moons' Dreaming*, written with Marguerite Krause, is a nominee for the Eppie, the e-publishing industries writing award.

Though "Dizzy and the Biker" is technically the first mystery story she's written, she's actually had the idea for Franciscan Place in the back of her head for several years. It's the sort of place she'd like to live if she lived in a city and kept pets. She'd had visions of Dizzy and Harley and their companion people for quite some time, but she had no idea for a mystery plot for them to solve until she started taking her own dog to a fenced-in dog park out in the country. The story that appears in this anthology fell into place while following her own very active greyhound-mix pooch around the paths in this wooded park, so she included the park as part of the setting for Franciscan Place. Only she took it out of an 800-acre forest preserve and put it in the heart of a city where it became the site of a murder and the beginning of a romance—between a pair of dogs, and their owners. According to Susan, "It was a great pleasure writing this story, and I hope to return to Franciscan Place again."

Susan's e-mail address is Ssizemore@aol.com and her web page address is: http://members.aol.com/Ssizemore/storm/home.htm

Early in life, **Deb Stover** discovered a passion for writing and an unwavering respect for honor and fairness. She left a journalism career to pursue her dream of writing romance, and editor Denise Little played a dual role as faerie godmother.

Stover's novels and short stories often include characters with disabilities. She believes strongly that individuals with disabilities must be included in society and fiction as people first, and her belief is reflected both in her writing and in her life. She strives to create characters readers will love and knows imperfection is a fact of life. A reviewer once said that "Ms. Stover's characters are so real—even the ghosts."

In "Keeper of the Well," readers meet Annie Campbell—a little girl with Down syndrome. One of Stover's own children has Down syndrome and served in some ways as a model for Annie. Deb also drew on her experience as an adoptive mother while plotting this story.

Stover is active in many writers' organizations, and has served as director of the Pikes Peak Writers Conference, held annually under the umbrella of the Kennedy Center Imagination Celebration. She has recently completed a two-year term on the Romance Writers of America's National Board of Directors.

Since publication of her first novel in 1995, Stover has received five award nominations from *Romantic Times*, including one for Career Achievement in Innovative Historical Romance. *Another Dawn* has also received the Dorothy Parker Award of Excellence from Reviewers International Organization, and was a finalist for the Colorado

Award of Excellence. In 1999 and 1997, she was chosen as Pikes Peak Romance Writers' Author of the Year. She has been a finalist for the Heart of Romance Reader's Choice Award twice, and won in 1998 with *Some Like It Hotter*, which was also a finalist for the Colorado Award of Excellence. *Almost an Angel* was voted Best Time Travel of the Year by Romance Readers Anonymous, and *Some Like It Hotter* was nominated for *Affaire de Coeur*'s Romance Novel of the Year and Best Time Travel. *Almost an Angel* was a finalist for Best Paranormal Romance, and Stover was a favorite author of the year. In 1996, her second novel, *A Willing Spirit*, was voted Romance Novel of the Year by readers of *Affaire de Coeur*.

Deb Stover is a native of Wichita, Kansas, but now lives near Colorado Springs with her husband, their three children, and a mutant dachshund.

For more information, visit her web page: http://www.debstover.com/.

Novels by Deb Stover include:
No Place For A Lady. Zebra Books, September 2001.
A Moment in Time. Zebra Books, 2000.
A Matter of Trust. Zebra Books, 2000.
Stolen Wishes. Zebra Books, 1999.
Another Dawn, Zebra Books, 1999.
Almost an Angel. Pinnacle Books, Denise Little Presents, 1997.
Some Like It Hotter. Pinnacle Books, Denise Little Presents, 1997.
A Willing Spirit. Pinnacle Books, Denise Little Presents, 1996.
Shades of Rose. Pinnacle Books, Denise Little Presents, 1995.

Novellas and Short Stories:
A Dangerous Magic, "The Enchanted Garden." DAW Books, 1999.

Diane A. S. Stuckart, who also writes historical romance as Alexa Smart and Anna Gerard, is a member of that proud breed, the native Texan. The oldest of five children, she was born in the West Texas town of Lubbock and raised in Dallas. She admits to crossing the Red River just long enough to obtain her degree in Journalism from the

University of Oklahoma before returning home for good to the Lone Star State. Now settled in a North Dallas suburb, she has worked as a purchasing agent in the electronics, aviation, and medical fields while writing fiction at night.

Diane's historical romances have been published in multiple languages and have garnered rave reviews from critics and fans alike. Her first book, *Masquerade*—written under the name Alexa Smart—was a finalist in the Romance Writers of America's Golden Heart competition. Pinnacle Books published that novel in December of 1994 as part of its popular Denise Little Presents line. Three other historical romances from DLP and Pinnacle soon followed: *Shadows of the Heart*, *A Touch of Paradise*, and *Roses at Midnight*. Diane's most recent novel, *Desert Hearts*, was a September 1999 release from Zebra Books penned under the name Anna Gerard. She has also made a foray into historical romantic fantasy. Writing as Diane A. S. Stuckart, she was one of several authors contributing to the DAW Books anthology, *A Dangerous Magic*. Now, with this book, she is taking her first step into contemporary romantic fiction.

Diane is a firm believer in research and visits her fictional settings whenever possible. She made three trips to New Orleans for *Masquerade*, prowling the French Quarter and old cemeteries, talking to convent groundskeepers and voodoo shop owners. For *A Touch of Paradise*, she journeyed to Bimini in the Bahamas, snorkeling to the underwater site of the "Atlantis Road" that some claim is a remnant of that legendary place. She also traveled the deserts and mountains of Arizona while researching for *Desert Hearts*, stopping in the town of Tombstone, once home to Wyatt Earp and Doc Holliday. Her most recent trip was to Colorado's cloud-high city of Leadville, where she explored silver mining and gold panning for a future historical romance. She was relieved, however, to realize she could do all her research for www.gonnahavekelly.com from the comfort of her own computer.

A fan of good books, bad movies, and '70s rock-and-roll, Diane is a longtime member of Romance Writers of America and a founding member of the Dallas Area Romance Authors. When not working on her next book, she is practicing Tae Kwon Do or yoga, or else wasting precious writing time surfing the Net. She shares her home with her husband, Gerry, and various other motley critters.

Mary Watson worked at a variety of jobs before selling her first romance novel to Harlequin Books in 1983—as patient-advocate at a large hospital, as a weekly newspaper columnist, a bank teller, a reading teacher for learning-disabled elementary school students, and a creative writing teacher.

Since that first book sale, Mary has had thirteen novels published under her Lynn Turner pseudonym, eleven series romances for Harlequin/Mills & Boon, and two single-title books published by the Denise Little Presents line of Pinnacle Books. *Forever*, her first book for Mills & Boon, received the 1986 Romantic Times Reviewer's Choice Award for best Presents. That same year, *Mystery Train* was a finalist for *Romantic Times*'s best Harlequin Intrigue title.

Mary's writing has focused primarily on romantic mystery/suspense. Her most recent books have also incorporated an element of the paranormal. *Race Against Time* was a time travel–romantic mystery story and a finalist for Romance Writers of America's RITA award, while *Dreamer's Heart* featured a psychic heroine targeted by a psychotic serial bomber. Lynn describes herself as a plot-driven reader and writer and loves stories that contain complex, tightly woven plots and lots of surprises. She describes "Hostage to Love" as a trial run for a few of the characters who will populate a novel presently in the outlining stage.

Mary and her husband of thirty-three years live in the southwestern corner of Indiana. Readers can send e-mail to marywatson@email.com.

Copyrights & Permissions

Printed in the USA
CPSIA information can be obtained
at www.ICGtesting.com
JSHW082156140824
68134JS00014B/262